PAUL E. HORSMAN

TRADE MAGNATE

BOOK 6

WYRMS OF PASANDIR

Book cover designed by Deranged Doctor Design
For more info: paulhorsman-author.com

There is a list of names at the back of the book.

Paul E. Horsman's books:

Zilverspoor Uitgeverij (Dutch Editions):
Rhidauna—Schaduw van de Revenaunt #1
Zihaen—Schaduw van de Revenaunt #2
Ordelanden—Schaduw van de Revenaunt #3

Red Rune Books (Dutch Edition)
De Shardheld Sage

Red Rune Books (English Editions):
Lioness and Warlock (Prequel to Wyrms of Pasandir)
The Road to Kalbakar—Wyrms of Pasandir #1
The Pirates of Brisa—Wyrms of Pasandir #2
The Bokkaners of the North—Wyrms of Pasandir #3
Building a Trade Empire—Wyrms of Pasandir #4
High Merchant—Wyrms of Pasandir #5
Trade Magnate—Wyrms of Pasandir #6
Jinnbane (2018) - Wyrms of Pasandir #7

Shardfall—The Shardheld Saga #1
Runemaster—The Shardheld Saga #2
Shardheld—The Shardheld Saga #3
The Shardheld Saga, trilogy

Rhidauna—The Shadow of the Revenaunt #1
Zihaen—The Shadow of the Revenaunt #2
Ordelanden—The Shadow of the Revenaunt #3
Vavaun—The Shadows of the Revenaunt #4

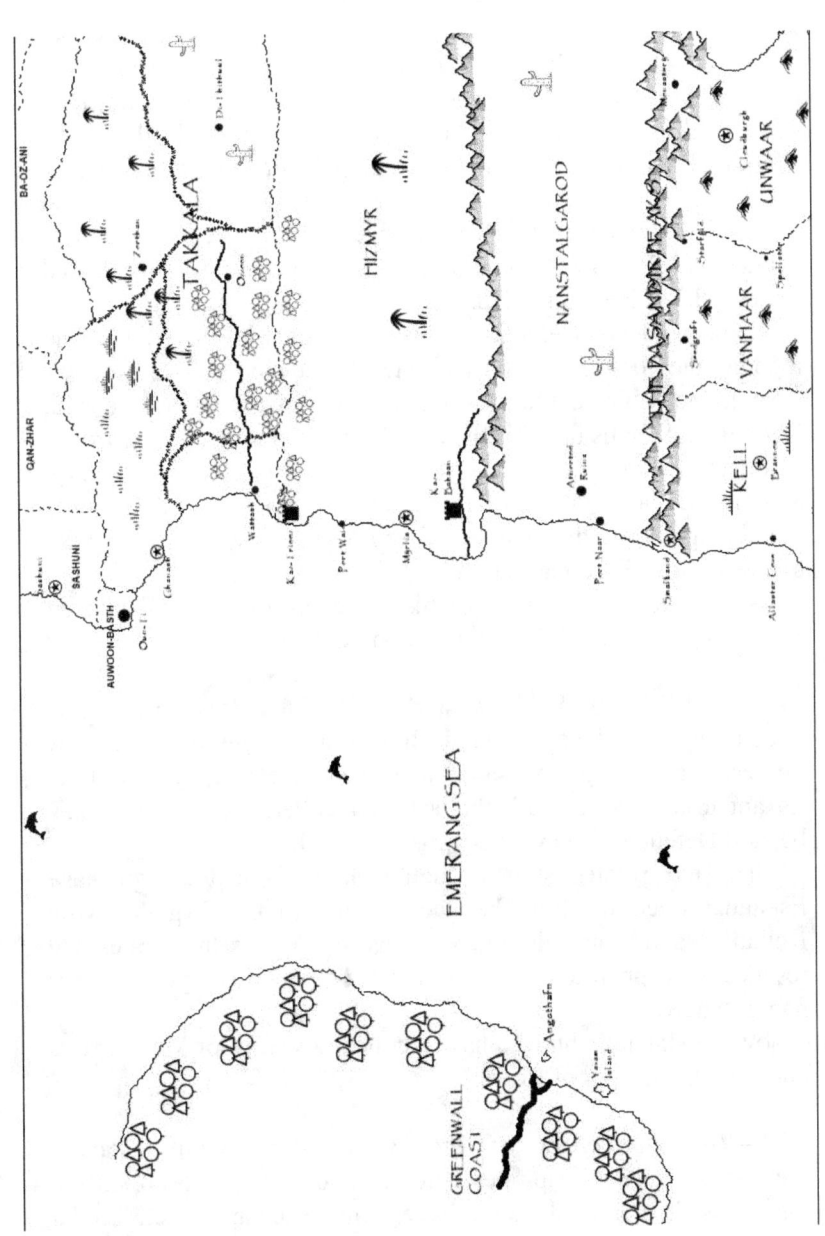

5

INTRODUCTION

The **WYRMS OF PASANDIR** - Series returns the reader to the colorful world of **Lioness and Warlock**, twenty-five years later, when the Lioness Maud has become the Queen of the Kell, and the Warlock Basil has settled down as the Spellstor, ruler of Vanhaar.

#1—The Road to Kalbakar introduces Eskandar, a young one-handed ship's boy serving in the old navy sloop *Tipred*, and Teodar, the voice in his head.

Eskandar meets Kellani, the daughter of Lioness Maud, and together they beat off a monster attack on the sloop.

No longer able to hide his magic, Eskandar goes ashore with Kellani, and teams up with Naudin, the son of the Warlock Basil.

Together, they discover a dangerous lich has escaped his crypt and is at large somewhere. They meet Jem, the bodiless granddaughter of the lich, and Lord Amaj, a warrior boy with connections to Eskandar's past.

Eskandar learns the roots of his secret history lie at Kalbakar Keep, a castle occupied by a mad monk cult...

#2—The Pirates of Brisa starts with Eskandar learning that Teodar and the Sleeping God Bodrus are being threatened by pirates, man-eating jinn, and their boss, the mighty lich lord. Eskandar has learned he is the last wyrmcaller, whatever that may be, and Defender of Divine Bodrus.

When the pirates start abducting kids from the orphanage Eskandar once lived in, he knows what to do. Together with Kellani, Naudin and his other friends, he defeats the pirates and rescues the orphan teens, among them a quiet fifteen-year-old girl named Shaw.

Now Teodar tells him he has to collect an army of kid warriors and fight the pirates of Brisa...

#3—The Bokkaners of the North starts with Eskandar victorious, the Brisan pirates defeated and their powerful ship in his hands. Just as he thinks to have some peace and quiet, Teodar sends him north, where another bunch of pirates roams.

Teodar knows of a stronghold at the foot of the Pasandir Peaks, Smalkand Keep.

This proves to be a rich former merchants' headquarters, and a veritable treasure room of gold and trade goods.

After Eskandar has secured the keep and the surrounding region, he travels further north, to the mighty kingdom of Hizmyr.

Before he leaves, he agrees to his Purser Shaw's plan to build a trade empire that can finance Eskandar's many plans for restoring the Peaks...

#4—*Building a Trade Empire* starts the tale of Shaw, the young purser who dreams of building a mighty trade empire.

She is the one who sells Eskandar's spoils of war, and as she follows the wyrmcaller north to find the old traders keep of Smalkand, she starts building her plans.

When the wyrmcaller Eskandar goes north in pursuit of his enemies, she obtains his blessing to realize her dream. Together with Nate, her business partner, she journeys back to Seatome, the capital of Lord Basil's Vanhaar.

Here, with the gold found in Smalkand's strongroom, and a load of valuable loot from a pirate vessel they had captured, she hires her first warehouse and makes ready to conquer the mercantile world...

#5—*High Merchant* sees Shaw at the head of a fast-growing transnational business. With the victory over the guild of Hizmyr, she is ready to grab the many chances the immense Hizmyran market offers her company. But just when she's getting into her stride, fate calls her to the town of New Winsproke, on Malgarth.

There is a lot amiss in New Winsproke. Here began the whole series of events told in *The Lioness and the Warlock** that ended with the liberation of Vanhaar. After that battle, most warlocks returned to the Continent, leaving New Winsproke without a useful job.

Shaw buys the Emporium, a nearly broke former arcane shopping center, and starts rebuilding it, bringing new life into the city.

#6—Trade Magnate starts with Shaw's determination to do what she came to New Winsproke for, get crystal cutters from the local mine for her own, new mine in Wattash. These crystals are the batteries powering ship's engines, airship drives, teleportals, and all other machinery. But of course things don't go as she planned—again.

CHAPTER 1 — THE WINSPROKE MINE

'We will go and hire some crystal cutter guys today,' Shaw said firmly, tapping the table with both index fingers to emphasize her words. 'I must be strong, no more distractions; our Wattash mine needs those workers.'

'Good,' Nate said with a hint of a smile in his eyes. They were in Wattash, sitting in *Royal Sashu*'s messroom, behind the remains of a kingly breakfast. Around them, the ship's crew babbled and laughed as free and happy youngsters do.

Shaw slapped Nate's hand resting on the table. 'I'm a girl of my word,' she said proudly. 'Don't you smirk at me!'

'Have another kipper,' Nate said.

She pulled a face. 'Kipper? At breakfast? Yech.'

'You ate three already,' Nate said calmly.

'I didn't! I... Ah, darn. Let's go to the mines.' She laughed and took Nate's arm. 'I'm horrible.'

'Mwah,' Nate said.

'Don't you dare say yes!' she exclaimed.

'I'm not going to,' Nate said. 'You are not horrible. Got your broom?'

'Of course,' she said haughtily.

'Sure?' he asked and handed her the riding broom. 'It hung on the backrest of your chair.'

With a cry she snatched the broomstick from his hands and stalked away to the portal.

'Lovely morning, guys,' young Portaller Elijan said cheerfully. 'The Emporium again?'

'Yes, please,' Nate said, and he winked at the boy.

'Wait, wait, *wait*!' Haai-Bo cackled as he joined them, wings a-flutter and eyes whirling. Then they whisked away.

The port to New Winsproke didn't make her surliness any better, nor did the sight of the Emporium portaller's round face, but Shaw didn't say anything.

'Good morning, Anna,' Nate said unperturbed. 'Any news?'

The stout girl sat on a display table swinging her legs as she looked up from the old tome on her lap. 'This is a great book.'

Nate frowned at the yellowed pages. 'What is it?'

Her eyes twinkled. *'Mathematical Substantiation of Fourth Level Spells.* Half of it is bunk. Magister Particulus disagrees with me, but I don't care. I'm going to *prove* I'm right.'

'Sound plan,' Nate said. 'Just don't ask us to judge between the two of you. Say, if anyone comes looking for Shaw or me, we're off to the New Winsproke mine today.'

Shaw felt her bad mood dissipating as Nate hooked his arm in hers and led her into the sunlight. She turned and touched his face. 'Sorry for being beastly.' She looked at the shadows playing over the mighty Warlock Tower. 'Don't know what it was, but it's gone now.'

'Up, up,' Haai-Bo said. 'Flying chases cobwebs away.'

Shaw mounted her broom and moments later the three of them raced north.

New Winsproke wasn't a big town. At its height, it had been home to twenty-five thousand souls at most and these days it held only half that number. As the wyrm flies, they passed the city limits, crossed some farmland and reached the outliers of the Winsproke Forest almost in the blink of an eye.

The forest was part of the wild Lornwood, but this stretch had been tamed by generations of foresters and farmers.

They followed the narrow path below them, leading to a stony hill and a dark pine forest.

Then Shaw saw a fence and a sagging gate, with a large sign, saying "No Trespassers! Winsproke Silvermine." Beyond that were two cabins, and a hole in the mountain, shored up with heavy wooden beams.

'*Wait!*' Haai-Bo said suddenly. '*Pirates.*'

'*What?*' Shaw said, reducing her speed to a crawl. '*Here in dull New Winsproke?*'

'*They're in the mine, stealing crystals.*'

Shaw slapped her knee. '*What the heck do they want those for?*'

'*Perhaps they captured a steamship? They'd need power crystals for the engines.*'

'*Curse them! How many pirates are there?*'

'*Twenty, twenty-five. No jinn.*'

'*Right, call to arms for our lieutenants Ber and whatsisname,*' Shaw said with a sideways glance at Nate's grim face.

Haai-Bo cackled. '*Ellogg? The broomrider?*'

'*That one.*' Shaw motioned to her partner, and they landed on the path.

'So we still haven't got all pirates around here,' Nate said.

'No,' Shaw said harshly. 'It is time to do something about that.'

Fifteen minutes later, both units came racing over the treetops and dropped down on the path.

Lieutenant Ber was already running before his broom had come to a halt. 'Pirates?' he said, his sixteen-year-old face livid with anger. 'They came *here*?' He was a local boy, trained as a New Winsproke defender, and this intrusion got him on the raw.

Broomrider Ellogg joined up with them. 'How many enemies are there?'

'Haai-Bo counted twenty to twenty-five of them, all over the mine,' Shaw said. 'We're going in and put them out of business.'

'Kill them?' Ellogg said, aghast. He was a nineteen-year-old battlemage and not yet used to the first half of his new title.

Shaw glared at him. 'You can't take them captive,' she said in a hard voice. 'They're drugged, their minds broken; they'll never submit. You think you can do it?'

Ellogg swallowed. 'If we must.'

'It won't be fun,' Shaw said. She was four years his junior, and she'd been fighting pirates for a long time now. 'Killing never is. But if you can't do it, you guys are useless to me.'

'We can do it,' Ellogg said hastily. 'It's just that...'

Shaw patted his arm. 'I know. The first time I had to kill one I was sick afterwards. Still, I did it; else he would have killed me.'

'*You* killed a pirate?' Ellogg said, surprised.

'They had abducted us,' Shaw said. 'Then Eskandar came to free us, and we had to fight. After that, I was in plenty other battles. We who follow the wyrmcaller are *all* pirate hunters, you know.'

She waved down the path. 'Over there is the mine. You broomriders will approach from the sky while Nate and I with Ber's guys go on foot. When you see us come out of the trees, you will swoop down and kill every pirate outside. When they're down, we will check the buildings, before we enter the mine. Let's go.'

The broomriders jumped into the sky, and Shaw trotted down the forest path, with Nate and Ber's Defenders in her wake.

When they came out in the open, sudden fire rained down from the sky. At the nearest cabin, two pirate guards turned into smoking heaps of blackened rubble.

Lieutenant Ber ran to the door. 'Locked!' he said. He threw his weight against the wood, and the door crashed open.

Inside, some twenty young men and women, bound with ropes, watched them anxiously.

'*Good* morning,' Shaw said. 'You folks are the crystal cutters?'

'Yes,' a bony Vanhaari woman said. 'Who the heck are you?'

'Shaw Harwans of the PTC. I came to see the mine, but when we discovered those pirates, we called in our troops to kick them out. Where are the miners?'

'In the next cabin,' the woman said. 'Those beasts came two nights ago, when we were asleep. Who'd expect flippin' pirates in Winsproke?'

'You people all live at the mine?' Shaw said.

'Weekdays, yes. The married cutters work in town, but not us.'

'All right,' Shaw said. 'Please stay here; I need to talk to you all later. We'll go clean out the mine first.'

'They won't get us a second time,' the woman said. 'We're all very wide awake now.'

Shaw hurried out to the next cabin and found Ellogg's broomriders had freed the miners, twelve men and a gnarly oldster in an often-patched woolen suit.

'Thank you, ma'am,' he said hoarsely. 'PTC? Never expected your people come here.' He held out a calloused hand. 'I'm Crimmon, owner and chief engineer of this here operation. How's the mine?'

'We'll attend to that next,' Shaw said. 'We wanted to make sure you people were alright first.'

'Oh, we are,' he said. 'Shaken and friggin' angry, but we're fine.'

Shaw grinned. 'Excellent. We'll get the mine done then.'

'Best o' luck, ma'am,' the mine owner said.

Outside, Shaw broke into a run. As she entered the mine, Ber's boys surrounded her, waving their swords. The corridor floor was flattened by the passing of countless cartloads of ore and the whitish-gray walls sparkled with the brilliance of myriads of tiny crystals.

Shaw barely noticed the splendor as she hurried on. Soon they came upon the first pirates, hacking away at a crystal cluster. Ber's men surged forward, and the three surprised ruffians fell without a cry.

'*Nineteen left,*' Haai-Bo said from somewhere above her.

They went on, more careful now, for the corridor was crooked and the floor uneven. They passed a dark opening from which the sound came of pickaxes striking stone. Ber gestured with his head, and his lads followed him in.

'Wait here for Ellogg's guys,' Shaw said to Nate, and went after them. The short corridor ended in a rough-hewn chamber with four pirates. One of them must be a mage of sorts, for he lifted his hands and moved his fingers in some spell, his face twisted in concentration. Then Shaw's knife buried itself in his shoulder and he screamed. Ber ran and silenced him with his sword. Shaw snatched up a mining ax and went for a second pirate. One of Ber's guys pushed her aside in his eagerness, his eyes fixed on the ruffian. Then he swung his blade, and hot pirate blood hit both the boy and Shaw.

'Duck!' Shaw yelled, and as the boy obeyed, she swung the pickax at another man just behind him. She broke his collarbone at the same time Ber rammed his sword into the man's chest. 'Finished here,' Ber said.

Shaw panted. 'My knife.'

'Here,' a boy said, and he handed her the blade.

'Thanks.' She put the knife into its wrist sheath and clutched the mining ax.

'*Fifteen!*' she shouted.

'*Fourteen,*' Haai-Bo answered, and then she saw the thin pirate in a blackened heap in the middle of the main corridor.

'Ah, good; Ellogg's joined us,' Shaw said, nodding at the broomriders. Then she hurried down the corridor. They all followed, kicking ass whenever they encountered a pirate.

'*Five left,*' Haai-Bo said sooner than she'd expected.

Shaw turned a corner and saw them. One last handful of pirates, and a monster.

It was big. It was a very big sort of beetle; a green, hairy monstrosity the size of an oxcart, with eyestalks and pinchers, and enough feet for a battalion. It oozed slime past its scales and smelled something awful.

'Undead!' Haai-Bo said. 'I didn't read its presence!'

'Ellogg,' Ber snapped. 'You first.'

'Lumentis aid me,' the broomrider said. 'Together, guys.'

A sea of fire engulfed the monster, killing all pirates but not the thing. It shuddered, meowed and lumbered forward on its many legs.

'Those legs,' Ber cried. 'Hack them off!'

His little troop ran, screaming at the top of their voices, and Shaw followed, waving her pickax. One of the monster's giant pinchers reached for a boy, and Shaw swung at the appendage. As she hit its hard shell, she felt the shock vibrating through her arm. She withdrew as the pincher let go of his prey, and the boy chopped off a hairy leg just below the monster's body before running back.

A hail of flaming balls rained down on the monster, and it screamed where the fire bit into its wounds.

'Once more!' Ber shouted and again they ran.

Nate skirted around the monster, jumped upon a rock, and from it onto the monster's back. With his sword he swiped at one of the eyestalks and chopped it off. The monster twitched violently, and Nate slid off the carapace. He hit the ground with a thud and sprang away.

'One last time,' Ellogg screamed. Mage fire washed over the monster, spluttered and died away.

Ber's boys ran for the remaining legs, and now the lieutenant mounted the monster's back. With most of its limbs gone, the beast lay on the ground, waving its pinchers. Ber raised his sword up and rammed it point-down between two plates of the carapace. The monster shuddered violently.

Ber lost his balance and tumbled as the beast imploded with a sucking sound that ripped their souls.

Then Ber landed, rolled away and came up on his knees.

'It's gone,' Shaw said, fighting for breath. 'You guys defeated it, whatever it was. Well done! Very well done, all of you!'

'You too,' Ellogg said. 'You and Nate were with us.'

'Gods,' one of the other broomriders said. 'I never spent so much power. I'm done.'

'Let's get out of here,' Shaw said. 'We need fresh air.' Then she thought of something. *'Haai-Bo?'*

'Present, ma'am,' the wyrmling said from the shadows.

'Those pirates, would they have a ship close by?'

'Goo-ood question! I will fly.' He wheeled around and shot off to the exit.

They walked the winding corridor back to the outside world.

'Ship!' Haai-Bo said, just as they stepped into the sunlight. *'You asked and there is a ship. Four pirates aboard, not doing much, like pirates always do. And prisoners.'*

'There is a ship,' Shaw said. 'Only four pirates aboard, but they've got prisoners.'

'Ah,' Ber said. 'Just one more go, lads.'

His boys cheered.

Ellogg glanced at him. 'You're not eager, are you?'

'This is what my dad trained us for,' Ber said. 'To fight and to defend what is ours. Of course we're eager.'

The broomrider nodded. 'For us it's different; we're brought up to study the elements. Using it for war is new— and fascinating.' He picked up a mining-ax. 'Power is spent, but there is always the uncivilized way.' The lieutenants exchanged grins.

'You guys go capture the ship,' Shaw said. 'I need to talk with the people here.'

'No problem,' Ber said. 'We'll have her in a jiffy.'

As troops raced off, Shaw hurried over to the big barracks. The cutters had cleared up their workspace and sat waiting for her.

'We finished the pirates,' Shaw said. 'Now I need a word with you folks. This mine has almost run out of crystals. That means you'll be out of a job soon.'

'We know,' the woman said. 'We've been talking it over often enough.'

'If you are willing to move to another country,' Shaw said. 'I have a job for you folks.'

'What job?' the woman said. 'Crystal cutting is all we know.'

'We recently bought a silvermine in Wattash. That's on the Continent. We discovered massive crystal deposits. The miners didn't know what it was, so they threw it all away. There are whole heaps of uncut crystals lying around, and the mine is still thick with them. I need cutters and cutter instructors, and I offer good wages. What are they paying you?'

'Twelve pennies for a six-day week,' the woman said.

'I'll make it thirty pennies, for days of eight-to-five. We have a teleportal connection, so you can be home here every Restday. Free company uniforms, free healers and meals.'

'That sounds grand,' the woman said. 'I think most of us will be interested. Only... old Crimmon holds our contracts. I dunno if he's willing to let us go.'

Shaw looked at Nate. 'Darn, I hadn't thought of that.'

'We'll have a word with him,' Nate asked.

Without a word, Shaw rushed outside and over to the smaller barracks.

'It's all done,' she said to Crimmon. 'You'll have to remove the bodies yourself, but they're dead.'

'We'll do that,' the mine owner said. 'We're mighty grateful, ma'am. I really can't use this sort of thing; it is difficult enough to keep the whole works rolling without pirates buttin' in.'

'The crystal is almost exhausted,' Shaw said. 'What will you do then?'

'Back to mining silver,' Crimmon said. 'There's plenty of that left. It'll be bad for the cutters, though.'

'I know,' Shaw said. 'That's what I came for. I want to buy off their contracts.'

Crimmon rubbed his unshaven chin. 'Buy their contracts? Well now; PTC is loaded with coin, ain't it?' He grinned, showing a mass of bad teeth. 'If we're talking money, why don't you buy the whole mine?'

'How much?' Shaw said.

'Eight thousand. Mine, barracks, miners and cutters 'n all. No debts, and no great profits, either.'

'How much silver is there left?' Nate said.

'Enough for the next twenty years, and I've got the reports to prove it. Only Winsproke doesn't need any silver, and my man in Towne is as active as a bear in winter. I'm sixty-seven, and of no mind to go lookin' for another agent.'

'Eight thousand is a bit steep,' Shaw said. 'Those contracts won't run into the thousands of libers, and the barracks aren't worth more than five hundred, and that's generous. The mine... I don't need another silvermine, but alright. Let's make it six thousand, and you have a deal.'

'And a thousand more for the goodwill,' Crimmon said.

Shaw smiled. 'What goodwill? Because we're nice people at the PTC, I'll make it six five hundred.'

The mine owner rose abruptly and walked over to a rickety cupboard. He came back with a sheaf of papers and dropped them in front of Shaw.

'That's the Winsproke Silvermine. Now gimme the money, you girl shark.'

Shaw adjusted her eyeglass to focus her lazy eye and leafed through the papers. The report on the mine's remaining ore was eighteen months old and signed by both an engineer and a dowser mage from a Towne company. She passed them on to Nate, who checked them over carefully.

'Seems all right,' he said finally. 'I'd say buy.'

Shaw got out her checks and wrote one for the agreed amount. 'There you are,' she said, as she pushed it across the table.

Crimmon carefully pocketed the little slip, and they shook hands. 'You're a sharp one,' he said. 'Had I had a daughter like you, I'd be a rich man.'

'Quite probably,' Shaw said. 'Now we'll need a foreman to run this place.'

'Young Naja can do that,' Crimmon said. 'She does it anyway; she's the most contrarian girl alive.'

'I'm not,' a slight Vanhaari girl with hair and face a startling ash gray said. 'I just don't think you're right most o' the time.' She threw Shaw a challenging look. 'You gonna tell me how to run this mine?'

'Sure,' Shaw said. 'I will tell you how I want you to run that mine, and then I'll go away.'

'Know anything about it, then?' the girl said suspiciously.

'Not a bit,' Shaw said calmly. 'Mining is your job, running businesses is mine. I'm going to move the cutters to our other place in Wattash. You put a handful of workers to getting out the last crystals. They will be cut by the elder cutters in the town. The other workers go back to silver mining. We will let you know about the specifics, and our terms of employment. That means things like working hours, safety, pay and promotions, schooling, and such. As forewoman you will follow these directions to the letter. You may tell me if you have any concerns, but the workers' rights are not something I take lightly. There are a few more things, but you will be a PTC company, and I expect a business-like approach. You have a clerk? If not, hire one. Can you work with that?'

'An orderly organization?' The girl gave old Crimmon a hard look. 'Sure, the muddling way of doin' things is my biggest gripe here. Do I report to you?'

'No,' Shaw said. 'We'll appoint a director and a small office to coordinate all our Malgarth businesses.'

'Good,' Naja said. 'I like a clear setup.'

'Then you're hired,' Shaw said. 'How many cutters are there?'

'Fifteen,' she said. 'There used to be sixteen, but one ran.'

'What do you mean "ran"?' Nate said.

'It was a young guy, one of the newer employees. At the end of the day he was there, the next morning he was gone. Left a little note he found a better paying job on the continent.' Naja gave Shaw a sharp glance. 'That weren't you by any chance?'

'Nope,' Shaw said. 'And we don't steal people away like that either. Strange; who else would have a job for a crystal cutter?' She shrugged. 'Gone is gone. How are you situated for money?'

'We ain't got any,' the girl said. 'Mr. Crimmon ran the mine out of his own pocket.'

The old man rose. 'That I'll do no longer. I will leave you folks to it. I'm going for a drink or two.' He went to the door, humming.

'He wasn't a bad boss,' the girl said as they watched him walk away. 'But his heart weren't in it anymore. You mentioned money?'

'So I did.' Shaw wrote a check for a hundred libers. 'Here, that'll tide you over until I have had a chance to arrange matters. I will tell the head cutter they can move to Wattash. For the moment, if there are any problems, you can call me. Either Portaller Anna or the manager Mage Leah at the Emporium will know how to reach me.'

Naja gave a curt nod. 'Understood. I'll get on with the cleaning-up.'

'Arrange for food first,' Shaw said. 'Free meals, and decent ones.' She hurried away to tell the head cutter she had arranged everything. Then she went out again and looked around.

'I...' All of a sudden she felt lost.

'Easy,' Nate said, gripping her shoulders. 'Breathe.'

'Yes,' she said. Then she twisted around in his arms. 'But I told you I'd get the cutters today, and I did.'

He kissed her. 'I never doubted you.'

'Shaw!' Haai-Bo's familiar cackle interrupted them. *'We gotta ship! Easy as mice-pie it was. Surprise! Found crew-kids on board. Stout kids though nervous-like.'*

Nate laughed. 'Come on, love. Let's go and see her.'

'Love?' she said, feeling heat rise into her face.

'Yes. Did I ever hide that?' he said.

The coast was much nearer than Shaw had thought. Then she saw the potbellied twomaster at anchor near the beach.

She dropped like a stone until she was just over the deck, landed like a feather and stepped aside to make room for Nate on the crowded deck. She put her broom away and looked around.

The ship looked slovenly. *That can't have been the pirates' work,* she thought. *She looks like she's been badly used for a long time.*

Ber came up with four Garthan boys dressed in dirty sailor's smocks. 'It wasn't much of a fight,' he said. 'Hardly a fight at all. Those guys could've done it alone, if they hadn't been tied to the deck.' He grinned. 'We cut them loose, and they joined the fight barehanded.'

One of them, a thickset red-haired fellow, bared his teeth. 'We were a bit pissed,' he said. 'Betrayed, we'd been, an' that made us unhappy.'

'Tell me all,' Shaw said. 'Who are you, what ship; everything.'

'Me? I'm Gunno, senior bilgerat of the *Grimrose* out of Dibloon. We're a supply ship, running food from Veurdel and Lismoor to the other towns. Me and me mates were half of the crew, the sail-raisers, anchor-haulers, cargo-loaders; the bilgerats. We're cheap, y'know, and so was our skipper, may Chottapan keep his soul—forever and ever and ever. The traitorous dog.'

'Quite,' Shaw said. 'I've known guys like that.'

'So we were on our happy way home, three days back, when a Brisan pirate came. Normally, the pirates don't bother us; we're feeding their towns, after all. But this one had his cannons out and fired a shot. Skipper lost his cool and took to the jollyboat. O' course the mate and the others followed, but they refused to take us. "Too full!" the poxy dogs yelled, as they rowed away. I told ya we were cheap, didn't I?'

He wiped his nose on his sleeve. 'We were 'bout three miles off the coast between Dibloon and Lismoor and we saw them rowing for the beach like mad.' He unexpectedly grinned. 'They didn't make it. "Too full" had been right; you won't fit six fat bums in a three-man jolly, not in a choppy sea. All their pushin' and shovin' did for them, and the boat turtled. I saw them waving' at us as they went down. Three miles out, and none o' them could swim.'

'So you had your revenge,' Shaw said.

'Sure,' the boy said. 'Then the Brisans boarded. They laughed when we told them where the skipper was. Their own ship left and those on board had us sail *Grimrose* to this beach. They needed the ship for a load of some ores, they said. Ores for Angsthafn. They weren't going to kill us, but they didn't want us to run. Did we believe them?' The boy shrugged. 'Dunno. Perhaps they wouldn't; perhaps they even would've returned the ship. Or perhaps not. We didn't fancy sailin' to Angsthafn to find out, so we're glad you guys came. You don't seem like the piraty sort.'

'We're not,' Shaw said. 'We're pirate hunters. Remember the burning of Brisa? That was us.'

Gunno gaped at her. 'The guys who stole idiot Luzon's *Drakon* and had her shoot up the town? Darnation! They still get nightmares of you guys!'

'They'll have much more than nightmares before I'm done with them,' Shaw said grimly. 'But for now, can you sail this ship to New Winsproke harbor?'

'Sure; *Grimrose* was built for small crews; we can sail her anywhere along the coast,' Gunno said. 'And what will happen then? We lose the ship?'

'You lost the ship when the pirates came,' Shaw said. 'You want a decent berth? We'll hire you. You want back to Dibloon? We'll take you there, but without the ship. Or if you want to join the army, speak with Lieutenant Ber.'

'Dibloon ain't got nothing we need,' the boy said. 'The army? We're not the salutin' types. What berths do you offer?'

'We can use *Grimrose,*' Shaw said. 'And you can sail her. We'll hire you to do so, if you want to. The ship will need dock time and a good clean-up; she is filthy, and I won't have that.'

Gunno shrugged. 'Four guys doing all the work; sail-handling, loading and unloading, steering her, you can only do so much in a day. Yeah, she's a mess. Gimme the hands and we'll make her pretty.'

'We'll find the hands. How's your navigating?'

'I can read a chart, find Towne and every port on Malgarth by day and night, and get there, too.'

'Fair enough,' Shaw said. 'How many hands does she need?'

'Eight, no more,' Gunno said. 'Could be less, but that's comfy-like, see?'

'All right,' Shaw said. 'We'll talk it over when you're in New Winsproke. Tell the harbor officials you're sailing under the flag of the PTC, with registration at Smalkand, in the Pasandir Peaks. Then report at the Emporium, on Tower Square.'

'Got that,' he said. 'We'll be there. Ma'am.' He grinned and gave a sketchy salute.

'I'll see you then,' Shaw said. 'We'll be flying back, guys.'

CHAPTER 2 — VISITING THE PAST

They walked into the Emporium, and then Shaw noticed the tables full of Nanstalgarodian artifacts, all polished and looking properly mysterious.

'Nicely done,' Nate said. 'Really cleverly displayed.'

'You like it?' Leah said. 'I tried to make it exciting.'

'You succeeded,' Nate said. 'What would this be?' He picked up a slender rod with wheels along its length.

'We don't know,' Leah said. 'That's the fun part. That ancient Nanstalgarodian secret artifact is over five hundred years old, sir, and it gives off an aura of powerful magic. Can you discover what it does? For fifty libers it is yours to find out.' She looked at Shaw. 'Even Jem couldn't identify much of it. She supposed many objects had been part of something bigger, but out of their context she didn't know what it was. Engineer Imooga took a whole box of objects they did recognize back with her. She was sure studying them would bring bigger discoveries.'

'That would be nice,' Shaw said, absently scratching her blood-drenched jacket.

'Shaw,' Nate said. 'Let's go to *Sashu* for a wash and change. You look like the centerpiece in a butcher's shop.'

'I know,' Shaw said. She looked aside at Leah. 'Pirates had captured the mines. We told them not to do that, but some of them bled a bit. We captured their ship as well. I hope to be back before her bilgerat crew report here, but if not, the ship is the *Grimrose*, and the senior boy is Gunno.'

A good two hours later, back in Wattash, Shaw sat in *Sashu's* mess, trying to contain her irritation as she wondered what kept Nate.

Finally he came hurrying in, all smiles. 'Hi,' he said, giving her a quick kiss.

'Huh,' she said grumpily. 'I thought you'd fallen asleep.'

'Nope,' he said. 'I've been ashore, having a quick word with Jassal, the new Director Mines. He only just arrived, but he seems a sensible chap. I thought it handy to tell him of the cutters in person. He had his eye on a large empty building nearby that could be converted into a workshop with small apartments over it, but he wasn't sure about money. I told him to go ahead; those crystals were too important to hang on some minor investments.'

Shaw felt a wave of guilt at her earlier irritation and gripped his hands. 'Yes, of course! I hadn't thought of that.'

'He needed transport as well; the mine had a small covered ore wagon, but nothing else. I told him he could go ahead to the sum of ten thousand libers and order what he needed, and I put it in writing for him.'

'That's it, I tend to forget such details,' Shaw said, and she bit her lip. 'Darn, you did all that, and I sat growling because you were late. I'm sorry.'

Nate kissed her fingers. 'No need. I had hoped to be quicker, but I stopped by Purser Ricco aboard *Drakon* to have him pass on my promises to Banker Wainschilt.'

'You always think of everything,' Shaw said. Her eyes sought his face, and she felt a hot glow in her chest. 'Have you eaten anything?' she asked quickly.

'I ate some buns on the way,' he said. 'As far as I'm concerned, we can go back to New Winsproke.'

She took his hand. 'All right; then we'll go.'

Portaller Anna at the Emporium greeted them, looking worried.

'What's wrong?' Shaw said.

'There is trouble at the harbor,' she said. 'Something to do with that captured ship you were expecting. Mage Leah went to see what was going on, but she hasn't come back yet.'

Shaw grunted. *Trouble at the harbor*. 'I'll have their ears,' she snapped and strode to the door.

26

But before she could storm away, Leah came in with Gunno and his friends. The mage looked grimly triumphant.

'Those idiots!' she said. 'They didn't want to let *Grimrose* inside. It seems her name was on some blacklist, and the harbor guard refused to lower the boom.' She sniffed. 'Well, I told them. The nerve, to blacklist one of *our* vessels. I mean, Gunno *said* she was a PTC ship. I warned those guards you would buy the whole harbor and kick them out if they persisted in their nonsense.'

Shaw blinked. 'I would what?'

'Of course you would have,' Nate said. 'You've got a big part of the harbor of Myrlia already, why not New Winsproke? It's not that they use it.'

Shaw knew he was funning. Still... She shook her head. It made her sound awfully bossy. 'Well done!' she said quickly, smiling at Leah. 'Those guards are fools. Gunno, are you guys hungry?'

'Most of the time,' he said. 'It's our natcheral state, so to say.'

'Let's see what our cook can do about that.' Shaw said.

They crossed the Arcane Hall, still largely bare of magic artifacts to sell, and entered the cafeteria to the side of the building.

This was a large room, three times as long as it was wide, and furnished in the glittering style the decorator had called arty. The woman in charge was a middle-aged former navy cook; a sparse, gray-haired and very un-arty widow, who had accompanied her daughter as she came looking for a job. Now both of them worked for the Emporium.

'Hungry boys?' Cook said. 'I fed whole frigates full of them, so I know. Wash your hands and your face first while I whip up something.'

'Wash me 'ands?' Gunno looked at his grimy paws. 'Why?'

Nate grinned. 'It's a small price for a meal. Come with me; I'll show you the restroom.'

Shaw sighed as she watched him go. Then she turned to the older woman. '*Grimrose* needs repairs. Does the town have a dockyard, or must I go to Towne?'

'We have one, in mothballs,' Cook said while cutting sliced of cold meat. 'I believe there's a caretaker, but that's all. It was owned by a shipping firm that was a WyDir property, but has been defunct for years.'

Shaw stared at her. 'WyDir? Would you remember the name of that shipping firm?'

Cook halted her knife. 'Something-Tinnacore it was,' she said.

Shaw groaned. 'Tell Nate I'll be right back, I need a word with Mr. Morgan.' She almost ran to the portal. 'WyDir Salmon Street,' she said to Anna.

Moments later, she found herself in the imposing stained-glass entry-hall of the WyDir head office building. She smiled and waved at the guards and office workers, who all beamed and bowed as she ran past, and took the tall stairs to her presidential office two steps at a time.

'Ms. Shaw,' Morgan said as she burst in on her manager. He was a pleasant chap in his mid-twenties, nattily dressed in a dark coat, striped pants and a very daring purple cravat. He rose as she came in and smiled, no longer surprised at her panting arrivals.

She grinned. 'Mr. Morgan. I just got informed we seem to own a sleeping dockyard in New Winsproke.'

'We do?' he said, startled. 'I have no idea. Mr. Wylmer Senior used to own a few other companies there, but as far as I know they're all gone.'

'This yard was the property of a shipping company with Tinnacore in the name,' Shaw said.

'Paden-Tinnacore.' Morgan walked to his tall filing cabinet and unlocked a bottom drawer. 'In here are Mr. Wylmer's files. He wasn't in the habit of archiving things. I organized them by date, several years ago.'

He leafed through the dusty maps. 'Spider, get out,' he said, and blew away a small insect from a faded yellow file. 'Here it is; Paden-Tinnacore International, Winsproke. Funny, Mr. Wylmer never terminated the firm. It is a subsidiary of WyDir Shipping, itself a sleeping WyDir Airships company. Paden-Tinnacore Shipbuilding and Repair, Winsproke, is a daughter. All three are inactive, but not defunct, per twenty-two years ago.'

He faced Shaw. 'Three years after the end of the Unwaari War, Mr. Wylmer moved the business from New Winsproke to Seatome. I was convinced he had terminated his other businesses; he certainly never did any business through them after that date. I will check the archives in case there are any more surprises. What do you want to do with this shipyard?'

'If possible, I want to reopen the place,' Shaw said. 'I'll go over and see what is left of it.' She smiled. 'Thanks. Should you find we own anything more, anywhere, however ridiculous it looks, let me know.'

'Of course,' Morgan said, staring at the file drawer with some resignation. 'Many of Mr. Wylmer's files make sense only to him. But I'll see what I can glean from them.'

Back in the Emporium, Shaw found Gunno's guys busily working their way through a huge meal. Nate sat watching them with a mixture of joy and recollection.

'Look at them,' he said as she joined them. 'How well I remember being starved.' Then he raised an eyebrow. 'What was the sudden hurry?'

'Something Cook said when I asked about a shipyard. There is one here, but it's been closed.'

'So we go and buy it,' he said.

Shaw couldn't hide a grin. 'It's called the Paden-Tinnacore Shipbuilding and Repair Yard, and we already own it.'

'That was it,' Cook said. 'I know the shipyard is still there, but I don't know in what state she is. The whole thing had gone under when I was a callow cook's helper.'

Absently, Shaw snatched a drumstick from a well-filled bowl and bit in the soft meat. 'I went to see Morgan. His files showed neither the shipyard nor its parent company was terminated. I got the impression old Mr. Wylmer just closed the door behind him when he moved WyDir to Seatome.' Shaw licked the red sauce from her fingers. 'So we go and have a look at this place.' She waved a finger at Gunno. 'You eat and relax. After that, you can go back to the ship and sleep. Return here tomorrow morning.'

Gunno, his mouth full, just lifted a hand as she hurried Nate away.

They found the shipyard in the southern part of the town, just beyond the harbor. From the air it looked deserted, but not the derelict she had half expected. There were several buildings, among which a three-story office of redstone and yellow bricks, bearing a faded sign with the name Paden-Tinnacore International. A high fence surrounded the whole property, with a locked gate and a bell.

Shaw didn't want to trespass, so they landed outside the gate and rang the bell. After a while, an elderly man in a blue workers' suit came from a cabin, cradling a gun.

'No sight-seers,' he said neutrally. 'We're closed.'

'I know that,' Shaw said. 'I am the owner.'

The man stared at her with watery eyes. 'Yet you're not Mr. Clanger, not Mrs. Lutai, nor even Mr. Wylmer.'

'No,' Shaw said with a smile. 'I admit I am none of these people. I am Shaw Harwans, managing director of the PTC and WyDir.' She pushed one of her visiting cards past the gate bars, and the old man studied it carefully.

'What happened to Mr. Wylmer?' he asked suddenly.

'I'm afraid he had a stroke,' Shaw said. 'He sold the company to us, because only PTC is large enough to run a great company like WyDir.'

'A stroke,' the man said pensively. 'Clanger and Lutai have been dead for years.'

'I'm sorry to hear it,' Shaw said.

The man nodded. 'Now you come to close us down, after all that time?'

'No, I come to see how the dockyard can be reopened.'

The caretaker stilled. 'Reopened? But who will want to repair ships here? Winsproke is as dead as Sparkling Jitter.'

Shaw had no idea who or what Sparkling Jitter was, but she shook her head firmly. 'We are busily reopening the Emporium,' she said. 'We have taken over Renquar's and we're making flying carpets again. We're traders and shippers, and we can use another shipyard.'

The man nodded slowly and got a bunch of keys from his pocket. Without a sound, the gate opened. Shaw and Nate went inside, and the caretaker locked the gate behind them.

'This way, please,' he said.

He waved a boney hand at the first cabin. 'That's where I live. Mr. Wylmer gave me a small sum as well, enough to live on. I don't need much.'

'I hope you will continue in your job,' Shaw said. 'So that stays your house.'

'The office,' the caretaker said, as they walked to the front door of the redstone building. 'I was inside only once since we closed,' he said. 'To refasten a window pane. The whole building is as it was twenty-two years ago.'

Shaw stopped in the doorway and stared at the desks covered in dust, with papers still filling in- and out-trays, and dead plants on the mantelpiece.

'Mountain's Breath,' she said. 'It looks like they just walked away.'

'They did,' the caretaker said. 'I was the shipyard's watchman and went round with Mr. Clanger as he told the people. He was the yard manager, you know, and Mrs. Lutai the head clerk. Mr. Clanger walked in like he did every end of day, in his natty suit and gleaming ankle-boots. "I have an announcement," he said in that low, steely voice of his. "Mr. Wylmer has decided to close the company down immediately. In your weekly pay envelope you will find an extra week's wages. Mr. Wylmer and I thank you for your loyalty and we wish you fast re-employment elsewhere." It was totally unexpected, and no one spoke. They all filed out with their hats and coats, took their pay and left.' He looked around the ghostly office. 'The whole scene stands etched on my brain; it was the weirdest thing.'

'But there must've been contracts, deals, whatever was going on. You can't just walk away from everything,' Shaw said.

'It was a strange time, ma'am,' the caretaker said. 'What with the Unwaari War and all that. Every eye was on the Continent, on Lord Basil's doings, and without us knowing it, our Winsproke died while over there Vanhaar came back to life.'

Shaw shivered and watched as Nate opened some drawers here and there.

'People even left personal effects,' he said.

'I know,' the caretaker said. 'A lot came asking for it later, but I had strict orders not to admit anyone back in.'

'Mr. Wylmer must have been an eccentric man,' Shaw said.

'Not so much that as focused, ma'am,' the caretaker said. 'He was very focused on his work and less so on his people.'

Focused on his work... Somehow, she felt her face grow hot. 'I see,' she said and there was a lump in her throat.

'Don't look like that,' Nate said. 'You're not like old Wylmer; you very much see the people. Gunno, Leah, that old spellscribe; you care for all of them. Wylmer didn't even accept his own son.' He knocked on a desktop. 'No woodworm,' he said. 'We'll have a builder check the place over, but it appears serviceable. What's next?'

The caretaker locked the door behind them. 'That'll be the tool shop.'

They walked across a carefully raked gravel path to a low, stone building with a shingled roof. Another lock, and then they were in a dim room.

Vaguely, Shaw could discern workbenches, cupboards and machines she couldn't identify.

'There is oil lighting,' the caretaker said. 'But no oil.'

After that they went to the sawmill, the ropeyard, the sail loft, the smithy and all other places that made up the shipyard.

'Everything seems sound enough,' Nate said. 'Now the people. Where would we find a manager in this town?'

The caretaker hesitated. 'Perhaps young Mr. Clanger,' he said. 'He worked here as the foreman's assistant, when he was a journeyman. He'd be forty by now and a carpenter. He still makes small boats, for fishing, and he is a pleasant man. He... visits me sometimes, to talk about the old days. I shouldn't let him in, but this place gets a little lonesome now and then.'

'Of course,' Shaw said. 'You have a right to visitors.' She took a deep breath. Somehow, the atmosphere of the place oppressed her. 'Where do we find this gentleman?'

'Not very far from here,' the caretaker said. 'Out of the gates to the left, across the bridge. It is the third house, with a wooden boatshed in the water.'

'We will see him,' Shaw said quickly, eager to get away from the gloomy atmosphere. 'Thanks for all your help.'

'This will be a much better place when we're back at work,' the caretaker said. 'You'll see the difference.'

Shaw nodded, and they shook hands.

As they walked away from the gate, they heard the key in the lock as the caretaker closed himself in again.

'Gods!' Shaw said. 'That place got me.'

'It was kind of creepy,' Nate said and put an arm around her shoulder. 'Let's see this Mr. Clanger.'

The bridge crossed a creek with a ramshackle houseboat amid a field of water lilies. Beyond was a stone quay with a row of houses and large sheds.

The third house looked neat and well kept, with green woodwork and red-flowering plants on the windowsills. The doors to the adjacent shed were open and showed a burly man at work on a small rowboat.

'Mr. Clanger?' Shaw said.

The man turned around. He had curly hair, uncommon for a Vanhaari, and a twinkle in his eye.

'That's me,' he said. 'Joswa Clanger, carpenter and boat maker.'

'I'm Shaw Harwans, of the PTC,' she said.

Clanger's face lighted up. 'The lady who bought the Emporium and Renquar's?' he said. 'An honor to meet you! How can I help you, ma'am?'

Shaw grinned. 'As it happens,' she said. 'PTC is full owner of WyDir. This morning I discovered we own Paden-Tinnacore as well.'

Clanger's brows rose. 'That company went defunct years ago.'

'We checked with WyDir's head office, but apparently the owner simply walked out. Neither the shipping business nor the dockyard were ever officially terminated.'

'That's surprising,' Clanger said. 'My late father was the dockyard manager. He never spoke of that time. All he ever said was "It was Mr. Wylmer's decision to stop". Of course he lost his job as well.' He hesitated. 'Now what are your intentions?'

'I want to reopen the yard,' Shaw said. 'The caretaker showed us everything, and it seems still in good condition.'

'If not slightly spooky,' Nate added.

Clanger smiled. 'I can imagine you think so. But to reopen the yard... Where would you get your business?'

'I've got one ship in the harbor in need of repairs,' Shaw said. 'We took her off some pirates recently. But in the long run we will have to concentrate on building steel ships. We own a revolutionary engine design that would make ours both the most economic and the fastest ships afloat. We already own a shipyard in Kell, and we can use a second one.'

'We're trying to put New Winsproke back on the map,' Nate said. 'The Emporium and Renquar both specialize in the arcane sector; we're opening a large weaving-mill for flying carpets, and a shipyard for steel ships would be another exclusive industry.'

'We need a manager,' Shaw said bluntly. 'The caretaker mentioned your name.'

'Dockyard manager?' Clanger ran a hand through his curls. He looked steadily at Shaw. 'What will your position be?'

Shaw laughed. 'I'm the general manager of PTC; I'm running around buying businesses and things. I'm not going to tell you how to run a yard. The general policy will be to repair and build ships, both steam and with our new mana drive. We have a set of guidelines for the workforce; six eight-hour workdays, free meals, healer and uniforms, standard PTC wage scales, schooling and age levels. The manager will be free to decide the rest.'

'Money?' he said. 'There will be money?'

'You will get a thousand libers cash to start the business up, and another nine thousand as a reserve in the bank.'

'That is ample,' he said. 'I'm in, if you still want me.'

'Excellent,' Shaw said as they shook hands. 'I'll write you a check for the first thousand. Ask Lady Ruth, our general secretary, about the exact guidelines; she is at our Old Wharf warehouse in Seatome. She can answer questions and give assistance. We have a portal at the Emporium that connects you to all PTC locations.'

'I'll start recruiting immediately,' Clanger said, staring at the check.

'The City Council should let the town criers announce it for free. You can also contact the Seatome office of the *Weal Gazette* for a newspaper advertisement,' Shaw said. 'They have special prices for PTC companies. We noticed there were quite a lot of personal things left behind that last day. Perhaps you can find a way to let it be known people can come and reclaim them.'

'That's a nice thought,' Clanger said. 'I will let you know when we're open for business.'

They shook hands solemnly and left.

'Great,' Shaw sand contentedly, as they walked back to the Emporium. 'He'll get that place up and running again.'

Nate grinned. 'Bodrus will be pleased.'

'Sure,' Shaw said, wrinkling her nose. 'But I'm doing it because it is sound business sense. I'm running a trading company; not a mission.' She looked up as she heard a faint, jolly laugh. *'My god?'*

But there was no answer.

CHAPTER 3 — OVERDUE RETRIBUTION

The next morning, when Shaw and Nate returned to the Emporium, they emerged in organized chaos. Sailors in PTC uniforms were carrying in boxes and bales for the general goods storeroom, stacking them left and right seemingly at random.

Mage Lea stood watching it all with visible satisfaction, with beside her Captain Leolynn of the *Maiden of Allastar*, PTC's big freighter.

Shaw looked at Nate. 'I didn't expect *her* here.'

'Morning,' Leolynn said, turning to greet them. 'Between us, our five ships carried so much cargo that Master Varan sent part of it on to Towne and here. *Hind* and *Lodestar* are in dock; Captain Olesha transferred crew and cargo into *Thistle Ivy* and sailed with me. *Lion* is here as well.' She grimaced. 'It took some time to find transport; the port seems unused to cargo ships. Such a big harbor and only one other ship in.'

'And that one is ours, too,' Nate said. '*Grimrose*; a recent capture. You're right; this place has been neglected far too long. For transport we'll be getting flying carpets; those should work for you as well.'

Shaw looked at Nate. 'With *Maiden* in port...' she said slowly, as an idea formed in her mind. Then she turned to the captain. 'Are you ready for battle?'

'Well,' Leolynn said. 'Our guns are clean, our girls are trained, and we've plenty of powder and shot.'

'With a bit of luck you won't fire a gun,' Shaw said slowly. '*Maiden*'s archeresses are the only fighting unit I've not yet seen. Kennan and his guys are marines now; I made him a captain.'

'I got a note to that effect,' Leolynn said. 'We wondered if that went for us as well. Our girls think of themselves as leopardesses.'

'And they get a leopardess' pay, which isn't all that much,' Shaw said. 'As PTC marines they'd earn more, and your lead girl would be a marine lieutenant, not a subofficer.'

'I'll ask them,' Leolynn said. 'But that wasn't what you wanted to discuss.'

Shaw grinned. 'No. I want to capture the Tradeports.'

Both Leolynn and Nate stared at her.

'I plan to stop their piracy once and for all. We've been moaning about their games long enough. Yesterday, we kicked them out of the local mine. I'm fed up with those drunken sods; let's go and wipe them out.'

'Aren't the Tradeports Malgarth lands?' Nate said. 'We don't want a quarrel with the high king.'

'They're not,' Mage Leah said. 'The Tradeports have always been independent, just like Thali is.'

'Didn't know that,' Nate said. 'How do you plan to conquer them?'

'I need to know more first,' Shaw said. 'Is Gunno here?'

'I saw him and his mates helping with the unloading,' Nate said. 'I'll call him over.'

He walked to the door and whistled.

Moments later, the bilgerat skipper came hurrying in, grinning and sweaty. 'We're earning our pay, see?'

'Great job,' Shaw said. 'But I got something else to ask. You guys are from Dibloon. Do you know the other ports too?'

'Of course,' Gunno said. 'We came there every month, mostly carrying foodstuffs. See, *Grimrose* was owned by the Table of Dibloon. The Table merchants are the rich guys who rule the town. Veurdel has the only farms in the land while Lismoor is cattle. Renvel has its fishing, but Dibloon and Brisa depend on us for their dinners.' He pulled a face. 'With *Grimrose* gone, they'll be getting hungry by now.'

'How are the defenses? Soldiers in the towns, artillery, things like that?'

Gunno shrugged. 'Veurdel is a hole. It's just a collection of farms with a pier; a thousand people, if it's that. Lismoor is about the same. Renvel is twice as big; fishing, canneries, smoke houses, things like that. Mostly closed down as the fishers joined the pirates. Last I was there they had two small pirate ships. Dibloon is bigger, but her harbor isn't too hot. Brisa is the main town, even with her port still in bad shape. Last I saw she had four ships and maybe five hundred pirates. If the ships are all in, of course.'

'How do the people think about the pirates?' Nate asked.

Gunno shrugged. 'What we heard is that most are fed up with the drunken sods. People are always talking about the good old days of trading and a bit of privateering. They had money then, and the freedom of the Wydemere. Now they're hungry, and no foreign town will receive them. Besides, many of those pirates aren't even locals; they're outsiders from the north.'

'So if we'd run in, kick the pirates into the sea and take over the government, the people would at least listen?'

Gunno gave a barking laugh. 'Promise them protection, vittles and some money, and they're yours.'

'That's the answer.' Shaw looked at Nate. 'We need food.'

'Don't look at me,' Gunno said. 'We're empty. *Grimrose* was on her way home after the last run.'

'When will they expect you back?' Nate said.

Gunno grimaced. 'Last week,' he said. 'They'll be feeling the pinch by now.'

'We'll have to hurry then,' Shaw said. She turned around to Anna, the Emporium portaller. 'Would you call Master Varan in Old Wharf and tell him I need his help right now?'

She giggled. 'I'll summon him.'

'Thanks,' Shaw said. 'The other captains?'

'Outside,' Leolynn said. 'Do you need them?'

'In a minute,' Shaw said. 'Haai-Bo?'

The wyrmling came drifting down from the rafters. 'Going to war we are? Good.'

'Ask Abbram, Kennan and Yens to come here for a council of war; that'll get their attention. Where are Ber and Ellogg?'

'All outside,' Haai-Bo said. 'They're working hard.'

'Let them be until the others arrive,' Shaw said.

A short hour later, all were present; the three merchant captains, Gunno as acting skipper, Master Varan, and the ten army and marine officers. From *Maiden* came an energetic young leopardess who introduced herself as Dryona.

'We want to join the marines,' she said, seriously. 'It is better to be an equal with the others.'

'Much better,' Shaw said. 'Gentlemen, this is Marine Lieutenant Dryona, of the *Allastar Maiden*.'

Kennan rose first. 'Another marine!' he said. 'Well met, I'm Captain Kennan.'

He was a male, of which there still weren't many of high rank in the conservatively female Kell army, but Dryona simply saluted and they shook hands.

'Good to see you, guys,' Shaw said, grinning broadly round at their expectant faces. 'Are you curious?'

'Of course; when you call a council of war,' Captain Abbram said pugnaciously. 'Are we going to attack somebody?'

Shaw smiled at his grim eagerness. 'We are; a long overdue matter. Yesterday, we discovered a party of Brisan pirates had captured the local crystal mine.'

Abbram frowned. 'You need us to get them out? Are they many?'

Shaw laughed. 'Hardly. Lieutenants Ber and Ellogg took care of that.'

Kennan made a thumb-up. 'Well done, guys.'

'They also captured the *Grimrose*, a merchantman acting as the Tradeports' supply ship. Gunno here is the senior of the four survivors and acts as her skipper.'

'Good for you,' Abbram said. 'Welcome.' He glanced at Shaw. 'Brisa? I don't know the place.'

Nate unfolded a chart. 'We're here,' he said. 'New Winsproke, a colony of the Weal of Four Nations on the west coast of Malgarth. To the northwest are five towns commonly called the Tradeports. They always were a bunch of privateers, but later they got taken over by the Bokkaners. Brisa is the leftmost town and the main port of the five. Some months ago, the wyrmcaller decided to stop their pirating. We sailed and in a night action conquered the *Drakon* and used her to shoot up the port. It bought us some time, but apparently not enough, for they are back at their games again.'

'This time we will sail north and conquer the lot,' Shaw said coolly.

Varan half-rose. 'You're going to *capture* the Tradeports?' he said.

'We don't want the pirates to come back again, so we'll make the place part of the Peaks,' Shaw said. 'Do you see any objections?'

Varan's face lit up in a smile. 'Not I,' he said. 'The Weal Council might.'

'Stuff them!' Shaw said. 'They could have done it themselves. Instead they sat on their hands and let their merchants suffer.'

'Hang those Tradeport rats and you'd be the hero of the Chorwaynies,' Varan said. Then he turned to Gunno. 'Your pardon; I meant the pirates, it wasn't personal.'

The boy spread his hands. 'We're with you,' he said. 'Most of common Tradeporters want to see them swing too.'

'You are the local expert,' Shaw said. 'Tell us of the Tradeports.'

For the next hour they discussed the ports, until Abbram leaned back in his chair. 'Thank you,' he said. 'You got your eyes open, mate; very useful information.' He looked at Kennan. 'I think it can be done.'

'So do I,' Kennan said. 'Among us, we can take those towns. But then what?'

Shaw smiled. 'We get them to agree to join the Peaks. To help them decide, we'll bring them a load of foodstuffs as a gift. After that... Dear Varan, what would you say to a job as director for Malgarth? It'll be mainly the Tradeports; unite the towns, set up trade, rebuild the lot and make them into something useful for the company and the wyrmcaller?'

Varan's face was blank, and he stared at her without seeing anything. Finally he stirred. 'It is tempting,' he said. 'I need to see the towns first, though.'

'We all do, of course,' Shaw said. 'But I want you to come with us and bring five capable managers to open a warehouse in each of the ports. The director will see to the election of town councils and will act as the coordinator.'

'That's quite a job,' Varan said pensively. He grinned. 'Those five managers; I'll have to beg some from Sylas and Amsalon. I can't take too many away from Old Wharf, especially not if I accept your proposal.'

'Start with Amsalon,' Shaw said. 'He must have lots of people looking for a high-class job. Tell him you need five warehouse managers, but keep the Tradeports a secret from all but the candidates. I will inform the company myself when we've captured the ports, not before.'

'All right,' Varan said. Then he frowned, as if considering something. 'Five new managers to break in is a lot. Perhaps you could write a list of do's and don'ts for them?'

Shaw sighed. 'Yes, that may be best. I'll put it all down and send it to Ruth. She can distribute it among the management for comments and make it all nice.'

'Transport,' Nate said. 'We have four ships. Gunno could use some spare hands, maybe?'

'I spoke to a few guys,' Gunno said. 'Fishers; their skipper went bust or got busted, something like that. The three o' them were hanging round in the harbor, throwing flat stones and being bored sick. I could maybe hire them if you'd fork over some money.'

Shaw took out her purse and shook a handful of pennies on the table. 'Here; pay them and your guys. Two pennies per day and four for you as skipper. When we get back, we'll make better arrangements.'

'Darn,' Gunno said, while he tied the coins carefully into an extremely dirty handkerchief. 'You're the first boss who actually pays us.'

Abbram laughed. 'Nice, ain't it?'

'Now,' Nate said. 'Which ship will go where?'

'Depends on speed,' Leolynn said. 'Gunno?'

'Twelve knots,' the boy said. 'I won't win the race, I think.'

Leolynn grinned. 'No, even *Lion* is faster than that.'

Captain Lowin snorted. '*Lion* is a pleasure yacht,' he said. 'Not a ruddy warship.'

'She's a lazy bucket,' Captain Olesha said bluntly. 'Perhaps Ms. Shaw will capture you a real ship; one that doesn't put all of us asleep watching her amble in our wake like some overfed lapdog.'

'Abbram's battalion will go in *Maiden*,' Shaw said quickly, before Shar Lowin could retort. 'How much food will Brisa need?'

Gunno took a slim booklet from his pocket. '*Grimrose*'s order book,' he said. 'Here's all which town gets what and how much.'

Varan held out his hand. 'Let me copy the details.'

'Then *Thistle Ivy* will take Ber's troop to Veurdel and Kennan's marines to Dibloon,' Shaw said. 'That settles the farthest towns. *Lion* will go to Lismore with Ellogg's broomriders, and finally Yens will go in *Grimrose* and capture Renvel. Dryona's marines will take the Brisan ships, while Abbram goes for Brisa town. If there is any trouble, opposition too strong, or whatever, don't play the hero. Take to your brooms and get out. We'll come with more troops to back you up.'

'Will we attack when ready, or wait for the other ships to be in position?' Abbram said.

'Attack when you're there. Do give Haai-Bo a shout when you go in, and when you've captured the town.' Shaw looked around. 'How much preparation time do we need?'

'Three days for the food,' Varan said. 'A lot of stuff will need to be repacked.'

'All right,' Shaw said. 'Then we'll sail the fourth day from now, at eight in the morning.'

CHAPTER 4 — SAILING FORTH

Promptly at the appointed time, the flotilla departed. Shaw stood on *Maiden*'s quarterdeck with Nate and Varan when the faraway pitch of the steam engine changed and New Winsproke harbor slipped away.

Shaw watched the other ships; fat *Lion* with her old-fashioned lines, the sleek schooner *Thistle Ivy*, and *Grimrose*, a rough workman barging his way through the waves. She saw figures running up the mast to lower the topsail as well. Gunno had found not three but seven seafaring kids, and they didn't do badly at all. *I'll send Gunno to Smalkand,* she thought. *Miyra or Wylmer must give him a crash course on what an officer needs.*

'We're on our way,' Nate said.

She leaned back against his shoulder and grinned. 'Fun, ain't it?'

Nate put his arms around her waist, and together, they watched the flotilla following them as the town disappeared in the distance.

'Strange ship at anchor!' the lookout in *Maiden*'s mainmast shouted. They were six hours out of New Winsproke, and about halfway to Brisa, the nearest of the Tradeports.

Shaw glanced at the coastline and the waning moon above it. *Moon or not, that lookout had good eyes to see an anchored ship in this darkness.*

'That should be Codnoallis; the chart says it's a fishing village,' Leolynn said. 'Shall we investigate?'

'We had better,' Shaw said. She would rather press on, but this close to the Tradeports, every ship was suspect, and she couldn't take the risk. '*Maiden* will do it. Tell the other ships to carry on; we'll catch up later.'

Soon they saw the ship, an old brig moored to a pier with two fishing smacks in company.

'Pirates aboard,' Haai-Bo said. 'Twelve of them, mostly asleep.'

'Pirates? Then it's a job for the marines,' Leolynn said. 'Tell Dryona to take the ship.'

It was as if they'd been waiting for action. Within five minutes, the Kell girls were in the air, and another twenty minutes later, Dryona's corporal returned to report, flushed and triumphant.

'We've got her,' she said. 'Those fool pirates couldn't fight their way out of a bottle of booze.'

'Fast work!' Shaw said. 'Tell the lieutenant I want the squad to go ashore and see if there are any more villains lurking.'

The corporal saluted and hurried back.

'It doesn't look much,' Shaw muttered, staring at the moonlit village. *What would a brig do at a flyspeck place like that?* 'What did you say it was called?'

'Codnoallis,' Leolynn said. 'It's on the map, but barely.'

Shaw grunted and got her broom. 'I'm going to have a look.'

'You surprise me,' Nate said.

She stuck out an undignified tongue at him and shot up in the air. Without waiting, she hurried to the dark shore.

Moments later, Nate appeared beside her, and together they landed at the beginning of the pier.

The village was smaller than its name. One large communal building, three dwellings and a barn, all with roofs looking in the dark like upturned rowing boats.

At the largest building, they found most of the marines outside.

'Where's the lieutenant?' Shaw asked.

'She went in, to question the locals,' the corporal said.

Shaw nodded and pushed open the door. Then the smell of rancid whale oil, wet furs and ripe humans in the low room made her gag. She swallowed, screwed her eyeglass in her eye and walked over to where Lieutenant Dryona stood talking with a gnarled man in an innkeeper's apron. Several young guys and a second man with a bandaged foot were listening.

'No pirates here,' the innkeeper said. 'We're honest folk, lieutenant.'

Dryona saluted Shaw. 'We got the ship, ma'am; I believe those pirates were all.'

Shaw nodded. 'Good evening,' she said to the locals. 'I am Shaw Harwans, of the Pasandir Trading Co. What was that brig doing here?'

'Waiting for a passenger,' the gnarled innkeeper said. 'Them dogs had nothing to do with us. We have no business with those blighters.'

'Do they come here often?' Shaw said.

The innkeeper shook his head. 'Not after they took all we had, last year. Now they leave us alone. They don't need our boats, they don't eat our fish an' we sent our women inland when they came, to a safe place.'

'They don't even take the boys?' Shaw said.

'They tried once,' a lad said. 'But we run faster and when we're in the fens, they'll never find us. So they let us be.'

'Who owns this land?' Shaw said. 'Are you part of Malgarth?'

'We're not,' the innkeeper said. 'We're a free port and always were. Everything between Winsproke to Brisa is ours, for what it's worth. We once thought to farm it, but every time we got something set up, raiders from Malgarth came an' ruined it.' He hawked and spat with practiced precision into a dented bucket.

'At least the pirate threat kept *them* away,' one of the boys said.

The innkeeper grunted. 'Yeah. But by now we're slowly dying out. Come in twenty years, an' we'll be gone.' He shrugged. 'Chottapan's Will.'

'We'll see about that,' Shaw said. 'What are your strong points?'

'We got plenty of fish,' a boy said. 'The sea's full of them, and so are the rivers. Salmon!'

'Salmon?' Nate said. 'We could open a small rest house and organize fishing trips. Rich guys pay a lot of money for good fishing.'

Lieutenant Dryona laughed. 'I've got an aunt like that. She's been all over the Weal; spear fishing at the Chorwaynies, ice fishing at Bitter'eights Lake, she'd be here in a shot if I tell her.'

Shaw grinned. 'Your aunt will have to buy a fishing license first.' She turned to the gnarled man. 'We'll talk about that later. Now I need some guys to guard the ship. Honest guys, who won't go pilfering.'

One of the boys looked at her. 'We're honest as newborn babies,' he said. His friends laughed heartily, but he waved them into silence. 'We're honest, as long as you pay us.'

Shaw mustered him, from his big feet in leaky boots, past his patched pants and tunic to the dirty lines in his face. 'Guy, I was raised in an orphanage,' she said softly. 'I know how it goes and I'll not demand anyone work for free, ever. Got that? Of course I will pay you. There are six of you; two pennies per day for each of you. You bury those dead pirates—and I mean bury in the ground, not throw them overboard—and I'll pay another two pennies per body. You clean up the ship and I'll add a penny per man per day. For a minimum of five days, that would earn you nineteen pennies each, half in advance, half when we return.'

'Deal,' the boy said quickly.

Shaw got out her purse and handed him half of the promised sum.

Then the boy came to his feet. 'Right, lads. We got a job to do.'

'The money!' a second boy demanded, holding up a dirty hand.

'I know you,' the first one said. 'Lemme see some work first.' He gripped the second boy by the neck and pushed him to the door.

'My grandsons,' the gnarled man said proudly. 'Two fine lads, as are the others.'

'They're all good fishermen,' the man with the bound foot said. 'I hope you're not hiring them away from us?'

Darn, Shaw thought. *He's right; I can't take them and expect the town to live.* 'No,' she said hastily. 'You need them more than we do.'

He nodded. 'With my gout, I can't sail anymore, so I depend on them.'

'You are the only fisherman left?' Shaw said. 'I mean adult ones?'

'The only skipper,' he said. 'I own those two boats at the pier. But we're none of us healthy, and we need those boys more than we like.'

'What you need is a healer,' Shaw said.

'One with a passion for fishing,' Nate said.

'While we're gone, discuss with the other folk what your needs are,' Shaw said. 'When we get back, we'll make a list and see what we can do. Now we must hurry.'

'What are you going to do up north?' the innkeeper said. 'Brisa is brimful with pirates.'

'After tomorrow it won't be,' Shaw said. 'We're going to put an end to the pirating business once and for all.'

'Going to raze them?' the gouty man said, suddenly anxious.

'Of course not,' Shaw said. 'We'll kill the pirates and take the towns. Then we're going to help them just as we'll do for you.'

'So fierce,' the innkeeper said. 'And such a wisp of a girl. I would laugh if it weren't for those Kell warrioresses.'

'Don't let them stop you,' Shaw said coolly. 'But remember I will have the last laugh. I run a large trading company with thousands of employees; I have an army sailing north and I will root out those pirates. Then I will show Brisa, Dibloon and the other towns doing it my way will be far more profitable and far healthier than terrorizing my friends.'

The innkeeper raised his hands. 'I ain't laughing. Will we see you again, ma'am?'

'We will,' Shaw said. 'I must take my leave now; I need to be in position by nightfall. Lieutenant, let's go back to the ship.'

'We will await your return then,' the innkeeper said. 'We all wish you the very best of luck.'

Shaw smiled. 'Thank you.'

Outside, she breathed in the clean air. 'Let's go.'

As they flew over the captured brig, the local boys stared up at them open-mouthed. Shaw waved and raced to the *Maiden.*

'We're done here for now,' she said to Leolynn as they had returned to the ship. 'Can you still catch up with the rest?'

The captain grinned and pulled the telegraph to Full Ahead.

Under Shaw's feet, the deck vibrated and spray came over the ship's high prow as Codnoallis disappeared into the distance.

'Well,' she said to Nate. 'Talk about a dying place. How many people did we see? No more 'n fifty.'

'If that many,' Nate said. 'You won't get anyone else living there. Not as it is. I've seen some miserable hovels in my life, but that place beats everything.' He glanced at Shaw. 'That fishing lodge idea sounds like a great solution.'

She nodded. 'It could be profitable. I can't think of anything else that would be.' She lapsed into silence and Nate simply drew his arm around her shoulders as she stared out over the dark sea.

Maiden easily caught up with the rest of the flotilla and a little past midnight they were off Brisa's harbor no more than a mile away.

'*Haai-Bo?* ' Shaw said. She wasn't a mindreader herself, but she could initiate contact with a few minds who probably where monitoring her anyway; her wyrmling advisor, Teodar the Kavid-Jar and of course Divine Bodrus.

'*Up, up, away; flying spy am I,*' the wyrmling said. '*Ship, moored to the quay; three men on guard, asleep, and four prisoner kids. Another ship, six men; drunk as can be, and five kids. Beyond them a third, a bigger one; ten men, more or less awake, and twelve kids. Am going to the town now.*'

Shaw repeated his words to the others on the bridge. 'It's the same as they always do; capture a ship, kill the adults and keep the youngsters to do the work their drug-ruined minds can no longer grasp.' She turned to the marine lieutenant. 'They're all yours.'

Dryona saluted and hurried away.

'*Town sleeps,*' Haai-Bo said. '*Only the pirates are busy; there's a row of warehouses where they booze and get drugged. One captain is sober, more or less; he is the commander. Five buildings are for drinking, with some hundred men inside each and little room for fighting. Other place is for making eggs; nude men and women twining necks and acting love.*'

Shaw grinned when she repeated that.

'We can't just run in if it's that crowded,' Abbram said sternly. 'We will surround the buildings, summon them to come out or we torch the tavern with them inside. Then we'll fight it out in the open.'

'Five hundred men,' Nate said.

'Drunk and drugged,' Abbram said. 'That halves whatever fighting abilities they have.'

'I seen all,' Haai-Bo said. 'No guards, no jinn. Some roaming parties, singing to the moon as they wander the streets.'

Shaw took a deep breath. 'That's it, then. Captain Abbram, go get them. Nate and I will follow you in. Good luck!'

She shook hands with Captain Leolynn and walked to the *Maiden*'s wide main deck. Nate gave her a quick kiss, and then they flew after the troops to the town.

She saw the shadowy form of a large threemaster vessel. While she looked, she saw the gangplank being drawn in and a tall Kell girl raise a hand in triumph.

Shaw waved back and grinned wildly at Nate.

On the quay, small figures ran towards the row of warehouses. As Shaw landed near the first building, the door opened and a fat pirate came weaving out. He must have seen the running soldiers, for he opened his mouth and ran back inside. Moments later, a stream of pirates came, brandishing swords, barstools and billiard cues, pushing and shoving to get past the door. Lieutenant Kashim, he of the innocent face and the many knives, shouted an order, and his guys went to the attack.

Shaw bit her lip. It wasn't a battle, but a massacre. The pirates may have been in the majority, but drunk and drugged, coming out one by one through a narrow door, they were next to helpless. It wasn't nice, it never was. Shaw knew there was no alternative; they wouldn't surrender. And even if they did, she'd have to hang them. Those guys were scum; murderers, butchers of innocent sailors and passengers, slave dealers and servants of man-eating jinn. Still, she wished there was another way. *Cursed jinn! They made those men and women what they were!*

Then, when the stream of pirates dried up, Kashim yelled, and they stormed inside. Shaw went with them, gripping the pickax from the mine and expecting opposition, but the barmen raised their hands. 'We only work here,' one of them shouted.

While a few men remained below stairs, the others ran for the staircase to the upper floor. Sounds of fighting told Shaw there were more enemies, but soon Kashim came back.

'We got them all,' he said with grim satisfaction. 'Those coyotes won't rob no more ships, ma'am.' He looked at the cowering barmen. 'Put them to work, Corporal. Let them collect the dead and clean up the mess. You guard the joint while we go next door.'

'Aye, we'll have a nice snort, sir,' the corporal said, grinning.

'All the booze is poisoned,' Shaw said. 'Drinking it would make you a jinni tool.'

The corporal paled. 'I was only joking, ma'am,' he said.

Shaw smiled grimly. 'I wasn't. Remember what they did to Guildlady Jathira.'

The corporal nodded vehemently, and Kashim gave him a scathing look before running outside.

From the third warehouse came the sounds of heavy fighting and without a word, Kashim led his men inside.

Before Shaw had decided whether to follow him or not, a window crashed open and a bearded giant Garthan in a fancy captain's coat jumped out. He bellowed as he saw them and his heavy ax swished as he swung it at Shaw's head. She dropped to the ground and rolled away while Nate lifted his sword. The Garthan ignored him and gave a triumphant grin as he saw Shaw pinned against a lamppost, unable to escape.

'Die!' he screamed, drooling spittle. Then Nate lunged and skewered him. Shaw gaped as she saw the point of his blade appear over the man's navel, with blood gushing down the pirate's crotch. The giant captain wavered, dropped his ax and tried to push back the sword punt. Then he grunted, tottered and fell down, pinning Shaw's legs to the ground.

Nate stooped and with a mighty heave, pulled the dead body aside. Then he dropped to his knees beside Shaw.

'You're all right?'

She nodded weakly.

Nate grinned at her. 'This time I protected you,' he said contentedly. 'Can you stand?'

She came to her feet and picked up the miner's ax she'd kept since the fight at the silvermine. 'That was a mighty blow,' she said softly. 'Darn! You really did him in!'

He laughed. 'The hidden power of the Vanhaari,' he said. He tried to pull his sword from the body, but it stuck.

'Wait, I'll hold him,' Shaw said. She gripped the dead captain by his coat while Nate tugged at the blade. All at once, the sword came free and Nate nearly fell on his back as it effortlessly slid from the body. Shaw began to giggle, and moments later she roared with laughter.

'What's wrong with you?' Kashim said as he came from the tavern.

Shaw couldn't stop. All the emotion she had so carefully kept in check this night came out as she sat and laughed till she cried.

'Oh,' the lieutenant said, nodding at the dead pirate captain. 'You got him? Good for you.'

Shaw hiccupped and took a deep breath. 'Your pardon,' she said. 'It's not him; I was laughing at myself. How's the tavern?'

'It's ours,' Kashim said. 'Some wounded, but nothing the healer can't handle. We've been darned lucky until now.'

A broomriding soldier landed beside them. 'Captain Abbram sends his compliments, and we took the last warehouse, ma'am. We got them all.'

'Well done!' Shaw said warmly. 'Any survivors?'

'Among the pirates?' the young soldier said. 'None. We couldn't have kept them alive had we wanted to. The last ones fought, so we *had* to kill them. The barkeeps and the friendly naked ladies are all fine.'

Kashim coughed. 'We've got an audience,' he said. 'There's a crowd gathering down the street.'

'Let's have a word with them,' Shaw said, and she took out her broom.

As she walked past the captured warehouses, she marveled at those people. To come out in the middle of the night to see what was going on, was that bravery or stupidity?

'News from the war,' Haai-Bo said suddenly. He was overhead somewhere, acting as her personal communications officer. *'Commander Yens reports he took Renvel and two small ships. They're unloading food and the town is at his feet.'*

'Tell him congratulations,' Shaw said. *'Great job!'*

By now there were almost a hundred people staring at the soldiers. Shaw saw desperation in their faces; many looked as if they hadn't slept for too many nights.

As she went up to them, more were coming. Men, women, elderly and children, many only half-dressed.

'Good evening,' Shaw said pleasantly. 'Your pardon if we woke you people up. We tried to do it silently, but those pirates; you know them. Always screaming; they can't even die quietly.'

Someone sniggered.

'Who are you?' an older man said. 'Them soldiers, they're all youngsters, but they fight like men.'

'We are the Pasandir Trading Company,' Shaw said. 'Part of the lord wyrmcaller's organization.'

'Gods!' a boy sighed. 'The guys who shot up the port.'

'The very same,' Shaw said. 'This time we're not here to shoot up anything. We want you all alive and happy, and free of pirates.'

'That won't happen,' the old man said. 'They're rats; the moment you leave, they'll be back.'

'But we won't leave,' Shaw said. 'We know far too well what those ruffians are. Do you have people who speak for Brisa?'

There was a silence while all townsfolk looked away.

'The merchants of the Table,' a man said reluctantly. 'The Table governs the town.'

Shaw looked at the shadowy faces. The people seemed cautious, even scared. 'Kindly send someone to warn the Table merchants I want to see all of them here in an hour's time.'

'Are the streets safe?' a woman asked.

Lieutenant Uzhan came forward. 'Our men searched the whole town from the air and took out every pirate we found wandering, mistress. As far as we can tell there isn't one of them left alive in the town.'

'Gods bless,' the woman said fervently. 'Gods bless and thank you.'

The townspeople dispersed and Shaw turned to the commanders.

'We will gather all bodies and collect their possessions,' Abbram said. 'After that, I suggest hiring some townsfolk to arrange for their disposal.'

Shaw nodded, suddenly sick of all the killing. Five hundred bodies... 'Carry on; I will have a look at the ships,' she said.

Abbram nodded and Shaw turned her back to the piles of dead pirates.

'You don't need to do everything,' Nate said. 'Let the army handle the clean-up.'

She shivered, grateful for his words. Silently, she mounted and waited for Nate to join her. Then they went over to the big steamship.

The ship was called *Wentiibi*, her name written on the bow. As they landed on the main deck, a group of youngsters silently gathered to stare at them.

'Do you bring food?' a wiry, very pale Garthan said. 'We haven't had anything in two days.' He was barefoot, dressed in a dirty smock, and smelled like a cesspool.

'How many of you are there?' Shaw said. 'And why? Are you the crew?'

'There are twelve of us,' the boy said. 'We were ordered to discover how this ship works.' He sighed. 'Ekiel is showing us all he knows.'

'Who is Ekiel?' Shaw said.

The first boy said something, and from the back of the group another came, bald-shaved and tense. Then Shaw blinked. In the light of the ship's lamps she could see him clearly. His face was Vanhaari, but his complexion was different; not stone gray like hers, or green like her Qoori friends, but a startling blue, while his eyebrows and the stubble on his head were yellow.

'Hi,' she said. 'Are you Ekiel?'

'Yes, high one, I am him, once Seeker-almost-Found of the Saeill Invincible Navy,' the boy said. 'Now I am Last of the *Wentiibi*.' His whole body seemed tense, but his voice was soft and steady.

'What happened?' Shaw asked.

'The First Steerer of the Saeill demanded to know what lay across the sea to the sunside of our island. So he ordered our First Wielder to go and discover. Many long days we sailed into an empty sea.' He swallowed. 'The horror of an empty sea... No land; nowhere. We thought us all alone, sailing into oblivion. Into madness.'

He swayed a little and his words came out in bursts, betraying the strain his face tried to hide. 'After a month, at night, they came. We kept no watch; why should we? We were all alone. Yet we weren't. Sea robbers boarded us before we knew what happened. Boarded us; the pride of the Invincible Fleet! We would have fought them off, were it not for the monster; a bloated, shapeless *thing* that refused to be killed. It defeated us and we were undone. All were killed but me. Why not me? Why not?'

A sob escaped him and for a moment he looked panicked as if he'd committed a breach of discipline, but when Shaw didn't react, he relaxed a little.

'For some reason, pirates don't kill youngsters,' she said. 'At least not out-of-hand. Go on.'

Her cool tone seemed to steady further, for he nodded.

'The sea robbers managed to reach this port,' he said. 'They drove the ship without attending to the engine, until the power stones gave out. Then, the shapeless horror told me to go below and see what was wrong. I went to the engine room and shut everything down. I told him the power stones were gone. He smiled—oh, that awful smile—and told me it didn't matter, he was returning to Angsthafn and would send a set of them down.' The boy lifted his hands. 'I bowed and said "Yes, Mighty Lord". What more could I say? That I do not know how to install power stones? That this is a task for the Wielder of Engines, not for one who is still Seeking? Such did not seem a wise course.'

'Best you didn't tell the beast,' Shaw said. 'You are a midshipman? A student-officer?'

He nodded. 'I am. I would have become a Finder, a... lieutenant, after we'd returned to the Saeill, but now I am still Seeker.'

'Yet you know how the ship works,' Shaw said. 'Could you sail her as an officer would?'

'Can, yes. But I lack the blessing of Finding.'

'We could arrange for an examination,' Shaw said. 'Passing it would make you a third officer. I will ask our ship's engineer to arrange for a set of new crystals. He can at least show you how to install them.' She looked at the other kids. 'You are none of you sailors?'

The boy who had first spoken shook his head. 'We are locals the pirates pressed to learn the way of this ship.' He was silent for a moment. 'We've never been to sea before. Ekiel showed us the sails, and by now we can handle them, if the weather stays calm. But we're not sailors.' He grinned mirthlessly. 'Besides being faint from hunger.'

'I'll get some food,' Nate said, and he mounted his broom. 'After you've eaten, we'll take you guys back ashore.'

The boy hesitated. 'Do we have to?'

Shaw stared at him. 'Why wouldn't you?'

The boy looked away as if ashamed. 'We weren't chosen for this job by accident,' he said roughly. Then he looked squarely at Shaw, his lips pressed into a grim line. 'You killed all the pirates?'

'Yes,' Shaw said. 'They didn't leave us any choice; they *made* us kill them.'

'They were mad,' the boy said. 'They had been our parents, once. We're of the Mihaal, the poor quarter. We live among the filth, the rats, and the stink of the town's slums. Many of our parents joined the pirates in the hope of loot and a better life. Instead, they found the free booze and... forgot us. Some lads tried to join, too, but the pirates didn't want us as equals, only as lowly scrubbers and bilgerats, and they didn't give us their rotgut to drink. Funny, ain't it? They didn't mind starving us to death, but no booze.'

Shaw grunted. 'Be glad,' she said. 'The stuff they drank was highly poisoned. The jinni, that's what that blob monster was, had mixed the booze with a drug that enslaved the mind. Those pirates had no choice but obeying their captains, and that was all.'

The boy stared at her. 'Poisoned...' he said slowly. 'So was that why our parents forgot us? They couldn't... help it?'

Now several of the other lads cried out, and a few stood wordlessly leaking tears.

Shaw felt a stab of remorse. She was so used to the thought of poisoned booze that she hadn't realized what it would mean for those guys. 'They didn't plan to forget you,' she said hastily. 'The stuff they drank made them obey the jinn blindly. After a few weeks, they had only just enough mind left to execute simple orders, but they couldn't sail the ship without guys like you, they couldn't truly think or plan, and they stopped caring about anything but their own desires.'

She slammed a hand to the railing, hating the jinn for what they did to people. 'Don't think of them as your parents; the ones you knew died long before today. These pirates were tools, brain slaves; they were ordered to fight to the death, so even the ones we managed to knock down, forced themselves to die.'

The boy bowed his head. 'Then it is... better so. We'd like to stay here and learn how to handle this ship.' He shrugged. 'The Mihaal ain't a happy place. It's filthy, a mess of crummy hovels without decent water or sani... Ah, places to crap, beggin' your pardon. We don't wanna go back there.'

'I can understand that,' Shaw said. 'Are there many people living in this Mihaal area?'

The boy shrugged. 'Some old folks and a double handful of younger children. Us here'd rather become sailors; Brisa has nothing to offer us.'

'All right,' Shaw said. 'If that's what you all want, stay on board. We'll discuss it later, when things are settled.'

A boy yelled and pointed at the sky.

Shaw looked up and her silly heart leaped as she saw Nate coming back. 'It's your food delivery,' she said with studied nonchalance.

Nate landed beside them, loaded with bread, bananas, milk and sliced meat.

'Mealtime, gents,' he said. 'This is for two days. After that, you will get new stuff.'

'This one is grateful,' Ekiel said. 'We will take the food to the galley, have our share and sit down in the mess. Understood?'

'Yep,' the other boy said. 'Let's go.'

'Thank you,' Ekiel said to Nate, before hurrying after the others.

'They want to stay aboard,' Shaw said tiredly. 'If they truly want to become sailors, I must find training for them.'

'And for Gunno's boys, and those other kid crews we liberated,' Nate said. 'We'd best have a word with old Wylmer.'

'He must be bored to tears, playing senior naval officer in Smalkand,' Shaw said. 'Teaching our guys how to handle his schooner should cheer him up.' She gripped her broom. 'We should go ashore; those Table merchants must be getting impatient.'

CHAPTER 5 — A NEW BEGINNING

It was still dark as they landed on Brisa's ruined quay. What little wind there was, brought a smell of death from the huge mounds of slain pirates, palely naked in the weak moonlight. Abbram's lads were sorting piles of arms, bloodied clothes and personal effects.

Varan sat on his knees, checking the rings, amulets and snuffboxes the soldier boys had collected.

'Magpies,' he said disdainfully. 'That's all those fellows were. Glittering rings and neck chains that are no more than baubles.' He came to his knees and dusted off his pants. 'What's the next step?'

'I asked for the Table merchants to come,' Shaw said. 'I had supposed them here already.'

'They're not,' Varan said. 'I haven't seen anyone yet.'

'Darn,' Shaw said angrily. She heard a shout, and as she turned, a smallish girl in an oversized man's jacket ran toward her, evading one of Abbram's guys as he tried to stop her.

'It's all right,' Shaw said. 'Let her come.'

'You're waiting for the Table?' the girl said breathlessly. 'They won't come. They're holed up in the Table house, discussing plans to cheat you.'

'Are they now?' Shaw said. 'Do tell!'

The girl looked grimly angered. 'When we heard you summoning them, my mates and I were almost sure they wouldn't come. They've been pulling the strings around here for too long, buying the pirates' loot and the booze they guzzled.'

'They're not pirates themselves?' Nate said.

The girl laughed harshly. 'Not them! They were Lord Nimmendal's mates—or that's what they thought. Those guys are all puffed-up with how rich and important they are and they're sure you will come to them.'

'Not me,' Shaw said. 'I will send some troops to fetch them.'

'Don't wait too long,' the girl said. 'Me and my mates kept an eye on them, and so we found out things. There's this ivy growing all over their building, see. Someone not too tall and heavy can go up all the way to their meeting room window, and if that's opened a little, it's as good as bein' in the room with them. They're planning to act like they're with you, while they send an agent to Renvel and tell the pirate captain there he's to warn Nimmendal.'

'Ha!' Shaw said. 'They think I'm an idiot? By now there isn't a pirate left alive in the Tradeports.' She looked around and beckoned to Lieutenant Uzhan and his men.

'It seems the town's merchants are playing us false,' she said. 'Would you have them brought here? This girl and her friends will show you where they are hiding.'

'Sure!' the girl said eagerly. 'I hope you'll hang those rats!'

'We'll get the fools,' Uzhan said. 'For fools they must be to think those ploys work.' He looked at the girl and his formerly frozen face smiled. 'Show us their hole, miss.'

Then his troop trotted away, with the girl calling for her friends as she went with them.

An hour or so later they came back, bringing five well-clad men with them. They were followed by a crowd, shouting abuse at the arrested merchants.

'Apparently those men aren't well liked,' Nate said dryly.

'It seems so,' Shaw said. She patted her pockets for her lazy-eye patch and her monocle. 'Did I put them...? Yes!'

'Not the patch,' Nate said. 'Not in a pirate town.'

Shaw stifled a giggle. 'You're right.' She put it away and screwed only the monocle in her eye. *'Haai-Bo?'*

'Look up, up!' he said.

Then she saw him perched on a lamppost, looking much like a vulture watching a parched animal die.

'What are they thinking, my wise advisor?'

'Treason,' the wyrmling said promptly. *'They do not understand their games are over.'*

'What is the meaning of this outrage?' an elderly merchant called as they stood before Shaw. He was a potbellied little man with gray sideburns and dressed in checkered trousers under a striped frock coat. 'We are the Table of Brisa, girl; not some common rabble!'

'You are cursed traitors,' Shaw said coolly. 'Pirate stooges. Tell them their sins, Haai-Bo.'

The wyrmling's sudden keening shocked even Abbram's guys, and all present stared up as he raised his wings, pointing his long-necked head at the merchants.

'You want to call back Nimmendal,' Haai-Bo said in a voice as cold as death. 'You want the jinni to return, to harass and eat your own people. You want the pirates to go on buying the Jabbi-drugged booze you have been smuggling from Kell. You want to go on selling children to the Angsthafn pirates. You want to continue stealing, taking poor people's property and wallowing in ill-gotten wealth. You are bad, bad men.'

'You hear the accusation. Do you have anything to say?' Shaw felt her voice and heart tremble with rage.

'That beast, a speaking parrot? It's nonsense!' the oldest said haughtily. 'We are merchants, girl. We dealt with the pirates; we couldn't very well do anything else. Everyone worked with them; why, Lord Nimmendal himself agreed we should do so! The First of the Table...'

'Nimmendal is a jinni,' Shaw said harshly. 'In associating with a monster like that, you prove yourselves the enemy of all the people.'

'Preposterous!' a purple-cheeked merchant in a long, caped driving coat said. 'Lord Nimmendal is an honorable man, a great merchant.'

'They're playing games,' Haai-Bo said. *'There's no trace of drugs in their minds, just greed. They think you're bluffing; that you will need their services. They're waiting to make a deal with the new masters.'*

'Bring me five sets of pirate shirts and pants,' Shaw said in a deadly tone. 'Not the cleanest ones. You traitors, take your clothes off. Quickly now!'

'What?' the oldest one said, aghast. 'But we're the Table! We...'

'You are nothing,' Shaw said. 'Everything you were is gone; all you owned has been taken from you. We will examine your trade books post for post and when we have our proof, you will hang. Undress or I will have you forcibly stripped.'

Blank-faced, the men took off their top hats and fine suits, their jewelry and purses. Shuddering, they donned the bloodstained pirate clothes and stood, unable to comprehend their changed fate.

Shaw nodded to Uzhan. 'Take them to *Maiden*. Ask the captain to lock them up somewhere safe and have them guarded. We'll attend to them later.'

'Hang them!' the crowd shouted, as the five were led away. Shaw's icy rage drained away and left her empty. She took a deep breath and turned to the screaming crowd. As she lifted a hand, the people slowly fell silent.

'Thank you,' she said. 'These five persons are under arrest. Their property has been confiscated, and they will be judged.'

'They are traitors and deserve to die,' an older man said loudly, as if he spoke for the whole crowd. 'They grew fat on our misery!'

'They will be judged,' Shaw said repeated.

Emboldened, the man stared at her. 'And what are your plans with us?'

'You are now part of the Pasandir Peaks,' Shaw said. 'That will bring you many advantages.'

The man's eyes were cynical. 'I am sure,' he said. 'Would you name some?'

'First of all, we won't burn this town to the ground,' Shaw said coolly. 'A great many people all over the Wydemere Sea have been dreaming to do so for many years.'

'Do they hate us that much?' a young man at the front of the crowd said.

'Yes,' Shaw said. 'They hate you that much. Tradeport ships have left too many gutted merchantmen sinking, with their crews either killed or abducted to feed the jinn. Your five towns are curse words in all the known lands.'

'But we have suffered too!' the young man cried, his face twisted in anguish.

'Possibly.' Shaw eyed him coldly. 'Yet you let those pirates come here. Had you people been strong, they wouldn't have settled among you. But you were privateers already, masquerading as innocent merchantmen, so the step to piracy was small. And didn't you all profit gladly from their work? You, too, are guilty; tools ready for the jinn's hands.'

'No!' the young man wailed, tearing his hair.

'Be silent, fool!' the older man snapped. 'The lady's words are true. We all did profit. We all did rejoice our pirates were bringing in so much loot. Until the Great Captain came.'

'Nimmendal?' Shaw said.

'Yes.'

'He is a jinni,' Shaw said. 'The Angsthafn pirate boss.'

'Now we know,' the older man said. 'At first we didn't. Nimmendal the Great Captain, chosen Chair of the Brisan Table, then of all the Tradeport Tables. He turned us into murderers and slave dealers. It's no wonder the other nations hate us.'

'Your becoming part of the Peaks is a new beginning,' Shaw said. 'That is the second advantage.' She looked at the faces before her; the tired, underfed, desperate faces. 'There are more. We will not levy taxes; the Peaks get their income through trade. We will invest in your businesses. We will set up a company to bring your wares to a great many markets. We will give you free healing and a good education for your children. We'll build airship towers and you shall be welcome visitors everywhere. You'll choose your own town council, and we will guarantee both your safety from your enemies and jobs for everybody.'

'Fine promises,' a woman said skeptically. 'What must we suffer for them?'

'You won't suffer at all,' Shaw said. 'We expect everyone to do their daily jobs; farm, produce goods, import and export things, raise children, be happy, and rule yourselves wisely.' She looked at the faces. 'How is the food situation?'

'Bad!' The woman's skepticism dropped away, showing her desperation. 'The supply ship should have been here weeks ago. *Grimrose* comes every month, to sell us the produce of Veurdel and Lismoor. She's nearly ten days late and only the children get what scraps we've left. We elders haven't had a full meal in two days.'

'*Grimrose* was captured by a Diblooni pirate,' Shaw said.

The woman screamed. 'No food? Those cursed dogs killed us!'

'The Diblooni didn't care for your lives,' Shaw said. 'They used *Grimrose* to attack New Winsproke. We found them out, killed them, and took the ship. Only the bilgerat boys were left alive, and you should be grateful to them. For it was they who warned us how bad the situation here was. Thanks to them, we knew we must bring you food, people! For free.'

A balding man in a checkered shirt stepped forward. '*You* bring us food?' he said, unbelieving. 'You really do?'

'I said there are advantages to being a Pasandir Peaks town, didn't I?' Shaw said calmly. 'We care for our people.' She beckoned to her prospective director. 'Mr. Varan Lomillor will organize everything.'

Varan came to stand beside her. 'Who is responsible for the monthly reception and redistribution of the stores?'

'That's me,' the bald man said. 'I am the last grocer still in business.'

'We will unload the food we brought onto the quay,' Varan said. 'As soon as we're done, you can take it away. For any further business, we will need a warehouse. Who owns those buildings our troops disinfected tonight?'

'They belong to the Table merchants,' the grocer said.

'Then they're confiscated property,' Varan said with a quick glance at Shaw. 'We will choose the ones we need, and buy them from the town.'

The grocer almost staggered. 'You will buy them?'

'We are a trading company,' Shaw said. 'We buy and sell things, not steal them. We will import everything you need and more and sell it through the local shopkeepers the normal way.'

'There won't be any money,' the grocer said. 'The pirate taxes took most of what we had.'

'We'll find a way,' Shaw said. 'What about business? How are the artisans doing?'

'No raw materials, no tools, no market,' a woman said. 'I'm a clothier; I used to have a store and two girls working for me. After the pirates came, I had to close my shop and dismiss my girls.'

'It became worse,' a man said. 'After the harbor attack, everything came to a standstill. Nimmendal never came back from wherever he was, nor did his tax collectors, and the pirates left us mostly alone after that.'

'We didn't have much,' another man added. 'So we were lucky they lost interest and spent the days boozing.'

'Their bottles were poisoned,' Shaw said. 'It contained a mind killing drug. Whatever you people do, don't drink the stuff in those taverns! It will turn you into slaves. Pour all of it into the harbor and be done with it.'

The woman gave a harsh laugh and several men turned red-faced. 'So that young captain was right,' she said. 'No free spirits, men.'

'Now first thing first,' Varan said. 'Once the sun is up, we want you to get together and choose a town council. Not another merchant Table, but a mayor and some councilors who represent all the people. When you have done that, I will discuss the next step with them. Go home now while we unload the food. Master Grocer, a word with you, please.'

Varan clearly had matters in hand. Shaw left the rest to him and walked back to the *Maiden*. Nate put an arm round her shoulder and she sighed.

'Curse those five traitors!' Shaw said bitterly. 'Now I must hang them, too. I... I *hate* that.' She gripped Nate's tunic. 'I must have proof of their guilt, not somebody's say-so. Not even my own! And their families? Do they have wives? Children? I can't ruin them all!'

'Easy!' Nate said, holding her tight. 'We'll let the town council handle that. The locals will hang those robbers with the greatest goodwill.'

'You're right,' Shaw said as they came to the ship. 'It's just a part I hadn't counted on.'

'You did great,' Nate said. 'I think you got old Varan hooked as well.'

'He needed something bigger,' Shaw said, angrily wiping the silly tears from her cheeks. 'I love Old Wharf, but anyone can run that place. This is a challenge and one near to his heart as a Chorwaynie. His people probably suffered the most from Tradeport piracy.'

'Action required!' Haai-Bo crowed, diving from his perch in the main mast. 'Kennan reports heavy opposition in Dibloon. There was a pirate schooner, which they took, but at least a hundred pirates still in the town. He requests assistance.'

'Darn!' Shaw said. 'Haai-Bo, tell Abbram to send two of his troops aboard. We'll have to sail to Dibloon immediately. Stop the unloading, we...'

'Wait!'

Shaw turned and saw a small Vanhaari girl in a red robe waving her hands at a boy aboard *Maiden*. 'I mean Ms. Shaw, not you, idiot!' As she spoke, a heavy wooden barrel appeared on deck and flew as if carried by invisible hands over to join the goods on the quay. Then the girl turned around. '*Thistle Ivy* is in Dibloon. I got a handportal for her.'

'What!' Shaw stared at the girl and she couldn't remember having seen her before.

'This is Margery,' Nate said. '*Maiden*'s portaller.'

'I can port you to *Thistle*,' the girl said. 'I prepared a handportal for every ship before we left. Just in case, like.'

'You *did*?' Shaw said. 'How absolutely brilliant of you! I never thought of that. Girl, you saved the day! Can you send over a hundred guys?'

'Easily,' she said, scratching her short black hair vigorously. 'I'll go get the right portal stick.'

She ran up the gangplank and shouted to the crew boy standing there. The boy nodded and yelled something down an opened hatchway.

'Margery,' Shaw said. 'Portaller? And she's a mover as well? And they thought her a hedgemage?'

'I saw her at work preparing those goods for unloading, and I had a word with her,' Nate said. 'She was kicked out of the Institute early, based on her lack of mana potential. No one discovered her mover talent. It's only short range; ship to quay and such, but for a trader ship she's very useful. I told Leolynn to adjust her wages; if she does a mover's job, she should get the pay as well.'

'Agreed,' Shaw said.

Then the girl came back waving a slender gold-colored stick.

'Got the right one,' she said, grinning. 'I labeled them. Now let's go send those guys over.'

Lieutenant Kashim joined them. 'Another hundred of those dogs, I hear? Generous of Kennan to share with us. Two troops stand ready, ma'am.'

'I'll activate the handportal,' Margery said, eying him brightly. 'Just walk past me slowly and mind you, don't pause to look around when you come out. Not unless you want a big pile-up.'

Kashim bowed gravely at her admonition. 'We will remember that, Mage Margery.'

Two by two, the soldiers disappeared from sight, until all were gone.

'There,' Margery said, as she put the handportal in her pocket. 'Let's go back to the unloading.'

'Thanks,' Shaw said. 'You made my day, girl.'

'Oscar Battlemage reports they're going to attack,' Haai-Bo said. 'He sounds relieved.'

'A perfect time for an early breakfast,' Nate said. 'Let's go to *Drakon*.'

'*Food?*' Haai-Bo said. '*How terribly mundane!*'

'*You ate already?*' Shaw said.

He chuckled '*Of course, I cannot serve well on an empty stomach.*'

'*Nor can we,*' Shaw said. '*Now do me a favor; what's the news from the other towns?*'

'*Oh, we got those,*' the wyrmling said offhandedly, as he returned to his high place. '*Lismoor and Veurdel both joined. They're happily discussing business. Lismoor got a ni-ice condensed milk factory. Good catch, that; very yummy, condensed milk. This Dibloon place is the last one and you'll be queen of the Tradeports.*'

'*I'll be not,*' Shaw said. '*Eskandar can be king, if he cares to; I'm a merchant. Let me know when they're done.*'

'*Sure. Now eat and let the boylings do their work.*'

'Smartass,' Shaw muttered. Then she laughed. 'I wonder how Eskandar will react when we tell him we made his country a bit bigger. *Teodar?*' she asked on impulse, sure he'd been following her expedition. '*What's your take on this?*'

'*I'm dumbfounded,*' the Kavid-Jar said immediately. '*Shocked. So many more people! And none of them has been following a god for a very long time.*'

'*We'll have to start them on our divine,*' Shaw said. '*But do you approve of me adding those non-Peak folks to Bodrus' flock or not?*'

'*Not that you care,*' he said grimly. '*If you did, you would have asked first. Formally, I do approve. Informally, I hope you know what you are doing.*'

'*I'm killing pirates,*' Shaw said. '*That's the idea, isn't it?*'

'*Killing pirates, yes. Taking their lands into Bodrus' realm is something else entirely.*'

'*But...*'

He sighed. '*It's all right. Perhaps our god wants it this way. I'm not sure I know his plans anymore. You and Eskandar between you are causing so many disturbances that my visions are all clouded.*'

'*Bodrus would tell me if I went against his intentions,*' Shaw said. '*We put a large dent in the number of pirates threatening you.*'

He laughed at that. '*True, those chaps with the lich lord are a lot quieter these days. They're less cocky and no longer jeering at me.*'

'*There! See I'm doing the right thing?*' Shaw grinned. '*Why don't you sit down and think up some ways to tell the tradeporters about Bodrus? Perhaps a miracle or two? Just a suggestion of course.*'

'Yeah, a miracle. As if those grow on trees. Well, if I think of something, you will find out.'

'Good,' Shaw said. *'Stay safe, buddy.'* She looked at Nate and shook her head. 'He may be a holy guy, but he ain't flexible. He wouldn't last a week in our line of work.'

'Nor you in his,' Nate said, taking her arm.

'I'd go stark raving bonkers,' Shaw said.

'News from the front!' Haai-Bo tweetered halfway their quick meal in *Drakon*'s mess. *'Oscar reports the Diblooni with their own grubby hands shredded their Table merchants. Then Kennan raised the wyrm flag and when he unloaded the food, the people joined the Peaks with glad cries and rumblings of stomachs.'*

'Gweat, they agweed!' Shaw managed to say as she swallowed her last bite of buttered toast. She gripped Nate's hands. 'We've done it! We've annexed all Tradeports! Now we should formalize it with a written agreement, a... a... *Haai-Bo, what's a treaty to join the Peaks called?'*

'Agreement of Admittance into the Domain of the Pasandir Peaks,' Haai-Bo said promptly.

'Darn,' Shaw said. *'What did you name your baby? Well, Agreement... Bah. All right; I got it and what does this paper say?'*

'Ask Ruth,' the wyrmling said. *'She must know the treaty between the Weal nations. You would want something similar.'*

Shaw sighed. 'We'll need Ruth.'

'Why not?' Nate said. 'Better her people hear the glad news from her than through their spies.'

'True.' Shaw drank the remainder of her cawah and jumped to her feet. 'Let's go to Seatome and surprise her.'

'Shaw!' Ruth cried as Shaw and Nate came into the Old Wharf office. 'You saved the Weal's crystal mine! Both my dads are grateful and shocked. Pirates in New Winsproke—it's an obscenity. Was that why you needed Yens' troops?''

'Only in part. Should your fathers be planning some sort of retaliation, tell them it's not necessary. We already did that,' Shaw said.

'They were discussing a bombardment,' Ruth said. 'What did you do?'

'We captured all of them.'

Ruth stared at her blankly. 'Say again?'

'We gathered our troops, sailed to the Tradeports and annexed the lot of them.'

'You didn't!'

Nate grinned. 'We most certainly did. The common people were very pleased with us, and they all agreed to join the Peaks.'

'But—you can't do that!' Ruth said aghast.

'Why not?' Shaw said. 'Those folks were starving. We brought them food, killed some seven hundred pirates with only scratches on our side, told the people to choose a council and mayor, and promised to protect them, trade with them and do for them the same we do for all our friends. Now I hoped you have the text of the Weal agreement we could use.'

Ruth sighed. 'You pulled a fast one there, girl. I'm not sure what Daddy Basil will say of it. Those agreements—do you want the same text?'

'As much as is applicable,' Nate said. 'Should Eskandar later decide to join the Weal Nations, it would be practical to have these things set up the same way already.'

'And should the Weal balk at our action, let's be clear about one thing,' Shaw said pointedly. 'They have had plenty time to do it themselves. The Weal navy, their army and the broomriders could have made matchwood of those pirates, even of one jinni prince. They never did. They let their own merchant ships be taken, and they did nothing. Nothing!'

'You're right,' Ruth said. 'But military actions need to be agreed on by all Weal Councilors. Every time a proposal to go against the Tradeports came up, Singer Eghol vetoed it. The last war had been enough, he said and he wouldn't sign for any more violence.'

'Fine,' Shaw said. 'If he can't see the difference between an unjust religious war and a punitive expedition against pirates, that's his problem. Now we did it, and I darn well don't need his approval.'

'Eghol is too old; he is unable to accept he should retire,' Ruth said.

'Until one of these days Divine Aera herself tells him,' Nate said. 'As she told Singer Wador.'

Ruth slapped the table. 'Those treaties; you want them now, I suppose?' Ruth said.

'Yes, please. While you work on them, we'll go and badger Engineer Oychak for some portals. Perhaps when you have time, ask WyDir to open up their old aerodrome in Brisa. You can tell them the field is there, but nothing else. I do want that aerodrome going and connected to New Winsproke.'

'I'll tell them,' Ruth said. 'Now let me be for a moment; I need to dig up my little-used legalese.'

Shaw waved and went to the entresol cantina. Young Cook's face lighted up when he saw them. He was a fierce Vanhaari boy, an out-of-work cook's assistant Shaw had hired to run Old Wharf's cantina and with her from the start of her business.

'Shaw!' he said. 'Are you coming back, or...? No, you're not, of course. Darn, I miss you here, you know, and all the excitement. It's grown dull.' He grinned at Nate. 'Glad to see you too, of course, boss.'

'I know,' Nate said. 'I haven't got Shaw's charms.'

She gripped Cook's shoulders. 'I know, guy. I'm running from madhouse to madhouse, and there are days I would love to settle down, but it won't work. Not yet; there's too much to do.'

He nodded. 'At least have a cawah and tell me what you two have been up to.'

So they sat down and Shaw told of New Winsproke, of flying carpets, the Emporium and pirates in the mine. 'There is more,' she said finally. 'But it's not yet time to speak about that.'

'So there are poor jobless kids over there too,' Young Cook said. 'Then it's good you went and gave them work. Better a dull job than the excitement of starving under a bridge.'

'Yes,' Shaw said fervently. 'I've seen too much starvation lately.' She put her mug down. 'That was lovely. Now I must have a word with our engineer.'

Nate made a slurping sound, and she looked quickly at his eyes smiling over the rim of his mug.

'Ah no, I wasn't thinking,' she said contritely and sat back in her chair, curbing her impatience while he made a show of savoring his cawah.

Finally he put his cup down and gripped her hand. 'It's all right. Let's go.'

Oychak sat hunched over a small object, prodding it with some tool Shaw didn't recognize. As they came in, she looked up and smiled. 'More portals?'

'Six, actually,' Shaw said. 'We've been busy.'

The Thali engineer pulled at her nose. 'I got one portal ready, and a portaller, but six will take some time. Where do you need them?'

Shaw told her of the Tradeports, and the engineer looked up in surprise.

'You took all of them? That will please our elders at home. Not that the pirates threatened Thali directly, but we always thought them a stain on the whole island. Of course you want to link the towns. But do you need a portal in every port? Say we install one main portal in Brisa, with a full mage in charge, and we put transferals in the other towns? They're something Imooga developed recently. A transferal has only one outgoing direction, but is open to all incoming portals, and it doesn't need anyone to operate. I could build you these in a jiffy and Mage Tomas is more than ready to get to work on the main one in Brisa.'

'That sound like a great solution,' Shaw said. '*Maiden* is in Brisa. Her portaller Margery was brilliant and prepared handportals to the other ships. Only Codnoallis will mean travel, but it's not all that far away.'

'Leave it to me,' Oychak said. 'I'll warn Tomas, and we'll put those places on the map.'

As they walked back to the office, a steamcart came to a screaming stop outside. Shaw glanced at the front door.

'Someone's in a hurry,' Nate said.

Then the door slammed open, and a boy ran in, dragging a large bag.

When he saw them, he stopped and grinned. 'Ms. Shaw and Mr. Nate! Tell me all about the scoop!'

'Good morning, Mr. Journalist Emmett,' Shaw said. 'What scoop?'

'Eh? Lady Ruth sent a message you had something big for the newspapers. What is it?'

'Did she now?' Shaw said, trying not to laugh.

'Actually that's a very good idea,' Nate said. 'The world will have to know the change as soon as possible and there's no faster way than the newspaper.'

'True,' Shaw said. 'Come up to the office and I'll tell you.'

'My, you're quick!' Ruth said as she saw Emmett.

'Fifteen minutes,' the boy said. 'Could have been here already, but some fool merchant stole the first steamcart I called and I had to look around for another one. Now; the scoop.'

Shaw told him.

When she was done, the boy looked up from his notebook. 'You captured all the Tradeports? Just like that? Wow! That'll make my readers sit up! I must go over and see the places for myself. Wow, this is really big! No one in the Weal saw the dreaded pirate towns before and now I'll bring them pictures! If I hurry, I can make it an extra edition. How do I get there?'

'Ask Mage Kier for a port to the *Maiden*,' Shaw said. 'Nate and I will be back later. Mr. Varan is in charge there.'

'I'm off then,' the boy shouted and ran to the stairs, his camera bag bumping on his back.

'And they call *me* impetuous!' Shaw said as Emmett's loud 'Kier! Mage Kier!' died away in the distance.

Ruth chuckled. 'Both the *Gazette* and the *Trumpet* are selling like mad. I heard rumors the *Dvarghish Legends* is slowly going broke.'

'If you get a chance, buy her,' Shaw said. She thought for a moment. 'Then put in some educated guys who will write thoughtful articles about what we're doing and the effects it has.'

'For the educated readers,' Ruth said.

'Yep,' Shaw said. 'Which I'm not.'

'They'll be critical,' Ruth said. 'Can you handle that?'

'They can be as critical as they like,' Shaw said. 'As long as they keep in mind Divine Bodrus is the judge of my actions. I'm following his goals, not theirs.' She glanced at Nate. 'Not always mine, either. Still, if their criticism is justified, I will act upon it.'

Ruth nodded. 'I'll put out feelers,' she said. 'I know a few of the *Legends'* financiers; perhaps they'd be interested to sell.'

'While there is anything to sell,' Shaw said blithely. 'If they wait six months, they might have nothing left.' She rose. 'We must go back.'

'I've got your treaties,' Ruth said. 'In triplicate. You won't find me copying books, but I don't mind doing some documents.'

'Thank you,' Shaw said gratefully. 'You're the greatest. I'll have these signed; then you will get one of each back for our archives; all nice and lawful.'

'Good luck; I'll read about it in the newspapers,' Ruth said.

'I suppose so,' Shaw said. Then she smiled. 'Emmett the Newshound will bring all the gory details. His readers seem to relish those.'

'There you are!' Portaller Margery cried when they returned to the *Maiden* in Brisa. 'Mr. Varan was asking for you. And Engineer Oychak came with Portal Mage Tomas, and a mad boy with a lot of questions.' Her gray face flushed darkly. 'Mage Tomas wanted all my handportals; he was very nice about them.'

'And so he should,' Shaw said. 'They're coming to install a portal and something called transferals in the other towns, and thanks to your preparations they won't have to go all the way by ship.'

'Oh,' she said. 'Good! The transferals? They're done then? Marvelous.' She grinned. 'You don't want to be portaller in a dull little *hole*, now would you?'

'Certainly not,' Shaw said. 'I wouldn't like that at all.'

'And that boy!' she said indignantly. 'Asking about me, and the ship, and what I thought of our being here. Who does he think he is?'

'He's the reporter for the *Weal Gazette*,' Shaw said. 'He comes to write a series of articles about the Tradeports.'

'Ooh, he's from the *Gazette*!' Margery said. 'I've read all those stories about your adventures! Is that him?' She got a crafty look in her eyes. 'I wonder if he'll mention *me* in his piece. I must... ask him.'

Shaw grinned. 'Good luck with that. We'll be going ashore and see Mr. Varan.'

'She'll have to be *very* lucky to catch Emmett standing still,' Nate said as they walked to the gangplank.

CHAPTER 6 — AN OLD MYSTERY REVEALED

Shaw found Mage Tomas standing a little forlorn, alone in the large, nearly empty warehouse.

'If you need Oychak, she just went to Dibloon to install the first transferal,' he said.

'Actually I was looking for Varan,' Shaw said.

'He is out, seeing someone about a house,' Tomas said. 'Staff accommodations.' He smiled. 'I never thought to end up living in Brisa.'

'I can imagine,' Shaw said. 'I was here the first time, with the wyrmcaller, when we shot up the port. I never thought I would be the one to come back with an army to conquer the place.' She shrugged. 'Bodrus had other plans.'

'But the divine is asleep,' Tomas said. 'How can he attend to his plans?'

'He's a god,' Nate said. 'As far as I understand it, he can influence things through his dreams.'

'That's it,' Shaw said. She didn't fully understand herself, but she didn't want to discuss Bodrus. She ran a trading company, and she still found it hard to accept how this brought her into the divine world of Eskandar, Teodar the Kavid-Jar and the Sleeping God. 'If anyone is looking for Nate or me, we'll be walking around town a bit, to get the feel of things.'

Back outside, Shaw looked around. To the right were the quay and the sea lapping against it, across the road the burned-out remnants of the slave-market and the tavern beyond it, and to the left, past the row of warehouses, was the town.

As they walked past, Shaw thought of the fight with the jinni slave master and his men, that night they'd shot up the harbor. He had used the form of a wizened old man, but when Eskandar accosted him, he'd turned into a burning figure nearly seven feet tall. Every step of the beast had brought more fire, and they'd fought his minions amid the flames. Then Eskandar had ported away with the jinni, dumping the creature into the harbor, and its henchmen had died. They managed to escape from the burning building seconds before the whole roof collapsed.

'Brisan Building Co.,' Nate said. 'Construction and Demolition Works.'

'What?' Shaw looked at him in some confusion. Then she remembered Nate hadn't been here, that night, and the ruins would hold no memories for him.

He waved a nonchalant hand at a wooden sign to the side of the ruin and now she understood.

'So someone was going to remove the rubble,' she said. 'Only they haven't started yet.'

'You need a guide?' A young voice made her start. She turned and saw a smallish local girl watching them, hands in the pockets of an oversized jacket as scruffy as she was.

'We meet again,' Shaw said, as she recognized the girl who had come to warn them about the Table merchants' plot. 'A guide would be handy. What's your name?'

'You don't wanna know,' the girl said. 'Just call me Wisp; they all do on account of my being not that tall, see. Where you want to go?'

'Show us around,' Shaw said. 'I'd like to see the Table merchants' properties, local businesses, shops and things like that.'

'That'll be a long walk,' Wisp said.

'In that case, we'll fly.' Shaw got out her broom. 'Sit before me and show us where to go.'

'Wow!' the girl said. She sat down gingerly. 'Ooh, that ain't as hard as it looks.'

Shaw laughed. 'You won't get a sore butt on a riding broom. Now, where to first?'

'A shop; at the crossroads to the left,' Wisp said. Shaw repeated that and obediently, the broom gathered speed.

The shop was a ship's chandlery, and Shaw noted with some surprise she could look at it without the familiar gut-wrenching sense of loss. She saw Nate glance at her.

'It's all right,' she said firmly.

The chandler stood leaning on the lower half of his double door, staring at nothing. When they halted, he looked up and started violently.

'Ma'am!' he said, bowing hastily. 'How can I help you?'

'It's the other way round,' Shaw said. 'I want to know what the people's biggest problems are.'

'Problems.' The man sighed. 'No customers, no stock, and I dunno what's happening with the seizure.'

'What seizure?' Shaw asked.

'I had a high-interest loan from the Table, but there's no money to be had from thieving pirates who ransack your stores for their needs. So I couldn't pay back anymore and the Table's agents were coming to seize my business. Instead, you arrived, and all is changed. But what will happen with the loan?'

'I'll have a word with Mr. Varan, who'll be in charge of our business in the Tradeports,' Shaw said. 'We will examine all the Table transactions, including the loans. How much of it did you pay off?'

'With interest added, nearly one and a half times the original sum, with another two installments to go,' the man said.

'That's robbery!' Shaw said, shocked. 'Over fifty percent interest is way too much. Leave it to me; I'll find out and let you know.' She turned to their guide. 'Would you know where those Table merchants kept their books?'

'They's got a big house in the rich quarter,' Wisp said. 'I guess that's where they hide their stuff, wouldn't it?'

'Let's go there first,' Shaw said. 'I should have thought of that sooner.'

'It's a good bit away,' the girl said, pointing down the street.

'Not for the birds,' Shaw said, and rose in the air. 'Now point me where it is.'

'Ooh, I never seen the town this way,' Wisp said, wrinkling her brow as she looked at the maze of streets below. 'Lessee... Go there, see that fat statue? The house is on the right beside it.'

Shaw waved at Nate and pointed. Together, they leapt over several blocks of non-descript dwellings to land at the feet of the portly bronze merchant standing in the center of a small square, facing a tall, three-story building with a redbrick, ivy-grown façade.

'That is it?' Shaw said.

Their guide nodded. 'The Table office.'

Shaw strode to the gleaming door and pushed. It opened soundlessly, and they stepped into a high corridor where every hand-painted tile, every portrait and colorful tapestry, breathed wealth and dark shadows.

In the first room they tried, they found a clerk at work. He was a gaunt, older man in a sober tunic, at a tall standing desk, copying notes from a document into a leather-bound trade book.

As they entered, he raised his eyes and calmly put down his pen.

'Ma'am,' he said politely. 'You come to drag me away too?'

Shaw lifted an eyebrow. 'Who might you be?'

'The Clerk of the Table, ma'am. Your soldiers passed me over when they came to arrest the Table merchants, but I supposed it was only a small respite.'

'Are you a merchant?' Shaw said.

'Not anymore,' the man said. 'I am merely an indentured servant. To pay off my debts to the Table, I have been their clerk for twenty-five years.'

'Then you must be the one who knows everything?' Shaw eyed the man pensively. He didn't look shifty, just weary and very much awake at the same time.

'About the Table? Yes, ma'am. The merchants didn't make a deal I do not know about. Every sordid detail, every ill-gotten coin, and every pirated treasure I noted in the Table ledgers. You won't find a penny not booked.'

'Every usurious loan?'

'Certainly, oh certainly those. Twenty-five years of the Table's growing malpractice, meticulously written-down. Twenty-five years of hoping my efforts would someday tell the people of Brisa how they have been cheated.'

'You are vindictive?' Nate said.

'Yes, very much so,' the clerk said. 'I once was a merchant like they, rich and successful. Until one of them accused me of evading taxes. I was brought down, lost all I had, and was reduced to this. To work off my debt to the Table, or be kicked out of the Tradeports, all because I helped an old friend's son.'

Some memory plagued Shaw, something someone had once said. Then she had it. It was a story Kellani had told her about how her father and mother had met in this same town.

'Jurgis,' she said.

The clerk frowned. 'That was the son's name.'

'I remember his daughter telling me,' Shaw said. 'Jurgis' father, stepfather I believe, was treated the same way as you were. Then Jurgis stole the accusing merchant's trade book and handed it to a friend of his father, before he left Brisa. He was sure that book would hang the false merchant. He never told anyone who this mysterious person was.'

'That friend was I,' the clerk said. 'I knew all Table merchants were crooked, but I believed they worked against each other as well as against the rest of us. They didn't.' He shook his head. 'I don't blame the boy; I should have been more careful. How is he, these days? Did he make something of his life?'

Shaw smiled. 'Jurgis proved a Spellstor, and a son of Prince-warlock Argyr. He married a young lioness who is now the Queen of the Kells. Their daughter is a good friend of ours.'

'That is surprising,' the clerk said without even a hint of emotion. 'Though he was a cheeky youngster and a very good thief. Or perhaps I shouldn't have said that.'

'He makes no secret of his past,' Shaw said. 'Lord Jurgis is commander of the Weal's broomrider corps these days. Broomriders aren't very stuffy.'

'I am glad for him,' the clerk said. 'What will you do with me?'

'I think you can help us. I want proof of the Table merchants' perfidy, so the new town council can judge them legally.'

'That is easy; the trade books show you the exact number of slaves sold to Angsthafn, the barrels of Jabbi imported, the false loans and illegal seizures, enough to hang them a hundredfold. I could make you a list.'

'Do so,' Shaw said. 'And I want another list, recounting all assets, all false loans and repayments received, all properties seized and all other Table crimes that can be corrected. If you aid us truthfully and faithfully, we will pardon your work for the Table and I will suggest to Mr. Varan, our Director Tradeports Co, that he might hire you.'

'I will aid you gladly,' the clerk said. 'I want to see those crooks hanged, you see. After that, my services are yours, if you would care to use them.'

'*Haai-Bo?*' Shaw said. '*Can we trust him?*'

'*He doesn't think deceit,*' the wyrmling said. '*He wishes revenge on those crooky merchants. He hopes you'll pay him, though he scoffs at the penny pittance the Table paid him for his efforts.'*

'I would like your lists as soon as you can manage,' Shaw said. 'Of course you will be paid a senior clerk's wages for your efforts. That's one silver per day, I believe.'

The man bowed. 'I will get onto it immediately, ma'am. You should have the proof by nightfall. The other lists will take more time, as there are a great many of them.'

'Start with assets,' Shaw said. 'Then the loans and seizures. Are there any outstanding loans?'

'Several, ma'am, including some who indicated they can't pay, but whose goods hadn't been seized yet.'

'Freeze all payments,' Shaw said. 'I will discuss this with our finance people.' She slapped her thigh. 'A question. How are financial transactions handled in Brisa? Large transactions?'

'The Table acted as money-lender,' the clerk said. 'This house has a secure vault where the Table merchants and the pirates kept their money.' He smiled. 'Of course the money is still there, and it is quite a sum. Around three hundred thousand pieces of gold, roughly said.'

'So Brisa has a bank,' Nate said. 'That makes matters much easier.'

'Every town has a money-lender, sir. We don't use the word "bank", because the Table merchants considered this gold their property.'

'But we will,' Shaw said. 'This money now belongs to the Peaks Bank, which is ours. We will use the gold to rebuild the town and invest in the people. I will have our chief banker Mr. Wainschilt contact you about the details; I am not involved in banking matters. For now I want you to handle our financial transactions.'

She pulled her checks from her pocket. 'These slips with my or Mr. Nate's signature can be paid out. They always need the amount of money written both in numbers and in letters to be valid, and bear the name of the recipient.'

The clerk studied the paper carefully. 'That doesn't differ much from the old system,' he said. 'It will give no problems.'

'Good,' Shaw said. 'You will need assistance. Would you know any both able and trustworthy persons who can assist you?'

'There are many ruined merchants and their clerks in our town, ma'am,' the clerk said. 'Several, in quite destitute circumstances.'

'Send them to me for an interview; I will take care being available tomorrow,' Shaw said. She smiled. 'I am glad to find an able man to undo this tangle of deceit.'

'I have long hoped for the chance, ma'am,' the clerk said. 'I am grateful you give me the opportunity—and your trust.'

'To our mutual profit,' Shaw said.

Once they were back on the street, Wisp looked at Shaw. 'Where to now, ma'am?'

'Those Brisan Builders guys,' Nathan said. 'We can at least see what they're planning with those ruins.'

'That's the east end of town,' the girl said.

Brisan Builders was a series of sheds on the edge of an enormous, fenced-in field full of stones; cobblestones, building stones, shingles, in various sizes and colors.

In the main shed, four men were playing some game of cards and none of them looked up when they entered.

'Gentlemen,' Shaw said after a moment's wait.

'Eh?' a tall, broad-shouldered man looked up, scowling. When he saw her, his face became puzzled.

'I've seen you before,' he said. 'Who're you, girl?'

One of the others turned around, a wizened old fellow in a workman's smock. 'Darn! It's her,' he said in the loud voice of the deaf. 'The gal with the soldiers!'

Shaw smiled grimly. 'So I am. You gentlemen are Brisan Builders?'

The big man came to his feet. 'Were,' he said. 'We're defunct. No money, no workers, no customers. I'm Cathew, the former foreman.'

'Who was the owner?' Shaw said. 'Who holds the assets now?'

'The owner is gone, like many who went against the Table,' Cathew said. 'His daughter inherited his stuff, but she ain't got no money, and she ain't interested in the business either.'

'Married to the Slim Street cobbler she is,' the third man said.

'What is this place worth?' Shaw said. 'Would two thousand pieces of gold cover it?'

'Ha!' the fourth man said. 'Two thousand pennies would do. These sheds, the stone field outside and an old cart. That's all what's left of Brisan Building.'

'We'll have a word with this lady,' Shaw said. 'Don't go away, gentlemen; I'll be back.'

'Slim Street isn't far,' Wisp said, as they walked out. She waved a hand to the south. 'Just a little hop on yer broom.'

They crossed over a row of workman's dwellings and landed in a narrow lane. The cobbler's house was a bit larger than the others, with a workroom below and probably some small private rooms on the first floor.

The cobbler himself was a tall, painfully thin man with a permanent stoop and a complaining mind. 'You want my wife?' he said. 'About the building yard it is? That cursed place! First her father couldn't stop jabbering how she married beneath herself. Then that row with the Table nearly dragging us down along with him. And now you? What more misery do you bring?'

'Don't you dare blame my father!' A tall, equally thin woman came in, hands to her hips and an angry glitter in her eyes. 'He didn't like our marriage, but he did his best by us. Loaned you money often enough, didn't he? Then those jackals of the Table screwed him because he wouldn't clear away the ruins on the quay for free. Ruined his business, those crooks did. And you didn't suffer from his fall. The Table didn't even look at you, so why do you complain? Because I lost my inheritance? Pah!'

'I understand you hold the ownership to the building yard?' Shaw said when the woman paused to take a breath.

'Yes!' the woman said. 'Though what worth they have I don't know.'

'One thousand pieces of gold,' Shaw said. 'That's what I offer for the place, the name and everything else that was Brisa Building Co.'

The cobbler and his wife both gaped at Shaw. 'A thousand gold? For a building company that's broke?'

'Sell!' the cobbler said urgently.

The woman inspected her husband, a calculating look on her thin face. 'Two thousand,' she said, without a glance at Shaw.

'Fifteen hundred,' Shaw countered.

The woman nodded curtly. 'Done.'

Shaw got her checks and wrote one out. 'You can hand this to the gentleman who was the Clerk of the Table. He will pay you the money.'

'He will, will he?' the woman said slowly. 'But how do I know...' She bit her lip.

'Mistress, I captured this town,' Shaw said. 'I could easily do it the pirate way and take your business and what else I want. But I run a large company and I do things legally. This check is as good as coin anywhere in the Weal and beyond.'

'Your pardon,' the woman said. 'A moment while I get the deeds.' In minutes she was back and almost snatched up the check. 'Here are the ownership papers.'

'Thank you,' Shaw said politely. 'May the money bring you both happiness.'

'She won't give her man the money,' Nate said once they were back on the street.

'No,' Shaw said. 'She'll keep it, to remind the cobbler she doesn't need him.' She made a gesture of dismissal. 'It's their life. Let's go back to the builder yard.'

They found the men still at their card game.

'All right, gentlemen,' Shaw said briskly. 'Play time is over. Brisa Building is now a daughter of the PTC's Tradeports division.'

Foreman Cathew shoved his chair back. 'You did it?' he said. 'You went and bought this place?'

'I did,' Shaw said, waving the deed of sale. 'And your first job will be the repair of the harbor. Clear away the burned-out buildings, repair all piers and cranes, warehouses and whatever more we find. You'll get it in writing, but start hiring workers immediately. You will report to the Director Tradeports, Mr. Varan Lomillor. Discuss with him all matters like wages, free meals and healing, and things like that. He'll want an estimate of costs, worker hours, materials and time as soon as possible. I'll write you a check for one thousand Weal libers. The former Clerk of the Table will exchange this for coins. Questions?'

'A great many,' the foreman said. 'But I need to chew this over first.'

'In that case, ask Mr. Varan. I will not be in Brisa long,' Shaw smiled. 'Welcome with the PTC, gentlemen.'

Then she walked out, leaving four stunned builders behind.

'That must be enough for today,' Shaw said. 'You were a great guide, Wisp.' She took out her purse and handed the girl a silver uni. 'You earned your pay. If you want a job, contact Mr. Varan and tell him I sent you. He'll need plenty people who can use their minds. Now, do you need a lift somewhere?'

Wisp shook her head. 'I live nearby,' she said, clutching her coin. 'Thanks! I'm glad I could help.' She took a deep breath. 'I wouldn't mind a job, but what can I do?'

'We'll need all kinds of people for the warehouse, from cleaning to sales to soldiers to magic users and many others. Discuss it with Mr. Varan. And if you need schooling, he can help you there too.'

Wisp nodded. 'I'll go see this Mr. Varan.'

'Good. I'll tell him you'll be around.' Shaw waved and rose up in the air.

Back at the warehouse, she sought out Varan, and found him inside, were a team of townspeople were building up storage racks.

'Look at that!' Varan said. 'The original warehouse foreman came seeing me about a job. He offered to bring in his whole team, so I hired them all. Then he told me they'd taken down and stored the inventory in the attic before the pirates moved in. Now they're building everything up again.' He smiled. 'I got us a house, too. Fully furnished, three stories, and only five hundred libers. Now I only need an office, and we're all set up.'

'I got you that one,' Shaw said. Then she told him of the Table house and the former Clerk of the Table.

'He's trustworthy?' Varan said.

'Haai-Bo said he wasn't planning to deceive us. He simply wants to earn his pay, and he seemed quite happy with a uni per day.'

'Fabulous,' Varan said. 'If the guy's acting as our bank that will make a lot of difference. I'll have Wainschilt in on it. And he brings us a vault full of gold, too.'

'Don't go spending it all,' Shaw said. 'I want those overpaid loans returned first; that will mean money for people and businesses. Still, three hundred thousand libers is a tidy sum.'

Varan grinned. 'You could say that!' Then he grew serious. 'I'll have my people find out how things stand in the other towns.'

'That's not all,' Shaw said. 'I bought you a building company, and I told them to restore the harbor first of all; the Brisan Building Co.'

'Well, I had planned to look in on those guys,' Varan said. 'With their name on that stinking ruin outside.'

'That's what made us go there,' Shaw said. 'So that sign had its use after all. And the girl who guided us all day will come to see you about a job, or whatever she needs. She's smart and knows the town. I'm sure you could use her.'

'If she knows her way around, she could assist in the sales department,' Varan said. 'Learning the ropes and perhaps become a sales girl herself. I'll see what she thinks.'

'Great,' Shaw said. 'Then Nate and I are done for today. I want a bath. See you tomorrow, Mr. Director.'

He grinned. 'You guessed I decided to accept?'

'I knew you wouldn't pass up the challenge,' Shaw said.

CHAPTER 7 — JONNA

'Ma'am! Ma'am!' The agitated voice and the persistent knocking dragged Shaw from her first sound sleep in days.

'Come in!' she shouted, sitting up in bed.

It was *Maiden*'s second cadet, the new one she had barely met.

'What is it?' Shaw said.

'First Officer Madogar's compliments; a ship came in,' the girl said. 'A worn-out tub and badly sailed. Whoever captains her ought to be ashamed of herself for such a bad show.'

Shaw grinned. 'Quite. And?'

'They landed a boy, a dirty, uncouth bilgerat.' The girl's indignity was clear in her voice now. 'And he's asking for you, ma'am!'

Shaw jumped out of the big bed and groped for her boots. 'Where is he?'

'At the gangway, ma'am. He won't speak with anyone else but you.'

'Wake up Mr. Nate, will you? Tell him what you told me while I go and see the boy.' She put on her coat and hung the broom on her back. Then she hurried on deck.

It was a quiet night. Rid of its pirates, Brisa slept peacefully. Bluewing gulls cried over the ship and as she glanced up at them, she saw Haai-Bo dancing in their midst. She had seen him do that before; perhaps it reminded him of the siblings he missed.

At the gangway a stocky dark shape waited. As she walked towards him, the boy looked up. It was the same fisher guy she'd left in charge of the ship at Codnoallis.

'Ma'am!' he said. 'We need help.'

'Of course,' she said. 'You sailed that old tub all the way here?'

'They forced us,' he said.

'They?' Shaw said. 'Who?'

'Malgarth soldiers! Six of them, all armed, with a kid prisoner. We *thought* the ship had been waitin' for someone; that must've been them. They came aboard and ordered us to sail for Brisa immediately.'

'They weren't surprised there were no pirates?'

'Those guys are drunk! They ne'er asked anything; just assumed we were the crew—we had the bodies taken ashore just that day—and told us to sail.' He lifted two fists. 'We did. None of us ever sailed something as big as that tub, but we managed. Barely.'

'The cadet on duty wasn't impressed with your mooring,' Shaw said.

The boy snorted. 'Nah, we got her to stop, didn't we? Well, they sent me ashore to tell the boss pirate they had somethin' for him. We hadn't told them you'd gone north, we just hoped you had taken the place. And you did!'

Then Nate appeared, and quickly Shaw repeated the boy's words.

'Six armed soldiers?' he said. 'What the hell...'

'We'll find out. Come.' Shaw hurried them aft.

'Ms. Madogar, call out Dryona's marines, please,' Shaw said to the first officer. 'Brooms, full armor, the works.'

Madogar gave her orders. 'May I ask what's going on?'

'Of course.' Shaw repeated the boy's story. 'So these fisher lads sailed the ship all the way from Codnoallis here. That explains their inexperienced arrival.'

'I'm sorry,' the cadet said with a Kell's frankness. 'I judged too quickly. It was very well done of you, boy.'

'We had to, see. Or they'd murdered the lot of us,' the fisher lad said. 'We ain't got no fancy arms to defend ourselves.'

Dryona's girls were quick, and within ten minutes all were assembled.

'I'm afraid you will have to take the ship once more, Lieutenant,' Shaw said. 'Only this time we added a double handicap.' She explained the situation, and Dryona nodded. 'Both armored and a prisoner; that's awkward.'

'*Haai-Bo?*' Shaw said.

'*I know,*' he said absently, still whirling about among the bluewings. '*Six soldiers, drunk and drugged as pirates were. Barely sensible, very distraught and dangerous they are.*' Then his voice changed as if he woke up from a dream. '*What am I dancing? They're gulls! I am not chummy with beasts like these!*' he said, and he sounded mortified. '*Your pardon, ma'am. I wasn't attending to my duty.*'

'*That's all right,*' Shaw said, hearing the shock in his voice. '*I think I understand. Better come with me. We're going to board the pirates.*'

'*I'm with you!*' he said quickly. '*We'll fight those knaves!*'

Shaw repeated his observations and Dryona gave a grim smile. 'All right gals, you heard the boss. Mount up.'

'I'll be coming with you,' Shaw said.

'I'll run back,' the boy said. 'Would someone have a club to spare?'

Madogar waved to a weapon rack at the back of the quarterdeck. 'Take your pick.'

The boy snatched up a solid bludgeon and grinned. 'That's the work,' he said. 'Be seeing ya on board.'

'Watch your back,' Dryona said. 'Up, girls, like eagles swooping.'

They went up, and high above the old ship, Dryona made a chopping move with her hand, and as one, the Marines dropped down onto the deck.

Shaw waved at Nate and followed them to land aft, near the deserted wheel. Below them on the main deck, the soldiers were being slaughtered by Dryona's girls and a bunch of fisher lads armed with boathooks, belaying pins and massive anger.

'Where is the kid?' Shaw said.

'Holed up in the captain's cabin with a big, mean fighter,' Haai-Bo said. *'Be in for a surprise.'*

Without a word, Shaw ran down the companion ladder to the great cabin.

It was a dark, cramped space of low beams and scant light.

As the door opened, a panicked voice cried. 'Help!'

Shaw fixed her monocled eye on the big soldier sitting on the captain's hammock and holding a boy's arm.

'Not another step or the kid dies,' he said.

The boy, a pale-faced about-fifteen-year-old with wavy blond hair and wearing a natty, dark blue tail suit, looked at the man. 'You would kill *me*, you knave?'

'Silence!' the man cried, the sweat dripping down his face making wet stains in his red frock coat.

'Lord Morthan needs me alive,' the boy said. 'It is your *duty* not to kill me.'

The big man shook him like a dog would a plaything. 'Shut up! Shut up!'

'The hammock lines!' Shaw cried as she threw herself on the big soldier. She wasn't by any means heavy, but her weight and the man's involuntary move sent the hammock swinging back. Then, Nate's hunting knife cut through the line fastening the bed to the cabin wall, and the soldier crashed down. The boy screamed, wrenched his arm away and jumped back from the fallen man.

Shaw knelt down astride the soldier and with a swift twist of her wrist, pushed her knife into his larynx. The soldier gargled, reared up violently, and flopped back, thrashing.

'Die! Die!' a voice screamed almost in her ear. Shaw turned and saw the pale, angry face of the boy staring at the fallen soldier.

'He will,' she said coolly. 'Now, calm down.' She peered at the guy's face and felt a jolt. *That's not a boy! She's not all that young either. Fifteen or sixteen at least.* 'Who are you?'

The girl began to shake. 'I can't tell you! Yet I must; I must. But I swore not to... Gods Together, what must I do?'

'Tell all,' Haai-Bo said firmly. He drifted in front of the distraught girl, his eyes whirling. 'I, the Lord Haai-Bo, advisor to the Most Puissant High Merchant Shaw, say you must tell all.'

'A wyrmling?' the girl said, blinking. 'Like in the books? You're real? I'm not... dreaming?'

Haai-Bo slapped the girl's cheek softly with his tail. 'Feel the reality of me,' he said.

'I will tell,' the girl said. 'I'm Jonna; the... No, not here with everybody listening.'

'Easy, gal,' Shaw said. 'Come to my ship. You need food and after you've eaten, you can tell me.' She took the girl's hand. 'You're cold.'

She nodded. 'I am not such a hero as... as...'

'Later,' Shaw said.

'My sword,' the girl said vaguely, and darted past the dead man into the shadows. Shaw heard the lid of a chest close and moments later, the girl returned with a small blade on a belt.

'There,' she said as she hung the belt over her shoulder. 'Not that I'm such a fabulous fighter, I prefer words.'

'Now come,' Shaw said.

'I'll arrange for food for the Codnoallis lads,' Nate said.

Shaw turned to the door and almost bumped into Dryona. 'What...' the lieutenant began. 'Darn, another soldier?'

Shaw grinned. 'You can have him; he's dead.'

'Well now,' Dryona said. 'And you with only a knife?'

'Two knives,' Shaw said, nodding at Nate. 'We're a team. And we got the captive out.'

Dryona nodded. 'Good that you're free, lad. We got the others. Soldiers or not, they went about it like drunken brawlers. It was barely a fight.'

Shaw laughed at the disapproval in the lieutenant's voice. 'It's the drugs ruining their minds,' she said.

'And how would Malgarth soldiers get those same drugs as the pirates?' Nate said. 'Are there jinn in Malgarth?'

Shaw glanced at the girl, but it was clear from her face she had no idea what Nate was talking about.

Jonna stepped from the cabin and cried out. 'We're in a town? I thought you boarded us at sea. This is not... Where are we?'

'You're in Brisa,' Shaw said. 'A pirate-less Brisa.'

'Oh gods! I'm not allowed to be here!' the girl said anxiously. 'Please, I must get back to Malgarth! I must find my... my friend. She's still out there somewhere.'

'You will tell me all,' Shaw said. She took the girl by the arm and led her across the quay to the *Maiden*. As they passed the mess, she ordered a platter of food and cawah brought to her cabin.

Jonna stared around the genteel comforts of the owner's cabin and slowly calmed.

'Sit down,' Shaw said, waving at a chair and mutely, the girl obeyed.

Shaw looked at her, at the silk cravat twisted round her neck, her expensive boy's costume looking like she'd been wading through mud pools, and her dirty, streaked face. 'Now tell me who you and your friend are, and why those soldiers wanted you.'

'I'm Jonna of Lammark,' the girl said. 'My father is a Court lord.'

'What is that?' Shaw said. 'I know absolutely nothing of Malgarth, so please explain things as you go.'

'It's politics,' Jonna said. 'Malgarth has two parties, the Barons and the Court. Barons are the provinces; the Court is the capital, Croncliff.' she pulled a face. 'We may live in the country, but my father is a Court lord, serving the high king.'

Shaw grinned. 'Politics are confusing. All right, I got it. Go on.'

'The High King lives in Croncliff and the law says the heir must live somewhere else. That's why Princess Agusta stayed in Lammark. She's only a year older than me.'

'Your friend?' Shaw said.

She nodded. 'We grew up together, and we know each other pretty well. She's a have-at-ye gal, headstrong and impulsive; I... well, I'm not.'

'You're doing quite all right,' Shaw said.

'But I'm scared all the time,' Jonna said candidly. 'Agusta is never afraid.'

'Heroes are always the scared ones,' Shaw said. 'Without fear there is no bravery. So what happened?'

Jonna took a deep breath. 'The high king died.'

'Oh, that must've upset your friend,' Shaw said.

'It sure did! Not that she was sad, for she wasn't. The high king never hid he couldn't stand his daughter; he had wanted a son. She was upset because it meant she had to go to Croncliff, and she didn't want to.'

'She didn't want to become high queen?' Shaw didn't find anything strange in that. A girl of seventeen, brought up in the provinces, wouldn't want to be shackled to a throne already.

The girl rubbed a smudge on her face. 'Agusta was very, very angry with her father for dying. Actually, she refused to go to Croncliff. My dad gave her no choice though. He bundled us into the royal steamcart and sent us away with the messenger and his escort.'

'That weren't the guys we killed, were they?' Shaw said.

Jonna looked shocked at the thought. 'No! Those were from Morthan; Barons men. They are greencoats, while the Court soldiers wear blue. Morthan is the leader of the Barons Party.' She hesitated, as if she sought for the right words to explain.

'There's this tradition,' she said finally. 'When a high king dies, his heir must be escorted to Croncliff by either the Court or the Barons faction. The side who manages that *and* holds the royal palace becomes the new ruling party. Things sometimes get rough.'

'Gods!' Shaw said. 'A free-for-all over the living body of the royal heir. And no high king thought to end that nonsense?'

Jonna looked her disapproval. 'I don't think any of them can. The power is in the hands of the ruling faction, not the high king.'

'Is that so?' Shaw filed the idea away. 'So you were going to Croncliff by steamcart. Is that far from where you live?'

'About eight hours,' she said. 'The roads are all paved, so a good steamcart manages at least twenty miles an hour.'

Shaw thought of the WyDir drivers roaring through Seatome at twice that speed. 'Then what happened?'

'We were ambushed,' the girl said. 'Morthan's men attacked our steamcart. Of course we expected them to, but not them slaying the royal messenger and his escort! That's dishonorable! Fighting is permitted, but killing is not. Yet they did.' she shivered. 'It was horrible.'

Shaw touched the girl's knee. 'I can imagine. What happened then?'

'The men of Morthan took the wheel, and we continued our journey north. After a few miles, Court soldiers counter-attacked and liberated us. For a while. We changed escorts another few times, but then Agusta had enough of it. By then it was nearly dark, and when the next attack came, she and I ran.'

'Good for you!' Shaw said, surprised.

'We ran and ran; the land around wasn't as swampy as some places, so we managed without drowning. There were soldiers coming after us; we knew not who, and we didn't care either. By then Agusta wanted to reach Croncliff on her own and to the hells with the factions. Perhaps we would've made it both, if...' She stopped, looking embarrassed.

'Something went wrong?'

'There was a river; a big one. I'm not much of a swimmer, so I hesitated. Agusta didn't, of course; she swam like a water rat. That's how Morthan's men captured me.' She looked at Shaw, her eyes big with remembered fear.

'They were very polite; only creepy, like they weren't human,' she said. 'They asked my name, and I said I was Agusta. We had agreed to that; if I was captured, I'd say I was the princess. They'd stop the search and Agusta would go on to Croncliff and the throne. Then the Barons would release me and all would be well.'

'The soldiers believed you?' Shaw said. She thought it brave of them, but quite foolhardy.

'Sure; apart from my family, only Rutus—that's Lord Wrache, the royal chancellor—knows Agusta. Besides, I'm blond like the late high king, while Agusta has her dead mother's red curls. The soldiers bundled me back into the steamcart and rode away. Darn if those guys weren't blind drunk already! They ran us into a ditch, and we had to walk, following the river until we came to a little fishing village on the coast.'

'Codnoallis,' Shaw said.

'Could well be; I didn't catch its name,' Jonna said. 'It was dark. There was the ship, and we went aboard. There were only some boys, who said they were the crew. The knight in command shrugged and ordered them to sail for Croncliff. Then he locked me into that stinking cabin.'

'And that's it?'

'Until the knight came to kill me, yes.'

'All right,' Shaw said. 'Let's find Nate and make some plans. *Haai-Bo?*'

'*The girl's a true voice,*' the wyrmling said. '*The whole story is open in her mind; no tricks, no deceits.*'

'Would you be able to find the queen?'

'Non-magic minds aren't easy to spot. Think of finding one particular gnat in a swarm of them.' He cackled. *'Gnats, gnats everywhere. But yes, I got a clear image from your gal's mind. If I concentrate, I should locate this fleeing royal insect.'*

'Good!' Shaw said. *'Then kindly advise Kennan I have need of his help. One of Abbram's squads can relieve him.'* She turned to Jonna. 'I've called our marines; once they are here, we'll go in search of Agusta. What about you? Do you need to sleep?'

'I did that on the ship,' the girl said. 'At first the stink kept me awake, but then I didn't notice it anymore and I fell asleep.'

She sounded ashamed, and Shaw smiled.

'Great; that means you're fit to go. Every good soldier will tell you to sleep when you get a chance.'

The girl brightened. 'Really? I felt I was deserting Agusta.'

'You weren't,' Shaw said. 'Now eat, while we wait for Nate and Captain Kennan.'

Half an hour later, Nate came in, with Kennan. The marine captain was stiffly formal, and his eyes were angry.

'How was Dibloon?' Shaw asked quietly. 'Apologies about that enemy ship; had I known, I would have given you more men.'

'Abbram's guys are good,' he said. 'Together, we got them.'

'You did the right thing,' Shaw said. 'No use risking your guys' lives for a gesture.'

'No,' he said grimly.

'If you had tried that, I would've kicked you all the way back to Port Dvarghish,' she said harshly. 'I need commanders I can trust, not glory-hungry idiots.'

He relaxed. 'Curse it, and you would, too,' he said. 'I know, but having to ask for help was the hardest thing I've done in a long time.'

'It proves you're a professional officer,' Shaw said. 'Now, to business. This gal is Jonna of Lammark, a noble daughter of Malgarth. I want you both to listen to her story. Jonna, please tell Nate and Captain Kennan all you told me, including the explanations.'

Jonna cradled her lemonade between her hands and hesitantly at first, she repeated the whole story.

When she was finished, she sighed. 'Now what can we do?'

'Well told and well done,' Kennan said. 'I suppose you want us to go and search for the queen, ma'am?'

'*Us* is the word,' Shaw said. 'Nate and I will be coming. We'll not only find the high queen; we will take both girls to Croncliff as well. That makes it political, and my job. Besides, I need to know if this is jinn business.' She grinned. 'And no, we're not going to fight a jinni right now. But we need to be sure whether one of the beasts is still around.'

'How will we find her?' Jonna said worriedly. 'Agusta can be anywhere.'

'I will locate her,' Haai-Bo said haughtily, and he landed precariously on Shaw's shoulder. He anchored himself with his tail around her neck and showed his two double rows of teeth in a crocodilian grin. 'I will find her mind; there aren't all that many in your froggy wetlands.'

CHAPTER 8 — AND AGUSTA

As they followed the coastline south from Brisa, the land unrolled below them as an endless panorama of swamps and water, dotted with copses of trees, and populated by birds and deer.

'Those lands, would they be Malgarth, or part of Codnoallis?' Shaw asked.

'The latter,' Jonna said without taking her eyes off the ground. 'The memory of our coming to Malgarth is unclear. It must've been five centuries ago that the first wave of settlers arrived and built villages on the northwestern coast. That's Codnoallis, Brisa and the rest. Later followed a second wave of colonists. They found Croncliff Island with the palace already there; empty, but just as it is now. Those second wave went inland and built Landfalln. Then they spread out and made what is now Malgarth. There were a lot of fights with the first settlers, but after a while the leaders sat down and talked, and drew borders. After that, we and they left each other alone.'

'Where did those colonists come from?'

'We don't know,' Jonna said absently. 'We know there were two groups, but none of the old records say where they came from.' She lapsed into silence as she studied the landscape.

After a while she sat up. 'There! That's the river.'

'And there's Codnoallis,' Shaw said. 'I hadn't noticed the river the last time. Haai-Bo, any enemies below?'

'None.' The wyrmling cackled. 'Engineer Oychak is there and the locals are all staring at her as she tries to explain her business.'

'We'd better say hello then.' Shaw gestured to Kennan and dove toward the village alehouse. There was a small crowd outside, and Shaw recognized Oychak.

'Wait here,' she said to the others, and walked over to join the villagers. 'Good morning. I stopped by to tell you that your lads are all safe and sound in Brisa; they did a grand and very brave thing. We will send them back to you as soon as they've rested.'

'They are safe?' the innkeeper said quickly. 'What happened? We only missed them when we saw the ship was gone. Why did they go to Brisa? And how?'

'In the middle of last night, a bunch of Malgarth soldiers arrived with a prisoner,' Shaw said. 'They boarded the ship and thought your boys were the crew, so they ordered them to sail north. The lads didn't want to endanger the village and obeyed. When they arrived in Brisa, one of them sneaked ashore and warned us. We went over, killed the soldiers, freed the prisoner and fed your boys.'

'They just sailed?' the fishing boat skipper with his gouty foot exclaimed. 'They took that brig all the way to Brisa?'

'They sure don't lack spirit,' Shaw said. 'And seamanship. Engineer Oychak here comes to install a portal to Brisa.'

'That's what we were discussing, like,' the innkeeper said. 'We didn't rightly understand her business.'

'Let me explain,' Shaw said. 'After we came here the first time, we did what we promised and captured all the Tradeports. Every one of them agreed to join the Peaks, so we distributed food, and began helping them to build a life without pirates. One of the first things we always do is to install a portal. That is simply a magic door. You can step inside, and you'll come out in Brisa. You can do your business, sell some fish, do some shopping, and when you're done, the Brisa portal mage will send you back here. Or if you want to, he can port you to Winsproke, or to the Continent, but that's only for official use.'

'Now I understand,' the innkeeper said with a nod to the engineer.

'Good,' Oychak said grimly. 'Back to my question; where can I put the transferal?'

'It needs to be inside?' Shaw said.

'Yes,' the engineer said. 'And preferably out of reach of stray cats, pigs and little children.'

Shaw managed to suppress a chuckle at the Thali's barely concealed disapproval of Codnoallis.

'Well, we have the old barn,' the innkeeper said. 'It isn't much, but nobody goes there. I'll show you.'

The whole village escorted them to an old wooden shed in a small field.

'Would that do?' the innkeeper said.

Oychak inspected the ruin with pursed lips. 'Barely,' she said.

'Put it in there, and ask Varan to send some builders to shore up the shack,' Shaw said.

The engineer sighed. 'I'll do that.'

'All right,' Shaw said. 'If that's settled, we'll be off again.' She looked at the innkeeper as the most likely spokesman. 'You can expect one of Mr. Varan's people shortly, to discuss your needs.'

Behind her, Jonna made an impatient sound.

Shaw grinned at the girl. 'I know; we're going.'

Joanna blushed. 'I didn't want to...'

'Don't worry,' Nate said. 'We sometimes have to drag her away; she's got a lot of things going.'

Shaw grinned. 'You don't want to know.'

In a few minutes they were all back over the river and flew east. On the upper side of the river was the wild Lornwood and on the lower the marshes. After a while they saw big doors closing off the river. The water on their side was lower than on the other side of the doors. A little village lay close by, with some pasturelands and a pier for fishing boats.

'What's that?' Shaw asked.

'It's the Klenmarro Lock,' Jonna said. 'It regulates the water levels on the river. Not that there is much shipping these days, but the lock is a royal charter, so its keeper gets their pay just for being here.'

'The river is navigable?' Shaw said.

'All the way. There used to be barges sailing from the trade center at Lake Ilguddie to Codnoallis. In those days that was a seaport of sorts. Tramp ships, mostly, sailing to the Tradeports and on to Towne. That all stopped when the pirates came.' Jonna frowned. 'I always thought those bandits were the Tradeports' problem; I never realized how much their skullduggery ruined our trade as well.'

'They ruined trade from Codnoallis to Seatome and everything in between,' Shaw said.

Then Joanna leaned forward. 'There!' she cried, banging Shaw's knee in her excitement. 'That's the place where they caught me.'

'The river is quite fast,' Shaw said. 'No wonder you didn't just jump in.'

'Agusta did,' Jonna said bitterly.

'*Haai-Bo, your turn,*' Shaw said. '*What can you do from here?*'

The wyrmling turned his head without missing a wingbeat and seemed to sniff the air. '*Faint...*' he muttered. '*Faint traces of precocious royalty.*'

In a wide curve he flew away from the river. Shaw gestured at Nate and Kennan. 'We follow him.'

Nate nodded, and Kennan exchanged some signal with his squad. Then they all went after the little wyrmling, winging steadily northeast.

After an hour and a half, they came to a collection of dwellings at a crossroads, boasting an inn of sorts.

'*I will scout around,*' Haai-Bo said. '*I go alone. You go catch mice or something.*'

Shaw pointed and led them to land in a grassy field beside a brook.

'Haai-Bo wants to look around. Meanwhile we'll visit the inn and get some local information,' she said. 'We are traders, after all.'

Nate grinned. 'True, though as a market it doesn't seem promising.'

They shouldered their brooms and walked the last half mile to the village. The few locals they saw eyed them with a mixture of surprise and suspicion, but no one said anything.

At the inn, a large woman in a stained leather apron met them, hands to her broad sides and her eyes inspecting them.

'Strangers,' she said finally. 'Passing through?'

'Yes, ma'am,' Shaw said. 'We're traveling your fine country to see what opportunities there are for trade.'

'Trade?' the woman said. 'With the folks from the Weal? Not bliddy likely.'

'We're not from the Weal,' Shaw said patiently. 'We are from the Pasandir Peaks, a land north of the Weal.'

'Never heard of it,' the woman said. 'You've a Weal face, and so has that chap behind you. The others? What are you? Tar Kell mercenaries?'

'No,' Shaw said quickly. 'They're Peaks marines. These days one doesn't travel without armed protection.'

'The gods' truth,' the woman said, relaxing slightly. 'Can I get you anything? Beer? Wine?'

'No alcohol,' Shaw said. 'That's a religious thing.'

'Tea then. Herbal teas strengthen the body and cleanse the soul,' the woman said.

'Excellent,' Shaw said. 'A good brew is worth traveling for.'

The woman went aft, to return with a large kettle and a stack of mugs. 'There y'have it,' she said. 'That's one silver.'

Shaw heard Nate cough at the ridiculous sum, but without blinking she handed the woman a silver Hizmyran half-falor.

The woman stared at the coin. 'What is this?'

'A good coin,' Shaw said. 'Almost pure silver.' The woman tapped the coin with her teeth. Then she snorted and pocketed the money. 'Foreigners!'

'How is business these days?' Shaw asked quickly.

'With all the trouble we have? Miserable,' the woman said. 'Since the high king died, it's nothing but misery.'

'We heard he passed away,' Shaw said soberly. 'There is an heir, I believe?'

'Agusta,' the woman said. 'As she's a girl, she can't become a ruler herself, so all the dogs are sitting up wagging their tails, hoping to marry her.' She slapped the table with her dirty dishcloth. 'She's out there, somewhere, they say. Staying with a court party lord she was, so she'll have to go to Croncliff to get the throne. That means the race is on.'

'A race?' Shaw said, curious how a local would explain it.

The woman waved her cloth in agitation. 'Between the Court party and the Barons. Which of the two will bring the child to the high castle will be the party in power. Last time it was the Court, so the Barons are all anxious to have their turn. Not that it'll make any difference to us what they're playing in Croncliff.' She clamped her mouth shut. 'Politics! I'll say no more. You said you're traders? Where are your goods?'

'We want to see the country first, meet the people and hear their needs. Then we'll open a warehouse somewhere and start bringing in our trade goods.'

'Our needs? Good copper pans,' the woman said promptly. 'Haven't seen a decent pan for sale in a very long time. Needles and colored thread, and those little beads for dresses.' She lowered her voice. 'And you know what? Narangos. We haven't had any fresh narangos in years. There's lack of a lot of things, but somehow I miss those fruits most of all.'

Then the arrival of a group of loud landsmen called her away.

'Narangos,' Shaw said. 'How the heck is it possible? The Chorwaynies grow loads of them. Why aren't they for sale here?'

'Too little profit, perhaps,' Nate said. 'On the other hand, pans and needles shouldn't be scarce either.' He looked at his empty mug. 'I'm all for discovering local delicacies, but we'll give this herbal tea a pass.'

'Yes,' Shaw said. 'It asks for a strong stomach, just like the cake. Let's go.'

As they walked to the door, a burly landsman barred their path with a muscular arm.

'Traders, eh? Be wary on the road, strangers. There's too many soldiers roaming about to be healthy. We've seen two small battles already, right there amid our fields. A dead king needs followers, I suppose, seeing that many are eager to hurry after him into the netherworld. Gorm and Otha must be busy.'

'Thanks for the warning,' Shaw said. 'We'll give them a wide berth.'

The man pulled his arm back. 'You do that, and next time, bring us some pipe tobacco. We're clear out of it.'

'I'll put it on my list,' Shaw promised. 'What's the name of your village?'

'Farnedde,' the man said.

'Got it,' Shaw said. 'You're on the top of my list.'

'Go with the gods then,' the man said.

'Pipe tobacco,' Shaw said once they were outside. 'That's something else the Chorwaynies grow.'

Outside, they found Haai-Bo waiting. *'Not far from here,'* he said. *'A few more miles. Girl is hiding. Hungry and cold she is. And suspicious. We must lure her out.'*

They took to the air again, and as they crossed the fields, they saw isolated groups of soldiers battling each other with deadly ferocity.

'*Some are like pirates,*' Haai-Bo said. '*Drugged and mad. Boar-head men they are, like those in the ship. The others are clean, but full of fear.*'

'*We can't help them; too risky,*' Shaw said, and they flew on.

They flew over a maze of little creeks until they came to a grassy hillock.

'*There,*' Haai-Bo said. '*That's our mouse-trap. Now we need a lure of fire and food.*'

They landed, and after the marines had collected a stack of wood from the local birches, Battlemage Oskar made a comfortable fire. They all sat round the flames, sipping river water with sweet syrup and eating finely baked ship's biscuits.

'What are these cookies?' Jonna said. 'They're good.'

'Sashuni emergency rations,' Nate said. 'A few are enough for a full stomach.'

'*Someone is watching us,*' Haai-Bo said. '*Someone wet and angry.*'

'*Where?*' Shaw said.

'Do come out,' Haai-Bo said aloud. 'No good standing in the water being cold and empty-bellied, when you could sit at our fire and eat.'

'Who are you?' a girl's voice said from inside the plumy reeds.

'Agusta!' Jonna cried. 'They're friends! They're here to help us.'

The reeds swayed and a soaking wet figure appeared. In the light of the fire they saw she was a straight-backed girl, with long red hair plastered to a round, pale face. She was dressed in a blue suit like Jonna's, covered to the neck in duckweed.

She had bound her cravat round her head and gripped a small saber that shook with the chattering of her teeth.

'Oh gods,' she said. 'You did it!'

Jonna ran to embrace her. 'We found you! Come to the fire; you're cold.'

The girl sloshed ashore, looking much like some mythical swamp creature.

'Come here,' Nate said. 'Sit down at the fire.'

Agusta dropped to the ground and stretched out her hands to the flames. 'How did you find me?'

'Our master spy did,' Shaw said. 'Haai-Bo! Please show yourself, great advisor.'

'A wyrm!' Agusta said, groggy with tiredness. 'It's a real wyrm? Looking for me?'

'Sure,' Shaw stroked Haai-Bo's neck. 'We all were looking for you.' She then offered Agusta some biscuits, and she wolfed them down as if she hadn't eaten for days.

Then the girl turned to Jonna. 'Why didn't you swim?'

'I was too slow,' Jonna said.

'You were scared.'

'Yes. And be glad I was, for now we have people to aid us.'

'True,' Agusta said. 'Will they help me get where I hate to go?'

'Croncliff?' Shaw said. 'If you want us to, yes.'

'Want?' Agusta rubbed her hands hard to get the blood going. 'I don't want to go there, but I must. Jonna told you, of course.'

It was a statement, not a question, and Shaw nodded. 'She had to, to get us out here.'

'Fine by me. If Jonna trusts you, so will I. She's the careful one. Can you understand my predicament? My father died. It wasn't expected; he wasn't ill or old, or something, it was just his heart stopped. Not that I grieve or anything; the last time I saw him I was little and I knew he hated me for being a girl. Then the god of foolish people—there must be such a god, mustn't there?—called him, and I was cooked. All my life, I loathed the thought of going to Croncliff and live in that snake pit of a palace; so his death scared the heck out of me.' The girl spat in the fire and stared at the hissing blob boiling away on a burning log. 'Those greencoats... What's *wrong* with the Barons soldiers? Killing your opponents isn't in the rules.'

'They're not themselves,' Shaw said. 'Those who had caught Jonna were drugged in a way we know all too well. Ever heard of the jinn?'

Agusta stared at her. 'There aren't any in Malgarth.'

'A lot of other rulers thought the same. Jinn are everywhere, masquerading as ordinary people; even people you know.'

'Don't worry,' Nate added quickly. 'Haai-Bo will recognize them immediately, and so will our Battlemage Oskar.'

'Yep,' Oskar said, bowing forward and smiling. 'Jinn have no mind, you see. No mind we can read. They stick out like an elephant in a chicken farm.'

'Jinn,' Agusta said. 'I thought they were legends, like...'

'Like wyrms,' Jonna said. 'But those are real, aren't they?'

'Yeah,' Agusta said. 'What do these jinn want? Land? Riches?'

'They eat people,' Shaw said.

'What?' The high queen sat looking at her. 'Say that again?'

'Jinn see humans as cattle. They want to breed us, use our lands as their farms and eat us,' Nate said.

'I cannot agree to that,' Agusta said. 'We are farmers, not cattle. And what is your part in this?'

'We fight pirates and jinn,' Shaw said. 'Have you heard of the burning of Brisa, some time ago?'

'Yes!' Agusta said. 'A Weal ship blew up those boneheads!'

'Not a Weal ship,' Shaw said. 'That was our lord wyrmcaller. I was there with him, that day.' She told of Eskandar, the orphanage and the pirates, up to their journey to Smalkand. 'Now the wyrmcaller has gone north, hunting the jinn in their homeland, while Nate and I are building up the Pasandir Trade Company. Some days ago, a Brisan pirate ship plundered a mine in New Winsproke and that was too much. To protect our people and our businesses, we went and annexed the Tradeports.'

Again, the high queen sat frozen. 'You *took* them?'

'We defeated the pirates and asked the common people to join us. The people liked the idea, and they joined us willingly.'

'Don't think we will do the same,' Agusta said in a high voice. 'We won't.'

'Of course not,' Shaw said. 'Don't worry; we're not in the habit of conquering nations! The Tradeports had stopped being one long ago. They were simply robber's nests, where the good people starved and the bad people prospered. At least we put a stop to that.'

'Now you want to go to Croncliff?' Nate said. 'We should make that before nightfall.'

'Yes, please,' Agusta said, relaxing as she turned her mind back to her own problems. 'But how will we get there? It must be quite a walk yet. Do you have a steamcart?'

'We'll fly,' Jonna said. 'They ride on broomsticks.'

CHAPTER 9 — CRONCLIFF

'There!' Agusta said with deep disgust in her voice as she pointed at a large rock in the distance, rising up from the sea bearing a many-towered castle on its back. 'Croncliff.'

'It's not all that far from Dibloon,' Shaw said.

'Thirty miles or so,' Agusta said. 'But the whole bay is Malgarth territory.'

'I'm sure we can discuss fishing, mooring rights, and details like that,' Shaw said affably.

Below them was a walled town with tall, narrow houses, and two small two-masted vessels moored to a rickety pier. Beyond the walls, on a grassy hill, was a sprawling mansion.

Then Kennan pulled up and pointed. Shaw nodded and followed him down, well away from the town, in a road between fields of corn.

'Why do you stop here?' Agusta asked. 'This is Landfalln; a dull place.'

'People who want to be sure the castle is safe stop here,' Nate said.

'Do you think...?' The girl's voice sounded strangled.

'We don't think, Your Majesty,' Kennan said with a smile. 'We make sure all is safe before we risk your august personage.'

'You two put your hoods up,' Shaw said. 'You never know who would recognize you.'

Obediently, the girls hid their faces as they walked towards the town gates.

Within a few yards, three soldiers came running.

'Halt!' the senior of them shouted harshly. He wore a blue uniform with silver piping, and Haai-Bo didn't react, so Shaw supposed him of the Court faction.

'Who are you and what's your business here?' the man snapped.

'We are merchants,' Shaw said. 'We are traveling through Malgarth to see what the populace needs in trade goods.'

'Traders! You picked a fine time for it. Those Kells in their fancy suits, are they mercenaries?'

'They are our marines. We were advised there was some trouble going on, so we took them with us.'

'Trouble? Ha! With the high king dead and the Barons gone crazy, I'd say we have trouble,' the soldier said. 'Come with me; the Lord Chancellor wants to speak with you.'

Shaw sighed. 'Fine, perhaps we can talk business.' She glanced at the two girls, but they kept their heads well down.

'I don't think he will, trader. Not at this moment he will.'

The soldiers brought them through a maze of small streets to a solid inn overlooking the pier and the bay beyond. There were two more guards at the door, and several others inside, all looking harassed and, Shaw thought, extremely nervous.

To the right in the common room, a tall man was talking to an officer. He was floridly handsome, with dark, graying hair and a blue velvet suit showing a heavy gold timepiece-chain.

The lead soldier saluted. 'We found these strangers entering town, your lordship,' he said. 'So we took them here, as per our orders.'

'Strangers, eh?' the big man said, turning his heavy head to look at them. 'And who might you youngsters be, with your Vanhaari faces?'

Shaw screwed her monocle in her eye and returned his stare. 'I am the managing director of the Pasandir Trading Company,' she said coolly. 'We are from the Pasandir Peaks, a sovereign country north of the Weal nations.'

'Never knew there were lands further away,' the man said. 'So you're not the Weal?'

'Most assuredly not. We came to see what needs the people have, and what trade opportunities there might be in your lands.'

The man gave a curt laugh. 'Leave us,' he said, both to the officer he had been speaking with and to the escorts.

Then he walked to the hearth, where several chairs stood.

Shaw sat down, with Nate beside her. Agusta hesitated for a second, but then she and Jonna plumped down on the ground. Kennan's men formed a half-circle round them, facing the room.

The big man gave them a quick glance and took the last chair.

'I am Lord Rutus Wrache, the high king's chancellor,' he said. 'We have a problem.'

'That crossed my mind when we traveled through the lands,' Shaw said. 'Bitter fighting and dead soldiers are bad signs.'

'You could say that,' Lord Rutus said. 'It started with the unexpected death of the high king. The heir, Princess Agusta, traditionally lived away from Croncliff, staying with a trusted Court lord. We sent for her to take over the throne. We know the princess and the lord's daughter departed for Croncliff with the messenger and his escort. The latter were all found dead, and the girls gone.

'We thought the Barons party, the rich landowners, who think it is the king's duty to make them even more wealthy, were up to their usual tricks and tried to lay hand on the royal person. But they went further and started killing our side. That makes it even more urgent to get the princess to safety. We know we don't have her. We know they don't have her. But what they do have is Croncliff.'

Shaw saw the hooded girl queen start. 'They do?' she said hastily. 'How did they manage that?'

'Deceit,' Rutus said with barely hidden rage in his voice. 'As the party last in power, we held the palace. This morning, Morthan sent me a message to parlay. I expected them to tell me they had the princess, and wanted to discuss terms, as is traditional. So I gathered up my men and came to Landfalln.

Then, creeping behind my back like the cockroaches they are, the Barons landed a team at Cronstliff and somehow raised their banner.'

'And they didn't have the princess?' Shaw said.

'No,' Rutus said.

Shaw stared at the chancellor. 'But you have your soldiers. Why don't you go and take the palace back?'

'Impossible!' the chancellor said. 'Neither faction is allowed to use violence inside Croncliff. That is the one firm rule that binds us all. Who flies his banner over the palace and has the heir holds the kingdom, no fighting allowed. Everywhere else battle is part of the time-honored tradition of the royal succession.'

'A tradition?' Shaw said. 'All the fighting, all those deaths, are a tradition?'

'The fighting, yes. That way we decide which of the two factions is in charge. The killings are a disgrace and unsporting.'

'And the high king?'

Rutus coughed. 'The high king always goes along with the winning faction's policies.'

'Now what will you do?' Shaw said.

'This is where you people come in. I want you to go to Croncliff, raise our banner and take the palace back for us. Then you fire off some fireworks and we'll come back.'

'Why us?' Shaw said. 'We are not part of your tradition.'

'No,' Lord Rutus said. 'And that is why you can do things we cannot. You can go there; if we do that, we will break the covenant. That would mean all-out civil war.'

'So we are supposed to fight for you?' Shaw asked. 'And what will we get out of it?'

'All the trade you want,' Lord Rutus said.

Shaw smiled. 'A powerful argument. How many opponents are there?'

'As yet only ten soldiers and a commander,' the chancellor said. 'We hold the ships, you see, so without a vessel of their own they can't get their troops inside. I'm sure they are searching around for a suitable ship, but for the moment they're stuck.'

So that was why they needed the Codnoallis ship, Shaw thought. She saw Joanna stir as if she realized it too.

'Agreed.' Shaw looked at Lord Rutus. 'We'll go to the palace, raise our flag and that's that. How will you get us there?'

'When it is fully dark, one of the ferry ships shall put you ashore. You can slip in through the side door. The flag staff is on top of the central tower, through the door behind the high throne.'

'All right,' Shaw said. 'You have a room where we can discuss the operation?'

'Yes,' Lord Rutus said. He beckoned to a soldier. 'Show the merchant and her people to the backroom. They are guests of the court.'

The backroom was a large, dusty place with a dining table and several chairs, smelling after cabbage and wet clothes.

'Why...' Agusta started as the door closed behind the soldier.

'Wait!' Shaw said. 'Is this room secure?'

Haai-Bo appeared in the room. 'Now it is,' he said. 'Snoops hear only murmurings.'

'We need a plan,' Shaw said.

'I have a company banner,' Kennan said. 'I always carry one, in case you want us to capture a ship or a fort.'

Shaw looked at the commander. 'That's it! You are a genius!'

'What are you thinking?' Agusta demanded, red-faced. 'I am very angry, you know. I don't want to be a mouthpiece for Rutus Wrache or any baron. I am the high queen. You must not declare for him.'

'Don't worry,' Shaw said. 'Let me tell you the plan.'

That night, the smaller of the two ferries dropped them off on a pier to the side of the Croncliff rock.

Shaw breathed in the smell of seaweed and brine, and walked up a path between rocks. After a hundred yards, they came to a door.

'It's not locked,' Shaw said with a grin. 'How very trusting.'

'Shaw,' Haai-Bo said, and his voice sounded strange. 'Something has happened here.'

'What?' she said surprised. 'You mean the Barons?'

'I cannot tell.' The wyrmling sounded scared.

'Is there any danger?' Shaw asked, startled.

'I don't know. What happened here blinds my vision.'

'All right, we'll find out,' Shaw said.

'I'm sorry,' Haai-Bo said piteously. 'I cannot serve you here.'

'It's fine,' Shaw said, scratching the wyrmling's head. 'If there is anything wrong, we'll find it.' Then she slipped inside. 'Stairs!'

In a long row they climbed up; Shaw with Nate behind her, followed by Kennan and a soldier. Then Agusta and Jonna, with the rest of the soldiers.

The air was coldly still and cobwebs betrayed the corridor had been little used. Past several unlocked doors, they came to a storeroom full of crates and barrels, and several large slabs of meat on hooks.

Beyond that was a kitchen, empty and well kept, that opened up on a tiled corridor.

'Still nobody?' Nate whispered.

'There are minds,' Oskar said softly. 'Servants hiding in their rooms, and piraty types. Ten or more, they're too close together to be sure. They are very, very drugged, with a thick fog in their heads.'

They came into a high hallway, with vaguely the outlines of a big door. Broad stairs to their left and then on the top of them a door opened, and a bundle of light shone out.

'Intruders!' a heavy voice said, dripping satisfaction. 'They are even bringing me the new high queen! How very generous.'

'Lord Morthan?' Agusta said.

A big man with a pale face and a dark beard stood looking down at them. He was dressed in a green Barons uniform with huge gold epaulets and carried a businesslike sword. At his back, twelve burly soldiers stood glowering at them.

'No-mind!' Oskar whispered urgently.

'It won't work, jinni,' Shaw said promptly. 'You're at the wrong place at the wrong time.'

'You know?' the big man said, and he raised a busy eyebrow. 'WHO ARE YOU?'

'Jinnbane's Sister,' Shaw said with a big grin.

'Impossible.' Morthan slammed the stones with his sword and sparks flew around. 'Impossible! There is no such creature.' He pointed a hairy hand at Agusta. 'Give me the high queen and begone.'

Agusta drew her short sword. 'Come and get me, false baron!' she said and her voice shook only a little.

'Attack!' the big man screamed, and his soldiers ran down the stairs.

Kennan plucked the high queen from the ground and put her down behind him. 'No heroics now. That's our job.'

'Hoppa,' Oskar sang, shooting a mass of lightning at the enemy soldiers, incinerating six men at the same time.

'Whoa,' Healer Suzie said. 'Mind your reserves.'

'I'm not that easily done,' Oskar said, and threw a wave of fire up the stairs. The remaining soldiers withered away and then the flames engulfed the armored man, burning away the outer shape, and in its stead was a giant, six-armed monstrosity, with horns, warts and whatever all over its overly muscular body. Where his navel should be, a horrible face leered at them, drooling and gibbering.

'Behold Awasuz!' the jinni cried. 'Almir of the Ninth Plane. Now die, cattle!'

His sword changed into an anchor-chain with links the size of feet, which he swept around like it was only a rope.

'Gods, oh gods,' Jonna muttered, sweat running down her face.

'Stand!' Shaw said. 'We'll get the beast. Mind that hideousness on its tummy is its weak spot.'

Kennan's men all took a small bow from their belts and took aim. Moments later, six arrows found their way into the disgusting face.

Awasuz roared. 'Useless!' he shouted. 'Just give up already!'

'Out swords!' Kennan said. 'Aim for the eyes.' His guys darted in, slashed twice at the face and jumped out of reach of the chain.

The jinni screamed as a blade entered an eye, and deep rents dripped green goo. Now Nate ran, his face composed. 'For Clam Street!' he yelled, as he hacked at the face.

The jinn slapped him aside and he fell heavily, but then Jonna and the high queen dashed forward with their pint-sized swords and struck at the face, drawing green blood. Bleeding all over, the jinn swung the chain and bellowed.

Oskar lobbed a fiery ball into the jinni mouth. Somehow, he didn't miss, and the monstrous head exploded. The body staggered and the heavy chain clattered harmlessly against the wall. Then, as one, every blade in the hall stabbed at the face. With a loud implosion, the body disappeared and only a whitish stain on the floor remained.

'Done!' Shaw cried.

Nate came to his feet, shaking his head dazedly. 'We got the beast!'

'So that was a jinni,' Agusta said. She gripped Jonna's shoulder. 'We killed a jinni!'

Jonna stared at her blankly. Then she giggled. 'You must be the first Malgarth ruler in centuries to kill something bigger than a fly.'

Agusta punched her shoulder. 'We girls will set them an example, you and I.'

'We must go up,' Shaw said. She grinned at Nate, who was cleaning his sword blade.

'Jinnbane's sister?' he said. 'You were joking, I hope?'

'Yeah,' Shaw said, patting his cheek. 'I wasn't echoing some prophecy.'

They ran up the broad stairs and into a large hall with a massive throne. At the back was an open door giving access to a narrow staircase. Shaw ran lightly up the stairs. It was quite a way up still, and then they came to the top of a tall tower. A flagpole carried a boar head banner, and quickly Kennan took it down. Instead, he hoisted the banner of the PTC.

'That's the best we can do,' Shaw said, as she sent three fiery rockets up into the air, signaling their success.

'But you don't want the high kingdom, do you?' Agusta said pointedly. 'It's mine.'

'We don't want it,' Shaw said. 'It's yours. We'll help you change some things, though. Come down to the throne room and we'll talk it over a bit more.'

CHAPTER 10 — CROOKED DEVELOPMENTS

With the jinni and his henchmen dead, and the high queen returned, the servants came out of hiding. In minutes, the large throne room bathed in warm light, refreshments appeared as if by magic and the dead Baron's men were discreetly removed from the hall.

'Bring a chair for the high merchant,' Agusta commanded. She glanced at Nate, who shook his head.

'Let's not confuse the scene,' he said. 'I'll stand beside Shaw, as Jonna does with you.'

'Do I?' the blonde girl said.

'You must,' Shaw said. 'Remember she is the high queen now. In public you are a courtier.'

Agusta gripped Jonna's arm. 'That's all show,' she said. 'Nothing else changes between us.'

You hope, Shaw thought, but she didn't say anything. She thought Jonna's face looked upset, as if she had her doubts as well. Agusta's crown would stand between them.

Ninety minutes later, Lord Rutus Wrache came bustling in, followed by several other nobles and a tow-haired boy of some sixteen years, who was enough like him to be a close relative. When he saw Agusta sitting on the throne, the chancellor stopped in his tracks and the blood drained from his face.

'Princess Agusta!' he said in a choked voice. 'How did you...? I...' He swallowed. 'How glad I am to see you, Highness!'

'I am the high queen,' Agusta said chilly. 'You will address me as such, Lord Rutus.'

'Your Majesty,' the chancellor said, quickly recovering his aplomb. 'Of course you are the high queen. You will marry my dear son, and then all will be well. Now, about those barons. This time we have to hang a few of them. Don't you worry; I will give the necessary orders.'

'Marry your son!' Agusta said in a voice of disgust. 'Don't you believe it, Rutus. I can rule my own kingdom.'

'But you're a girl, a woman! You *can't* rule unsupervised. My son is a personable lad and I'll take care he will govern well. You can sit back and do... well, whatever girls do.'

They all looked at him, Shaw with raised eyebrows and a blistering remark on her lips. But she saw Agusta's face and swallowed what she was going to say.

'I will not be your puppet, Rutus,' Agusta said furiously. 'I am the high queen and I give the orders. And I won't marry your son even if he was the last male on the planet.'

'Father...' the tow-haired boy said, but the chancellor waved him away.

'We won, Your Majesty,' Rutus said. 'The rules say I... we Court nobles rule. It is our banner on the tower.'

'I'm afraid I must disappoint you,' Shaw said. 'It is our banner on the tower, Lord Rutus. After all, *we* won.'

Rutus stared at her, his eyes bulging. 'But we agreed... Who are you?'

'I am the High Merchant Shaw Harwans, managing director of the Pasandir Trading Co., speaking for the Lord Wyrmcaller, sovereign ruler of the Pasandir Peaks,' Shaw said. 'We helped the high queen to her throne, so we are her advisors.'

At that moment, Haai-Bo flew in through the open door. 'I saw... I saw her shadow. A vision. Big she was, very oh so big. And even more beautiful than I dreamt. I...' He sighed deeply and shivered. 'You were successful then. Good. Lord Rutus is a silly man, but he is not a no-mind. The castle is clean.'

Shaw had no idea what he was talking about.

'A wyrm!' the chancellor exclaimed, his hand clasping his sword. 'Wyrms must be killed, Your Majesty.'

'Do not even think to draw your blade in my throne room, Rutus!' Agusta snapped. 'Else I will have your head on a pike outside this instant! The Lord Haai-Bo is a very highborn wyrm; he is extremely powerful and a good friend. He and his kin are welcome in our land and at my court. Prepare for changes, Lord Rutus.' She slapped her armrest. 'To business; Baron Morthan is dead. Where are the other leaders of the Barons faction?'

'They are camped nearby, Your Majesty,' Rutus said faintly.

'Bring me pen and paper, somebody,' the high queen commanded. 'Who has the royal seal?'

'I do,' Rutus said. 'Keeping the seal is part of my duties.'

'Father...' the tow-haired boy tried again.

'Not now, Gerben,' the chancellor said as a lord came hurrying back with writing materials.

Agusta wrote a short note in a handwriting that needed all the paper. Then she scrawled her name underneath.

'Seal it,' Agusta commanded. 'Then have somebody bring it to the leaders of the Barons faction. And tell them to hurry.'

Rutus obeyed and one of the nobles hurried out, clutching the high queen's note.

'While we wait, you may explain to her majesty who does what at court,' Shaw said. 'Who handles the royal finances?'

'Actually most of the work is done by the royal chancellor,' Rutus said. 'Finances, foreign affairs, defense, trade and internal affairs are all his responsibilities.'

'Yours, you mean?' Shaw said.

'Ah, yes. Yes, actually, that is correct.' Rutus tried a smile. 'To have it all in one hand makes oversight much easier, you see.'

'No,' the high queen said bluntly. 'Remember these are all *my* prerogatives, Lord Rutus.'

'Of course, Ma'am,' Rutus said smoothly. 'I execute these offices in your name, to lighten your load.'

'Very kind of you, I'm sure,' Agusta said. 'I will discuss this later in more detail, my lord chancellor.'

Rutus bowed. 'As you command, Ma'am.'

Shaw looked at his face, and saw the anger hidden behind its hard lines. Lord Rutus was definitely not pleased with the turn of events.

It took another hour, which the courtiers spent in soft discussions, and the high queen dozing on her throne with her arms crossed and her eyes sternly open.

Shaw sat with Nate on a wooden bench in a window and rested with her head against his shoulder. She watched the faces of the worried courtiers, Rutus' mounting anger and the tow-haired boy's confusion. *He seems a nice chap,* she thought. *The honest, upright sort, he's hearing things he doesn't like. His old man is a crook; didn't he know that?*

Finally, servants ushered in a baron in a stained green uniform, who was wild-eyed and shaking as if suffering from a great fever. Behind him were four officers looking even worse.

Rufus stared at them and frowned. 'Ungreff, what have you been doing, man? Been on the booze?'

The baron shook his head wildly. 'N-n-no,' he said. His chin trembled and there were tears in his eyes.

'I know,' Shaw said. She looked at Healer Suzie standing with the marines. 'Can you do something for them?'

The healer came forward and put a small hand on Ungreff's shoulders. Slowly, the trembling left the shocked baron, his reddened eyes cleared and his stance straightened.

'For the moment he'll be alright,' Suzy said, stepping over to the officers. 'Sleep must do the rest.'

'Thank you, lady healer,' the old baron said. 'I haven't been clearheaded in days.' He turned to the high queen and bowed.

'Your Majesty; I respectfully bend my knee to you. It seems Lord Rutus won the race again.'

'He did not,' Agusta said. 'High Merchant Shaw assisted me in getting my uncomfortable seat of power. No doubt she wants to address both factions now.'

'Be sure I will,' Shaw said. 'But first Baron Ungreff's men need medical attention.'

'I shall call Healer Tymon and explain the situation,' Suzie said. 'He will send help.'

Shaw nodded. 'Thank you. Then, my lords, I will inform you of my part in this political farce. First, for your information, my army defeated the pirates in the Five Tradeports and Codnoallis. The local populace was relieved and decided they would be pleased to become part of the Pasandir Peaks. This will give them a great many advantages, which I will explain to you later.' She smiled. 'Don't worry; I fear the high queen's anger too much to even suggest her mighty kingdom should follow the Tradeports' example.'

'Rightly so,' Agusta said. 'My wrath is terrible. After all, I killed a very large jinni.'

Jonna coughed, and the high queen grinned at her. 'Yes, you helped. Our bravery was astounding.'

'We all gaped in awe at your courage,' Shaw said calmly. 'Let me continue.' She told of the Codnoallis ship, and freeing Jonna. 'As good neighbors do, I answered Lady Jonna's call for help and came to her majesty's aid. Lord Haai-Bo's massive powers enabled us to find the high queen, who had bravely evaded her captors and was making for Croncliff on her own. Her majesty told me of the situation, and we decided the PTC was to act as a third faction. Lord Rutus unwittingly gave us an opening, by requiring us to go to Croncliff and hoist his party's banner.'

'And you promised!' Rutus said bitterly. 'You broke your word.'

'I promised quite clearly to hoist our banner,' Shaw said. 'As we were not of your party, "our banner" was obviously mine, not yours.' She smiled sweetly at the chancellor.

The high queen laughed. 'Foiled, my lord Rutus.'

'Your ship brought us to Croncliff,' Shaw said, ignoring the chancellor's chagrin. 'We made our way inside. Only then we discovered that Baron Morthan, who had taken the castle with his men, was something else entirely. And that explains the sad state of Lord Ungreff's party. Morthan's person had been taken over by a very powerful jinni lord.'

Rutus turned pale and then red. 'A jinni? Here? Gods! Where is he? We must flee while we can!'

'The beast is dead,' Agusta said with satisfaction. 'I and Jonna killed the jinni, Lord Rutus.'

Shaw bowed. 'We were pleased to assist Your Majesty in this matter. The jinni was a powerful one. He had used a forbidden drug to poison the minds of his faction's followers. We know this drug well; the jinn use it to enthrall their pirate underlings. All Barons' soldiers were enslaved, what explains the ferocity of their fighting. The jinni's death broke the enslavement spell and his victims suffer from the effects.'

'They are lucky,' Healer Suzie said. 'They have been drinking the poison for a few days only. Had it been weeks or longer, no healer would have been able to restore them. That stuff is a mind killer.'

'It was horrible,' Baron Ungreff said. 'Now I realize what we did was wrong, but when Morthan explained it, everything sounded so logical that we couldn't do anything else.

'He went to Croncliff and raised our banner. Then, suddenly, it was as if our minds exploded. Many of my brethren are much worse than me; that is why only a few of us could answer your summons, Your Majesty.'

'I understand,' Agusta said. 'Well, my lords; the race is over. Neither of you won; I did. I rule and any man I choose to marry—in the far distant future—will be prince-consort; *not* high king.' She uncrossed her arms and gripped the small saber on her lap. 'I cannot accept factions fighting each other for the right to govern. That tradition is over, my lords. In the future, we will do it the normal, civilized way, like other countries.' She waved at Shaw. 'The high merchant has a few proposals. I suggest you listen to her.'

Shaw screwed the monocle in her eye and lifted her chin in the air. 'Once again, we are not going to take over the government. Her Majesty will appoint ministers to do her bidding, and they will be chosen from both factions. I run a trade empire, and to me Malgarth is important only as a new market.' She gave the lords a small smile.

'You need the things I sell, gentlemen. You don't know yet how much you need them. But before I can begin trading, I need a place to work from. Lord Rutus, we would buy a headquarters with a warehouse, preferably in Landfalln.'

Rutus sat up. 'Buy, you said? I'm afraid we won't be selling any property in the town right now, high merchant.'

'The Landfalln Estate, my lord,' a young man said.

'That's mine!' Rutus snapped. 'I mean, I would...' He faltered.

'What's with the Landfalln Estate?' Jonna said.

'Nothing,' Rutus said hastily. 'Nothing at all, girl.'

'Mind your manners,' Agusta said. 'Lady Jonna is my chief advisor, not merely a "girl". Now, what about that estate?' She pointed at the younger man. 'You! Out with it.'

'Lord Landfalln died recently, Ma'am,' the young man said. 'As there are no heirs, the estate reverts to the crown.'

'To the crown,' Jonna said. 'Then what did Lord Rutus mean with "it is mine"?'

'The chancellor was interested in acquiring the estate, Ma'am.'

'Nonsense!' Rutus barked. 'Landfalln is for the high king... queen to give away, like...'

'Like Roseborn, Marshfield and Towsend,' the young man said. 'You took them, yet his late majesty never did sign their deeds. Their transfers were handled by the chancellor. In Lady Rutus' name.'

'You're fired,' Rutus said harshly. 'Guards! Take this traitor to the dungeons. I...'

Shaw noticed the aghast look on the tow-headed boy's face, as he stared at the chancellor. *Father!* his lips mouthed, but no sound came.

'Stop!' Agusta said. 'One last time, I give the orders. These are serious accusations. Who are you?'

The young man bowed to the high queen. 'I am the Chancery Clerk, Ma'am.'

'Can you prove your claims?'

'Yes, Your Majesty. There are copies of the deeds in the archives.'

'I want to see them.' The high queen jumped to her feet. 'Show me those copies.' She turned around. 'Captain Kennan, may I request you to keep an eye on my lord Rutus? We will all go to the Chancery.'

Shaw nodded at Kennan, who gave a quiet order. His guys moved to surround the chancellor as they all walked down the corridor to a large stone room.

An enormous wooden desk dominated the room, with a high chair backed to the fire. To a side was a standing desk, and beside it several file cabinets.

The young man went to the first one and returned with three slim files.

'Give them to me,' Jonna said. She opened the first file and scanned the documents inside. 'A gift deed for the Roseborn estate with as beneficiary my lady Efena of Rattspir-Volgan, dated two years ago.' She looked at the young man, and then at Rutus. 'This lady...?'

'She is Lord Rutus Wrache's wife,' the young man said.

'Curse you!' Rutus said. 'It was a gift! A reward for all my toil. The high king was agreed, but unable to sign that day. So I handled it myself.'

'Father!' the tow-haired boy cried desperately. 'What means this? You said...'

Rutus slapped the boy. 'Quiet!'

His son closed his mouth and stared at his father with a mixture of anger and pain.

'A gift?' Jonna said as she flipped through the other two files. 'Marshfield and Towsend. Both to the same lady, and both signed by the chancellor alone.' She handed the deeds to Agusta. 'You must toil hard, to warrant three estates, Lord Rutus. But without the royal signature, these deeds are...'

'Theft,' Agusta said. 'That's what it is. Barefaced theft. Misuse of my father's trust. I need no more proof. You're done, Rutus. Hand me my seal and your ring of office.'

Deadly pale, Rutus undid the seal from his fob and moved to give it to the high queen. Then, with a swift flick of his wrist a knife appeared in his hand and he lurched at the girl, to die with Kennan's sword between his ribs and Jonna's blade in his side.

'No you don't,' the captain said. He looked at Jonna. 'You're fast, my lady.'

'No!' his son cried and fell on his knees beside his father.

'He's dead,' Suzie said. She crouched beside the fallen councilor. 'You pierced his lungs, Captain. Coupled with my lady's abdominal stab that was fatal.'

'My father... What did he do?' The tow-headed boy's voice was full of the same pain and anger Shaw had seen earlier.

'He appropriated three vacant demesnes that should have reverted to the crown,' Jonna said. 'He signed them over to your mother, under his own signature and the royal seal. That's a crime, you know.'

'He said...' The boy stumbled over the words. 'He said the high king gave them as a reward for his services. I... was so proud of him. It was all untrue? He *lied* to me?'

Shaw watched the pain and the shame rise in his homely face as the truth sank in.

Jonna put a hand on his arm. 'Steady, Gerben.'

'My father... dishonored us.' The boy stared down at Rutus' body. 'He ruined our name, he broke the high king's trust, he... he was a swindler. A traitor.'

He looked at Agusta, his face puffy and gray. 'I do not know what he meant with marriage, Your Majesty. He had never spoken of it to me. I... with all respect for the crown, I will not marry you, Ma'am.'

'Gods Bless,' the high queen said. 'We are of one mind then.' Her color was high, Shaw noted, but her eyes steady. The first crisis under her young rule and she took it well.

'I do not hold it against you, Lord Gerben.' Agusta looked at Shaw, her narrow face drawn. 'This is a darnable situation. Who can I trust?'

'That chancellor had great control of his mind,' Haai-Bo said, chagrined. 'I was skimming all brains, not watching him close enough. I need permission to dig deeper.' He turned his long neck from courtier to courtier. 'Who objects to my reading minds?'

A few courtiers looked troubled, but none dared to refuse.

Haai-Bo stilled in the air, defying gravity without a single wingbeat. Finally he cackled. 'All clean.'

'Thank you, Lord Haai-Bo,' the high queen said.

She looked at the clerk. 'You did me a service. Have you worked for that man long?'

'Six years, Ma'am. I saw enough. Rutus — your pardon, Lord Gerben, but your father was a villain, and the kingdom suffered for his misdeeds. His late majesty didn't care, so I couldn't speak out. But our new majesty seemed different.' He spread his hands. 'It was on impulse. Had I been wrong...'

Agusta gave a curt nod. 'You weren't. Now I need replacements for all those jobs he held.'

'Chancellor, high steward, treasurer, high chamberlain, keeper of the seal, chief justice, and several minor offices,' the clerk said.

Agusta sighed. 'I want to see all nobles here, with their families,' she said. 'Both Court and Barons, at Croncliff next week. Can you arrange that?'

The clerk bowed. 'It will be done, Ma'am.'

Agusta looked at the other nobles, who stood together, looking pale and sick. 'I will not hold you responsible, either. Yet you know the rules. A new government, a change of functionaries. I thank you all for your efforts, and all that. You may leave the palace now. Not you, Lord Gerben.'

She pointed at the officer Shaw remembered seeing in discussion with Rutus at the inn. 'Who are you?'

'Colonel in command of the Croncliff Guards, Ma'am.'

'Have these men escorted aboard the ferry. I don't want a Court noble left in the palace.'

The colonel beckoned an adjutant and passed on the orders.

'It will be done, Ma'am.' He hesitated. 'Will Lord Gerben...'

The high queen looked at the boy. 'You have a choice. Go back to Wrache with your father's body, or stay at court. I would prefer the latter, to show the world there is no quarrel between us, but you decide.'

The boy looked down at his fallen sire, his face hard and pale. 'He betrayed all I thought he stood for; his queen, his honor and his family. I do not... need to bury him. I will stay.' He turned to the colonel. 'I will write a letter to my mother. Have it delivered to her, please.'

He walked to the desk. 'Pen and paper?'

Without a word, the clerk helped him and with a steady hand, the boy started to write.

Agusta took a deep breath. 'On to other matters. Colonel. Let one thing be clear—your forces serve the crown, not any faction. I want a list of names, ranks, and pay of all your men. And a list of the fallen. Their deaths were senseless, and their families must be recompensed.'

'Yes, Ma'am,' the colonel said. 'Your pardon, but not all the fallen have been found yet.'

'Send out search parties,' Agusta said. 'Search for both your men and Barons soldiers. I expect the latter will be sick and confused. Remember whatever they did was done by the jinni that had enslaved their minds. The men won't remember much, I think.'

'Vaguely,' Baron Ungreff said. 'As if it was someone else who did them.'

'That's what I supposed. Those men are not guilty, not even Morthan. And we executed the jinni, so justice has been served. Ungreff, with Morthan dead, who commands the Barons men?'

Ungreff hesitated as if seeking for words. 'Ours was not a unified command like the good colonel's Guards. Morthan brought in five hundred men, and the other seven hundred came from ten different barons. They all have their own commanders.'

'That will change,' Agusta said firmly. 'Please return to your camp and tell the other lords I will be along later today. I need to prepare, and see young Morthan first.' She flicked a finger at the clerk. 'You send out messengers to the nobles. Tell them to come today next week, if they want cookies and see me crowned at the same time.'

The clerk bowed. 'Immediately, Ma'am. If Lord Ungreff and the colonel can lend me some officers.'

Ungreff turned to his lieutenants. 'You go,' he said. 'Tell every lord the news. Ask them all to look out for any wandering men.'

'We mustn't forget High Merchant Shaw still needs a headquarters in Landfalln,' Agusta said with an attempt at brightness. 'I would gift her the Landfalln Estate.'

'No gifts; we hire or buy it,' Shaw said firmly. 'I prefer to buy if the property is suitable.'

'It is the mansion on the hill, with several buildings in the town, including the harbor,' the clerk said. 'The whole estate is valued at fifteen thousand pieces of gold. The mansion comes fully furnished and staffed, but I have no information about the other property. I can make you a list.'

'Consider it sold,' Shaw said. 'Inform the servants they can stay on. I will provide the gold as soon as her majesty's finances are settled.'

CHAPTER 11 — THE BARONS FACTION

Shaw noticed Agusta's thoughts weren't on money matters. The girl plucked at her filthy suit with something like disgust on her face.

'I won't walk around in this any longer. I want to see the Barons' soldiers, but not looking like the Frog Princess from those old fairytales. I must have a chamberlain, I suppose?'

The clerk smiled. 'I'm afraid you just dismissed him, Your Majesty. But I will call one of the bedroom servants.' He stooped to pick up the ring and the great seal Rutus had dropped when he pulled his dagger and offered them to Agusta.

She stared at the slender stamp. 'For the moment I will leave both with you,' she said to the clerk. 'As soon as I've appointed a new chancellor, you can hand it over, but until then I suppose you need it.'

The clerk bowed. 'I will not betray your trust, Ma'am.'

The high queen gave a grim smile. 'Wise; I'm not in the mood for more traitors.'

A servant appeared in the door and waited unobtrusively. Shaw saw her and opened her mouth, but Jonna was faster.

'Her Majesty needs a change of clothes,' she said with a smile.

Agusta turned around. 'What? Oh, yes; show me to my father's rooms.'

The woman bowed and led them past the throne room to a large apartment with a big double bed and windows with the heavy drapes drawn.

'Not bad,' Agusta muttered. She pulled aside the curtains. Light streamed into the room and the high queen stared at the wide expanse of sea outside. 'Why shut the world out? Leave them open by day,' she said to the servant. 'I don't want to hide.'

'Yes, Your Majesty,' the woman said.

Agusta went to a tall closet. 'Lessee what we got.' She took out a blue brocade jacket and held it against her chest. 'Gods! Had he grown that stout?' she said, aghast at the expanse of cloth.

Without a word, the servant opened a door to a connecting room. 'Beyond is your mother's apartment, Ma'am,' she said. 'Her clothes are still there.'

'I want a uniform,' Agusta said. 'A uniform that is neither Court nor Barons. Is there such a thing?'

'Uniforms have trousers,' the woman said.

Agusta guffawed. 'So they do. Look at High Merchant Shaw. Rich, powerful, and she wears trousers. I don't want a skirt, I want a uniform.'

The servant folded her hands in acquiescence. 'Yes, Your Majesty.' She walked to a large trunk. Inside, neatly packed, were suits in many colors, all smelling vaguely musty, but more of a normal size.

'These are all from your late father's earlier years, Your Majesty,' the woman said softly. 'I will have them aired for your inspection.'

'There's no time; I need one now,' Agusta said. 'It will air while I wear it.' She stared down at the chest. 'Are there uniforms among all those?'

'His late majesty had one made. It might fit you as well, Ma'am.' The servant laid out a long red coat with two rows of gold buttons, matching epaulets, and crowns on the lapels and cuffs. With it came black pants with gold stripes down the outside legs. 'If you would try these on?'

Agusta sighed. 'You sound as if you disapprove,' she said.

'It's not my position to disapprove of Your Majesty's wishes,' the servant said primly. 'I remember your late mother was a very well-dressed woman.'

'I never knew her, or my father either,' Agusta said. 'I only know I am the high queen and I rule here; not the nobles or anyone else. I have the same duties as any of my predecessors, and if they could wear a uniform, so can I.'

The woman bowed. 'Then I will assist you to the best of my ability.'

'I prefer to dress myself,' the high queen said. She shrugged out of her soiled clothes. 'I would have loved a bath, but there is no time.' She did up all the buttons on her fly and picked up the double-breasted jacket. 'My,' she said, as she fingered the gold crowns on the lapels. Then she put it on and went to the mirror.

The servant came with a black sword belt. 'Allow me,' she said, and with deft fingers buckled it round Agusta's waist. 'Your late father always wore this.' She took a saber from a hook on the wall. 'It shouldn't be too long; he wasn't that much taller than you, Ma'am.' Then she went to a side table and picked up a heavy gold ring. 'It's your father's small seal. Should you want to send a letter or something.'

Agusta shoved it on her finger. 'It fits,' she said surprised.

'His majesty hadn't been able to remove it for years,' the servant said grimly. 'They had to cut off his finger to get the ring back.'

The high queen looked at the seal ring and swallowed. 'Ah. I see.'

The woman took a box from the top of the closet and handed Agusta a flat cap with a wyrmling's nest of braid on the visor.

The high queen walked to the tall mirror in the corner.

'Hmm... Yes, that's more like it.' She turned to Jonna. 'You pick something to your taste. You're not that much smaller 'n me.'

Jonna sighed. 'I'm not that fond of your father's choice of clothes,' she said. 'But if you want to wear trousers, I won't go in a skirt either. I'll take this.' She held up a black, high-necked jacket and pants.

'Dull,' Agusta said critically.

Jonna smiled. 'But of course. You don't want me to outshine Your Majesty,' she said slyly.

As Agusta's cheeks turned red, Jonna patted her shoulder. 'You look fine!'

The high queen grunted.

Shaw hid a smile. *Both girls look splendid. I'll take them on a round of the Continent. Malgarth has been isolated long enough. Let Basil, Maud and the others meet her; they need to put an end to those silly old quarrels. It will strengthen Agusta's position when she meets her nobles.* 'If you're both ready?'

Agusta cast a last glance at the mirror. 'Thank you,' she said to the servant. 'What do I have for my coronation?'

'The crown, the robe and the sword of state,' the servant said. 'They were the charge of the former high steward, but I suppose the attendants will know how to prepare matters as well. Does Your Majesty want me to see to it?'

'If you please. A week from today I'll need all that stuff, and someone to tell me what to do.'

'You need a priest to officiate.' The woman gave a barely perceptible sniff. 'I'm afraid your late father chased the last one away.'

Shaw grinned. 'We have a priest,' she said. 'Lieutenant Uzhan is the high priest of Bodrus. I'm sure he will be honored to assist you.'

'Ask him,' Agusta said. 'Then all is settled.'

'Your cloak, Ma'am,' the servant said, and handed the girl a heavy black riding-cape. 'I believe we have a second one for Lady Jonna as well.'

'Let's go get Gerben,' the high queen said. 'I don't want him moping.'

Once they were in the air, Agusta relaxed. 'Is it so strange I want a uniform? What do the other rulers wear?'

'Proprietor Darquine uses a merchant's uniform,' Shaw said. 'Queen Maud was born in the army; she wears old-fashioned leather armor. As a warlock, Lord Basil wears suits. Further north the Hizmyran king is worse. His people adore uniforms; he looks like a display for an accoutrements maker. Look, I was thinking to take you and Jonna on a round of the countries we do business with; a sort of unofficial state visit to meet the other rulers.'

'You know them?' Agusta said.

'Yes,' Shaw said. 'Much of my work is on government level.'

'I would like that,' Agusta said. 'I feel there's so much we don't know.'

'All right. As you have to be back next week, I suggest we'll leave this afternoon.'

Agusta nodded slowly. 'I can't do much before I've met the nobles,' she said. 'I'd rather be out and away than biting my nails for next week.'

'There's the Barons camp,' Haai-Bo said. *'Healer Tymon is below.'*

Shaw saw an army camp with large striped marquees, and smaller tents for the men, all in a large field bordering on a stream close by the bay.

They landed and stared around at the chaos.

'It looks trampled,' Nate said. 'As if someone ran a herd of cattle over it.'

Shaw saw Tymon's pudgy figure among a group of armored people, and she hurried over.

'There you are,' the young healer said. 'By Lumentis, Shaw, you know how to hand me the dramas, don't you? This camp is a mess.'

'I believe you,' Shaw said. 'I saw their leaders before Suzie got her hands on them, and they looked awful.'

'So do these,' Tymon said. 'The officer gents are more or less serviceable again. My guys are working on the soldiers now. The jinni?'

'We killed the beast,' Shaw said. 'It was a big one; not a prince, but definitely a higher-up. Still, we know their weaknesses by now, and it's gone.' She looked around at the milling soldiers. 'I fear there are several small groups of soldiers like these wandering around,' she said.

'I'll leave two of my healers here,' Tymon said. 'I was training them for our various posts, but I can hire more.'

'In that case I would like them stationed in our new headquarters in Landfalln,' Shaw said.

'Landfalln. Strange; I never thought I'd ever set foot in Malgarth,' Tymon said. 'It always had an aura of forbidden lands, you know.'

'I know,' Agusta said. 'But no longer. I will change all that, lord healer.'

Tymon looked at her without expression. He wasn't one to suffer clever-mouthed strangers patiently.

'This is the High Queen Agusta,' Shaw said. 'Her father died recently, and she's just ascended the throne.'

'Then well met, Ma'am,' Tymon said, his face softening slightly. 'These men have been lucky their enslavement didn't last too long. They're shocked, but all will recover.'

'I'm very grateful for your help,' Agusta said.

Someone shouted and Tymon waved back. 'Pray excuse me, Ma'am.' With a wink for Shaw he hurried away.

'He is good?' Agusta said. 'Most of our healers are so-so, but he sounds very sure of himself.'

'Tymon is the wyrmcaller's chief healer,' Shaw said. 'He's one of the best in the world, and that's no boast.'

'I'm glad,' Agusta said. 'My people need the best help available.' She turned to the huddling nobles. 'Rest easy, my lords,' he said. 'I do not blame you for what happened.'

'Your Majesty?' a cadaverous young man said. 'You're here? Did we win, this time? But Morthan...' He shook his head. 'No, no, no... Morthan is gone. He...'

'I know,' Agusta said. 'We killed the jinni, Jonna and I — with the High Merchant's people. Rutus Wrache is dead. No party won; I'm the high queen and I rule. There will be no more faction battles.' She looked at the gaunt lord and the others behind him. 'Do I have your loyalty, my lords?'

The young noble went down on his knees, and the others followed as one man. 'Unto death, Ma'am!' he said. 'No more horror; I am your man. Not Court, nor Barons, I'm a noble of the high queen.'

'I embrace your service gladly, my lords,' Agusta said gravely. 'I have summoned all nobles and their families to Croncliff, to honor my late father's memory and celebrate my ascension. My lord Ungreff is on his way here. He will inform you of all that has passed at the palace. I must leave you now, but know I ask the gods for your speedy recovery. I will now go to Morthan to tell them the sad news.'

'Go with the gods' speed, Ma'am,' the gaunt lord said. 'It will be a blow to his wife and son.'

'I'm afraid it will,' the high queen said somberly.

They took their leave of the lords, waved at Tymon, and went up in the sky.

'How am I doing?' Agusta said suddenly. 'I'm feeling so funny all the time, commanding left and right. Luckily there's Jonna. She is my sister in all but blood. I want to make her chancellor; she's a lot cleverer than me.'

'She's a bit young for the job,' Shaw said.

'I want my court to be young,' Agusta said. 'All those old men held us back, isolated us. Now let the young people do it for a chance.'

'I think you're doing fine,' Shaw said.

'Jonna's dad taught me a lot. He never said so, but I think he wasn't happy with my father's rule. Perhaps...' She frowned as she looked at Shaw over her shoulder. 'He always told me to stand up for myself, and how a ruler should behave. Even if she's a girl.'

Then Agusta sat upright. 'Look!' She pointed to the ground, where a group of soldiers with drawn blades had surrounded a second group. 'Trouble; we must go down.'

Shaw turned to the others. She saw Jonna arguing with Nate and gestured to land. Nate nodded. They turned and came down in the road, several yards away from the men.

Agusta was running even before they had fully stopped.

'Put up your swords!' she yelled. 'No more fighting!'

'Who're you?' a blue-clad officer said. Then he took in the girl's uniform and came to attention.

'I'm Agusta,' the high queen snapped. 'The fighting is over.'

The officer saluted. 'Honor to Her Majesty!' he shouted. 'It's done then? Did we win?'

'I won,' Agusta said. 'You may return to your lord. Tell him I want all Malgarth's nobles and their families in Croncliff in a week's time. The summons will reach him yet. Leave these men to me; they are ill and need help.'

'Yes, Your Majesty,' the officer said. 'But those broomriders? They're not the Weal, are they?'

'They are the wyrmcaller's people,' Agusta said. 'Allies of Malgarth.'

'These are strange times.' The officer saluted again and boarded his steamcart.

Meanwhile Healer Suzie had seen to the Barons soldiers.

'I can give them only a little relief each,' she said.

'They're Morthan's men,' Agusta said. 'Can we take them along?'

'Sure,' Shaw said. 'Leave it to Captain Kennan.'

Agusta smiled at Kennan. 'Thank you.' Then she went over to the soldiers. 'You,' she said to a burly young man with a lieutenant's insignia. 'You're one of Baron Morthan's officers?'

'Yes,' the young knight said with difficulty. 'What... what happened? Why are we here?'

'You have been enthralled by a jinni,' Shaw said, and she quickly explained the situation.

'We are on our way to Morthan,' Agusta said. 'We will take you with us; you're in no condition to walk right now.'

'Those men are... Kells,' the knight said. 'How come they're here?'

'Allies of the crown,' Agusta said. 'Captain Kennan, take up those brave soldiers, if you please.'

It took a while, but finally all were back in the air.

Another twenty miles on they saw a large walled estate, with farms and orchards, and a great many barracks.

They landed outside the gates.

'On your feet, men of Morthan,' Agusta commanded. 'Lieutenant, take us to your lord.'

Wobbly, the men made their way to the gates.

'Open...' the knight said to the gate watch. 'Open and t-tell my lady the high queen is here.'

One of the watchmen ran to the house, to return moments later with a tall woman in a stern dress and a boy of about sixteen.

'Dear gods!' the woman said. 'What happened?'

'They are sick,' the high queen said. 'You will be Lady Morthan? I'm Agusta. I bring you bad news, my lady.'

'Your Majesty,' the lady said, curtsying. 'Liom, make your bow.'

The boy was watching the soldiers with a puzzled face and balled fists. At his mother's voice he started and turned. 'The high queen? And Gerben of Wrache to ruin my day,' he said.

Then he bowed. 'Your servant, Ma'am.' He shook his head. 'What happened to these men?'

'We will tell all, Lord Morthan,' the high queen said. 'But better not here.'

At her use of the title, boy and lady gasped.

'My husband?' she said, staggering.

'I am afraid he is dead,' Shaw said. 'Let us go inside and speak in private.'

'Did your dogs kill him?' the son snarled, waving his fists in Gerben's face. 'I will get you for this! I swear you'll...'

'No man killed him,' Shaw said. 'Wait with your oaths until you heard what we came to tell you.'

The boy clenched his teeth; his face deep red with rage.

'We'll need you to calm down,' Jonna said. 'There's a great deal of work waiting for you and anger won't help.' She touched the boy's shoulder. 'We're all very sorry about your father's death. You're Liom? I'm Jonna, Lord Lammark's daughter.'

Shaw gripped Lady Morthan's ice-cold hand. 'Let us go inside.'

'Lead the way, my lord,' the high queen said.

Past shocked servants and soldiers they entered the house and followed Liom and his mother to a high, sunny parlor room.

Once inside, the lady recovered her poise. 'Please be seated,' she said. 'Then tell me.'

Shaw sat down, and so did Agusta. Nate and Kennan had stayed behind, probably to help the soldiers. Liom stood looking at the flames in the hearth, hands clenched to his back and legs apart.

Shaw began by introducing herself and, skipping over the Tradeports for now, went on with meeting Jonna and their search for the high queen. She described going to Landfalln and meeting Lord Rutus. 'So we went to Croncliff,' she went on. 'We expected to find ten men from the Barons faction, and a knight. Instead, it was Lord Morthan who greeted us. Or so we thought. He commanded us to hand over the high queen to him. Her Majesty refused, and Lord Morthan showed his true shape of a high-level jinni.'

The lady gave a high cry, and Liom wheeled around. 'A jinni!'

'We have seen it before,' Shaw said. 'Jinn are shapechangers. They murder a person and take their place. We don't know when it had happened, but as none of you people here seem affected, it probably was after the troops left Morthan.

'Once the jinni had taken on Morthan's countenance, he poisoned the water and the wine of his troops, and turned them into his will-less slaves. Then he sent them out to capture the high queen, and murder as many Court soldiers as they could. The moment we killed the jinni, the spell broke, and the Barons faction became as the men we brought back to you.'

'Where are they?' the boy said. 'Where are our soldiers?'

'A few are still wandering the lands,' Shaw said. 'Her majesty has sent out search parties. The others are with the Barons forces camped near Croncliff. Our healers are attending to them and they will all recover.'

'I must go to them,' the boy said. 'Mother?'

Lady Morthan sat up straight. 'You go and do your duty. I will take care of matters here. There is no body?'

'No,' Shaw said. 'There never is.'

The lady shuddered. 'I want to know, but later.'

'I will go north,' the boy said. He made a curt bow to the high queen and strode to the door.

'Were you going to walk, or something?' Agusta said. 'Do you think we're not about to help you? Don't be silly, idiot. We'll fly you north. After that, we'll discuss what's next. One thing; in a week's time I meet all the nobles and their families at Croncliff. I will excuse my lady, but I want you there.'

'I can't,' Liom said.

'You must.' Agusta walked over and gripped the boy's shoulders. 'I'll say to you what I said to Gerben. We have to show the kingdom all is well between us. That there's no blame attached to your name, Lord Morthan.'

'Her Majesty is right, and it's a noble gesture,' Lady Morthan said. 'I, too, will be there, Ma'am. House Morthan will not be amiss in their duty.'

'You will be all right here?' Shaw asked the lady.

She nodded. 'Don't worry about me. I have my work, and the estate; once the shock has passed, I will settle down quite happily.' She watched her son walk out with Agusta and Jonna.

'My husband was an impetuous man, quick to anger. His son has more self-restraint, and he lacks the hardness of his father. My husband was... difficult.' She looked at Shaw. 'He had a great appetite for love and enough pride not to indulge himself here. We both lived our own lives. Nevertheless, his habits and our troops cost us more than we can afford. Five hundred soldiers we muster because my lord was the leader of the Barons.'

Shaw thought the lady didn't sound very enthusiastic about their army.

Lady Morthan gave a small sigh. 'This unexpected fight for the throne meant a lot to my husband. Given Her Majesty's young age, it might well have been his last chance to rule, and he went into the fight with iron determination. So much, both Liom and I were afraid he'd go too far and ruin our name. Instead a cursed jinni... I don't want to think too much about it. Go; attend to whatever brings you here. I'll be fine.'

Shaw nodded and let her alone.

Outside, she found the others waiting.

'What kept...?' Liom bit his lip. 'Your pardon, ma'am; I should mind my manners.'

'It's all right,' Shaw said. 'You're taking it well.' She looked at Nate. 'We'll go back to the Barons' camp. Agusta, you ride with the captain, Liom goes with me. Ready?'

Liom took a deep breath as they shot away. 'That's a useful trick,' he said. 'I...' His voice faltered.

'Hey,' Shaw said. 'If you've got any crying to do, do it now. I don't mind; I've gone through the same thing.'

'I can't believe it,' the boy said. 'He was so strong. To be murdered by a jinni... Why?'

'The jinn want to be boss,' Shaw said. 'They're playing these tricks in other lands as well.' She told him of the jinn she had fought and of the wyrmcaller's battles in the north.

'Lord Eskandar is under oath to kill them all,' she said. 'Every jinni in the world. In the north are the beasts' homelands, so he is there, while we are guarding his back in the south. We just captured the Tradeports, killed the pirates and had the common folks join us.'

'You did?' he said, his face wet with tears.

'Pirates are the jinn's bullyboys,' Shaw said. 'They are drugged as much as your men were, but far longer. Too long; their minds are gone. Your men were lucky we came in time to save them.'

'How come you do all this?' Liom said. 'You're not any older than me.'

'I'll be sixteen soon,' Shaw said. *Sixteen!* 'The wyrmcaller is only seventeen himself. I don't know how; it's because of a prophecy. We all of us are kids; several hundred by now. We're following the wyrmcaller and some big plan Divine Bodrus, the Sleeping God of the Mountains, has made for us.'

She shrugged. 'I don't want to know the details. I'm doing what I like to do; running a trade empire. You know something? I'm going to do a round of our holdings in the world, to show Agusta and Jonna how people live there, and to meet the other rulers. I'm taking Gerben, and I think you should come, too, when you've seen to your men. What they need most is rest; our healers will see to their care.'

'Me? Go abroad?' the boy said. 'Go with the high queen?'

'Yes. Agusta has decided to do away with the factions battling for power. She rules the lands and will appoint ministers to do her will. If you aspire to a position at court, now is the time.'

'Yes, but our men...'

'They must cost you a lot of money.'

'Nearly fifteen hundred a year,' Liom said. 'For five hundred men.'

'I believe the high queen wants all Malgarth's troops serving the crown rather than a handful of barons.'

'It would make things easier at home,' the boy said. 'But what could I do at court?'

'The high queen has sacked all courtiers,' Shaw said. 'Lord Rutus proved a traitor; he had been swindling the late high king.'

'Old Rutus?' the boy said. 'Of course we all knew he was crooked, but we had no proof.'

'His clerk had.'

'Darn,' Liom said. 'My father would've liked to know that.' He wiped his nose on his hand. 'What's going to happen to Rutus?'

'He attacked Her Majesty with a dagger,' Shaw said. 'Both my commander and Lady Jonna stopped him fatally.'

'Rutus a traitor!' Liom said. 'That must hurt poor Gerben. He's such a square guy, so proud of his father and always gabbing how well the high king liked him. All those gifts and things...' He stared at Shaw. 'They weren't gifts?'

'Nope. Rutus used the royal seal and his authority as the chancellor. The high king never knew a thing about it.'

'Darn, what a mess.' Liom sighed and let his silent tears flow.

'We're at the camp,' Shaw said. Before her, Liom straightened. His face became expressionless, a lord's face, without a hint of emotion.

Shaw landed near the banner of Morthan. The boy sprang lightly to the ground, and without a word strode over to the command tent, where the officers sat staring at the ground.

As he entered, they all jumped to their feet.

'Lord Liom!' an older man said. 'What are you doing here?'

'I am baron of Morthan now,' the boy said harshly. 'I want to see my men are well, Captain.'

'As well as can be, thanks to Healer Tymon and his colleagues,' the captain said.

'They will need another day or two of rest.' A young woman in a light-blue robe stepped from the shadows. 'It will take time for their minds to be fully their own again. Healer Tymon taught us it is better for the men's sanity to let their own minds dispel the last of the curse. Even so, they will not fight any battle soon.'

'They won't need to,' the boy said. 'Not unless the high queen commands it.'

'The high queen won't command any fight,' Agusta said as she came in. 'I want peace and prosperity, not war.'

Liom bowed his head. 'I will follow you into battle, and even more eagerly into peace, Ma'am.' For a moment, both youngsters looked at each other searchingly.

'Then we are of the same mind, my lord of Morthan,' Agusta said. 'That is good.'

'Captain,' Liom said carefully. 'How many men are missing?'

'Twenty-four, my lord. We don't know how many of those have fallen in battle.'

'The high merchant brought back one knight's squad she found on her way to Morthan. That would mean eighteen unaccounted for.' Liom balled his fists. 'As soon as the men are able to, send out squads to search for them, both the dead and the living. We must know. Muster the troops, Captain. I want to address them.' He turned to Agusta. 'Will you join me, Ma'am?'

'Of course,' Agusta said.

'Captain, warn the men Her Majesty will be inspecting them.'

The officer saluted and snapped an order. Several young knights hurried away.

'How many men did you bring afield?' Agusta asked.

'Five hundred,' Liom said.

'And the other barons?'

Liom looked at the captain. 'You will know the numbers better than me.'

'The total force was twelve hundred strong, Your Majesty. The remaining seven hundred come from ten different lords.'

'I don't want any private armies, Morthan,' the high queen said. 'Not from either faction. I want a national army, serving the crown.' She turned to the captain as she had asked the lords before. 'Are your men loyal to the high queen, Captain?'

The officer stiffened. 'We are loyal to Your Majesty,' he said stiffly. 'Yet Morthan is our lord.'

'Are you men of Morthan?' Jonna asked curiously.

'Some, but not all of us, my lady,' the captain said. 'We all swore allegiance to the late lord, though, and of course my lord pays our wages.'

'I understand,' Agusta said. 'Thank you, Captain.'

A knight came in. 'The whole army is lined up, sir. The other lords are with their men.'

'Thank you,' Liom said impatiently. 'Let's go.'

Agusta chuckled. 'By all means, my lord.'

'Your pardon,' Liom said. 'I'm not used to this.'

'Neither am I,' Agusta said, and she put a hand on the young lord's shoulder. With the other hand she gripped Jonna's arm. 'Let's go together.' Side by side the three stepped from the tent, followed by the captain and his knights.

Shaw had watched everything with a great deal of approval. Both the high queen and the young lord were handling the situation excellently. She looked at Nate and Kennan. 'We'll wait; it's their show.'

'I wonder if the lords will freely do away with their little armies,' Nate said. 'And how will Agusta pay for her forces?'

'We'll do the same as we did in Hizmyr,' Shaw said. 'We'll offer her a concession for an airship monopoly. In Hizmyran crowns.' She thought for a moment. 'I've no idea how things are financed here. They will collect taxes, I hope.'

'All is well.' Haai-Bo materialized inside the tent. 'I sense a feeling of relief. No more fighting, no silly king and no bullying baron; the men are glad to see Agusta and young Morthan being friends.' He was quiet for a moment. Then he cackled. 'She's told the soldiers she needs their service! Just like that, she told them they are now soldiers of the crown. She enlisted them, officers and all!'

'And the lords didn't protest?' Nate said.

Haai-Bo crowed. 'No! Unwittingly the queen uses the yet undissolved remnants of the jinn spell to hammer her commands into their tiny brains. They wave their swords and cheer her.'

'Good,' Shaw said. 'Let's hope they won't feel tricked when their minds clear.'

CHAPTER 12 — AGUSTA'S GRAND TOUR

After the muster, Shaw took the four back to Croncliff and the throne room.

Agusta summoned the colonel of the Guards, who by now was looking somewhat harassed.

'I'll be away for a week,' the high queen said. 'I want the court to prepare for my coronation, but no one is to go in or out but our own servants. No nobles, no merchants, nobody. Take care of that if you value your commission.'

The colonel saluted grimly. 'It will be done, Ma'am.'

From Croncliff they flew across the bay to Dibloon. To Shaw's mind it looked much like Brisa from the air, though smaller and less worn.

Kennan took the lead, and landed in front of a small, two-story warehouse.

'Welcome to Dibloon,' he said. 'This is our local headquarters.'

'The Tradeports?' Agusta said. 'I never imagined they were such big towns.'

'Yes,' Jonna said. 'My dad told us the Tradeporters huddled together in their villages, while we of the second wave spread out from Landfalln and conquered the whole land.' She grinned. 'But this isn't exactly a village; it's as big as Landfalln.'

Shaw exchanged glances with Nate and smiled. 'There won't be much to see here, I suppose?' She looked at Kennan, who shook his head.

'It's a dull place.'

'Then we'll go on to Brisa.' She led them inside. 'Where is that transferal?'

'At the back,' Kennan said.

The warehouse wasn't very large, and most of the racks were still empty.

'I'll be visiting this place later,' Shaw said. 'Now we're going to teleport.' She looked at the youngsters. 'You don't have these in Malgarth yet. It's a magic invention for fast travel, and for the first time it can be scary. We go through a place without air, light and warmth. It will be a second, no more, but you must remember to take a breath first. Hold on to each other and to me.' She grinned at the four anxious faces. 'Ready?' Then they ported.

'Gods!' Agusta said when they came out in the Brisan portal. 'That was... awful.'

'Where was that place?' Jonna said. 'It was creepy.'

'That was the Intermedium,' Shaw said. 'Another universe. People can't live there; but we use it to make a shortcut from one place to another.'

'This is Brisa?' Agusta said, dismissing the multiverse. 'The place you shot up?'

'The same place,' Shaw said. 'Come outside for a moment; I'll show you the ravage.' She waved at Portal Mage Tomas. 'We'll be right back.'

Outside, all was still the same, only the dead pirates were gone.

'That's it,' Shaw said. 'Our ship, the brig *Marigold*, lay out of sight, about a mile away. There, at that ruined pier, lay the *Drakon*, a very powerful ship. The ruins right here were the slave market, beyond that the tavern. That heap of stones over there was the powder magazine. Those two smaller ruins were casemates, each with a gun inside.'

'And you shot up all of that?' Agusta said eagerly.

'First, we visited the slave market. There was one girl for sale, and then the slave master proved to be a jinni. A big, burning beast from some faraway desert. In moments, the whole building was ablaze. Then the wyrmcaller ported with the jinni into the sea. Neither could swim, but the wyrmcaller could port himself back. Then we freed the girl slave. She

156

proved to be an officer of the *Drakon*, and together we attacked the ship. We freed her crew, she was a school ship, and her sailors were about as old as any of us. Then we shot up the whole works and sailed out in triumph. It was a fun night.'

'I believe you,' Jonna said. 'It's as good as those adventure books at home.'

'You do a lot of magic?' Liom said.

'Yes,' Shaw said. 'Nate and I haven't got an ounce of it, but magic is very common in the lands.'

'We don't approve of it,' Liom said. 'It's not the Garthan way.'

'Perhaps not, but it is very much our way.'

Liom shrugged. 'I can bear it.'

'Wait,' Shaw said. She suddenly remembered something. 'Lieutenant Uzhan around?' she asked of a passing soldier.

'He was changing the guard, ma'am,' the boy said. 'You need him?'

'Yes, urgently.'

'I'll go get him.' The boy ran off, clutching his saber.

'Are all your soldiers like him?' Liom said.

'In age, yes. He's of Captain Abbram's battalion, soldiers from Hizmyr.'

'He looks capable.'

'They're very tough. They were trained as a suicide command. I changed that; we don't fight that way. But those guys aren't afraid of anything.'

'They're good soldiers,' Kennan said. 'The only non-Kells who are as good as Kells.' He smiled politely and Liom knew the Kell reputation well enough not to mention his own men.

Uzhan came hurrying, in that easy gait of the trained runner.

'Ma'am,' he said, saluting, his once empty face now shining with holy joy.

'Lieutenant,' Shaw said. 'I've gone and done something that may appall you.'

'That must have been a particularly gruesome murder, then,' he said. 'I don't appall easily.'

'Not like that at all,' Shaw said. 'I promised you will do the coronation ceremonial for Her Majesty the high queen of Malgarth, next week. You, being the high priest of Bodrus, would be the very best person for the task.'

Uzhan's face lighted up and he positively glowed. 'It would be an honor!' he said. 'Next week? That is a short time. I have no robes and no idea about the way those people do things. This queen? Who is she?'

'If you can keep a secret, she is right here,' Shaw said.

Agusta studied the lieutenant and smiled. 'This is perfect. You're not some stodgy priest or haughty prelate at all. Why don't you go to Croncliff, speak with the servants and see what you can do? There must be oodles of robes hanging around the place.'

'If Captain Abbram won't mind, I will,' Uzhan said. 'The Breath of the Mountains will bless your reign from the start, Your Majesty.'

'Make it convincing; all the kingdom's nobles will be watching,' Agusta said. 'Wait, I must write a note, or the guard won't let you in. Somebody got paper and sealing-wax?'

Jonna sniffed. 'Of course. I carry my notebook, and I filched the wax from the chancellor's desk. If I am not prepared, who else is?'

Quickly, Agusta wrote a few lines. Then she looked around. 'Something to melt the wax.'

Uzhan produced a flame in the palm of his hand.

'Thank you,' Agusta said. 'Doesn't that hurt?'

'No, Ma'am,' the lieutenant said. 'Not my own spell.'

With the sealed note in his pocket, Uzhan hurried away.

Both Liom and Gerben stared after him.

'I'm impressed,' Liom said. 'He looks absolutely deadly, but there's such a feeling of jollity to him.'

'That's Divine Bodrus' doing,' Shaw said. 'Uzhan was a dangerous kid; dead-eyed, full of magic he wasn't allowed to use, and terribly bitter. He didn't care about life or anything but his mates. Until Bodrus came along and chose him as his own priest. That saved his life, I think.' She sighed. 'Let's go to New Winsproke.'

'The warlock town?' Agusta said, and she swallowed. 'Malgarth parents threaten their children the warlocks will get them if they don't behave. It must be a dark and dismal place.'

'Those ports are still awful,' Agusta said, shivering, as they arrived in New Winsproke.

'Complaints to the management, gal,' Portaller Anna said. She sat in a chair, with the backrest tilted against the wall and her feet upon a second chair, with a heavy tome in her lap.

'I'm not complaining, I am stating a fact,' Agusta said.

Anna cast a lazy eye at the two lords. 'Welcome, guys,' she said. 'I like a presentable young fellow as much as the next girl.'

'As long as you know they're mine,' Agusta said coolly. 'I'm not the sharing type, *gal*.'

'Boils on your nose,' Anna said darkly. 'I'm a mage.'

'Enough,' Shaw said. 'Behave towards important guests of the company.'

'They're not our kids then?' The young portaller blushed slightly. 'I'm sorry, I'm sure.'

'They're not; we are going to Old Wharf. In a minute; I want to show them the view first,' Shaw said.

She waved at Mage Leah and greeted the workers as they went outside.

'Is that...' Jonna fell silent and stared goggle-eyed at the tower across the square.

'The warlock tower,' Shaw said.

'Big,' Agusta said faintly. 'It's darned big, isn't it?'

Liom gave a harsh laugh. 'Warlocks are the masters, so all things theirs are big and powerful.'

'No longer,' Shaw said. 'Before the war, maybe, but warlocks are no longer what they were.'

'Why not?' Gerben said. 'I know you people had a war, but that's about all.'

'I'll tell you when we have time,' Shaw said. 'Not now; we'll be going to Seatome, on the Continent. That's where Nate and I were born, and where we opened our first warehouse. We're having an important meeting there tomorrow, and I want you four to attend.'

'A meeting about Malgarth?' Agusta said, warily.

'Yes. It's all business; you'll profit from it. Come, one more port.'

They walked back to Anna and the portal.

'Old Wharf, please.'

'A busy place, this,' Jonna said, as they stepped from the portal. The Seatome warehouse wasn't as large as the Emporium, and every foot was used. Cheerful workers hurried to and fro, preparing orders.

'This is the main warehouse for Vanhaar,' Shaw said. 'Mage Kier is the portaller. He can take you to a million places.'

'Not a million,' Kier said, looking up from his book. 'Seven hundred eighty-five thousand and twelve.'

As she saw the youngsters' faces, Shaw laughed. 'He's got an eidetic memory. That means he never forgets anything ever and ever. He knows all of those locations and he's probably visited each of them at least once.'

'Yes,' Kier said as he drew a hand through his hair. 'And I remember the lot of them. Luckily I've learned to blanket it all out, or I'd be a raving lunatic.'

'It sounds awful,' Jonna said.

Kier shrugged. 'I don't know any better.' He grinned. 'And I couldn't do this job without it.' He looked at Shaw. 'Good to see you and Nate. You want Ruth? She's still upstairs.'

'Still? What time is it here?' Shaw said.

'Almost nine in the evening.'

'Drat, I always forget the time differences. Let's go up then.'

'You go on,' Nate said. 'I'll arrange for some grub. Kennan, your guys can put up their feet for the next two days.'

'You're great,' Shaw said and she gave him a long kiss. 'There, I missed that.'

'Oh,' Agusta said, looking at both of them. 'It's like that? I didn't know.'

'We're very discrete when we're on business,' Nate said. 'Don't scandalize the customers, and all that.'

'Don't mind me,' Jonna said. 'I promise I won't look.'

'Come,' Shaw said, unexpectedly embarrassed. 'I want you to meet Ruth.' She hurried past the cantina and burst into the office.

'Hi,' Ruth said, as she put down a many-paged file. 'You bring us new recruits?'

'Oh no, this is a visit of state,' Shaw said. 'Lady Ruth of Spellstor, Warden of Winsproke, meet Her Majesty Agusta, High Queen of Malgarth.'

Ruth stood up, looking from Shaw to the girl. Then she bowed. 'An honor to meet Your Majesty,' she said. 'You came to the throne recently?'

'Yesterday,' Agusta said. 'My father passed away; his heart, you see.'

'We'll tell you,' Shaw said. 'The others are Lady Jonna of Lammark, who is the high queen's chief advisor, with Baron Morthan and Lord Wrache. Lady Ruth is the Lord Spellstor's daughter. We're doing a round of the known world, and I want the high queen to meet the other rulers. I'm sure your father, Queen Maud and Darquine are eager to meet her as well. The high singer... I'd rather not see him if it can be helped.'

'After that business with Singer Wador at Smalkand he's gone into hiding,' Ruth said. 'So you can forget him. I'm positive the Family is all agog to meet Her Majesty.'

'In a week's time we need to be back in Croncliff, so I want to make it quick. Perhaps tomorrow, after our meeting? I prefer to go to Spellstor and Brannoe. It's just to say hi, the court will send diplomats as soon as matters are settled.'

'Sure. Lunch at Spellstor, the next morning cawah at Brannoe, with dinner at Towne. Will that do?'

'Perfectly,' Shaw said.

Then Nate came in, followed by Cook with a large platter of eats, which he unceremoniously plunked down on Ruth's desk. 'There y'are, mates. Fill up. If you need more, just holler.'

'Strange,' Liom said. 'I shouldn't feel hungry, but I do.'

'Then eat,' Shaw said. 'I will tell Ruth the story.'

And she did, this time in detail, while Ruth sat still, her fingers intertwined on the desktop as she listened.

'Well,' she said when Shaw was done. 'That's quite something.' She stared at the wall as she let it all sink in. 'We should have expected the jinn would target Malgarth,' she said. 'With the Tradeports in their possession, it was the logical next step. Only what could we have done? The high king... the late high king I mean, wouldn't have listened.'

'Probably not,' Agusta said around a chicken bone. Then she put it down and licked her fingers. 'And even if he had, his courtiers would've pooh-poohed it. I won't miss those guys.'

'You sent them all packing? Who's running the court?' Ruth said.

'The servants, for the moment,' Agusta said. 'They do most of the running anyhow.'

'Will the jinni who...' Liom coughed. 'Would the jinni have been the only one?' His face was red, but composed.

'Probably,' Nate said calmly. 'Every jinn project we found had only one beast in charge. A few times we encountered a mage of sorts, but never two of them. I think there aren't all that many jinn and most are centered up north.'

'That's a... relief,' Liom said.

Shaw glanced at him, wondering if he secretly had wanted to go and kill a jinni himself, as a form of revenge.

'Indeed it is; jinn are far more dangerous than people think,' she said. 'Their strength is immense, their cruelty unpredictable and they won't stop fighting.'

Agusta nodded and kept on nodding.

'Bedtime,' Nate said. 'Do we have some free guestrooms?'

'We have no staterooms for visiting royalty,' Ruth said. 'There are two double bedrooms free in the left house.'

'I'll show them,' Nate said.

'Thanks,' Shaw said. 'I'll be in the cafeteria, spending some hours in my own world.'

CHAPTER 13 — LUNCHEON AT SPELLSTOR

'Good morning,' Shaw said, looking round the circle of faces. They sat in Old Wharf's meeting room; Shaw at the head of the long table, with Nate on one hand and Agusta, Jonna, Gerben and Liom on the other. Ruth sat on the opposite side, with her notebook, and the others were crammed in between them.

'You have another surprise for us?' Mr. Morgan said. 'I don't know how you keep doing it.'

'Of course I have a surprise,' Shaw said. 'Both walking around on two legs and in the realm of business. First let me introduce my guests. You may all stay seated; there isn't enough room for ceremonial. I am happy to introduce you all to Her Majesty Agusta, High Queen of Malgarth.'

Both Varan and Leah stared, open-mouthed.

'Malgarth?' Varan said. He coughed. 'High *Queen?* Welcome, Ma'am. As a Chorwaynie, you find me flabbergasted.'

'I don't blame you,' Agusta said magnanimously. 'I had never expected to be sitting here either.' She grinned at Shaw. 'It's all her fault.'

'It beats wandering the marshes, I'd think,' Shaw said. She then introduced the other three and went on to name the company people. 'Mr. Wainschilt is our chief banker; he knows all about money.'

The high queen eyed Wainschilt, a nattily attired mid-twenty from a long line of Seatome bankers, appraisingly. 'Does that mean there is more to money than keeping it secure in a stout chest and buying what you want?'

Wainschilt smiled tactfully. 'Keeping it secure is very important, Ma'am. But you also want to know how much money comes in and goes out, what you spend it on, and many other details. That means you need a clerk to keep count. And stout chests have their limitations; nowadays we have a bank to take care of the coins. I could send someone to explain these things in more detail, if you'd like.'

'We would like that,' Jonna said decisively. 'It would be very kind of you.' She glanced at Agusta's dubious face. 'Don't worry; I will handle this one.'

The high queen snorted. 'All right; when you have done, you tell me how it works.'

'Next is Mr. Morgan, who represents WyDir,' Shaw said. 'Does your majesty know the principle of airships?'

'We've seen them,' Agusta said, brightening. 'Jonna and I made up whole adventure stories around them. I would like to have them, too.'

'That's the idea,' Shaw said. 'In Hizmyr we have a royal concession for ten years, for which we pay the king ten thousand pieces of gold per year. If we can agree on the same, Mr. Morgan will be more than happy to send people along to discuss a plan.'

'Most certainly,' Morgan said. 'We can fit your realm into the network even faster than Hizmyr, because we already have a presence in Malgarth.' He looked at Jonna. 'Lammark. The name is familiar. I seem to remember we have a field nearby. A grassy land with wooden towers.'

Jonna and Agusta exchanged glances.

'It's there,' Jonna said. 'The field, not the towers. They were dangerously rotten, so my father had them chopped down when I was small. We keep goats out there, and a small farm. Father said it was the property of a fellow in Winsproke.'

'Old Mr. Wylmer,' Morgan said. 'That means it is ours. We will have to discuss this with Lord Lammark.'

'What exactly does that field do?' Jonna said.

'It's called an aerodrome,' Morgan said. 'Those towers are for the airships. These cannot land, you know, so they hook onto a platform to load and unload passengers and goods. We'll build a small office building, perhaps an inn with meals and bedrooms, a repair shed, and of course we'll need the goat farm to keep the grass short. That is a small field. The main location will be at New Winsproke. I suppose that will have to expand now.'

'We can visit the aerodrome at Seatome, then you'll have an idea how a large one looks like,' Shaw said. 'I think Mr. Morgan will be pleased to send someone over as well.'

'Would we need a minister for that?' Jonna asked.

'I don't think so,' Shaw said. 'WyDir handles those matters. It would be something for a Minister of the Interior.'

'The most important thing we need Your Majesty's government to supply is the location of the places you would want connected,' Morgan said.

'My place,' Liom said. 'If you do Winsproke in the west, Lammark in the center, then Morthan is in the east. From there you could fly to Landfalln.'

'Tar Kell would be first,' Morgan said. 'But I see what your lordship means. It would make a circle over the whole of Malgarth.'

'And Thali?' Shaw said.

'They have a separate connection,' Morgan said. 'The Thali government restricts entry, so we run a daily ship from Brannoe, Dvarghish, Seatome, Towne, to Thali-the-City.'

'We lack the infrastructure for foreign visitors,' Engineer Imooga said. 'Thali is an ice city; our life support machines can handle a fixed amount of people, but a load of foreigners who are unused to the conditions wouldn't be wise. So one needs a permit to enter our city.'

Morgan nodded. 'As yet they are the only nation with their own crews, from captains to cabin servants.' He smoothed the table with his hands. 'Lord Morthan's suggestion has merit. It would mean a change in schedule. The Trans-Wydemere line would go to Landfalln, what means we would move our maintenance there. The Towne location really was too small, so that's a bonus. At Landfalln, passengers can change to the Malgarth-Circle line, what will be a series of short hops.' He stared at his papers for a moment. 'Very short hops. I think we'll need smaller airships.'

'Why?' Agusta said.

'An airship has an average speed of three hundred miles plus,' Morgan said. 'The distances between the Malgarth aerodromes will very short, especially in the north. Our large airships can't handle stops every twenty-five miles; it would ruin the engines.'

'I've been working on a mana-drive for carts,' Imooga said. 'I'm sure I can adapt the design for airships. You can go as slow and as fast as you like with them.'

'Then between us, we'll get this done,' Morgan said. 'You will get your airships, Ma'am.'

'And you want more portals, too?' Imooga said. 'Give me a week and I'll have one for you. We even found another portal mage. That is, Kier found him. He's an Institute dropout of an earlier generation, name of Cornal; the guy's in his thirties at least. He worked, if you can call it that, peeling shrimps in the Seatome fisheries. Tymon had to keep him tranquilized for a week, he was that ecstatic to get relief of his overloaded memory. After that he went to work. My, did he pick it up fast! Another week and he'll be ready.'

'Excellent!' Shaw said. 'News like this makes my day! Peeling shrimps, of all the most boring jobs.' She shuddered. 'Next, Captain Wylmer of the Pasandir Navy. With Flag Captain Abia away, he is the senior naval officer. Captain, her majesty wants a navy.'

'Yes,' Agusta said. 'It's too stupid that an island kingdom doesn't have a fleet.'

'I understand completely,' Wylmer said. 'It makes you very vulnerable. Do you have any ships?'

'The Croncliff ferry,' Shaw said. 'Two ships dating from before the war. They wouldn't last in a moderate breeze, should they leave the shelter of the bay.'

'That won't do,' Wylmer said. 'I would suggest starting with at least two small vessels; brigs or schooners, to act as coastguard.'

'We captured some ships at the Tradeports,' Shaw said. 'No big ones, but well enough for what you describe. We should be able to find people to man them and I'm sure we can prevail on Captain Wylmer to set up a training scheme. In the meantime we can discuss building something bigger. Our dockyard at New Winsproke can do that.'

'You got another dockyard?' Wylmer said, surprised.

Shaw nodded. 'We didn't know we owned it. Ever heard of a thing called WyDir Shipping? They owned Paden-Tinnacore International, which in turn owned Paden-Tinnacore Shipbuilding and Repairs.'

'Never heard of them,' Wylmer said. 'Before my day?'

'Several years. Your father owned those businesses. When he decided to move WyDir to Seatome, he sacked the shipyard workers, closed the door and left. Everything is still there; it truly is the weirdest thing. Anyway, we hired the original manager's son, who is a ship's carpenter, and he's reopening the yard.'

Wylmer cursed softly.

'I know,' Shaw said. 'Our Malgarth center of operations will be Landfalln. That is a historical landmark; the place where the Garthan people first set foot ashore. It is a small town on the bay across from Croncliff. We bought the local mansion, with some other buildings, and the little harbor. Now, Mr. Varan, your job as the director for Malgarth just expanded a little. Are you game?'

The young director sat up straight. 'Of course.' He chuckled. 'How shall we name it? Proprietor Darquine already uses the name Malgarth and Continental.'

'Paden-Tinnacore International,' Shaw said offhand. 'We got that one already. Offices in New Winsproke, Brisa and Landfalln. Oh, and until Eskandar decides otherwise, you'll be the unofficial Peak's ambassador to the high queen's court, just as Amsalon is our man in Hizmyr.' She turned to Agusta. 'If you think that is a good idea. Varan can advise you on a lot of things your own nobles aren't familiar with.'

'Do we need to send an ambassador to you in return?' Jonna said.

'We can speak of that later,' Shaw said. 'We don't really have a government yet, or even a capital.' She looked round the table. 'I have invited her majesty to a round of the nations, and to meet the rulers. We have a meeting with Lord Basil, so we will leave you now. I hand over the meeting to Mr. Varan.'

With a bit of a wriggle, Ruth and the youngsters got out of the crowded room.

'Do we get a copy of your notes?' Jonna asked. 'I wrote down what I could, but I'd like to make sure I ain't forgotten anything.'

'Of course,' Ruth said. 'I'll send it after you.' Outside, she produced a handportal. 'The rulers aren't in the portal,' she said. 'So we'll do it my way.' She grinned. 'With a Casterglade handportal.'

It went just as fast, and then they stood in a high, cool white hall.

'Welcome to Spellstor,' Ruth said. 'Home to our family for over a thousand years. Though we had to rebuild it from scratch a few times. But every time was a faithful copy of the original.'

The three looked around.

'This ballroom is huge,' Jonna said carefully.

Agusta nodded.

Ruth coughed. 'This is the entry hall. The ballroom is, ah, bigger.'

Then the awkward moment passed as the still youthful figure of the Spellstor stepped from the next room.

Precisely on cue, Shaw thought. *How tactful of him.*

'Your Majesty,' Lord Basil said, holding out his hands. 'Most heartily welcome. This is a truly unique moment between our peoples. We have always been grateful that your forefathers received us when we were fugitives. I am more than pleased to welcome you on our soil.'

'You are figures of awe for me,' Agusta said. 'Mighty warlocks clad in lightning, and all that. I think our folks are secretly a little afraid of you mana users. I am glad you don't wear that stuff now.'

Basil grinned. 'It's so hard on the furniture, you know. No, I fear us warlocks aren't all that awe-inspiring. But come inside. Mr. Nate, Lady Jonna, Lords Wrache and Morthan, welcome.'

'Do you read our minds?' Jonna asked curiously.

'Certainly not,' Basil said. 'That would be extremely discourteous. No, Ruth told me.'

Then, draped in a mass of green and blue cloth and shawls, Siolde came forward. The mother of Basil and Yarwan's children was a stout lady with a dark gray complexion. For some unknown reason she always made Shaw think of Eskandar.

'Your Majesty,' Siolde said, with a small curtsy. Then she embraced the girl. 'I'm so glad you are here. All those silly frictions between our nations should have been buried long ago.' Then she released her and briefly hugged the others.

Basil turned to the high queen. 'My husband, Commodore Yarwan.'

The commodore, stiffly handsome in his white ceremonial uniform, saluted before holding out his hand.

Shaw glanced at Agusta and saw her easy smile as they shook hands.

'That's what we need,' she said. 'The navy.'

'We're the backbone of any realm, Your Majesty,' Yarwan said gravely. 'Lady Jonna, Baron Morthan, Lord Wrache, pleased to meet you.'

Basil grinned and relaxed. 'Our daughter told me you've an overloaded schema,' he said. 'So we better get to the table, or you will never make it.'

'It is all a bit hurried,' Shaw said. 'But her majesty has her coronation next week, and I thought it wise she had something to show her people.'

'Of course,' Basil said as they all sat down at an elegant table laden with an enormous light luncheon. 'Help yourselves. I thought we would speak more free without servants in attendance. High Merchant Shaw, knowing you I am sure there is a rousing tale to her majesty's succession.'

'There is,' Shaw said. 'It all started with our capturing the Tradeports, in response to a Brisan attack on New Winsproke territory.' She looked squarely at Basil as she said it.

'That certainly was surprising,' Basil said, smiling over a spoonful of delicious soup.

Shaw told of the mine and the *Grimrose*. 'With those scoundrels defeated, I decided I was absolutely fed up with Brisan pirates. So when three of our ships arrived with goods for the Emporium, I collected my troops and sailed north.'

'Just like that,' the commodore said.

'That's how it mostly goes,' Shaw admitted. 'Strange enough it works every time.' She spoke of Codnoallis, the taking of Brisa, and the other ports.

'It was quite a night, but when morning broke, we had the towns. We unloaded the food we'd brought and told the people we were willing to take them into the Peaks. I couldn't see an alternative. If we just left, the pirates could slip back in, and even if they didn't, the towns were impoverished, hungry and damaged; they wouldn't survive on their own. It will cost a lot of money, but we'll get them back on their feet.'

'Why do you do this?' Basil said. 'They were murderous brutes, who terrorized the Wydemere for years. Why do you spend money on them?'

'Partly because it is sound business; a long-term investment. And partly because we're not only fighting pirates and jinn, we must heal the damage they caused as well.'

'You are doing Bodrus' will,' Siolde said.

'Yes.' Shaw pulled a face. 'I'm a merchant, not a missionary. But somehow, both come together.'

Siolde bowed her head. 'I understand. The Sleeping One's ways are different, but then, he is... Bodrus.'

She had wanted to name him differently, Shaw thought. *She knows something.*

'So he is,' she said coolly. 'Well, the next night the ship from Codnoallis bumpety-bumped into the Brisan harbor. One of the fisher lads came to find me.' She spoke of the soldiers, of Jonna, and of their search for Agusta. 'Haai-Bo managed to locate her, and we lured her majesty from the waters with a fire and cookies.'

'A great fire and delicious cookies,' the high queen said. 'It was wonderful, to see Vanhaari and Kell so cozy and comfortable in the middle of that swamp.'

'How well I know that feeling of relieve,' Basil said. 'So you joined them.'

'She did,' Shaw said. 'Then we rode on to Croncliff. Or rather, to Landfalln.' She went on with Lord Rutus, the jinni, and raising the PTC flag.

'Ha!' the commodore said. 'A clever ruse. Would that old ceremonial have been valid for you as a foreigner?'

'It would,' Agusta said. 'The custom mentions only parties. The party who brings the heir to Croncliff and raises their flag over the palace will guide the high king. Ms. Shaw definitely was a party, so the others couldn't protest.'

'But you won't be the power behind the throne?' Basil said.

Shaw shook her head. 'We will not. Her majesty made it clear she would rule, not any faction. We will advise her once in a while, but the high queen will decide what to do with it.'

'And showing her majesty the world is part of that advice?'

'Of course,' Nate said. 'No one can rule well locked up in a castle on an island.'

'True.' Basil laughed. 'You are a lucky ruler, high queen. Shaw's slender figure casts a mighty shadow.' He studied the light playing through the red fluid in his glass.

It is not wine, Shaw thought suddenly. *The commodore drinks wine, but not he.*

'Lemonade,' Basil said. *'I rarely drink alcohol. I find it plays the deuce with my magic. I'm very fond of cherry syrup.'*

Shaw nodded. *You're much like Eskandar, listening with your ears and your mind. It must be a habit.*

Basil smiled. 'Are your people all loyal?' he said, turning to the high queen. 'Given the circumstances, wouldn't someone try something?'

'I don't think so,' Agusta said. 'Lord Morthan's father was the Barons party and Lord Wrache's father the Court. They are both out, and their heirs are with me. Besides, I ordered the castle locked until I return.'

'I left Haai-Bo in Croncliff,' Shaw said. 'He is monitoring the situation and will warn me if anything untoward happens.'

'He's a most powerful spy,' Siolde said. 'Your advisor is probably the mightiest wyrm alive, barring the Princess Lothi-Mo.'

'I know,' Shaw said. 'He's very devious. He's not like Lothi-Mo at all. She and Eskandar are friends, partners. I sometimes have the feeling Haai-Bo merely tolerates me.'

'He is an advisor. All non-royal wyrm advisors are first and foremost loyal to the queen,' Siolde said. 'After all, they are her mates.'

'Oh,' Shaw said. 'So that's it. He is besotted with Lothi-Mo, drooling over her like any boy.'

Nate coughed, and Shaw felt her heart grow cold. She looked at him, but he grinned back in that easy way that always put her at rest.

'Boys do that. I've been drooling over you for years,' he said. 'You never noticed?'

She gripped his hand. 'Idiot,' she said tremulously. 'Not here!'

'Why not?' Yarwan said gravely. 'After twenty-five years I'm still drooling over Basil.'

'Dad,' Ruth said reprovingly. 'Don't embarrass our guests.'

'We're not embarrassed,' Jonna said. She grinned. 'At least the high queen and I are not; I can't speak for my lords, of course.'

'I'm not,' Liom said. He glanced at Gerben, who was studying the best way to eat a somewhat overloaded roll of tuna salad. 'Nor is he, I deem.'

'Not at all,' Gerben said absently.

'Better use your fingers,' Basil said kindly. 'That tuna is looking for a way to escape.' He turned to Agusta. 'I gathered you dismissed your courtiers. How will you replace them?'

Agusta picked up a double cherry and let it swing from her fingers as she gathered her thoughts. 'I'm going to take a sheet from High Merchant Shaw's book,' she said. 'I have summoned all nobles and their families to Croncliff for my coronation. I ordered my clerk to tell them to come if they want a cookie. I'm sure he'll find a more dignified description, but the point is, they will come in the expectation I will choose a new chancellor and all that lot from their midst. Well, I will. From among their children. So if you send me an envoy, Lord Spellstor, make them young.'

Basil put his elbows on the table. 'An interesting thought,' he said. 'Do you think they have the experience?'

The high queen laughed. 'Not of the way it was. That is just the point; I want a fresh start. The last adult bunch wasn't very able and as a result we became more and more isolated. Citizens weren't allowed to leave the country, and though visitors were not forbidden, I guess no one was interested enough to come in. I fear other elders would only repeat those mistakes. So give me their kids and we'll set up a new system we can grow into.'

'Indeed interesting,' Basil said. He studied Agusta briefly. 'I mean that in a positive way. I was barely eighteen when I became the Spellstor. We, Yarwan, Queen Maud, my brothers Jurgis and Saul, were all young when we fought to liberate our countries. It was—I'm not going to call it a glorious time; I leave that to Justin—a hard-fought battle. Both Vanhaar and Kell were in very bad shape, after a century of bondage and ruin. Being young certainly helped. Of course we had a lot of old hands to fall back upon.'

'I've those too,' Agusta said. 'But I won't have them in any executive position. As advisors perhaps; people like Jonna's father, and Lord Ungreff.'

'Dad won't hang around at court,' Jonna said.

'Gods help me, no! I'd consult them when I need advice,' the high queen said. 'They are quite welcome to do something else with their lives the rest of the time.'

Basil smiled. 'You are gracious. I will be awaiting your envoys with...'

'Trepidation?' Shaw said.

He chuckled. 'That, too.' He left it at that and the rest of the lunch was filled with small talk, until servants came to clear the table.

'Time to leave,' Shaw said. 'I'm taking her majesty on a visit to a clothier. All she has now are the wardrobes of her parents.'

'I don't want a dress,' Agusta said. 'I'm much more comfortable in a uniform.'

'But a dress *is* a uniform,' Siolde said gently. 'Sometimes it is even a weapon. A fine dress is a silk sheath around a steel blade to blind and lull your opponents.'

The high queen's face turned thoughtful. 'I never looked at it that way,' she said. 'Fine, show me what the girls wear in the Weal.'

'Vanhaari girls,' Nate said. 'You don't want what Kell girls wear. All that leather is smelly and uncomfortable, besides we're not built for it.'

They took their leave and Ruth ported them back to Seatome.

'That went different from what I'd expected,' Agusta said once they stood in the Old Wharf portal. 'Very friendly and relaxed. Lord Basil didn't do a single bit of magic.'

Shaw glanced at Ruth. She was sure Basil had been doing heaps of magic, to set the guests at ease, and get as much information as he could without violating their privacy.

Ruth gave her the tiniest of winks. 'I'm glad,' she said aloud. 'We're not the nasty warlocks of legend.'

'Now, let's get our steamcart and I'll show you round the town. We'll start at the Sewery, were they make, among things, all our company uniforms. Our seamstresses are high-class artisans. Let's see what they can do for you.'

'They do a creditable line of men's clothes as well,' Nate said to Liom and Gerben. 'You can look through their catalogues and see if there's anything you fancy.'

'Who makes your dresses?' Shaw asked as they went outside.

'Most nobles retain their own dressmaker,' Jonna said. 'It's not very fashionable, I fear.'

The steamcart was waiting, a large, gleaming vehicle with a driver, all in the WyDir livery.

'Smart,' Gerben said appreciatively. 'A very handsome cart.'

The driver smiled and saluted as he opened the door. They got inside and settled down in the soft leather. Then, without a whisper of noise, the vehicle spurted away.

'Hey!' Nate said. 'This isn't a steamcart!'

'No, sir,' the driver said, clearly enjoying their reactions. 'We just got the next model, with the new mana drive installed. I believe this is the first in its sort.' He gripped the wheel and the cart gathered speed.

'Eighty miles an hour,' the driver said without taking his eyes from the road. 'Her top is a hundred miles, but I won't try that here.'

After another minute they entered the town and he slowed down to the usual forty. Every now and then he honked his horn.

'I must warn the other road users,' he said. 'With this motor they won't hear us coming.'

They stopped in front of the Sewery and for a moment Shaw marveled at the change. All lights were on, and the whole interior had been wainscoted in some reddish wood, with the upper half papered in a flowery pattern.

'That's become very classy,' Shaw said.

They stepped inside, to be met by the head seamstress, a stout woman in her late thirties.

'Ms. Shaw!' she said. 'You come to inspect the house? You will find it much changed, ma'am.'

'It looks wonderful,' Shaw said. 'Very nice and chic.'

'We're getting first class customers as well,' the woman said. 'We're giving Clarkill of Fisherman's Lane a run for their money. Masters of Elegance they call themselves. Pah!'

'I'm bringing more potential customers,' Shaw said. 'My guest is High Queen Agusta of Malgarth. She wants a new wardrobe, and so do her noble companions.'

The woman curtsied, flustered. 'Your Majesty!' she said. 'But of course! Please, allow me to show you our collection. They are all our own designs.'

Agusta allowed herself to be sat down. Jonna pulled up another chair, and the two entered another world, of fashion and elegance.

Liom and Gerben looked at each other. 'That's all very nice, of course, but...'

A young seamstress brought another catalogue. 'Perhaps I might advise you as to the latest fashions for gentlemen.' She put the heavy book on a standing desk. 'There have been some important changes lately. You see how the stiff stand-up collar has disappeared for all but the most formal occasions. The same goes for the cravat. Everything is much more designed for comfort, without losing the stylish look.'

Shaw glanced at Nate. 'Let's step outside for a moment,' she said. 'Our friends will be busy for a while. I want to have a look-in at Mackerel Square.'

Nate nodded. He beckoned another woman. 'We'll be out for a moment. We will be back in an hour. Put whatever our guests might order on a bill for the company.'

They went out and walked away briskly. It wasn't far, and within twenty minutes they entered the square.

'It's gone.' Shaw stood stock-still, her heart racing. Every sign of her family's burned down chandlery had been cleared away. In its stead were the contours visible of the new building that would be Harwans Workery. Builders were hard at work and for some moments Shaw watched them silently.

'It's good,' she said, turning away. 'My heart says it's good.' She felt strangely at peace, as if with the blackened remains, her sense of loss had been—not gone, but eased.

Nate put his arm around her shoulder, and slowly they went back to the Sewery.

Here they found the royal companions arguing over an image of a naval uniform much like the one Commodore Yarwan had worn.

'It's beautiful,' Agusta said stubbornly.

'It's *navy*,' Gerben said, showing clear signs of exasperation. 'You can't wear a navy uniform when you inspect the army.'

'Why not?' Agusta retorted. 'Give me one good reason why I can't wear that?'

Shaw grinned. 'You can, of course. Only the soldiers would hate it. It would suggest you liked those ferry boat sailors better than them.'

Agusta scowled. 'Why?'

'Army and navy are factions,' Shaw said. 'You wear your army uniform to military occasions, and naval uniform to nautical occasions. That's polite and tactful, and prevents making them all mad at you.'

'Oh,' Augusta said. She turned to the boys. 'Why didn't you *say* so?' she snapped.

'We tried,' Gerben said with visible restraint. 'But Your Majesty didn't listen.'

The high queen snorted. 'So I *can* buy a naval uniform?'

'Sure,' Shaw said. 'I think you should, it would set a good example. Just remember when to wear it.'

The lead seamstress bowed. 'We will have it all done and delivered to your court in time, Your Majesty.'

'We'll open a portal shortly,' Shaw said. 'I suppose you shall send somebody along to see if it all fits?'

The woman smiled. 'In this case, of course we will.'

'Excellent. And why not have a nice sign made?' Shaw said. 'Couturiers to the Royal Court of Malgarth.'

'Ah, that will poke old Clarkill's eye,' one of the seamstresses said a little too audibly.

The head woman frowned at her, but Shaw laughed. 'So it will.'

They went back to the steamcart, chatting more like friends than a ruler and her retinue. The two boys had moments of silence and gloomy thoughts, but then one of the others said something that distracted them.

'We'll drive you round the town,' Shaw said. 'And I'd promised to show you the aerodrome.'

Traitor Field Aerodrome was a busy place. They walked into the high entrance hall, a near copy of the one in Port Dvarghish, with marble columns and copper-potted flowering trees. A guide led them around, to the offices and the control tower, where they spoke with the manager and the controller.

They walked round the field, looking into the hangars and the airship yard, where workers were busy on the frame of a new ship.

'That one won't be for us?' Jonna said.

'It's probably meant for Hizmyr,' Nate said. 'I believe your ships will be built in New Winsproke.'

They had a look inside a liner for Brannoe, where the captain and his officers explained some of the wonders of the airship's bridge.

After that, they drove to the *Grand Argyr*, Seatome's most luxurious hotel, where they had dinner in style.

While they ate, Shaw told the story of the Unwaari War, of Basil and Yarwan, Maud and Jurgis, Saul, and all the other heroes.

'So this place is named for Lord Basil's father?' Lion said.

'The *Grand Argyr*?' Nate said. 'Yes, there is a statue of him in the hall. It is said the likeness is good, what we can't say of the Liberator.'

'That's an image of Commodore Yarwan, the Liberator of Seatome. We suspect the town bought it second-hand somewhere, for it doesn't look like him at all.' Shaw grinned. 'That's typically Vanhaar. They're cheapskates.' She looked at Nate's face. 'Not us, we're Peak citizens, remember.' Then she quickly went on to Eskandar's story, the prophecy and all that followed.

'You live exciting lives,' Gerben said. 'I'm not sure I'd be cut out for that.'

Shaw shrugged. 'Neither were we. You grow into the role, or...'

'Or you die?' Liom said quickly.

Nate laughed. 'No, or you spend your life washing dishes at Smalkand. Not all of us kids are heroes; most are good guys doing useful jobs; dull but safe.'

'Still, they will fight when they must, and have done so before,' Shaw said. 'And so will you.'

'Yes!' Liom said. 'I certainly would.'

'Of course,' Gerben said. 'But I won't go looking for it.'

'Neither do we,' Shaw said. 'Most of the time we stumble over it. By accident or by divine will, we're not sure about which.'

Then the waiters brought the dessert, a burning castle of ice cream that had them gaping in wonder.

'Why don't we have a place like that?' Agusta said as they finally returned to Old Wharf.

'We couldn't pay for it,' Jonna said. 'I think the bill for that dinner could feed the whole royal household for a week.'

Shaw didn't say anything, but she agreed it probably could. 'I think it's time to retire,' she said instead. 'We've got two high level visits tomorrow.'

'Two more big meals,' Gerben said, and he smiled.

CHAPTER 14 — CAWAH AT BRANNOE

The next morning, the royal company rose and sluggishly sat down in the cafeteria. Shaw grinned at their faces as she sat with Nate beside her and his hands kneading her shoulders.

'Gods,' Lord Gerben said. 'I thought I'd spent the night wide awake with all those new experiences, but I slept like a marble crocodile.'

Liom looked at him. 'So did I,' he said. 'I'm ashamed. My father died, and I'm here amusing myself.'

'Did you love him?' Gerben said, as he stared at the cawah in his mug. 'I did love mine, do I still? I'm not sure. He lied to me and my mother. Again and again. I believed him... Now? I don't know what I feel about him, other than anger and disgust.'

'My father wasn't a man to love.' Liom smeared some honey on a bread roll. 'My mother certainly didn't, father lived in a different world from us. He had his position as the Barons' leader and his many, many loves. His anger was always close to the surface and terrible. Am I a beast if I say that now the shock has passed, his death is a relief?'

Agusta hid a royal yawn. 'I'll not judge you. My father had wanted a boy to succeed him. Instead, he got me. That I could succeed him just as well never occurred to his tiny brain. It was easier to forget I existed. Ah, but I grew up with Jonna's father, so I shouldn't complain. He's the nicest and most honorable man in all Malgarth.'

'And your parents?' Jonna asked of Shaw.

Nate's hands on her shoulders froze, but Shaw found she could handle the question.

'I lost them when I was ten,' she said calmly. 'We had a ships' chandlery; ropes, tar, biscuits and stuff like that. One day when I was out, there was a fire. When I came home, all was gone. I loved them very much.'

'I'm sorry,' Jonna said awkwardly. 'I shouldn't have asked.'

'That's all right,' Shaw said. 'After nearly six years, I can cope with it.'

Ruth came in and grinned at the tired faces. 'Better wake up,' she said. 'Queen Maud is a Kell of Kells, a physical exercise demon. Should you come in like that, she'll put you through the mill and believe me, you don't want to do gymnastics the Kell way.'

'I'm going to take a cold shower,' Liom said. 'That should do it.' He looked at Gerben. 'Coming?'

The other boy sighed. 'I guess.' Then he slapped the table and sprang to his feet. 'Let's go and wake up.'

The girls exchanged a smile and followed them.

'What more did you do, yesterday?' Ruth said, staring after them.

'We went to the Sewery, after that a round of the town and a visit to the aerodrome. Dinner at the *Argyr* and home. Nothing but lemonades. It's all the new impressions on top of their private troubles. I felt like that, after Eskandar had saved us with the *Marigold*. They'll get over it.'

'Basil was quite pleased with the young queen,' Ruth said.

Nate kissed Shaw's neck and sat down. 'So he should; Agusta's a very determined girl. She's going to revolutionize her country.' He sat back, munching a dry slice of toast.

'You know,' he said. 'It was the ice cream. Or rather, the brandy to make it burn. On top of a busy day and two heavy meals there was enough left to make us all feel a bit heavy-eyed.'

Ruth giggled. 'Fun! You kids got a hangover on ice.'

Two hours later they were spruced up and eager as Ruth ported them to Brannoe.

They arrived in an immense hall of heavy redstone blocs and massive pillars.

183

'Brannoe Hall, Kellhome,' Ruth said. 'These are Aunt Maud's own quarters. She rarely receives people here; she's very protective of her privacy.'

A door opened, and Lord Jurgis appeared, clad in the full sky-blue glory of his broomrider uniform.

'High Merchant,' he said with a smile. 'Once more we meet.'

They shook hands and Shaw smiled. 'It is always a pleasure. May I present you to High Queen Agusta of Malgarth? Your Majesty, Lord Jurgis of Kell-Spellstor, Consort to Queen Maud and First Broom of the Weal.'

Jurgis gave a little bow and a broad smile. 'Welcome, five-fold welcome. To receive the ruler of Malgarth in our abode is an unexpected pleasure.'

'I never thought to be here, my lord,' Agusta said. 'The Weal was a place of strange, powerful beings; fearful warlocks and towering Kell.'

'Oh, we are,' Jurgis said easily. 'Warlocks are powerful and Kell do tower. But we're quite nice people as well and I hope we can convince you of that. Come inside and meet the wife.'

Shaw grinned. 'The cats are out of the room, I hope?'

'Cats?' Agusta said. 'I love cats.'

'So does my wife,' Jurgis said. 'I've grown used to them, but two prowling beasts the size of cows don't instill fond feelings in me.'

'The queen keeps two black lions. They're local and rather on the big side.'

'Like everything local,' Jurgis said.

They entered a large, comfortable room with easy chairs, a billiards table and a fire in the hearth.

Queen Maud rose from her chair in all her seven feet of glory. She was a massive, handsome woman, impressively muscled, and her short hair dyed the red of active military service. She didn't wear uniform, but her smart sleeveless leather tunic and pants weren't exactly civvies either.

'Welcome to Kell,' she said. 'High Queen Agusta? I'm Maud. It is good to see another female ruler come into her own. I hope you will tell me all about it. Shaw, thank you for bringing the queen here.'

'My pleasure, Ma'am,' Shaw said. She introduced the other three, and they all sat down.

A knock on the door heralded the cawah, and Jurgis took over the load. 'No servants inside,' he said. 'We really want to be alone, the rare moments we can.'

'Which isn't all that often,' Maud said. 'Even after so many years Kell is still like a peat fire, trouble flaring up where you least expect it.'

'And no one can wipe their... noses without crying for the queen,' Jurgis said. 'She still is the mother of them all.'

'I'm not sure I would have the patience for that,' Agusta said.

'Of course not,' Maud said. 'You're not old enough to be their mother. I remember your father inherited the throne fifteen years ago. You must have been very little then.'

'A little over a year,' Agusta said. 'Father became king, mother died, and I moved to Lammark.' She grinned at Jonna. 'A happy change.'

'I met with your father once,' Maud said. 'When he threatened to annex Tar Kell and Winsproke I told him those towns were ours and he'd better keep his hands in his pockets or else. After that we haven't had any further contact.'

Agusta smiled. 'I don't want them; I always considered those towns Weal territory. I've got my hands full already; I'm not at all happy with the way my father let his barons run the country. I'm going to do it very different.'

'That sounds promising,' Maud said. 'You succeeded only recently?'

'Not a week ago,' Agusta said. 'And a lot has happened already. Perhaps I'd leave it to Shaw to tell all; it's her story.'

'She's got a lot of those stories,' Jurgis said. 'She's a gal on the move, and fast.'

'Things happen around me,' Shaw said. 'I'm not looking for them.'

'Mwah,' Nate said.

Shaw gripped his hand. 'Not often, then.'

'Well...'

She kissed his fingers. 'Hush.' Then, still holding Nate's hand, she once more told of the Tradeports, and all that happened after that.

When she came to Brisa, she saw Lord Jurgis' face grow still, and she went on carefully.

'When I visited the Brisan Table house, all the Table merchants had already been arrested. I spoke with the clerk, and he mentioned he had once known you. He spoke of a book you had given him.'

Maud made an involuntary move. 'That secretive fellow.'

'He was a friend of my stepfather,' Jurgis said slowly. 'How did he fare?'

'He told me he had misjudged the situation then. The Table merchants were not working against each other, but together against the rest. When he tried to use the book, he was treated like your stepfather before him, only he was forced to work as indentured clerk to the Table merchants. He kept meticulous accounts of everything, which was a great help to us.'

'They got him, too? Darnation! I must go and see him.' Jurgis stared hard at Shaw. 'What did you do to him?'

'My wyrmling told me he was not thinking to harm us; he wanted the Table merchants punished. I kept him on, against a more appropriate wage, and I suggested the Peak Bank director to appoint him the Brisan branch manager. That is as well-paying as a merchant's position, and far less risky.'

'Thank you,' Jurgis said, relaxing. 'I will pay him a visit. You don't know his name?'

'I didn't ask,' Shaw said. 'Banker Wainschilt will, I'm sure, but I didn't want to hurry him.' She smiled at Jurgis. 'We have a portal in Brisa. Our Seatome warehouse will be pleased to port you there.'

'You are well-organized,' Maud said.

'Thanks to our engineers,' Shaw said. 'I wouldn't know what to do without them.' She drank her cawah. 'Anyway, we got the Tradeports, and the people were eager to join the Peaks.'

'So you got your own colonies already,' Maud said.

'We offered them an equal relationship. Brisa is as much the Pasandir Peaks as Smalkand or Kalbakar and they get all the goodies.' She grinned. 'Citizens don't pay taxes, get free healing and education, free investments in infrastructure and rent free business loans.'

'Gorm and Otha!' Maud exclaimed. 'How do you *pay* for all that?'

'Trade,' Shaw said. 'All our income is from trade. Employees get healing and schooling, clothes and meals for free.'

'Will you be able to keep that up?' Maud said.

Shaw laughed. 'We're making money. How things develop we'll know when we're done fighting and settle down. After all, Eskandar is the boss. And he has no idea what I've been doing.'

'He won't mind,' Nate said.

Shaw liked the feeling of his hand in hers. 'No, he better had not,' she said with a chuckle. 'But I'm boring the high queen.'

'Boring?' Agusta said. 'Not at all; you give me loads to think of.'

'Good,' Shaw said. Then she went on to Jonna's arrival, and everything that happened in Malgarth, only glossing over Rutus' death.

'Another jinni,' Jurgis said when she was done. 'Those pests are everywhere.'

'They keep trying to destabilize us,' Shaw said.

'I am sorry about your father, Lord Liom,' Maud said. 'A most grievous murder.'

For a moment there was silence.

'And then you fired your whole court,' Jurgis said.

'That is the rule,' Agusta said. 'A new monarch brings changes. Before, the party that won brought their own officials. This time, it was I who won.' She glanced at Shaw. 'So I'm doing the same. I will bring in my own people. Next week, after my coronation, I have them all in one room. Then I'll have a good look at my loyal nobles' families. There must be a few promising ones among the sons and daughters, and I will appoint those. Together, we'll build a new organization.'

Jurgis burst out laughing. 'You! You'll have them tearing their hair, girl! All those hopeful lords, coming to pick the royal plums, to be passed over for their kids! With a bit of luck we'll be able to hear their howling over here.'

'A shame, isn't it?' Agusta said.

Shaw leaned back against Nate's arm and listened to the easy banter. Here, in their private apartment, Maud was much warmer than she appeared as queen, and Jurgis showed he still was that cheeky street kid inside, now and then reverting to the vernacular Shaw remembered from Wisp, the girl who had guided her through Brisa.

The time passed quickly, until Ruth signaled it was time to go.

As they rose and walked back to the hall, Maud touched Shaw's arm.

'You have not been to Tar Kell?'

'It's on my list,' Shaw said. 'But I haven't had time yet. I will go there next.'

'I would like your opinion.' Maud frowned a little. 'It is a very old-fashioned place, the refuge of Queen Hilda, my late predecessor. She was a kind woman, but very set in her ways, and so is Tar Kell. I fear its people don't tell me everything. They say all is well, but so did the Port Dvarghish commander. It took you and young Kennan to show the underlying insubordination.'

'You fear something like that in Tar Kell?' Shaw said.

'I'm not sure. I haven't been there a long time, and I'm confident I won't discover anything amiss if I went. Should your unorthodox approach find anything, I would appreciate it if you would let me know.'

'After the coronation I should have time,' Shaw said. 'I haven't got a warehouse in that town, so that's a logical argument.'

'Good,' Maud said. 'Queen Agusta, I suppose Basil will send you an envoy. May I add a military advisor? I have a young lioness-cadet in need of foreign experience.'

'Of course,' Agusta said. 'I have no idea of our military prowess. I certainly could use advice on how to turn a house guard into a standing army.'

'She will report to you the day before your coronation,' Maud said.

They shook hands and returned to Old Wharf, straight into the chemicals-stained hands of the press.

'Wait!' young Emmett shouted. 'Hold it right there!' His flashlight blinded them all for a moment.

'What the heck?' Liom cried, and his hand went to his saber.

'It's all right,' Shaw said. 'Emmett, warn people, if you don't want to be killed on the spot.'

'Apologies,' the boy said from under the black cloth of his camera. 'Wait for the next one.'

A second bright light, and the young newsman smiled at the blinking royals.

'A fine picture and another scoop for the *Gazette*. Read it all tomorrow!' He pulled out some newspapers and gave one to the bemused high queen. 'A free copy of today's news, with the compliments of the *Weal Gazette*.'

'What's this?' Lord Gerben said. 'Some sort of book?'

'It's a newspaper,' Shaw said. 'Emmett Barnet here is a journalist. He writes of what is happening in the country. His readers buy his newspapers every day to keep up with matters. He just made a picture of you, so you will be on the front page of tomorrow's issue.'

'The high queen of Malgarth visiting Seatome! Sure my readers want to know all about it. They love beautiful queens and handsome courtiers; it's a certain seller,' Emmett said. 'Subscriptions are only five libers per year.'

'You should come to Croncliff next week,' Shaw said. 'You could get some nice pictures of her majesty's coronation.'

'Next week? I'll be there,' Emmett said. 'All three of us, for the *Trumpet* and the *Tidings* will want their own stories. Only I will do the pictures.' He shouldered his camera and made a sketchy bow. 'Y'r servant, ma'am queen.' Then he ran to a waiting steamcart and roared off.

'Well,' Agusta said, staring after the disappearing vehicle.

Jonna chuckled. 'He's funny. A newspaper? And people pay money for it?'

'They do,' Shaw said. 'It's free advertisement for us, our business, and the wyrmcaller's side of things.'

'I've got a stack of them in the office,' Ruth said. 'If you're interested. That guy writes a good story, and he was an eyewitness of several battles. With pictures.'

'I'm interested,' Gerben said.

Jonna nodded. 'Me too.'

They all trooped off after Ruth, and Shaw stayed behind with Nate.

'Phew,' she said.

He grinned. 'Yes. Let's have a quiet walk up the quay to the Liberator and stare at the sea for a bit.'

Shaw drew an arm around his waist. 'Great idea.'

CHAPTER 15 — DINNER IN TOWNE

Around seven, Shaw collected the royal company for their dinner appointment with Darquine.

'Nervous?' Nate said softly as they herded Agusta and her friends to the office.

Shaw moved her shoulders. Somehow, she did feel some trepidation at the coming meeting. All her life, the Proprietor had been an almost mythical figure of wealth and economic power. Her parents had mentioned her in hushed tones, praising her graciousness and full of awe for the power of her Malgarth and Continental Trading Co.

Then Shaw met Darquine, when Eskandar took her along on his first visit to Towne, and not only did the great lady know who she was, she even offered her a position with the MCTC! Shaw had declined; she wanted to stay with Eskandar, and besides...

'She's a challenge?' Nate said. 'Or a goal to reach?'

'Both,' Shaw said. 'I wanted to be like her; the powerful proprietor.'

'You did that,' Nate said. 'The Pasandir Trading Co. is probably even bigger than Darquine's organization. And now you're not sure how she will react.'

Shaw gazed darkly at him. 'Am I that obvious?'

He grinned and gave her a quick hug. 'I know you, gal.'

'Darquine wants to meet us at the *Drunken Peacock*,' Ruth said. 'For personal reasons she cannot receive visitors in the Overhouse, the official residence.' She activated the portal and moments later they came out in the MCTC warehouse.

Ruth greeted the secretary who rushed out to receive her.

Shaw grinned at her guests. 'This isn't ours; the PTC doesn't have an office here. We're in Towne, capital of the Chorwaynie Archipelago. Officially, the ruler is Overcaptain Wallanck, but he is in his eighties and his health has deserted him. His daughter Darquine is his deputy, besides being the proprietor of the Malgarth and Continental Trading Co.'

'Are you competitors?' Jonna said shrewdly.

Shaw managed a smile. 'Yes and no. Yes, because we're in the same markets, and no, because the MCTC is for the Weal what we are for the Peaks, and our countries are friends.'

'That must make it awkward,' Gerben said.

'It asks for circumspection,' Shaw said.

They went outside in the full sun.

'My,' Gerben said. 'It's hot here.'

'So near to home and yet so strange,' Agusta said. 'It's only a few hundred miles northeast of Croncliff; I didn't expect it to be this different.'

'The gods created it as a tropical paradise,' Shaw said. 'It is a beautiful place.'

They passed a grim-faced patrol of the harbor guard in blue uniforms and black hats. Their leader saluted stiffly.

Shaw lifted a hand in return and looked at Ruth. 'Was that for you?'

'I haven't been here for ages,' Ruth said. 'I don't think the guards even know me. They saluted you.'

'Oh,' Shaw said, staring in surprise. 'Why?'

'Because you're the badass Shaw Harwans, conqueror of the Tradeports,' Nate said.

'It was in those newspapers,' Gerben said. 'A big story all about you subduing those nasty pirates. With gruesome pictures.'

Shaw sighed. 'I forgot Emmett was there. I never sit down long enough to read the papers, so I missed it.'

'A lot of folks do read them,' Nate said. 'There are probably a lot more people who know you're here.' Then he waved a hand at a large, low inn. 'The *Drunken Peacock.*'

'It's not the *Grand Argyr*,' Ruth said. 'But the food is fabulous.'

They went inside and found the whole dining room empty but for a table for eight.

'Did they kick all other diners out?' Shaw said.

A slender, boyish figure in a trim merchant's uniform came forward. 'Of course I reserved the whole establishment,' Darquine said. 'We don't want any onlookers when we eat.' She held out her left hand. 'Your pardon, but the right limb refuses to serve. High Queen Agusta; what an incredible pleasure to meet you. I never thought hidebound old Malgarth would allow a woman to rule.'

'Nor had they planned to,' Agusta said. 'They even had a husband at hand to take over.'

'Me,' Gerben said. 'Though they had forgotten to inform me.'

'Lord Gerben is a nice enough chap, but he won't get my crown,' Agusta said.

'Nor would I want it,' Gerben said. 'I'm quite willing to serve my queen, but not that far.'

'Ha!' Darquine said as she guided Agusta to the table. 'You must tell me all; I so love a good adventure.'

'Not "good",' Liom said.

Darquine glanced at him. 'No, that was an unfortunate word,' she said. 'Adventures can hurt terribly.'

They sat down and servants brought a grand repast of grilled, baked and broiled fish, the specialty of the archipelago.

While they ate, Shaw once more told her whole tale, and had Darquine listening spellbound, not interrupting her until she was finished.

'Yes,' she said finally. 'A grand but painful story. My condolences to Lord Morthan, and to Lord Wrache.' She drank her wine and ate some morsel of fish.

'Now where does this leave us?' she said finally. 'Two of our nearest neighbors have changed government. The Tradeports — they are part of the wyrmcaller's realm now?'

'Fully,' Shaw said. 'Eskandar doesn't know it yet, but they are.'

'Then we must open our port to them. I will let the harbormaster know.'

'All trade goes through our warehouses,' Shaw said. 'They act both as independent traders and as agents of the local industries.'

'You don't allow the towns to sell directly to third parties?' Darquine said, curiously.

'For now, no; we want our share in the deal. Instead they pay no taxes, get free schools and healers, and more,' Shaw said.

'A fair exchange. And Malgarth?'

Jonna put down her fork. 'We will trade with the merchants who give us the best deals,' she said. 'Not necessarily the cheapest, but preferably the most comprehensive.'

'I see,' Darquine said. 'I'm not sure I can compete with Shaw.'

Shaw looked up in astonishment. 'What?'

'Does that surprise you?' Darquine said. 'I can see it does. Gal, if ever we had a contest, you won it long ago. When you acquired WyDir, I knew it was done. Then you started those businesses up north in places I'd not even heard of, and I decided I'd better scale back. So I closed our warehouse in Port Naar and focused on the Weal. One thing I don't understand; you haven't opened a warehouse in Towne.'

'That's your territory,' Shaw said, a little awkwardly. 'I'm working for us, but not against you.'

'You mean that?' Darquine searched Shaw's face. 'I see you do.'

'Sure I mean it,' Shaw said. 'The Weal and the Peaks are friendly, so I just went ahead and built my companies, careful not to steal business away from you. Though there were moments I wondered what you were about.'

Darquine carefully removed some bones from her fish. 'When?'

'When we got complaints about the bad service of your warehouse in Port Dvarghish. Long overdue deliveries and such. Then we found your agent in town had been taken over. That had me wondering why you hadn't acted. You must have heard the same complaints.'

'No,' Darquine said. 'That is, they reached my in-tray, but I didn't see them until it was too late. My father went through a bad time then — he is old, and his mind has gone. He can be very difficult, and that period was particularly troublesome. So I wasn't attending to the business much. What exactly happened?'

Shaw told her of the Jelvaren take-over, Brynnyr Gunny Co, the robber cave and the captured guys from Spellstor.

'So that was it,' Darquine said. 'Young Ms. Jelvaren's death caused all the delay. And then the Gunny kid — poor boy; he and his friends must've been shocked out of their wits.'

'They recovered quickly enough,' Shaw said. 'B.G., as he's called, is in Port Naar, where he found the river back. The stream went underground, and now he and his team are trying to make her flow again.'

'Will that work?' Darquine refilled her glass, apparently glad to change the subject. 'Will you try to fertilize the desert?'

'If it can be done, Princess Jem would like us to restore her homeland,' Shaw said. 'We'll see how it goes. Much is possible if the gods favor it.'

Darquine turned to Agusta. 'Your pardon for talking trade,' she said. 'Shaw and I meet so rarely we almost automatically speak of what we are full of.'

'Do go on,' Agusta said. 'It gives a rare insight on your world. All those businesses and things are strange and fantastic.'

'And we're sorry about your father,' Jonna added. 'It must be difficult to care for him if you have both a country and a business to rule besides.'

'It is; I lack the time and the joy to battle it out with Shaw. That's why I'm concentrating MCTC's business on trade between the Weal countries. All else must go. Shaw, I made a list of companies I wish to dispose of. Some are moribund, others are quite lively. You can make me an offer piecemeal or buy the whole list for twenty thousand libers.'

'Full ownership?' Shaw said. She glanced through the list. 'I must study this. I will let you know shortly, if that's all right.'

'That's fine,' Darquine said. Suddenly she sat up, her face drawn. 'I fear I must go. Nurse mindspoke me I'd better come home.'

They all rose.

'Take care,' Shaw said urgently, feeling very sad all of a sudden.

Darquine nodded. 'I will see you all another time,' she said and hurried out.

'This is worrisome,' Ruth said, as from the street the roar of a steamcart died into the distance. 'I wonder if my dad Basil knows how bad it has become.'

'Well, tell him,' Shaw said. 'She's exhausting herself and ruining her business. He should at least be aware of it.'

Ruth nodded. 'I'll call him later.'

'About tomorrow,' Shaw said. 'The Allastar Castle?'

'Up and running,' Ruth said. 'It was the fastest restoration possible. The Institute sent some mages, and the builders hired most of the townsfolk to help. The first students arrived two weeks ago while the paint was still wet.'

It was, what? A month? Shaw thought. *To have the whole castle turned into a school in that time... the Institute must be eager to be rid of the hedgemage problem.*

'All right,' she said aloud. 'Then we'll have a look at our new school for mages. After that, we'll check up on B.G. in Port Naar, and then on to Smalkand, our headquarters in the Peaks.'

'Now we'll return to Old Wharf?' Ruth said.

Shaw looked at the royal companions. 'I'm sorry about this. We'd better go.'

'I feel for the proprietor,' Agusta said. 'In our stories the Overcaptain was a powerful ruler, a bearded giant who could kill with his voice alone. It is a pity to know such a man brought low.'

'He was,' Ruth said, soberly. 'That is how I remember him too.'

Without another word, they gathered, and she ported them back to Seatome.

'I'm for bed,' Agusta declared, as they arrived back in the almost deserted warehouse. 'It sounds like another well-filled day tomorrow.'

Jonna looked at the two young lords.

'I'm not sleepy yet,' Liom said. He glanced at Gerben. 'Let's stroll along the waterfront.'

'I'll be in the office,' Ruth said.

Alone for once, Shaw and Nate sat down in the cafeteria.

She pulled Darquine's list from her pocket and sat staring at the scrawled names.

'I feel strange,' she said.

Nate took her hands. 'About Darquine?'

'Yes. All this time I wanted to be as good as she was; the rich and successful proprietor.'

'You were better, more successful, and probably richer.' Nate cradled her hands between his. 'Disappointed?'

'Deflated,' she said. 'And I feel sorry for her. She wanted so much, and she never got it. No adventures, no partner, instead she's left with a lame arm and a demented father, and now I ruined her business as well.'

'She's too much a loner,' Nate said. 'Our PTC is full of people who all feel responsible for their companies. If you decided tomorrow to quit and go live on a deserted island, guys like Amsalon, Varan, and Morgan would all carry on. I never saw the same spirit with MCTC. Darquine's people don't care. It's not their company; it is hers.' He looked at her. 'I agree coping with a dotard for a father ain't fun, and she's probably darned lonesome. She's a nice person, but she's a ruler and a big business owner. She employs several thousand workers and she simply can't afford letting MCTC run aground. The Weal has trouble enough getting back on its feet; if she goes broke, the gods know what will happen. We don't want to take over; we *need* competition to stay sharp. So we should see if there's a way to help her.' He took a deep breath and grinned. 'That was Father Nate's evening sermon. Now, let's see that list. What goodies does she want to sell?'

CHAPTER 16 — TO SCHOOL

'Castle Allastar?' Portal Mage Kier said the next morning. 'I'll send you to the dockyard. We'll be installing some transferals shortly, but the Tradeports came first.'

'No matter, we'll fly to the castle,' Shaw said. 'Kennan knows the way.'

The marine captain raised an eyebrow. 'You want to go there?' he said. 'Is it still empty?'

'They should've turned it into a school,' Shaw said. 'Let's go and see.'

Kier looked over the group. 'Take a deep breath, royals and nobles all,' he said with a grin for Agusta and her friends.

Moments later, they came out in the portal shed at Allastar Dockyard.

'Ms. Shaw!' someone cried as they stepped outside in the light of day. Moments later, she was the center of a small group of workers, who all wanted to shake her hand.

'How are things going?' Shaw said. 'You're all back in your old jobs?'

'It's a marvel, ma'am,' a carpenter said, hooking his thumps behind the straps of his apron. 'The schooner is nearly finished. We've been working on her for nigh on a month, and she's as new.'

'Good job!' Shaw said. 'I'm glad for you all. Now, I came for a look at the castle.'

He grinned. 'The school! They're all wee kids, but they liven up the town for sure.'

'I like that,' Shaw said. 'I'm afraid I must go, for I've got visitors to show around. Have a good day, all.'

The workers stepped aside and Kennan's men lifted first. Shaw rode with Agusta. 'We're in Allastar Cove; a clanhold on the west coast of Kell. Almost everyone you see here is related to each other. Apart from the dockyard, PTC acquired the town's castle, and that's where we go now.'

'It's a real castle!' Agusta said. 'We don't have those, unless you'd call Croncliff one, but we know them from the adventure books.'

Minutes later, they landed on the edge of the courtyard where a bunch of youngsters in short blue robes was playing some ball game.

A stout boy ran backwards, arms outstretched, and caught the ball. 'Still in!' he cried and passed the ball with an overhand throw to another kid. Only then he noticed Shaw and her people, and he stopped in his tracks, the game forgotten.

'Ooh, soldiers,' he said, grinning hugely. 'We're under attack!'

'Yes!' Shaw said lugubriously. 'We come to arrest *you*.'

'Aiii!' he said in mock terror. 'What did I do?'

'You know your own misdeeds,' Shaw said sternly. 'Now, all funning aside, I'm Ms. Shaw, the school's owner. I think you can show us around.'

'That'll make me late for class,' he said dubiously.

'Then let's start with the Headmaster. I will tell him I kidnapped you.'

'The Head's doing a demo class on lightning,' the boy said.

Shaw looked at him. He was eleven or twelve, a rotund Vanhaari with short dark hair and quick, light eyes.

'That sounds exciting,' Shaw said. 'Lead us to him.'

Past the high castle entrance, they were stopped by a tall person in a handsome uniform Shaw didn't recognize.

'No visitors allowed without an appointment,' he said sternly.

'This is Ms. Shaw, Beadle,' the boy said quickly. 'She's the lady who owns the school.'

The man glanced quickly at Shaw and unbent miraculously.

'Pleased to meet you, ma'am!' he said. 'I'm the school's beadle, responsible for order and discipline.' His eyes twinkled. 'And as I'm a hedgemage myself, I well understand our pupils' present high spirits. You did a wonderful thing here, Ms. Shaw.'

'Writing off those kids was the most stupid misconception; we need those mage artisans,' Shaw said. 'I have guests who are interested, and I asked this young man to show us around. Kindly advise his instructor he will be late for the next lessons.'

'I will pass the word, ma'am,' the beadle said. 'Young Brigg's in Room 8 when you're finished with his awesome services.'

She smiled at the beadle. He seemed an alright type for her school. 'Thank you. Now, Mister Brigg; the Head.'

The boy nodded. 'This way. You're in luck you asked me, ma'am! I've been here two weeks already and I know everything.'

'Two weeks!' Shaw said, properly impressed. 'Then you were among the first students.'

'I am,' he said proudly. 'And it's great. Much, much nicer than the Institute.'

'I'm glad to hear that,' Shaw said. 'Could you explain to my guests exactly what you are doing here?'

'Sure,' the boy said. 'This is a mage artisan school. All kids with magic get sorted out when they're small. Those with heaps of mana go to the Institute to become mages. Those with less magic come here to learn a trade and be mage artisans. I am going to become a confectioner. My cakes will enhance your magic, my wafers will feed you on the trail, and my sweets will sharpen your spells.'

'That's a great pitch,' Shaw said. 'When you graduate, call on me. I will have a job for you.'

'I'd like to open my own shop,' Brigg said.

'You got a lot of money?' Shaw asked.

The boy sighed. 'Ah well, that's the rub.'

'That's why we must talk. I'm opening the Emporium; a big store for all things arcane. I could use a magic sweetshop.

You'd draw a handsome salary and be your own boss. Think on it. Now, the Head.'

'I heard of the Emporium; they say it's a posh place. That would be just the spot for my arts.' He waved a hand. 'For sure, the Head; follow me.'

Shaw remembered the way from her first visit, but now it looked very different. There were mage lights on the walls, and the great hall had been transformed into a messroom where meals were served to students and staff.

'Well,' Gerben said. 'How many students are there?'

'Thirty-seven of us, and seventeen wavies,' the boy said.

'Wavies?' Nate said.

'That's the nautical bunch, on account of them sailing the waves.'

'Ah, and what do they call you?'

Brigg looked disgusted. 'Wrigglies. Because they think we wriggle our fingers with each spell. That would make a fine mess if I were kneading spelled dough.'

'It's a higher number than I thought,' Shaw said.

'There will be more once people hear of it,' the boy said. 'I mean, school, our uniform, meals, all are free!'

'That's generous,' Agusta said. 'It will cost a lot of money.'

'It does,' Shaw said. 'It's an investment. We hope to employ all those kids when they graduate. They don't have to, but we offer good money for mage artisans. Before, those same kids had barely any future.' She explained the problems hedgemages faced. 'To PTC, all mana is an asset to be used, and being a full mage isn't the way to riches many people think. These kids are needed. They run our portals, they work with our engineers, and shortly they'll make our cookies, too.'

They walked through a long corridor until they came to a door with a big sign "Practice Room; KEEP OUT!"

The boy opened the door just wide enough and stuck his head inside. 'Headmaster, sir! Visitors!' he yelled over the crackling of lightning.

Shaw smelled ozone and singed hair. The sounds of fury died down and a balding man in a stained robe appeared.

'Who is disturbing my demonstration?' he said in a deep voice. 'Speak loudly, my ears are deafened.'

'Your pardon,' Shaw said with a smile, and she handed him her visiting card.

The headmaster glanced at the name and started. 'Ms. Shaw!' he said. 'Happy to meet you, ma'am.'

'I wanted to show my visitors the school,' she said. 'I impressed this young man's services as a guide, but I don't want him to get into trouble.'

'Brigg can do that well enough by himself,' the headmaster said. 'But his innocence is noted. He knows his way around. I can't join you, I'm afraid; those rapscallions inside would burn down the keep if I left them unsupervised.'

'I'm only doing a quick tour,' Shaw said. 'I'm impressed and pleased with both the building and the atmosphere. This is what I had in mind when I launched the idea of a mage artisan school.'

'Thank you,' the headmaster said gravely. 'I used to be a master at the Institute, and I never agreed with the way hedgemages were treated. The Institute is merely producing high-level warlock's assistants. Here we school our students for a place in society.' A loud bang inside the room made him smile. 'Your pardon; I'd better return to my class.' He hurried inside and closed the door.

'I don't do that course,' the stout boy said regretfully.

'What classes do you do?' Nate asked.

'The usual, manapool enlargement, concentrate and manipulate, spell copying, and the school's pastry woman teaches me how to make cakes and such. Next year I get herbs, alchemy and potion making. That will be fun.'

They walked past several doors.

'Classrooms,' Brigg said with a grubby finger to his lips. 'Better not disturb them.'

After another bend in the corridor, they came to a double door with a heavy wooden sign reading "Nautical School".

'That's the Wavies Hell,' the boy said. 'Hall, I mean.'

Beyond the doors the color scheme changed subtly from vaguely yellow-orange to vaguely blue-green.

'More classrooms,' the boy said.

Then a door opened and a lad in a blue sailor's uniform came out, a squarely built Kell with short, dark hair.

He grinned as he saw them.

'Kicked out of class?' the stout boy inquired.

'No! It's emergency training. Now the others are thinking up a disaster, and then I'll be officer of the watch and I must prove I know what to do.'

'And do you?' Shaw asked.

The boy shrugged. 'Hope so; I'm a M'Dvargh, from a long line of mariners. I've been to sea as a ship's boy for three years, before they sent me here to become an officer.'

Then an older woman in a merchant officer's uniform came out. 'You can go in,' she said. Then she turned to the visitors. 'Ms. Shaw,' she said. 'I recognize your face from the newspapers. Are you inspecting the school, ma'am?'

Shaw smiled. 'I'm showing round some important guests. Do you mind if we watch the exercise?'

'Not at all; that young fellow should take it all in his stride. Please sit at the back of the class.'

They filed in, and no one paid any attention to them. They all watched the M'Dvargh boy.

'Well, mister,' the instructor said. 'The class dreamed up an impossible situation for you. They are sure you will go down with your ship this time. Listen: You are in the middle of a violent storm, some thousand miles from the nearest coast. Your masts went by the board, your pumps are clogged, and you're making two feet of water per minute. You have no boats, and the sea around you is packed with hungry sharks. You may retain one other person, crew or passenger. What will you do?'

The boy smiled. 'That's easy,' he said. 'With me is the ship's mage; a clever chap. I will tell him to go into the hold and shield up. A large forcefield will keep the ship afloat, while he can spend his time unclogging the pump. Every hour or so he'll renew the spell, until the wind lessens. In the meantime I've jury-rigged a mast, and when the storm dies down, we'll sail home again.'

'I'm not sure your mage can do that,' the instructor said slowly. 'No spell would be strong enough to keep a ship from sinking.'

'It has been done,' the boy said stubbornly. 'I heard my first officer tell the story.'

'Wild tales,' another boy scoffed.

'He's right,' Shaw said slowly. 'It has been done.'

The instructor looked at her. 'Do you perhaps know the details, ma'am?'

'It happened a hundred miles out of Towne Harbor,' Shaw said. 'A burned ship, with enough planks sprung to sink her ten times over. The only survivor was a young Unwaari singer, who did just that trick. He kept his shield up for two days, until he was rescued. I know, for I was there when the lord wyrmcaller brought him in.'

'See,' Brigg murmured. 'Your mage is your best friend in need.'

'Yeah,' the scoffing boy retorted. 'Every ship should keep one in glass, next to the life buoy.'

'Watch your tongue,' a bony Vanhaari said. 'I've got just enough magic to try that trick as officer of the watch. It's a good story; I guess you wormed your way out of it again, mate.'

The instructor nodded. 'It was a good answer. I didn't know a thing like that was possible, but I'll discuss it with the other instructors whether we should add it to the curriculum. There aren't many mages at sea, of course.'

'But there ought to be,' Shaw said. 'It should be just as normal for a mage or mage artisan to choose a career at sea as for any other person. That's just what this school is about. You're not restricted to some professions as a mage; you can wriggle your fingers on the waves as well as anywhere else.'

That had the whole class laughing, and the instructor smiled.

'I suppose there will be some demand for nautical mages.'

'Demand? I will hire every single one of them,' Shaw said. She grinned at the suddenly thoughtful faces. 'Don't worry guys; I won't send *any* of you lot away. We need a great many capable ship's officers, both merchant and navy, and so will other nations.'

'I most certainly do,' Agusta said. 'The high kingdom of Malgarth wants you.' She looked at Shaw. 'Can we send you pupils? I'm sure I will find you likely candidates.'

'You should discuss this with Ruth,' Shaw said. 'We better leave now; we've disrupted enough of the instructor's class.'

'Not at all,' the woman said. 'We'll now be discussing magic at sea and its uses. Thank you for making this point clear.'

'Ma'am, before you leave,' the M'Dvargh boy said urgently. 'The chap who first did it, what was his name?'

'Justym,' Shaw said. 'Why?'

'Then we should call it the Justym Trick. That's only fair, isn't it?'

Shaw hid a grin. 'It sure is. He is with the wyrmcaller now; when I see him again, I'll tell him how he has been immortalized.'

'Perhaps he could come and tell us himself,' the boy said. 'That would be grand.'

'I'll ask him,' Shaw promised.

Outside the room, she looked at their guide. 'Is there anything else we should see?'

'We've done all the important places,' Brigg said.

'Then you may bring us back to the exit,' Shaw said.

He had another, faster way back, and soon they were at the now empty courtyard.

'You were a great help,' Shaw said. 'Remember to call me when you're a graduated mage pastry cook. Here's my card, it will get you past any who try to guard me.'

'Fabulous,' Brigg said, as he took the visiting card reverently. Then he bowed. 'Thank you, ma'am.' Clutching the card, he hurried back to his own class.

'What a great place this is,' Jonna said. 'All our youngsters are home schooled; they miss out the contact with the other kids.'

'Our noble youngsters, you mean,' Gerben said. 'These weren't highborn, I think?'

'Probably not,' Nate said. 'We don't have many kids you'd classify as noble.'

'That's what I mean. Our commoners don't school their children.'

'My father pays for classes for our servants' children,' Jonna said.

'Can I make that mandatory?' Agusta said.

'We don't have the teachers,' Liom said. 'My mother taught me; I'm not sure she would have time to do the same for two hundred demesne kids.'

'No,' Agusta said. 'Jonna's father paid his clerk to do it. But only the house servants' children; not all in the village.'

'One teacher can't handle two hundred kids. We'd need two per demesne. That's four hundred teachers. What do we pay them?'

'A silver coin per day,' Shaw said. 'Roughly estimate of six thousand pieces of gold per year for the lot of them.'

'Or thirty gold per demesne,' Jonna said. 'That's a bit steep for a mandatory rule.'

'Do the nobles pay taxes?' Shaw asked.

Jenna hesitated. 'Yes, but I've no idea how much, or for what. The Chancery Clerk will know. When we're back, I will have him show me.'

'All right,' Shaw said. 'Then we'll go back to the dockyard portal and on to Port Naar. If you thought Towne was hot, prepare for a shock. Naar is far worse.'

'Gods!' Liom exclaimed, as they appeared in the Port Naar warehouse. 'It's like walking into our bread ovens!'

'The Hellesands, they call it,' Shaw said. 'This was the kingdom of Nanstalgarod, ruled by very powerful mage kings. Somehow, they ruined their soil, and as a result the desert ate their lands.'

She led them outside, into the heat of the day. 'This is a Weal navy base. The land beyond is mostly uninhabited. The Weal maintains reclaimer camps at the ruins of several major cities. They seek for magic artifacts the original inhabitants left behind. I'll not tire you with the local authorities; they are of no interest. We'll have a word with B.G., the warlock leader of the team that searches for the lost water around here.'

They mounted up and rode in search of Gunny's camp, and found him not far off, standing on the banks of a dry river.

As they landed, they heard him yell. 'Hold!' He turned to them, his face streaked with sweat and dust, and his eyes glittering. 'Shaw!' he said. 'I've been trying to contact you, but Ruth sent a "don't disturb" sign, and no one else knew where you was. Yet here you are, as if the gods sent you.'

'I'm showing the new high queen of Malgarth around,' Shaw said. 'Agusta, this is the warlock Brynnyr Gunny, one of the few real, live warlocks of our generation. He's a dowser, searching for water.'

'High queen?' B.G. said, and he bowed. 'You are in time for a very important happening, Ma'am. After a long search, we will try to get this part of the river back onto the surface.'

'What river?' Gerben asked, looking at the stony lands.

B.G. smiled. 'Ah, that was our question. If you know what to look for, you can vaguely see the ancient riverbed, but it's as dry as they come. However, a dowser will find water, wherever it is hiding. The whole stream went underground, centuries ago, but she is still there. Let's join the others.'

Only now Shaw saw Lord Amaj and Jem waiting under a striped awning.

'Hi, Shaw,' Amaj said. 'Come to see the show?'

'By accident,' Shaw said. She introduced the royal company. 'Agusta, Jem is the bottle girl I told you about. With her creepy lich grandfather still around, she won't claim her title, but she is queen of all Nanstalgarod. You can't touch her,' she added hastily, as the high queen held out her hand. 'Her corporeal body was turned into a bottle; only her ethereal form is here.'

'It's a bother,' Jem said grandly. 'Malgarth are you? Were you a kingdom when I was born, half a millennium ago?'

'We'd just arrived then,' Agusta said. 'We don't know much of that time. You look well for such an old lady.'

Jem's laugh startled them all. 'I do, don't I?'

'Now we're all here, let us continue,' B.G. shouted. 'Phynn, our engineer, and Latharom, our mover mage, will together open up the bottom of this river arm, and we should see the water come welling back to the surface.'

He lifted his arms as if about to cast a spell. On the other bank, Latharom waved. A long series of explosions rocked the river bottom and an immense mass of water burst forth, boiling and hissing as it spread out over the bone-dry river bottom.

'Gods!' B.G. yelled. 'I didn't expect *that*!'

In minutes, the water lapped against the stony banks and rose a foot, two feet, five, six feet.

'WHEEEE!' an exultant voice from nowhere cried, and grass sprang up on the banks, a copse of tall trees appeared, and a stone bridge spanned the river.

'That's how I saw it!' Rhila stared around wildly. 'Now it's real; my vision is gone!' The young Port Naar portaller had been helping B.G. because she saw memories of this place from before the desert.

'Gone?' Shaw said.

Rhila gripped her arm. 'They're no longer here! What I saw... came back.' She waved an arm at the grass growing under their feet, for a stretch of several yards from the river.

'Teodar!' Shaw said. *'What's happening?'*

'Zenyunthalata doing a miracle,' the Kavid-Jar said. He sounded scared.

'What's wrong?'

'I always thought the Hellesands was a natural disaster,' he said tersely. *'Now I wonder if it wasn't a Divine Punishment.'*

'You mean the God of the Lands deliberately killed Nanstalgarod? His own people?'

'Yes,' he whispered. *'In a fit of anger. Remember Bodrus wasn't there to stop him.'*

'As he wasn't when Aera turned her back on her people,' Shaw said. *'Our god does have some things to answer for.'*

Teodar didn't say anything and Shaw broke contact.

'What the heck is all that?' B.G. said, staring at the grass and the trees.

Shaw watched Jem's strained face. *I'm not going to tell her that her god killed her people — if she doesn't already suspect...*

'Somehow, Rhila's visions returned,' she said calmly. She held out her hand. 'Congratulations, B.G. You did it.'

He shook hands absently. 'Grass and trees,' he said. 'I wonder what would happen if we dug small channels inland.'

'First you will have to explain things to the locals,' Nate said. 'There's a crowd of them coming this way.'

'Oh, gods,' B.G. muttered. 'That idiot captain.'

'I'll take her majesty to Smalkand,' Shaw said. 'She has silly court people of her own, and doesn't need ours.'

'Amaj, you go back, too,' Jem commanded. 'I'll be along later.'

The young lord stretched a hand out to her and dropped it with a sigh as Jem faded away.

'She wants to be alone,' he said with an attempt to a smile.

Shaw took his arm. 'Escort us, my lord,' she said. 'Rhila, we need a port, gal.'

The portal mage looked away from the river and the bridge. 'Yes,' she said dully. 'I don't understand what happened.'

They rode back to the portal, and flashed to Smalkand.

In the hall of the cave keep they ran into Willow, who stopped and beamed at Shaw.

'Hi, good to see you! And who are you bringing us today? Guests?'

'Yep.' Shaw grinned. 'Visiting royalty. Agusta, High Queen of Malgarth, Willow is the keepmistress of Smalkand. She rules all with an iron hand.'

Willow managed a curtsy without losing an inch of her authority. 'Welcome to Smalkand Keep.'

Shaw quickly introduced the others. 'We're doing a grand tour of our main centers. Can you put us up for the night?'

'Of course,' Willow said. 'Your Majesty is right heartily welcome.'

'We're just back from Port Naar, so we're dying for something cool first of all,' Shaw said. 'And you should send someone to check up on young Rhila. She seemed a little upset at the way B.G.'s spectacle turned out.'

'Oh dear, didn't the river thing go well?'

'All too well,' Shaw said, and she told what happened.

'Grass and trees?' Willow said. 'They just... sprang up?'

'Whatever happened, that river became just as the visions Rhila always saw of it. Now her visions are gone, and the whole thing unsettled her.'

'I'd say it would,' Willow said. 'I'll tell Portal Mage Beth to send a relief and have Rhila come back to report. Let her pour her heart out.'

Shaw led the royal company to the bar, nearly empty at working hours.

'Hi,' the serving boy said. 'Good to see you two, and your guests, of course. What can I get you?'

'Ice cream,' Shaw said. 'Big ones. They're on me.'

'A remarkable place, this,' Liom said. 'All that marble and those copper chairs. This is the keep you just happened to find?'

'The wyrmcaller found it,' Shaw said. 'It was a Nanstalgarodian trade center. From here, they sent caravans into the mountains, to trade with the keeps and villages. They left it well protected, and it came to us as they had last seen it, five centuries before.'

'And now it's your seat of government.'

Shaw looked at Agusta. 'Actually, we don't have a government. Eskandar is head of state, but he'd stare if you called him that. Lord Amaj is the commander of the Pasandir Armed Forces, Flag Captain Abia is the senior naval officer, and that's about it. Of course there is the Kavid Jar, but he is the mouth of Bodrus, not a civil servant.'

The high queen rested her elbows on the table. 'Then who governs the people?'

'Nobody,' Nate said. 'The Peaks are a collection of ancient castles, each with a village and its own lord. As far as I understand it, in the old times before the wyrms went mad, every keep had their own wyrmcaller. He, I don't know if there ever was a female one, was a combination of mage and defender, who could speak with the local wyrms. The keep's lord cared for the people and the crops.'

'A mage defender and a farmer,' Liom said. 'Do I say that right?'

'That's how I remember it explained,' Nate said. 'The wyrmcallers formed a council, and their head was the Wings of the Mountains, who coordinated all defense. He and the Kavid Jar were Divine Bodrus' agents in the Peaks.'

'Eskandar is the present Wings of the Mountains,' Shaw said. 'Defender and disciple of Bodrus.'

'Then the wyrms went away, and the whole wyrmcaller thing toppled,' Nate went on. 'Kambish, Eskandar's grandfather, was the last of them. Twenty-five years ago, Jem's long dead grandfather returned as a lich. Somehow, he got chummy with the jinn and their pirates, and he's beleaguering the Kavid Jar's sanctuary. It is a stalemate, and we're killing pirates to keep them from getting the upper hand.'

'Why does he want that sanctuary?' Gerben asked.

'That's where Divine Bodrus' sleeping body is,' Shaw said. 'We suppose he is after the powers of our god. We won't allow that, of course.'

'So you're gathering strength?' Agusta said. 'Troops, gold, friends?'

'Yes,' Shaw said. 'And we're gathering kids. It is in the prophecy we need them.'

Then the ice creams arrived in large glasses, with fresh fruits and syrup, and that got their attention.

'Well,' Gerben said. 'Those look yummy.'

'And no alcohol,' Shaw said. 'We don't even serve that to our guests.'

'This alone is worth coming for,' Jonna said. 'How do you make something this deliciously cold?'

'Ice machines,' Shaw said. 'That is one of our inventions; a machine that can make a well-isolated room freezing cold.'

She steered the conversation away from the prophecy; it wasn't something she liked to discuss with outsiders.

After the ice cream, Shaw showed them round, before handing them over to Willow.

'The keepmistress will point you your rooms and where to wash. I suggest you just walk around and talk to the kids. Mind they aren't very impressed by titles; don't expect many "majesty's" and all that stuff.'

Agusta grinned. 'I can live without that.'

Shaw gripped Nate's arm, walked outside and sat down on the wheel of one of the big guns guarding the entrance. She felt depressed, as if a black cloud hung over her.

'What's wrong?' Nate said.

'That bit at Port Naar,' she said. 'When all those trees were popping up, I asked Teodar, and he was clearly shocked by it. He suddenly wondered if Zenyunthalata had killed Nanstalgarod on purpose, in a fit of pique.'

'You mean that he had sent the sands?' Nate stared out over the bay. 'And after that he brought his faithful to Yavam Island, and disappeared.'

'Until today.'

'You think the God of the Lands brought the grass and the trees?'

'Teodar thought it was him that did it. I didn't dare tell Jem.'

'Nice of you, but I knew,' Jem voice came from nowhere. Then her form shimmered before them. 'Those sands... It went all too fast to be natural. I knew the Divine and my grandfather... Let's say they didn't like each other. Grandfather's hobnobbing with the jinn was the ultimate insult. After Yavam and that book I read for them... There were passages I didn't translate... Those that suggested

Zenyunthalata had caused the sands, because he was blinded by anger. Later, I confronted my god with the accusation. He didn't deny it. The process was natural, only it would've taken centuries and it could have been averted. So he hastened the process to mere years.'

'And now?' Shaw said.

'He will not undo the harm just like that. He's afraid to lose face. But if we show we are willing to work for it, he'll aid the process, bit by bit. We must not talk about this again; it's very sensitive, because he is ashamed. You needed to know, as you are the ones, you and Eskandar, who are fighting the gods' fight.'

Shaw growled softly. 'I'm a merchant.'

'Jinnbane and the Trade Magnate, Zenyunthalata called you two. You're both parts of the prophecy.' Jem drifted up, much like a ghostly apparition. 'That's all he said. Now I'm going to cheer up Amaj. And thanks, you know; I'm grateful.' She waved, and disappeared.

'Trade Magnate,' Shaw said with something of disgust in her voice.

'Part of the prophecy,' Nate said with a sigh. 'Darn!'

'It's nonsense,' she said as she drew her arms around his neck and kissed him. Her black cloud dissipated.

CHAPTER 17 — RUCKUS AT A COURT

The next morning, Shaw collected her royal visitors, and they ported to Yavam Island.

'Where does the surprise tour bring us this time?' Agusta said as she looked around the large barn full of weaponry. 'It looks like an armory.'

'It is,' Shaw said. 'This is Yavam Island. It's across from Port Naar, on the other side of the Emerang Sea. We captured it from pirates. Then we found the people here are descendants of Nanstalgarodian refugees. Jem considers the kids here her kin. Like the Tradeports, the island is part of the Peaks.'

They went outside in a sultry drizzle and walked the path between the hills to the town. Here and there, they saw boys and girls at work in the fields, oblivious to the weather as they toiled.

'They're not slacking,' Liom said. 'Aren't they bothered by the rain?'

'Why?' A broad-shouldered boy had been half hidden behind a parked farm cart, but now he straightened and when he recognized her, he smiled broadly. 'Shaw! Welcome back, ma'am! You come to see how we're doing?'

'Uthur,' Shaw said, awestruck as she peered at the boy's face. 'What a terrific beard!'

The Yavam Island boss stroked his dark growth. 'Our elders hid their origins out of fear. We won't; we're from Nanstalgarod and by the gods, we'll look the part.' He spread his hands. 'Don't worry; we won't behave like them. That's not how we've been brought up.'

'I have the greatest trust in you guys,' Shaw said.

'Thank you,' Uthur said. 'And to answer your question,' he added to Liom. 'We're all working for ourselves. Those guys are tilling their own fields, for the food we all live on. Why would they slack? If they did, they and we all would go hungry.'

'I get it,' Liom said. 'For our field workers it should be the same, but somehow they don't see it that way.'

'Perhaps because they don't feel responsible?' Uthur said. 'Your field workers are servants. These guys are not. They're all friends and equals.'

'And who owns the ground?' Gerben said.

'Every business, the farms, the mill, the inn and all others are collectively owned by the people who work there. They share the work, the costs, and the profits.'

'I don't think that will work with us,' Liom said.

'You're a landowner?' Uthur said. 'Then I suppose it won't.' He smiled. 'You won't give up your gods' given ancient rights, of course.'

Liom grinned back. 'No way.'

'Still,' Gerben said. 'Would it help if I were to parcel up my acres and rent them out to my workers, instead of paying their wages?'

'You mean they pay you?' Liom said skeptically. 'Why would they do that?'

'If they could earn more money by selling their beans and stuff directly, it would be in their interest,' Gerben said. 'I must think on this. Thank you for your advice, Supervisor Uthur.'

'You're welcome. If you folks want to see how we do, I'll walk with you. We're quite proud of our progress.'

'You're rightly proud,' Shaw said when they had seen all. 'Last I saw this place it was halfway to a ruin. Broken windows, sagging roofs, rubble and desolation. Now it's all neat and tidy.'

'Divine Zenyunthalata is with us,' Uthur said. 'He made the grass grow on the hills, and the fields sprout corn and bean stalks. We worked hard, of course, thatching and glazing, But without our god's help we wouldn't have come this far.'

'You have earned his help,' Shaw said resolutely. 'I am proud of you all.'

'It is a pretty place,' Agusta said to Uthur. 'And your enthusiasm is an inspiration.'

They walked back to the armory, and when they came to the cart, shook hands with the Yavam island boss.

Inside the barn they found a young Vanhaari portaller busy polishing a stack of tools, mumbling by herself.

'Oh, there you are,' Shaw said. 'I hadn't seen you when we arrived.'

The girl blinked as if she woke up from a dream. 'Did you port in? I'm sorry; I didn't notice you. There isn't all that much traffic, and when I'm working I only hear magic.'

'What are you doing?' Nate said.

'I call it spell-polishing,' the girl said self-consciously. 'I find when I rub them and mumble my spell, the tools work better. We did a test, and my polished hoes stayed sharp much longer than the unpolished ones.'

'That's useful,' Nate said. He looked at Shaw. 'Would that be teachable, or is it a unique talent?'

'Don't ask me,' the girl said. 'I don't know what I'm doing. Only what it does.' She grinned at her own logic.

'That's not unusual,' Shaw said. 'It's something the Institute should've noticed, but they didn't. Don't break your head over it; Lady Ruth will send someone trained to find out. I'd like you to port us to the Myrlia warehouse.'

'Just a moment,' the girl said. She put down the tools and the polishing cloth, and stood with her head bowed. 'There,' she said brightly. 'Now I can leave them. Myrlia coming up.'

Seconds later, they were in the portal room of the immense warehouse. Portal mage Enric received them with a smile and a bow, with the young mage Aliq at his side.

'Ms. Shaw,' Enric said. 'Lord Amsalon advised us of your coming, and of the royal visit.'

'Perfect,' Shaw said. 'Your Majesty, Mage Enric is our portaller here, and Mage Aliq works with him.'

The boy bowed almost double. 'I am most honored to find your mighty gaze notice me a little, Your High Majesty.'

'Are you the one who foiled that infamous bombing attempt?' Agusta said. 'Then I am glad to meet you, Mage Aliq. We of Malgarth are unused to magic, but we adore heroes.'

The boy blushed furiously, and Enric came to his aid. 'Mage Aliq has offered to lead you around the warehouse. After that, I will port you to Illansor House, where Lord Amsalon will handle the rest.'

'A round of the warehouse will mean a few miles' walk,' Shaw said. 'This is easily our biggest place, after Smalkand. You will find treasures here most in the Weal have never seen.'

They walked into the warehouse proper, and Agusta stopped in her tracks. 'Oh dear,' she said, gazing at the many hurrying workers amid the rows upon rows of racks stretching out in every direction.

Aliq waited patiently until the impression had sunk in. He didn't speak; being born into the lowest Hizmyran caste had taught him to keep his mouth shut until it had become a habit.

When Agusta sighed and relaxed, he bowed and led them past stacks of hand-painted porcelain, gleaming copperware and delicate glassworks.

They tasted glazed fruits, pieces of spicy dry sausages, and at the specials section, Shaw offered her guests a light brown sweet.

'Hmm, nice,' Agusta said.

'I could eat a box of those,' Jonna said happily.

'I wouldn't advise it,' Nate said. 'These are toffees. Converted to your coinage, ten of those would cost a merchant six thousand pieces of gold.'

'You mean...' Agusta said in a strangled voice. 'I just ate six hundred gold coins?'

Shaw nodded. 'Yes. It's a rare delicacy, mostly bought by people who want to show off their wealth.' She glanced at the high queen. 'Don't worry; we pay our suppliers much less for it. It's a fool's price, but at the last sale, merchants came to fisticuffs over the remaining ten.'

After that, Aliq brought the shocked royals back to the portal.

'I hope Your Majesty enjoyed the sight?' Enric said.

'Her Majesty is a bit upset by the price of sweets,' Liom said. 'So am I, by the way.'

'Toffees?' Enric said. 'It is idiocy. But apparently people *want* them, and as long as they aren't necessaries of life I don't really care.'

'It's decadent,' Gerben said. 'If you're that rich...' He shook his head angrily.

'Let's go see Lord Amsalon,' Shaw said quickly. 'Thanks for the tour, Aliq.'

The boy smiled and bowed again. Then Enric ported them away to the hall of Illansor House, where Amsalon stood waiting to receive them. At his back was Captain Hizar, the royal adjutant.

'Welcome, Ma'am,' he said. 'His Majesty the King is all agog to meet with his sister from the south.'

'Sister?' Agusta said, lifting an eyebrow.

'Not really; King Rashaunt is in his sixtieth year. It is the royal kinship he claims.'

'Ah,' Agusta said. 'Kinship is not a Malgarth ruler's strongest point. Our upbringing doesn't favor such ties.'

Captain Hizar bowed. 'I informed the crown prince of your remark, Ma'am,' he said politely. 'His royal highness will no doubt pass it on to his father.'

'Mindspeak,' Shaw said.

Agusta smiled. 'Discrete of you, Captain.'

'I have a motorcade waiting,' Amsalon said. 'I was certain Prince Meshan was about to send his own, and I was just as certain you wouldn't like their driving. So I asked Captain Abbram, and he sent Lieutenant Kashim with his troop to do the honors.'

'Good of you and Abbram,' Shaw said. 'Meshan's men are road devils.'

'The prince is an impatient man,' Hizar said.

Shaw pulled a face. 'Let's keep it at that.'

Outside, a long row of steamcarts waited. Kashim stood at their head and saluted as they came out of the gate.

'Good to see you, Kashim,' Shaw said. 'I know you will keep the drivers from racing though busy streets at sixty miles an hour. Her Majesty would like to see something more of this city than people scrambling for safety.'

The lieutenant chuckled. 'I told the lead driver to keep the meter at thirty, on pain of instant death. I'm a former Disposable; he believed me.'

They got into the center cart, and slowly the motorcade rode away. Near the market, the first driver had to use his bullhorn to get the masses step aside.

'How big is this place?' Jonna whispered.

'About two hundred square miles,' Nate said.

Agusta didn't speak; she looked at the teeming masses with something akin to horror.

'There seem to be more people in this city alone than we have in the whole of Malgarth,' Liom said.

'I don't know the exact number,' Shaw said.

'One million sixteen hundred fifty,' Amsalon said. 'About one-eighteenth of our total population.

'I see,' Liom said. He stared out of the window, arms crossed, and outwardly calm.

Suddenly there was a loud noise of a trumpet screaming in rage and with a rough bump, the steamcart came to a halt.

Amsalon cursed. 'Stay inside,' he said curtly, as he jumped from the cart.

'What's wrong?' Liom said.

'Elephant trouble,' Amsalon said, and closed the door.

Then the whole cart rocked violently as something gray and massive pushed past. Something heavy slapped the roof. The driver, seated in the open front of the cart, had disappeared.

Loud voices shouted, and Kashim's boys appeared at the other side of the steamcart, their blades in their hands.

Others screamed, and then men with long stakes clambered over the steamcart, prodding at the enormous gray shape and yelling incomprehensible curses. The beast backed away, still trumpeting and waving his ears big as a threemaster's spritsails.

Then the driver reappeared as from nowhere, and Amsalon dove in just in time before with a jolt, the steamcart moved forward. The engine roared as they rushed off fast, to get the royal visitor to safety.

'Well,' Agusta said in a cool voice. 'You won't meet this in Landfalln.'

'My apologies, Your Majesty,' Amsalon said stiffly. 'This shouldn't have happened.'

'What was the matter with that beast?' Gerben said.

'It probably was our lead cart's claxon,' Amsalon said. 'It must have startled the elephant as we passed.'

'You have *no* idea how difficult it is to bring a bit of adventure into your visit,' Shaw said with a straight face. 'What's the use of going abroad if it is just as tame as staying at home?'

'True,' Liom said with a hint of a smile. 'It is very considerate of you, Shaw.'

'It will give us something to boast of to all those homebodies in Croncliff,' Jonna said.

'Would your soldiers have attacked that walking mountain with only their swords?' Gerben said.

'Yes,' Shaw said.

'You once mentioned they were trained as suicide soldiers?' Liom said.

'Disposables,' Nate said. 'Lightly armed troops that storm a breach to catch the fire from the enemy. Cannon fodder. The crown prince offered them to us, and we took the whole half-battalion. They proved extremely tough and brave soldiers.'

With a screech of brakes, the motorcade came to a halt in front of the stairs leading to the royal palace.

'Guys, full court ceremonial,' Jonna said. She looked the two lords over and nodded. 'It will have to do. You know your positions. Ready?'

Amsalon and the adjutant got out first, followed by the two lords, then Jonna, Nate, Shaw and finally Agusta.

Then, in the opposite order, they ascended the stairs.

Agusta's face was as expressionlessly royal as any coin, with Shaw at her side trying not to give in to a fit of the giggles.

At the top of the stairs the crown prince waited to receive them.

'Your Majesty,' he said with a stiff bow. 'You honor us with your presence.' His greeted Shaw with a handshake and a smile. 'High Merchant, it is good to see you again. Please, my father is eagerly awaiting your arrival, High Queen.'

'I am very happy to visit your beautiful country, Royal Highness,' Agusta said.

They walked down the long corridor until they came to the throne room.

'Her Majesty Agusta, High Queen of Malgarth!' a herald's loud voice cried, and the room went silent. All present bowed as Agusta strode between them toward the throne with Amsalon, Jonna and the two lords behind her.

Shaw gripped Nate's arm and waited until the king had greeted his royal guest, before she followed inside.

'Don't announce us,' she said to the herald. 'I prefer to slip in silently.'

The man frowned at the breach of protocol, but held his mouth when Shaw and Nate walked past to stand watching Agusta exchange pleasantries with King Rashaunt.

She seemed to have herself well in hand, and Shaw was glad to stay where she was. The Hizmyran king wasn't a bad man, but he bored her to tears, as did his whole useless court.

After an endless time, the king led his royal guest away.

A servant came and bade Shaw and Nate to attend, so they followed him to a pleasant room where a table full of refreshments waited.

Stifling a sigh, Shaw went to greet the king.

'High Merchant,' Rashaunt said chidingly. 'We can't have you hiding in our court, ma'am.'

Shaw smiled. 'I didn't want to detract from her majesty's visit,' she said.

'Now sit you down and enjoy some of our specialties. Both on the table and on the floor.' The king clapped his hands, and from behind a curtain musicians began to play. A group of scantily clad dancers came in, both male and female, and brought a spectacular series of acrobatic feats.

After that three men with dancing snakes and a lady who swallowed flaming swords. Then a man in desert robes brought a basket from which came a singing voice. It brought a seaman's shanty in a high, slurred voice.

'Behold!' the man cried. The basket opened and a winged, snakelike figure came out. It was a dull yellow and tried to fly as it sang pathetically. It looked sick, too thin and utterly unhappy.

Shaw's chair crashed back. 'A wyrmling!' she cried. *'Haai-Bo? I have need of you right now!'*

Seconds later, he teleported in over the table. *'Ma'am?'* Then he cried out. 'Wiu-To? Cruel! Who dares? WHO DARES?'

225

The man dropped the basket and stared with open mouth at the wrathful wyrmling, big as a thirty-pound tabby cat, with a mouth like a crocodile.

'But... but... The beast's mine!' he stammered. 'I caught it. I taught it to sing. It's... it's a sort of parrot.'

'You cannot possess a wyrmling,' Shaw cried. 'That is a crime! They're people, not beasts!'

'YOU... MADE... HIM... DRUNK!' Haai-Bo thundered. 'Alcohol is poison to a wyrmling. Murderer! Assassin!'

'Guards!' the king commanded. 'Arrest that man.'

Haai-Bo spoke quickly to the yellow wyrmling. Then the little one was sick on the floor.

Shaw hurried around the table and picked him up.

'Hot milk,' Haai-Bo said. He craned his long head at a servant. 'Bring lots of creamy hot milk. Hurry!'

The servant ran.

'You there!' Shaw said to the shaking man in the grip of two big soldiers. 'Where did you find this wyrmling?'

'I... I... I bought him,' the man whispered. 'From a hunter who had captured the beast up north.'

'Not a beast!' Haai-Bo snapped. 'Are your children beasts? Neither are our young.'

A servant hurried in with a bowl of hot milk. 'Here,' Shaw said. 'Milk for you, little one.' She held the wyrmling while he drank greedily. 'You know him? Is he one of your kin?'

'He is Wiu-To, of my sept, a warrior wyrm,' Haai-Bo said. 'This is disgraceful.' He hissed at the shaking man. 'You will not harm a wyrmling! None will harm a wyrmling! Or else face the wrath of Haai-Bo.' He waved his wings, and wild flames engulfed the man.

All in the room cried out, but when the flames died, the man was still there, unharmed.

'Next flames will be hot!' Haai-Bo said. 'Let him go, king. The man is a fool, but if we kill humans for being fools...' He looked round the table and his cackle was somehow icily disturbing. 'Let him go.'

Rashaunt made a furious gesture. 'Take that man away!' he said, his brown face livid. 'High Merchant, I am deeply sorry.'

'Don't,' Shaw said quickly, realizing the king was feeling mortified. 'It is no fault of any but that man. Thanks to you we discovered he had one of those we seek.'

'Get meat,' Haai-Bo said to the room. 'My sept brother hungers. He is too small for his age.

Amsalon handed Shaw a platter of meat sticks in thick gravy.

'Here,' Shaw said. 'Open your mouth, Wiu-To. Fill your belly with food.'

Ravenously, the wyrmling gobbled up several of the sticks. Then he burped and fell asleep.

'Nate and I will take the little one to Smalkand,' Shaw said. 'No need for her majesty to break off her visit; Lord Amsalon will see about her return to our headquarters later.'

The king sighed and there was a hint of relief on his face to be spared the humiliation of a visiting queen leaving halfway the feast in her honor. 'Of course,' he said gravely. 'You must care for the young wyrm.'

Shaw rose and bowed to the king. 'We are glad to have found Wiu-To,' she said. 'You have our gratitude, Your Majesty.' She gave Agusta another bow. 'We will await your return in Smalkand, Ma'am.'

The high queen smiled a little shakily. 'You care for the little one, Trade Magnate.'

Shaw turned. 'Haai-Bo, could you...'

They flashed away to reappear in Smalkand's entry hall.

'Let's see what Tymon can do,' Shaw said as she walked through the messroom to the healer's little office.

'Hello,' Tymon said. 'What have you...? A wyrmling? I never...'

He put two gentle fingers on Wiu-To's tummy.

'Bad man made him drunk,' Haai-Bo said. 'Wyrmlings can't handle alcohol.'

'He has eaten?' Tymon said.

'Hot milk and meat in sauce,' Shaw said. 'Was that wrong?'

Tymon didn't answer. He closed his eyes and a white light appeared, enveloping his hand and the little wyrm body. Then a divine chuckle filled the sickbay and Wiu-To opened his eyes.

'Haai-Bo?' he said. 'Was no fever dream? Haai-Bo came?'

'Of course I came,' Haai-Bo said. 'You are safe now, sept brother.'

'Others?' the yellow wyrmling said.

'Tiu-Ti is all right, too. He is with the princess.'

'Oohh, Tiu-Ti good! And princess? You found princess?'

'The lord wyrmcaller found her, but the princess has come. She and I, we have different duties, but we will meet. Later. Can you fly?'

'Don't know. I was sick, sick, long time soo sick. No more. Hunger now.'

'Then go and eat,' Tymon said. 'You need to grow fast.'

'Thanks,' Shaw said. 'Do you heal with Bodrus now?'

'Sometimes,' Tymon said. 'Only in special cases. Lumentis doesn't mind; he accepts Bodrus is stronger.'

The little wyrmling hopped and flapped his wings once, twice, and the third time he lifted off the table. 'Fly, fly, Wiu-To fly!' he yelled.

'So you do, sept brother,' Haai-Bo said. 'Is he well enough for duty, Healer Tymon?'

'As long as he feeds regularly, he is,' Tymon said.

'Then we return to observing Croncliff,' Haai-Bo said. 'Come, I will show you the fat mice.'

Both wyrmlings winked out and Shaw burst out laughing helplessly.

'Poor Rashaunt,' she said. 'He had this lovely repast arranged for Agusta, with wonderful artists, and everything so fine. And then this. A sick wyrmling, Haai-Bo terribly angry and me shouting; how horrible for him.'

'He is a fool,' Nate said. 'Why didn't his people screen the artists? If they had rescued the wyrmling and given him over to us, we would have been profitably grateful. Rashaunt ought to sack the lot of them.'

Shaw whirled around. 'I'm going to have a cawah. I've got a bellyful of those royal meals.' She gripped Nate's arm and walked to the door. Over her shoulder she said to Tymon, 'Thanks. I said it before, and I'll say it again. You're the greatest.'

That evening, Lord Amsalon found Shaw and Nate in the library. 'I brought the high queen safely back,' he said. 'And I must give you this.' He handed her a large box. 'It's from the crown prince; a letter of apology for the little wyrmling, and two pounds of the choosiest meats. King Rashaunt made a proclamation to the populace, saying wyrms are allies, not beasts to be hunted. He fined the idiot who had bought the little one ten gold and enclosed them with the letter, "for the lord wyrmling to dispose of".'

'Give them my thanks,' Shaw said. 'I don't think Wiu-To can write, but I leave that part to him and Haai-Bo. I'll put the meat in the freeze room until we go back.'

'You've got more visits planned?' Amsalon said.

'We'll look in on the *Drakon*. I'm not sure what to do with Kas-Triooz. Do you think you could find fifty armed guys to act as garrison? Abbram's men are not going back there,' Shaw said. 'After that, Wattash. Then we're going back to Croncliff and prepare for the coronation.'

'Fifty soldiers? I can do that, but they'll be garrison grunts; you won't use them for a battle,' Amsalon said.

'I'm not going to; it's just I want to hold on to that keep as a base when we go north again. So I would like it fully functional, with a healer and a transferal. I will tell Abia she can return to Myrlia when your troops arrive.'

Shaw walked with Amsalon back to the portal and saw him off. Then she returned to the mess. Agusta and Jonna were nowhere to be seen, but the two lords sat at the bar.

'You look kind of worn-out,' Shaw said as she joined them.

Liom looked at her. 'That Hizmyran court! Of all the terrible places...' he said. 'What a bunch of useless, vapid...'

'Fatheads,' Gerben added. 'We won't do it that way. I swear to you we won't.' He snorted. 'Agusta wanted to scream, she said. She's probably gone to bed. That idiot Rashaunt with his endless piffle.'

'How's the little wyrm?' Liom said.

'He was in a bad state, but Healer Tymon restored him. Haai-Bo took him back to Croncliff, to feast on your mice.'

Gerben chuckled. 'What a disaster it was. Your big wyrmling looked really angry.'

'He was,' Shaw said. 'Wyrms of his rank have a high sense of their honor, and Wiu-To is his sept brother.'

'What exactly is that?' Gerben said.

'I'm not quite sure,' Shaw said. 'Kinship in wyrms isn't as clear as with us. They are born in the same lay, but I'm not sure whether they are full kin or clan kin. Haai-Bo is the eldest of their sept, the first-born, and of the highest rank.' Shaw frowned, trying to make sense of what was an alien culture. 'Their status isn't inherited; it depends on the number of digits on their hands. Haai-Bo has four fingers, which makes him comparable to a duke. Wiu-To has three, and he is a warrior, while Haai-Bo is a mana-user. Lothi-Mo, the wyrmcaller's companion, has five digits. She is a princess, of the Royal sept of Ancho Dar, the vanished Wyrm

Queen. I believe in the old times the Wyrm Queen decided which ranks would be born, but these new births were random.'

'Nothing what happens these days is random,' Nate said. 'I wouldn't be surprised Divine Bodrus arranged for those wyrmlings to be hatched. They're his creatures, after all.'

Shaw grunted. *Nate could well be right; it all stank.*

CHAPTER 18 — FRIGATE

'The last visit,' Shaw said. She looked at Agusta's face. 'We'll not see any more rulers; Wattash is a province of the Grand Principality of Takkala. Most of the other provinces are in hands of the jinn, but the wyrmcaller liberated Wattash some time ago. Its duke is not an inspiring character to meet, but you should see a bit of his town. And you will like our two warships in the region.'

They flashed away to arrive in *Drakon*'s familiar portal and the heavy smell of blackpowder.

'Something's wrong!' Nate said.

A terrible crashing shook the ship around them, and sent Agusta reeling into Liom's arms.

'What the heck...!' Gerben cried, but the deafening roar of *Drakon*'s artillery drowned his words.

One of the messroom attendants dashed up to them. 'Enemy vessel!' he said breathlessly, his fingers clutching an old boarding pistol. 'A big one!'

'Where's Captain Abia?' Shaw said, trying desperately to appear composed.

'Quarterdeck,' the boy said, and his whole face quivered.

'Nate, take Agusta into the mess and see that she stays there. I'll go find Abia.' Shaw whirled around and ran off.

Once on deck, she stopped in her tracks. The enemy ship was Qoori like theirs, but bigger; a veritable warship, its bridge towering above the smoke perhaps a mile away.

'Bodrus aid us,' Shaw muttered, and she went up the stairs to the quarterdeck.

Beside the quartermaster at the wheel, Abia stood watching the enemy ship, her legs apart and arms crossed. A few feet away, Miran, the midshipman mage, leaned motionless on the railing, his eyes seemingly fixed to the ship's side.

'Shaw!' the flag captain exclaimed. 'You bring reinforcements?'

'I'm sorry,' Shaw said. 'I didn't know. How does it go?'

'She outguns us,' Abia said curtly. 'Three to one, I'd say. Their guns are heavier as well. Xailin said they're operated by the engines instead of their crew's strength. Their broadsides are as regular as clockwork.'

'Qoori navy?'

'Pirates,' Abia said. 'Bokkaners and prisoners.'

'How many pirates?' Shaw said.

'At least fifty; far too many for a boarding party,' Abia said. 'I need all able hands for our own guns.'

Of course, I stole away Kennan and all her marines, Shaw thought.

The enemy ship fired again. Twelve guns belched fire, and Miran waved his hands. Most of the shot crashed into the *Drakon*'s side, and the ship rocked violently. Shaw gasped, expecting flames, gaping holes in the side, and kids dying. But there wasn't any sight of damage, no telltale smoke, no sounds of renting metal and splintering planks; nothing but the banging of some loose gear somewhere. 'What is Miran doing?'

'Shielding the ship,' Abia said. 'He's mind-talking with Portaller Sem, who is with the gunnery officer on the main deck, observing the enemy. Miran has thought up some sort of portable forcefield, and every time Sem warns him of a broadside, he activates it long enough to deflect the shot. Split-second work, but up to now they've kept us afloat. I don't know how long they'll keep it up, though.'

Shaw stared at Miran's face and saw the strain he was under. The midshipman came from the Weal navy, where he'd had to keep his magic a secret, and he lacked any real arcane training. Shaw had no idea of his limits, and the boy probably never before had a chance to find out. And Sem, who was barely fourteen and a portaller, was one of those kids kicked out of the Institute. Today those two had the fate of the flagship in their hands.

Shaw turned away. 'We never counted on the mages being out of action.' Then another broadside crashed into *Drakon*'s side. Miran caught it, his face twisting with the effort.

Drakon fired back, but the smoke from the shots drifted between the ships like a thick fog and hid the results from the eye.

'*Haai-Bo?*' Shaw thought urgently. '*You hear me?*'

'*Of course I do,*' the wyrmling said stuffily. Then he squawked. '*Sea battle?*'

'*Sure thing,*' Shaw said. '*Going badly. I need Kennan and one of Abbram's troops aboard* Drakon *right now.*'

'*Give me a moment,*' Haai-Bo said.

Five minutes later, he and Wiu-To popped out of nowhere over Shaw's head.

'Troops are grabbing their gear; will arrive soon,' he said. He cackled. 'We'll be scouts now. Sept brother, you follow me, but fly high, high. No silly risk takings, hear?'

'I'll be sneaky shadow wyrm,' Wiu-To said. 'Observe only.'

'Good,' Haai-Bo said, and they shot away.

Then the sound of cheering came from below, and Kennan came running aft, with Lieutenant Kashim of the innocent face on his heels, while their men gathered on the main deck.

'Reporting for orders, Flag Captain,' the marine said.

Abia answered his salute calmly. 'I'm glad to see you gentlemen,' she said. 'We're sorely beset.'

Behind her, Miran waved his hands and caught another broadside on his shield.

'You want us to go and put an end to that nonsense?' Kennan said.

'If you'd be so kind.'

'Do you have any info about the enemy?' Kashim said.

'Haai-Bo just went over there with his sept brother,' Shaw said. 'We should await his return.'

'Return!' Haai-Bo cried, as he came swooping down. 'We're the fastest spies in the whole world. Fifty-seven pirates, light on the booze and drugs; these are Nimmendal's own men. The gunners are seventy-nine Qoori; cowed and blindly obeying man-boys they be.'

'We'll concentrate on the pirates,' Shaw said. 'Forget the Qoori, unless they prove bothersome. Just be careful; if those Bokkaners are sober, they'll be dangerous. We...' She looked at the two expressionless officers. 'But I don't have to tell you that.'

'No,' Kennan said drily. 'But we don't mind you warning us. Kashim, let's go.' He shouted an order and, squad after squad, over a hundred brooms rose into the air.

Without a word, Shaw followed the two officers as they flew their troops to the enemy ship.

In the air over the frigate they stopped for a few seconds until Kennan waved his hand and they dropped down to the deck.

For a moment, Shaw was disoriented. Then she recognized the ship had a similar layout as *Royal Sashu*.

There was no proper deck, but a gangway round the superstructure. The guns... under other circumstances Shaw would've stared. No brass cannons and carriages; all artillery was part of the superstructure and of a type she hadn't seen before.

The Qoori gunners were all classless peon kids, hardly more than uniformed slaves. They ignored the boarders and worked their guns feverishly.

A pirate subofficer screamed orders and a mass of Bokkaners came running.

'At them!' Kennan snapped, and grimly silent his forces went to battle.

Those cannons must stop, Shaw thought and she ran past the fighting men into the ship's superstructure. She found the stairs and went down. A pirate shouted from below and ran to intercept her. Shaw didn't think; she jumped on top of him, her knives ready, and he went down screaming, gushing blood. Shaw ran on until she reached the engine room. Here was another pirate, a thin man in a fancy hat, brandishing a gun at a Qoori boy.

Neither had seen her come in, and Shaw's first knife entered his back. The man staggered around, cursing. A shot rang, echoing wildly through the room. Shaw struck, her knife went into his breast, and his hands gripped her wrist. Then, from behind, the engine room boy brained the pirate with a large monkey-wrench.

For a second, she and the Qoori stared at each other. Then, a loud crash shook the ship. Lights flickered and somewhere, an alarm blared. *Drakon* was still shooting and Shaw saw a flash of fear cross the Qoori boy's face.

'Cut the power!' she said.

The boy frowned.

Darn, he doesn't speak Vulgar, Shaw thought. She pointed at the power crystals and pantomimed pulling them out.

The boy nodded and went to the control panel. He pushed a series of buttons, and around them the sound of the engines died.

The ship shook as she fired another broadside.

Curse it; isn't that artillery powered from here? Shaw turned to the Qoori engineer and imitated firing a gun. The guy hurried to a set of stairs at the back.

Shaw retrieved her knives and followed him. Halfway up was a second room, with another white-clad boy, and an unshaven pirate with a dirty yellow cloth tied round his head.

The first boy screamed something incomprehensible and dragged the pirate away. The second lad calmly gripped a lever and pulled. Lights flashed, a clamoring siren fell silent, and over their heads, the cannons fell silent. Together, the two boys bashed the pirate against a bulkhead until he stopped moving and let him drop.

Shaw slapped their shoulders, grinned, and ran all the ladders up to the bridge. Here, a tall pirate in a captain's coat was screaming orders at two Qoori boys in officer uniforms. One of them was speaking urgently over the intercom, his face puzzled as if he didn't understand what he heard. The other boy had the wheel. Shaw didn't hesitate and jumped on the pirate's neck. Pulling his head back with one arm, she slit his throat with her other hand. The pirate's handgun went off and the midshipman at the wheel yelled. Then Shaw dropped back to the floor and watched the pirate fall, his blood spreading over the deck.

'Who - are - you?' the first midshipman said in careful Vulgar.

'Friends,' Shaw said. Then Kennan ran onto the bridge, his blade dripping blood.

'Been doing it again?' he said, grinning. 'Captured the ship all on your own?'

'All those big guns are such a waste of power,' Shaw said loftily. 'I asked the engine room to silence them. Such obliging boys, they immediately saw it my way.' She clenched her fists to stop them from shaking.

'Trembling is a natural reaction,' Kennan said. 'You're not a killing machine, after all.'

'Are we done here?' Shaw said.

'The ship is ours,' the marine captain said. 'No serious wounds.'

Then one of the Qoori midshipmen screamed. Shaw turned to see what was wrong and saw the dead captain woodenly stagger to his feet.

'You!' a heavy voice said from the dead mouth. 'I see you now, Trade Magnate. You thwarted me once too often. The temerity to attack my flagship! I will hunt you now, like the cattle you are. I, Nimmendal, Prince of Angsthafn and Lord of the Seas will hunt you myself, and when I have you, your carcass will make a nice side dish at my next banquet.'

'Hide and cower, fat fool,' Shaw said contemptuously. 'We of Jinnbane's people will come for *you*, Nimmendal. Prince and lord of nothing you are; a windbag, a has-been with a lot of silly tricks.'

'You dare!' The bellowing voice sounded strange from a dead mouth and the blood-drenched body of the slain pirate shook with the jinni's rage. 'Die, cattle!'

The dead captain had a dagger in his bloodless hand and sprang at Shaw. Kennan pushed her roughly aside as he hewed at the reanimated body. The pirate head bounced off the stiff shoulders, but still the body came on.

Shaw backed away, feeling sick to her stomach at the sight of the headless corpus. It waved a nonchalant arm and moved Kennan aside.

One of the midshipmen came running with a long boathook in his hands, his face twisted in fear as he struck. The dead body disregarded the pole sticking into its back and came at Shaw, the knife in its bloodied claws pointing straight at her.

Shaw's own dagger flashed, but she knew it wouldn't save her. She backed away, and he followed, slowly as if walking asked for a lot of effort. Her legs were stopped by the steel binnacle beside the wheel, and she raised futile hands.

Feeling strangely impassive, she noted the bit of backbone sticking from the headless neck, and the bits of severed arteries and *things* and...

With a flash of waving wings, Haai-Bo appeared on the bridge.

'This won't do,' the wyrmling said disdainfully. 'Such foul jinni magic will not threaten the noble Magnate.' There was an echo of jolly laughter in his voice, and a bright light exploded all over the dead pirate. At once, the body slumped to the ground, and the knife clattered away.

Shaw stared at her advisor, and Haai-Bo, eyes whirling, looked back at her.

'Thank you,' she said finally.

'It is not part of an advisor's duties,' Haai-Bo said haughtily. 'But that reanimation spell is an abomination to Divine Bodrus.'

'I'm sure it is,' Shaw said, and her voice shook only a little.

She turned to Kennan, who had come to his feet, blood running from his nose. 'My thanks to you as well, Captain Kennan. You have a mighty cleave.' Lastly she looked at the two Qoori boys, one clutching a bleeding arm. Both were palely blue and shaken, but in command of themselves.

'It's over, gentlemen,' Shaw said. 'Well done. Is your arm still bleeding?'

The wounded one opened his mouth, but no words came.

'It is,' the other said. 'I will attend to him later, if I may.'

'I will send our healer up,' Kennan said, and he left.

Shaw looked around at the spacious bridge, much like the one of *Royal Sashu*, with a grand view over the whole vessel and the surrounding sea. 'What ship is this?'

'His Imperial Majesty's Frigate *Glory of Xalt*,' the first boy said, standing at attention. 'I am Aspirant Huono. If you are in command of the boarders, may Tahin and I be permitted to kill ourselves?'

Shaw looked at him gravely. 'No. Neither the emperor nor I would be served with your deaths. We need you alive to help officer this ship and fight back against our mutual enemies.'

Both boys nodded expressionlessly. 'We are your slaves, so it will be as you say,' Huono said in a toneless voice.

'You are not slaves, either,' Shaw said. 'We will discuss this later. Tell your crew to secure the guns, power up and close on *Drakon*. Can you manage that?'

Huono saluted. 'Most certainly, ma'am.' He gripped the wheel, while the other aspirant gave a series of orders over the intercom, cradling his bleeding arm against his chest.

The deck trembled and slowly, the ship turned to the ordered position.

Then the troop healer came in, a sparse chap Shaw had only seen from a distance.

'Tsk, tsk,' he said, looking Tahin over. 'Another tough guy going on with his duties while bleeding to death. Your turnover in crewmembers must be quite high. Now come here.'

He gripped Tahin's shoulder and pulled down his shirt. With two fingers over the wound, he smiled grimly at the boy. 'It will leave a scar,' he said. 'An honorable wound to boast of.'

'They're not feeling very honorable,' Shaw said. 'Yet they should; under duress they behaved like responsible officers.'

A buzzer sounded and Tahin managed to activate the speaker with his good hand.

'Boat alongside,' he said to Huono.

Shaw looked through the large windows at the ship's entry port and the officer stepping aboard. It was Xailin, *Drakon*'s third officer. Of course Abia would have sent her. She was the Qoori girl they had saved from the burning slave market at Brisa; the ship's original junior officer, who was the Qoori Emperor's heir to boot. She was a straight-backed girl of some twenty years, with the blue complexion that was the only difference between a Qoori and a gray Vanhaari.

She entered the bridge, and both aspirants turned to stone. Huono spoke in stiff Qoori, but Xailin interrupted him.

'We will speak Vulgar,' she said. 'I am *Drakon*'s third officer, Xailin za-chan-Qoor.'

Huono's eyes turned glassy at the mention of her imperial title, and for a second Shaw thought he was going to faint. Then he crashed to his knees, touching the deck with his forehead.

'Don't you dare,' the healer said, and he gripped Tahin to stop him from doing the same.

'Stand up, Aspirant,' Xailin said sternly. 'I serve as a naval officer; a salute will suffice. Nor will you be permitted to commit honorable suicide. You shall regain your honor through faithful service to the ship and to the lord wyrmcaller.' She gave a rare smile. 'And of course to his most honorable partner, High Merchant Shaw.'

'But I told you *that* already,' Shaw said, as Huono came to his feet, looking dazed. 'I will return to *Drakon.*' She looked at Xailin. 'Will you take command here?'

'No, ma'am,' Xailin said. 'I am a technician and not qualified to be a frigate captain. I came to speak with the crew.'

'Perhaps you will inspect the ship,' Shaw said. 'There is a boy in the engine room, and another one in the room where the guns are controlled. Are they apprentices too, Mr. Huono?'

'Yes, ma'am,' Huono said. 'Engineering Apprentice and Gunnery Control Apprentice. The others are the Junior Bos'n's Mate, the Gunner Apprentice and the Purser's Apprentice.'

'Purser?' Shaw said. She didn't suppose it was the same job as the PTC pursers. 'What does he do?'

'At present, he keeps us fed, ma'am,' Huono said earnestly. 'The pirates weren't very active in ship's handling and they didn't seem to require food. As his department's duties include overseeing the cooks, the purser's apprentice took over the organization of the galley. The results aren't very good, and we're all out of fresh produce, but thanks to him, we have our daily meal.'

'You can sail the ship, Mr. Huono?' Shaw asked.

'Yes, ma'am,' the boy said. 'Though we are in strange waters and I have no charts. But both Tahin and I can sail her; we have been standing watch and watch ever since it... happened, taking short naps in a corner.' He pointed at a heap of coats at the back of the bridge.

'How did you manage that?' Shaw said. 'It must be exhausting.'

'We applied *Ai-zu-Yoh*, Calm the Mind,' the boy said. 'The ritual kept us going.'

That name Shaw remembered. When they had cut out *Drakon* in Brisa, Lieutenant Chagan had been walking around with a broken leg, thanks to that same ritual. Still, it couldn't be healthy in the long run.

'When *Xalt* has moored, I want you and Tahin to see me aboard *Drakon* to discuss the situation,' she said. 'Meanwhile Lieutenant Xailin can explain to you how we arranged matters with the *Drakon*'s original crew.'

Shaw walked down to the deck, noting the wooden, fearful way the young Qoori sailors went about their duties. They must've seen Xailin come aboard, and probably expected to be shot, or worse. The imperial navy maintained a rigid discipline, and these boys would have been treated more like serfs than seamen.

We'll change all that! Shaw thought. Then she got her broom and flew back to *Drakon*'s quarterdeck.

'Shaw!' High Queen Agusta cried as she landed. 'You're covered in blood.'

Nate gripped her hands. 'Been playing marine again, love?' he said lightly.

Shaw grinned, then started to shiver. 'But we got the ship. It's another bunch of kids, just like *Drakon*'s guys used to be.'

Captain Abia watched her in silence. 'Thank you,' she said finally. 'You and Kennan's lads saved the day for us.'

Shaw smiled waveringly. 'It gave me a chance to show off my awesomeness,' she said. 'Not that I'm feeling very formidable right now.' She stared at her bloodied uniform.

'Didn't you have a spare one on board?' Nate said.

Shaw tried to focus her thoughts. *Did she?* 'I think so. I... I'm going below. There are two midshipmen left alive; I told them to report to me once they had anchored. Please show them to my cabin.'

'In an hour's time,' Nate said. 'Come.' He took her arm and together they walked to the great cabin reserved for either her or Eskandar. At the door he stopped.

'Don't be silly,' Shaw said. 'Come inside. You've seen me undressed often enough.' Nudity hadn't been a problem in the orphanage, and later at Fort Jamril they always swam naked.

'You sit on the bed,' Shaw said. She opened the closet. 'You were right! It's not my best, but it is a uniform. I'm having a quick wash and meanwhile I'll tell you all.'

And so she did, in all the gory details. Suddenly she faltered. 'Nimmendal spoke to me!' she said urgently. 'He reanimated the pirate captain whose throat I'd just cut. Called me Trade Magnate! He threatened to come after me himself. Then the dead pirate attacked me with a knife. Kennan decapitated the body, but it just came on. Then Haai-Bo appeared and did something magic, and it was over.'

'Nimmendal finally reacted?' Nate said. 'I wondered why it took him so long.'

'My attacking his flagship did it,' Shaw shouted over the noise of running water as she washed her hair. 'All the other matters weren't personal, but this stung him.' Quickly she went on with the rest of her tale.

Nate listened and when she was done, he was silent so long it scared her.

'Nate?'

'Next time I'm coming with you,' he said calmly. 'You can go fighting pirates as often as you like, but I'm not staying behind anymore.'

'I don't want you hurt,' she said.

'I'm not that interested in getting hurt myself,' he said. 'But there it is. You're not going without me.'

His tone told her he wasn't going to budge on this one and without a word she gave in. Grabbing a dry towel, she rubbed her short hair dry, and went into the bedroom, clean and naked.

'You've grown,' he said impassively.

She couldn't help but grin. 'That happens when you're nearly sixteen. Do you mind?'

'Nah,' he said. 'It suits you.'

She dressed quickly. Then she walked over and gripped his shoulders. 'Nimmendal attacking me was the blippy limit! We must attack. We can't afford to put it off any longer; Angsthafn must fall.' Then she gave him a quick kiss.

There was a knock on the door. Nate started, and she grinned. 'Guilty conscience?'

Outside were Abia and Xailin with the two Qoori boys.

Shaw went to her table, and the others joined her. Only the aspirants remained standing stiffly at attention.

'Sit down,' Shaw said patiently.

Huono stared as if he'd misunderstood. 'High Merchant, Ma'am?'

'Sit down,' Shaw repeated. 'We're not that formal.'

Gingerly, the two perched on the edge of their chairs.

'Now tell me what happened,' Shaw said. 'In your own words.'

Huono swallowed. 'Two months ago, the *Glory of Xalt* was stationed at Oun-ti, his Imperial Majesty's southern naval base. One evening, while out on patrol, we were hailed by a trade schooner. She showed the flag of the Aincham Commerciality, a very great trading house, so the captain let them come alongside.'

The Aincham Commerciality. Shaw remembered that name; they had been *Drakon*'s original owners. The greatest trade house of Qoor, Xailin had called them. Of course they would have waited for her.

'Then a boat drew alongside,' Huono said. 'A person came on board, wearing a long riding-cloak. He spoke with the captain, and shortly after he went back to his boat, to return with fifteen men dressed like pirates. Of course we were alarmed, but the captain said they were sent by the Emperor's tihang; agents of the Imperial secret service, going to infiltrate a pirate base.'

'An uncommonly clever trick,' Shaw said. 'Especially with a letter from the Emperor's secretary.'

Huono nodded. 'All was false,' he said softly. 'We sailed across the Emerang Sea until we were utterly alone. Then the slaughter began. First, they locked the bulkhead to the day crew's quarters. Then, while they held the night crew at gunpoint, they killed the officers and the subofficers. After them, they killed every sailor of both watches; all but the young ones.'

'That's what they always do,' Shaw said. 'What then?'

'They ordered us south,' Huono said. 'Then we sighted this ship. The *Drakon of Ilzhar!* Everything is such a chaos, we didn't know she and the Son of the Gods' heir had gone missing. The pirates were very excited at the sight of her and had us attack as soon as we were in range of our new long guns. Only...' He sounded puzzled now. 'Our so fine guns didn't do any damage. Yours did to us, but our shots appeared to bounce off.' He hesitated. 'I'm not sure we could have kept it going much longer.'

Shaw glanced at Abia. 'That was a very clever trick of young Miran.'

'It's good to know it worked,' Abia said.

'Anyhow, you finally got your frigate, love,' Nate said.

'Is *Xalt* still seaworthy?' Shaw asked.

'We had a quick look,' Xailin said. 'Our gunners scored some holes, and one compartment is flooded, but her bulkheads are holding. If we take it slow, she should reach Myrlia.'

'In that case, Captain Abia, would you escort *Xalt* to Myrlia and arrange with Lord Amsalon for a dockyard priority appointment? Kindly tell *Sashu* to return to Myrlia as well; we'll find another solution for Kas-Triooz. I want to hold on to that keep, but there's no need for Tamyas' kids to hang around there doing nothing.'

'Are you coming back here?' Abia said.

'I sure am,' Shaw said. 'I have the coronation business in Malgarth, but after that I want a look at Sashuni. If *Xalt* is repaired in time.'

Shaw looked at the two midshipmen. 'Now you, gentlemen. Did Lieutenant Xailin tell you your choices? Return to Qoori as dead men with your honor in shards, or join the wyrmcaller's service and be reborn as Peak naval officers?'

The two looked at each other.

'If the Heir of Qoor chose for your side, who are we to refuse?' Huono said. 'We will join you, ma'am.'

Shaw held out a hand and the boys hesitantly took it. 'Welcome.' She came to her feet. 'I leave it to you to convince the crew. Are they *khuial* — bondsmen?'

'Not all, but many of them, ma'am,' Huono said. 'Such is common for the lower ratings.'

'Does that mean those will never get a promotion?' Nate said.

'The khuial? Never, lord.'

Nate nodded. 'Tell them they are all free men here. To Qoor they are dead, and so are their bonds. Here they start afresh as free sailors of the Peaks Navy. They will draw the same pay as every sailor, and in due course the able ones will be promoted.'

Xailin gave Shaw a hard look. 'I thought that idea disgusting,' she said. 'It went against all I believed in. I knew khuial were failed men, and to give them responsibility was foolish.'

She turned her glance to the two midshipmen. 'I have seen those same sailors in action since. I have seen the change in them. They became two, maybe three times better at their tasks than they had been. The ones Captain Abia promoted never failed us, and even the others outshone all but the best Qoori sailors. When I become Daughter of the Gods, I'm going to look long and hard at the whole khuial system.'

Shaw put a hand on Xailin's arm 'Thank you,' she said. 'I think the results will surprise you.' She came to her feet. 'Now I must pick up my guests. Have you been able to meet my main guest?'

Abia shook her head. 'I've barely seen her. Who is she?'

'The new high queen of Malgarth,' Shaw said.

'Oh gods,' the flag captain said. 'What must she think?'

'She's an adventurous girl,' Nate said. 'She won't mind a bit of excitement.'

'At least I must make my bow,' Abia said. 'Xailin, you'll want to meet her too. Malgarth and Qoor are about as far apart as you can sail.'

'As far from home as I am,' Xailin said with a sigh.

'Mr. Huono, Mr. Tahin, you return to *Xalt* and prepare the ship for a five hundred mile journey south,' Abia said. 'Show me you can do it, and a lieutenancy will be yours.'

The boys saluted and hurried away.

Back on deck, Shaw looked around and found the royal companions chatting with Purser Ricco and Midshipman Miran.

As they joined them, Miran thought to slink away.

'Wait,' Shaw said. 'That was a good show, you and Sem did today. This shielding, was that your idea, Miran?'

The midshipman nodded. 'Sem and I discussed it one day, just as a fancy. Now we had a chance to try it for real. I made a very flat shield to cover the side. It took good teamwork, but Sem and I know each other. I don't know if it would have worked much longer.'

'You have a word with those two chaps of *Xalt*,' Shaw said. 'It looked dicey for you, but I believe you guys were close to sinking them. Don't forget *Drakon* was shooting back all the time.'

Miran blinked. 'We were?'

'Yes. Take your broom and have a look at those holes in their side.'

'I want a navy,' Agusta said. 'I really, really want a navy.'

Shaw grinned. 'I thought you wouldn't be bored. Before we go, you should meet our flag captain Abia. She is the Peaks senior naval officer. Beside her is *Drakon*'s third officer, Xailin. In her spare time she is the heiress to the Emperor of Qoor.'

'In exile,' Xailin said. 'The jinn are in my father's palace.'

'Cursed jinn,' Liom burst out. 'Are they everywhere?'

'Around here?' Shaw said. 'Yes.'

Ricco stretched himself up on his toes and coughed.

'What?' Shaw said innocently. Then she grinned. 'Your Majesty, this is Mr. Ricco, our purser. He is my agent aboard the flagship, and the guy who brought us the Hizmyr contracts. You can shake his hand, but count your fingers.'

Then Abia was called away, and Shaw led her guests down to the portal.

Young portaller Sem sat cross-legged on the ground, staring in front of him.

'Hey,' Shaw said. 'I heard how you and Miran saved the *Drakon* with your teamwork. Well done, mate.'

He looked up. 'It *was* a good show, wasn't it?' he said. 'And now I'm so darned tired.'

'That's normal. I hope you can port us back to Smalkand, and then you tell Captain Abia you close up shop and go to bed. In your job you must be clear-headed.'

He nodded. 'I'll do that.' He smiled. 'I can manage one port.'

'Good. And know I'm proud of you, Mr. Sem. Sleep well.'

A short flash and they were in Smalkand. Portal mage Beth had the coordinates for the new transferal in Croncliff, and in seconds they found themselves in the hall of the palace, frightening the stuffing out of the servants.

'Don't be foolish,' Jonna said sternly to the shaking footmen. 'Weren't you told what this thing is and that people can pop out of it?'

'My lady,' an older man said, aggrieved. 'So we were told. But we didn't know it was awake yet.'

'Now you do,' Agusta said. 'I'm in my office. Tell the Clerk in Chancery I want to see him.'

With head high, she strode through the throne room, with a smile and a word for all she passed.

Behind the throne, next to the tower stairs was another door. On the threshold Agusta stopped and sniffed. Then she went in and pulled open the curtains. Sunlight entered and showed a somber, wainscoted room with a large desk in the center and a row of chairs along one wall. Some gloomy tapestries covered the walls and from the center of the ceiling hung a large brass gas lamp. The room smelled dusty and long unused.

'Help me with this window,' Agusta said, as she tried to open a pane. It didn't budge.

'Your pardon, Majesty. They are sealed shut.' A servant had pussyfooted in. 'His late majesty felt uncomfortable with the idea of burglars.'

'Out here?' Agusta said. 'I want them opened. Let a builder attend to it, both here and in my quarters.'

The man bowed and left.

Agusta dropped down behind the desk. 'Take a chair,' she said. 'It's all horribly uncomfortable, but I'll wait with any other changes until I know where I stand, financially.'

'Do we open our doors again?' Liom said.

'Business visitors,' Agusta said. 'I'm not seeing any applicants for court functions.'

Then the clerk came in, carrying a stack of papers. 'Welcome back, Ma'am,' he said, bowing. 'I prepared some reports for you. Finances; tax incomes, rents, wages and other state revenues and expenditures, plus a list of your majesty's personal possessions.'

The high queen glanced at the totals and pushed the list to Jonna. 'That's your department; we will discuss it later.'

Shaw rose. 'You won't need us nosing around in your state secrets,' she said. 'Nate and I will go attend to our own business for a while. We will be back in two days for the coronation.'

Agusta studied some long list and waved absently.

Shaw grinned. 'She's glad to be boss again, after those days following my lead.'

'And you are glad to have no one tagging along anymore,' Nate said.

Shaw took his arm. 'True. Just the two of us, that's how I like it.' She laughed aloud. 'That is, where is Haai-Bo?'

'Tagging along,' her wyrmling said out of nowhere. 'Young sept brother got the hang of stealth quickly.'

'Me fly, me invisible warrior,' Wiu-To said. 'Assassin I am now.'

'You're feeling better?' Shaw said.

'Much, much better,' the younger wyrmling said. 'Mice are good here, and the kitchen stocks endless.'

'Moochers!' Shaw said. 'Did anything interesting happen?'

'Nothing,' Haai-Bo said. 'Some nobles tried to get inside, but the colonel was stern and did his duty. No treason, no bad thoughts against queen.'

'Good of them,' Shaw said. 'Darn, I forgot the parcel. King Rashaunt sent two pounds of fine meats for Wiu-To, with a So Sorry-letter, but I left it in Smalkand, in the freeze room.'

'Meats? For me?' Wiu-To said excitedly. 'Nice! We must get.'

'We'll all go,' Shaw said. 'I'm sure Haai-Bo won't mind porting all of us for this once.'

'Don't mind,' Haai-Bo said. 'Smalkand good place. Watch how I do it, sept brother.'

CHAPTER 19 — CORONATION AND AFTER

On Coronation Day, Shaw and Nate arrived in Landfalln. The portal mage was a gaunt fellow with sparse dark hair and a brand-new robe. He stood in a group of agitated nobles, looking both bored and irritated.

'There will be no ferry ship?' a richly clad man exclaimed in a loud voice. 'You mean we're to trust ourselves to that... that...' Then he saw Shaw and Nate standing in the transferal's circle and he frowned. 'How did you get there, girl?'

'My colleague and I just ported in,' Shaw said, as she screwed her monocle in her eye. 'It is perfectly safe.'

'I saw them arrive,' a boy said. He looked about fifteen, dressed in fine clothes that looked crumpled and slightly stained. 'One second the place was empty and next they were there.' He grinned. 'Seems the thing works.' He dropped on his knees and stared at the visible cables. 'There must be an engine of sorts.'

The portal mage touched a square protrusion no bigger than a toddler's hand. 'In here,' he said. 'It is not an engine, though. It is a spell converter.'

The boy narrowed his eyes. 'It's not a technical thing, then.'

'Only in part. This portal is simply a door through the Intermedium. At this moment, it opens on Croncliff, but I can change that to over seven hundred other destinations.'

The boy sniffed. 'That's a salesman answer, not a technical one.'

The portal mage gave a small bow. 'The technical answers are a secret of the PTC. I assure you it works unfailingly, young lord.'

At that, the boy laughed. 'Ah well, secrets!'

'You can safely trust the portal, my lords and ladies,' Shaw said. 'It brought us over a distance of four thousand miles, no less.'

The loud-voiced lord scowled. 'That's impossible,' he snapped. 'Four thousand miles? Pshaw! There is nothing in the world that far away! Who are you, girl?'

'I am High Merchant Harwans,' Shaw said coolly. 'Managing director of the PTC and Landfalln Enterprises. My headquarters is in the Pasandir Peaks, and that, my dear lord, is four thousand miles to the north.' She smiled. 'Now, my colleague Nate and I are on our way to join the high queen. Please gather round me. Portal Mage Cornal is very experienced; he will send us to the palace in the wink of an eye.'

She noted Cornal's flash of surprise as she mentioned his name, but he regained himself quickly and nodded gravely.

'Faster than a wink, my lord. Now, take a deep breath, please.' He sounded like Healer Tymon as he said that, and automatically they all obeyed.

Then they were in Croncliff.

'And that was all,' Shaw said.

The lord stared at her, for a moment at a loss for words. A stout woman who could well be his wife stifled a giggle.

'Thank you,' she said. 'I'm sure we will get used to this porting thing.'

'I think that portal is quite handy,' the boy said. 'We should have one at home. That beats hours on the road, I'd say.'

'I'm afraid these portals are too expensive to supply every lord,' Shaw said. 'We will probably install some at strategic places around the country.' She gave a small smile. 'Now you must excuse me; the high queen expects me.'

She hooked her arm into Nate's and hurried away.

'Her Majesty is in her office, ma'am,' a servant said.

Shaw thanked her and entered the throne room.

'You, girl,' a tall noble said, gripping Shaw's arm. 'Bring me something to drink, and make it snappy.' The woman at his side pressed her lips together, and the two girls... *His daughters?* Shaw thought. *They seem extremely unhappy. Darn the useless slob!*

She used her monocle to look the noble up and down without speaking.

At her side, Nate stepped forward, his face hard with anger. 'Your hand, sir! The Magnate Shaw is not to be accosted in any way,' he said coldly. 'Besides, the high queen's throne room is not an alehouse.'

The man's face became a hot, flaming red and he snatched his hand back. All three women looked at him in apprehension, but he turned away, fists clenched.

Nate offered Shaw his arm and together they entered the royal office.

'Fool,' Nate muttered.

'Who?' Liom said. He stood at the window looking out at the sea, and now turned his head.

'Some idiot lord,' Nate said. 'He had the gall ordering Shaw to fetch him a drink.'

'A tall guy with a face like one of those Hizmyran camels?' Gerben said, looking up from the book he was reading. 'That's Lassonder. Even my father didn't want *him* at court. His daughters are all right, though. Twins. But their old man is an offensive idiot.'

'Why the "magnate"?' Shaw said. 'Wasn't high merchant bad enough?'

Nate patted her arm. 'Jinnbane and the Trade Magnate,' he said. 'They were a Divine's words. I think the title fitting, now even Darquine admits your success.'

Shaw made an indelicate sound, then laughed. 'Fine; if it pleases you. You put him in his place nicely. *The high queen's throne room is not an alehouse* indeed!'

'Well, it isn't,' Agusta said. 'My people aren't serving drinks there.'

Jonna came in. 'It's filling up quickly,' she said. 'My family just arrived amid a whole crowd.' She glanced at Agusta. 'It's time to dress.'

The high queen pulled a face. Then she relaxed. 'It is a nice dress,' she admitted. 'Those women at the Sewery did an amazing job.'

The two girls slipped away through a side door.

It took them a good part of an hour before they returned. Agusta had changed into a long dress of creamy silk, patterned with small birds in gold and silver, and encrusted with pearls. Around her neck was a long, intricate chain of more pearls, and she wore a dark blue robe with a long train.

They all bowed as she entered. In front of her desk she halted.

'Well?'

'Beautiful,' Shaw said. 'Stunningly beautiful.'

'Good,' Agusta said firmly. 'Jonna?'

The other girl came in, wearing an elegant dress of pale blue, a short robe in the same color as Agusta's, and a tiny tiara in her hair.

'A picture,' Shaw said. 'Very, very elegant. There will be a great many jealous ladies in the room today.'

'Then we will proceed,' Agusta said.

Liom hurried outside to warn the master of ceremonies.

As they filed out, Shaw heard a mighty choir burst into some song of praise.

'Where...?' Agusta said.

'It is the Lord Advisor Haai-Bo, Majesty,' a servant said. 'He and the high priest of Bodrus devised a new ceremonial.'

Head high, Agusta strode to the throne room, while little Wiu-To dove and gripped the end of her train in his claws.

Escorted by Lady Jenna and the two young lords in fine new court dresses she entered.

There went an audible gasp through the massed nobility as they beheld their new ruler. Then all bowed or curtsied as Agusta walked to the throne while the grand choral came to its jubilant crescendo.

A flash of light nearly had her falter, but it was young Barrett doing his journalist duty. The high queen gave him a fleeting smile before going on.

In front of the throne she remained standing. The choir changed into a march, both martial and divine.

'His Eminence the High Priest of Bodrus, Sleeping God of the Mountains,' a great voice intoned.

From outside, Uzhan strode into the throne room. Not a soldier now, but an ordained priest, dressed in many-colored robes, and infused with a holy joy.

He stopped before Agusta and waited for the choir to finish. Then he spoke and as the words rolled from his mouth, a divine light flowed from his being, enveloped the high queen, and spread out over the watching nobles.

Shaw felt an overpowering rightness gripping her. She didn't hear a word of the ceremonial, as she bathed in the presence of Bodrus. Vaguely, she saw Agusta kneel. Then a spark sprang from priest to queen. Agusta's face was filled with awe and resolve, and Uzhan's battered countenance glowed with light. Then, a thousand musical instruments played, and a multitude of gold and silver birds sprang from Agusta's dress, singing of divine glory as they winged a round over her head and flew out of the throne room, out of Croncliff, to tell the people of Malgarth they had witnessed their high queen crowned.

Uzhan's light slowly faded. He bowed for Agusta, and stepped back to join Shaw.

'Wow,' he whispered. 'Wow.'

Shaw gripped his hands. 'You were great.'

'I was a vessel,' he said simply. 'The will of Bodrus filled me. I was one with my god.'

Shaw held both his hand and Nate's, and then she became aware of Agusta speaking.

'My lords and ladies, that I am here today — that we all are here today, we thank to Magnate Shaw of the PTC and her people. Her bravery and unselfish assistance saved us all from a terrible fate we weren't even aware of. I would ask the magnate to tell you herself.'

Shaw blinked, lifted her chin and walked to stand beside the throne.

'I thank your majesty for your kind words,' she said. 'My story is a long one, my lords and ladies. For to inform you of what happened here, I must first tell of the state of the world outside Malgarth. I ask you all to bear with me.'

She then spoke of Eskandar, how he became Bodrus' Defender. She named the pirates and the jinn, and the lich lord eying the Sleeping God's power, and explained the prophecy and the army of children.

'At the moment the lord wyrmcaller is in the north, battling the jinn on their home ground,' she said. 'He is fighting for all of us; the Pasandir Peaks, the Weal Nations, the northern lands, and the high kingdom of Malgarth as well.'

'There are no jinn in Malgarth,' a boy in the front row protested. He had been staring at Shaw, listening intently, but now he found the courage to object.

'The jinn are everywhere,' Shaw answered him gravely. 'I will come to that.'

She went on with her trade efforts, how she had fought jinn and pirates in too many vital places, and went on to the taking of the Tradeports.

This caused a stir just short of an uproar.

'You captured them?' a noble said. 'That is brutal!'

'My dear lord,' Shaw said. 'We defeated the pirates, not the townsfolk. The people suffered under the Bokkaner yoke,

257

seeing their business ruined, without food or income. They were overjoyed to join us as equals.' Shaw paused and smiled. 'You will understand the time for raids into the lands of Codnoallis and the other ports is now past.'

A few lords looked discomfited, but no one spoke.

'Then we come to the present,' Shaw said. She told them of the Codnoallis ship, of Jonna and their search for the high queen. She spoke of Lord Rutus, who had sent them to Croncliff. Then she dwelled at some length on the fight with the jinni and the fate of Lord Morthan.

'So you see,' she said to the boy in the front row. 'There was a jinni in Malgarth, and he was the cause of much grief.'

The boy nodded. 'I'm sorry, Liom,' he said.

At that, many eyes turned to the young lord behind the throne and Liom bowed; his face a hard mask.

Shaw then briefly mentioned Lord Rutus' malversations and his subsequent death, and went on quickly to the high queen dismissing her court, and the grand tour.

'So it will be clear the world is not as safe as many of you might have thought. The jinn threat is very real. They are nonhumans, who see us as cattle. The wyrmcaller is under a divine obligation to kill them all, but he cannot be everywhere at once, so we will have to be alert. One of the safest precautions is a trained mage. Any mage will be able to recognize a jinni. I understand the use of the arcane has not been popular in Malgarth, but I strongly suggest it could mean the difference between life and death to you. Should you know anyone who is a mana-user, let me know. It is not a shame and besides, mages earn very good incomes.'

Shaw grinned and stepped back.

'Thank you, Magnate Shaw,' Agusta said. 'The old custom made the party who escorted the heir to Croncliff would be the new ruling party. Yet the magnate and her people are here to trade, not to meddle in our government. I hereby declare this custom abolished.

'Let no one be mistaken; I rule in Malgarth. I will choose my councilors from among you, to become my ministers of the crown.'

All nobles sat up now, trying to look wise and ministerial.

Agusta had seen it, too, and she didn't even smile. 'My lords and ladies. When my father died, and I was called to the throne, government skipped a generation. So in choosing my advisors, I will do the same. I am fully assured of the immense wealth of experience among you, but that is not what I wish. I want young minds, young ideas. Therefore I turn to your sons and daughters to find my ministers.'

The silence in the throne room was deafening as they all struggled to understand.

Then the boy Shaw had met with his reluctant father at the portal rose. 'Does your majesty mean... us?'

'As long as you are between fourteen and nineteen, yes,' Agusta said.

'Preposterous!' his father said in a loud voice. 'My son is a child. He knows nothing.'

'If he knows nothing, you have clearly done something wrong in his upbringing,' Agusta said. 'I assume he has been schooled.'

'Of course I have been,' the boy said quickly. 'For years and years.'

Several nobles shouted at once and Agusta raise a hand. 'Quiet, please. My father was "advised" by older men. As a result, Malgarth is poor, isolated and backwards. The last week I made a tour of the great courts of the known world. I spoke with the Lord Spellstor, the Queen of the Kells, the Chorwaynie Proprietor, and the King of Hizmyr; I met the heir to the Emperor of far-off Qoor, and the princes of Sashuni. I discussed business with leaders of large companies, with generals and admirals, and I returned, realizing how much my father and his advisors have held us back.'

She slammed the armrests of her throne. 'I will not accept this. I want a fresh look at things. I saw how Magnate Shaw's enormous organization, her trade posts, her merchant and naval ships are run by people my age. If she can do it, so can I. My lords and ladies, I have arranged a grand buffet in the ballroom for your enjoyment. Meanwhile I want those of your sons and daughters interested in a court position stay behind.'

A noble with a blond beard and a marked likeness to Jonna rose. 'Come, my lords. Not so crestfallen. Think of the honor to your family if your boy or girl becomes a minister of the crown. You will bask in their glory, without having to lift a finger. Now to the buffet. When was it last our late high king fed us?'

'You don't need me right now,' Shaw said to Agusta. 'I will go with the lords and have them cry on my shoulder.'

The buffet was sumptuous. Far too sumptuous for the palace kitchens. Then she saw Varan, and the owner of *The Merchanteer's Rest*, New Winsproke's famous restaurant, and she smiled. So that's where it came from.

'Magnate Shaw,' a voice behind her said. 'And you must be Director Nate.'

'Lord Lammark,' Shaw said, turning to the noble with the blond beard.

'A surprising development,' Jonna's father said. 'I've known our new majesty for most of her life, and I knew her for a headstrong girl. But her decision surprised even me. For a moment I wondered if it had been your suggestion, but I find you here and not with Agusta.'

Shaw smiled. 'It was her idea. When Lord Rutus turned traitor, she felt she couldn't trust any of the Court and Barons lords. Barring your person, but she knew you didn't want a job at court.'

'No,' Lammark said. 'Most certainly not. But to trust our untried youth is... extreme.'

'She saw it worked with us. Our whole organization from the lord wyrmcaller down is governed by young people, yet we are acknowledged allies of the Weal nations and business partners to several other countries. Besides, the queen is not planning to replace her clerks and other professionals. She is just going to modernize the kingdom.'

'And what will be your part in this?'

'Mine?' Shaw laughed. 'I'm not about to have a part in anything. We will open a warehouse in Landfalln and start trading with any who has need of anything. We will build an airship network, connecting you to the Continent, and add some strategically placed portals for official use. There will be some other matters, but they will all be in the line of business.

'We will not tell her majesty how to run her kingdom. My company is here for trade, and the man you should meet is our Mr. Varan, the young gentleman standing to the back of the room. He is our director for our Malgarth companies, and all business matters on Malgarth are in his hands.'

'Shaw?'

She froze at Healer Tymon's unexpected voice in her head. *'What's wrong?'* she said, worried what could have happened at Smalkand.

'Nothing bad,' Tymon said. *'Your pirate boy regained consciousness.'*

For a moment Shaw didn't know what he was talking about. Then she remembered the red cutter they'd sank on their way to Yavam, and the boy she and Nate had picked up from the sea.

'He is? And is he well?'

Tymon sounded puzzled. *'Strange enough, he is fine. No weakness, no harmful effects; nothing. He asks for you. By name. It's urgent, he says.'*

'Me?' Shaw said. *'Does he say why?'*

'*All he says is "Shaw, I got something urgent to tell Shaw".*'

'*Darn,*' Shaw said. '*I'm at a coronation.*' She looked at Nate. '*I'm on my way.*'

She turned to Lord Lammark. 'I am called away. Would you give my respect to her majesty? By now she will know me well enough not to be surprised.'

'Of course,' Lammark said. 'I understand you lead a hectic life.'

'You could say that,' Shaw said with a grin. '*Haai-Bo? We must be leaving, my friend.*'

'*Leave the eats?*' he said, shocked. '*Why?*' Then he sighed. '*Fine, we will starve, then.*'

'*At Smalkand? Don't be silly.*' She gripped Nate's arm and as they hurried to the transferal portal she told him about Tymon's message.

'That long-haired guy?' Nate said. 'I wonder what he has to say.' He cocked an eye at Shaw. 'You're not sorry to go, are you?'

'I find courts are not my favorite place,' Shaw said. 'Most nobles are extremely dreary. Besides, there's still so much to do; I'm wasting my time there.'

Nate laughed and drew her close. Then they stepped into the transferal and ported away.

CHAPTER 20 — THE JINN BOY

'He couldn't possibly know my name,' Shaw muttered, as they emerged from the portal.

'Lots of people know your name,' Nate said. 'You'll be surprised how many.'

'But pirate kids? That doesn't fill me with gladness.'

'Shaw and Nate!' Smalkand's keepmistress Willow must've spied them porting in—it was a clever visitor who escaped her eye—and she hurried over.

'Hi, you got Tymon's news?' she asked. 'I'm so glad that boy woke up after all; many of us have been nursing him, and we were worried.'

Shaw nodded. 'So he wakes and immediately asks for me.'

Willow grinned. 'Strange, isn't it? Perhaps he wants to marry the girl who saved his life.'

'Not a chance,' Nate said firmly. 'I'll kick him back into the sea first.'

'I am too young to marry,' Shaw said primly. After all, she was still some time short of her sixteenth birthday.

'I'll wait,' Nate said. 'But no competitors.' He took her arm. 'Let's go and see this bold fellow.'

The boy was younger than she remembered. Twelve, maybe thirteen years old; a slender lad with the dough-pale skin of a Garthan or Takkalan — or a pirate.

He sat stiffly propped up by cushions, his long hair making something unworldly of his face. His eyes lighted up as he saw her come in, and he relaxed. 'Yes; it is you. I must tell you about Angsthafn.'

She stared at him. *Angsthafn, the dread pirate base.* She pulled up a chair and sat beside his bed. 'First tell me of yourself. Who are you and all that stuff.'

'You want to know that?' he said, clearly surprised anyone would be interested in him. 'I'm Villaume, and I'm an Isdoran.'

'And that is?' Shaw said.

'The Isle of Isdor,' the boy said. 'That once beautiful place the Bokkaners call Angsthafn.'

'Angsthafn is inhabited?' Nate said.

The boy glanced up at him and was silent for a moment as if he tried to decide Nate's right to ask questions.

'Yes,' he said finally. 'It has been for a very long time.'

'And you know where it is,' Shaw stated.

The boy turned his eyes back to her with something like relief and nodded. 'I do.' His hands moved over the blanket as if they had a will of their own. Then he looked at them and they stilled. 'There is a spell that keeps it hidden, but it doesn't work on us who were born there. I wouldn't have been allowed off the island if I hadn't been Amir Sostaz' own calf.'

'Calf?' Shaw said.

'That is how the jinn call the young of their cattle,' the boy said. 'I was Lord Sostaz' pet calf.'

Nate's face tautened. 'Curse those cannibal jinn! You are a boy, a young human.' He took a deep breath. 'Who was this Sostaz?'

Again, the boy hesitated. 'The noble Sostaz was one of great Nimmendal's adjutants.'

'A jinni?'

'I was a jinni lord's c... boy. He was a puissant master and a terrible foe.'

'Who couldn't swim,' Shaw said.

That brought a smile to the boy's face. 'He could not. I felt him go and for the first time since I could remember, I was free. It was a terrifying moment, alone in the sea. I should have allowed myself to die then.'

'But you didn't,' Shaw said. 'I saw you waving. You didn't want to die.'

'I did not,' Villaume said. 'Your mind, and that of the others I could sense were free. You were your own beings, not pets, not cattle. I wanted to be like that.'

'A sensible idea,' Nate said, relaxing.

That earned him another smile. 'I have much to learn,' the boy said. 'It is bewildering to voice-speak with so many people at once. Do I answer all of them?'

'That wouldn't work,' Shaw said. 'Start with the ones you are directly speaking with. In this case that's Nate and me. We will explain this to the others not to bombard you with questions. I take it you can mindspeak?'

'I would be dead if I couldn't,' the boy said. 'My master only mindspoke me; it was my duty to convey his orders to the other cattle.'

'People,' Shaw said.

'Your pardon, yes.' Villaume sighed. 'I have much to unlearn as well.'

'So you can take us to Angsthafn,' Shaw said. 'Can you describe the place? Lay-out, defenses, and things like that?'

The boy closed his eyes, and for a fleeting second Shaw wondered if her questions had overtaxed his strength.

'No,' he said. *'Watch.'*

In her mind, she stood on a ship's prow, watching a tall volcano rise up from the sea; a brown cone streaked with green, reaching to the clouds from a circle of jungle growth maybe ten miles wide. As she approached the island, the volcano grew to huge proportions and the jungle a tangled mass of impregnable density.

Her vision turned to port, as the ship passed close to golden beaches, where what looked like crocodiles lay, just out of reach of the breaking surf. Her sight wavered. All at once, the near-perfect symmetry of the cone was marred, as if a sharp knife had cut away a slice. Her ship moved toward it, and she saw the jungle end sharply in foam and rocks. Past it, she entered a channel between the high, smooth sides of the cleft. On both sides, ships without masts but bristling with cannons, were a formidable barrier against intruders.

Past them, she entered a circular bay at least a mile wide, lit by the sun peering into the volcano's wide mouth, high overhead.

All around the bay was a stretch of land perhaps half a mile deep, with palm trees, overgrown fields and a large village of wooden houses and a big keep built against the volcano wall.

Mountains Breath! Shaw thought. *How will I manage taking that place with only my guys? Wait, what's that?* She had spotted a giant wyrm sitting on the deck of an old ship.

They've got an adult? How the heck...? As they sailed past, she saw the cage the wyrm guarded, a large iron prison with a heavy lock, and inside four wyrmlings no bigger than Wiu-To. They huddled together without moving, totally miserable.

Hostages? Was that how they kept the elder wyrm subdued? Villaume's visualization gave her no time to think; it walked her all around the base, past apathetic slaves, swaggering pirates and several tall, cadaverous beings dressed in gleaming armor. Only when she came to the keep, the vision stopped.

'Great Nimmendal's headquarters,' Villaume said. 'I am not allowed inside.' The pirate base faded and she was back in the sickbay.

'That was very good,' Shaw said. 'A mighty harbor; who built all that?'

'Our people,' Villaume said sadly. 'Over a period of centuries. They were a strong, proud folk then.'

'They will be again,' Shaw said. 'Perhaps not immediately, but their children will return to their former greatness.'

She sank into thought. *It's a clear vision. But I can't attack that place with only my guys. I must call in the Weal. Commodore Yarwan...*

'*No!*' a voice shouted in her mind.

'*Teodar?*' she said, surprised. She knew the Kavid-Jar followed her as well as Eskandar, but he never spoke unless she asked him. '*Why not the Weal?*'

'*It's your show, girl. The commodore and all those other bigheads wouldn't serve under your command, and the prophecy wants you to be the one to take this place. Just think of a way, mistress merchant.*'

Shaw knew he was right. Commodore Yarwan was a nice man and a friend, but she couldn't expect him and his captains to follow her orders like their own guys did. It would go against all their instincts. So no Weal. Then what? That wyrm. If she could convince her to join them...

'*I think I have a plan,*' Shaw said pensively. '*One thing; the prophecy may forbid me asking the Weal forces to join us, but Lord Jurgis would never forgive me if I left him out. I'll invite him; unofficially, of course.*'

'*If you must,*' Teodar said grudgingly. '*But tell him he's just a — what do you call it? A grunt.*'

Shaw grinned. '*Jurgis can come as a grunt; he isn't as stuffy as Commodore Yarwan.* Villaume, are you fit enough to get up and visit people?'

The boy nodded. 'I have been abed long enough.'

Shaw looked at Tymon, who had been watching her without a word. 'What do you say?'

The healer smiled. 'His body is strong enough. His mind? Only the gods know that. As far as I'm concerned, he is fit for duty. His clothes are in that cupboard; clean and repaired, but they *are* pirate togs.'

'He will need them yet. Get up and dress, friend; we've got a big shot to visit.' Shaw hesitated. 'That tour was impressive. Can you do it again?'

'It isn't difficult,' Villaume said. He drew back the blankets and put his feet on the floor, pushed himself up, and stood swaying for a moment. He was thin; not food-starved, but wiry. His brows furrowed as if he was angry at his weakness. Then his face cleared, and he straightened as he went to get his clothes.

'Well done,' Tymon said. 'You would make a healer yourself.'

Villaume grimaced. 'Great Sostaz chose me for my strength. Not that I could touch *him,* of course.'

'We found the jinn are masters in bluffing,' Shaw said. 'By now we have killed several of them.'

Villaume stopped with one leg down his pants and looked at her. 'Several?'

'Killed in a straight fight,' Nate added. 'But then, we're followers of Jinnbane and hunting jinn is part of our duty.'

'Jinnbane is dead,' the boy said, as he pulled up his pants. 'You can only follow his memory.'

'He is reborn in our boss, Wyrmcaller Eskandar, who is of his kin,' Shaw said. 'Now Jinnbane is in the north, fighting jinn in Takkala. That makes killing Angsthafn our job; we've been fighting Nimmendal's minions for a long time.'

'And we took Brisa away from him,' Nate added.

Villaume shook his head. 'You speak of impossibilities,' he said.

'You will find out they are truth.' Shaw looked him over. He was dressed as a pirate, but his clothes were of better cut than most. 'Ready?'

Villaume turned to Tymon. 'My thanks for your good care, Master Healer,' he said with a strange formality.

'My pleasure,' Tymon said.

'Come with me,' Shaw said. 'We'll go to Seatome first.'

'Is that far?' Villaume said, as they crossed the mess to the entry hall. 'I can walk.'

'Several thousand miles to the south,' Nate said. He stopped at a table and took out the map he always carried.

'We're here,' he said, pointing at the little symbol that was Smalkand Keep. 'Our warehouse in Seatome is in the very south.'

The boy studied the map. 'I have never been that far from the island. We go by boat? How many days will we travel?'

'No boat,' Shaw said. 'We teleport.'

'How? That is something only high jinn can do,' Villaume said, surprised. 'It is a very special magic.'

'Nope,' Nate said. 'That's one of their bluffs. We have a machine that does it.'

Villaume looked shaken. 'All those things you tell me; is everything I believed false?'

'If the jinn told you, it probably is,' Shaw said. 'They are first class liars.' She touched his arm. 'I'm sorry; it must be terribly confusing. Best to accept you have to change your thinking on a lot of things. Luckily, most of it will be for the better.'

'Much better,' Nate said. 'Now, can you tell me where is Angsthafn?'

Villaume hesitated, touching the left side of the map. 'This land here, with those tiny trees drawn in?'

'The Greenwall Coast,' Nate said. 'This speck is our local base, Yavam Island.' He grinned. 'We captured it after we picked you up. So technically you were at the famous Battle of Yavam.'

'There was a jinni,' Shaw said. 'He died, just like yours.'

Villaume swallowed. 'Good.' He tapped Yavam. 'Go north by northeast until you come at a river delta. Steer well around it, or you find yourself on the Deathwood Sands. That truly is a deadly place, crawling with poisonous snakes. When we're close, I can break the spell of concealment, so you can see the island. Before your ships can enter, you must eliminate the gun platforms, or they'll sink you.'

'Any air defense?' Shaw said.

'Izo-Ky,' Villaume said. 'She is their wyrm. I don't know how they captured her, but they have a hold on her.' He lowered his voice. 'They keep her young in a silver cage.'

'We saw them!' Shaw said. 'This wyrm; isn't she mad like every other adult wyrm?'

'Not that I noticed,' the boy said. 'I spoke to her two or three times, and she answered very clear and precise.'

'Strange.' Then they came to the Smalkand portal, and Shaw filed the wyrm question away for later

'So that was a teleport,' Villaume said when they had returned to Old Wharf, their Seatome warehouse. 'Fascinating.'

'Most people find it creepy and cold,' Shaw said.

'Cold, but not creepy,' the boy said. 'Different.'

They went up the stairs and on the entresol Villaume halted and looked out over the warehouse, the compact hall filled with storage racks and kids whistling and joking as they collected orders.

'This is much different from Smalkand,' he said. 'More home-like. Those workers are clearly happy.' He sighed. 'It must be nice to have no cares in the world.'

'They have had their problems,' Nate said. 'But now they have a job, regular food and a place to sleep. That makes a lot of difference.'

They walked on to the office at the end of the entresol.

'Haai-Bo?' Shaw called to her wyrmling advisor. *'I need you, m'dear.'*

'Ooh, yes! the wyrmling's mind voice came immediately. *We're flying; coming back.'*

As they entered, Ruth of Spellstor, Shaw's management secretary who kept the whole of PTC running smoothly, looked up from a stack of reports.

'Hi! I hadn't expected you back already. What did that boy have to say?'

'He's here,' Shaw said. 'He will tell you himself.' She introduced Villaume. 'He is an important chap; he knows Angsthafn.'

Ruth opened her eyes wide. 'Gods! So he can show us how we get there? And now?'

'We will go and capture it,' Shaw said.

Villaume choked. 'How?'

'We'll discuss that later,' Shaw said.

Then the two wyrmlings popped in.

'We're here,' Haai-Bo said. *'Wiu-To getting stronger every day.'*

'Me great warrior,' Wiu-To said complacently. He turned a toothy smile to Villaume, who sat staring at the two wyrmlings as if stunned. *'Surprised?'*

Then Haai-Bo squawked and waved his wings in agitation. 'What's this in your mind, Villaume boy? An adult wyrm? Captured by jinn? This cannot be! We must go there; free her and her brood, lest all fails.'

'We will,' Shaw said. 'We're working on it. Ruth, I want all steamships in Smalkand; *Drakon*, *Maiden*, *Sashu* and of course *Marigold*. I want *Wentiibi* at Brisa to sail as well.'

Ruth made a note. 'I'll pass on the orders.'

Shaw narrowed her eyes as she remembered the Angsthafn vision. 'I'll need Keena and Callogan. Ask them to be in Smalkand by the end of the week and tell them why.'

'What are you planning?' Nate said.

Shaw told them.

CHAPTER 21 — PREPARATIONS

The company cart dropped Shaw, Nate, Ruth and Villaume off at the Broomrider H.Q. in the center of Seatome, and they hurried inside. The boy seemed oblivious to his surroundings. Where other newcomers usually goggled and gaped at the sights, he simply walked past.

'I notice,' he said when Shaw asked him. 'Too many new things at once. I accept and later, I will ask.'

He listened intently for a moment, then shrugged and walked on.

'Did you hear anything?' Shaw asked.

'When bosses speak, cautious cattle listen,' the boy said. 'This boss is concerned about Angsthafn, but no threat to us. He is waiting for us; shouldn't we hurry?'

Shaw grinned. 'That will be Lord Jurgis. Don't worry; he is a friend.'

'Ms. Shaw?' a uniformed guard said as they crossed the hall. 'The First Broom is awaiting you in his office.' He called a guide, who took them up to the top floor. Neither man stared at the two wyrmlings flying circles over Shaw's head.

Lord Jurgis had been walking the floor, and he stopped abruptly as the guide announced them. 'There you are! Angsthafn! I wish we could have done it. Now you youngsters are going for the glory.' He waved at several chairs. 'Sit down and tell me.'

'Not for the glory,' Shaw said, as she leaned back in her chair. 'We need the jinn exterminated.'

'I know,' Lord Jurgis said. 'You want the Weal to join you?'

'The prophecy forbids it,' Shaw said. 'I must do it myself. Of course, should you personally want to come with us, you are most welcome.'

'Yes!' Lord Jurgis said fiercely. 'And so would Maud, but her position wouldn't let her. I will bring a handful of volunteer broomriders as well.' His face was uncommonly grim. 'I've hated that place forever. When Maud and I had just met, we'd shipped as passengers in *Daisee*, out of Codnoallis. Its crew proved pirates, and they planned to sell us as slaves to Angsthafn. Then we ran into Basil and Yarwan. Together we killed the pirates and took the ship. I swore to capture that slavers nest somehow.' He grunted. 'With the war and the rebuilding afterwards it never happened. But my oath still stands.' He slammed his hands together. 'What can you tell us about Angsthafn?'

Shaw smiled and introduced Villaume. 'He is the expert,' she said. 'He was a jinni's slave; we sank his ship and found him the sole survivor. He's been sick for quite a while, but now he's up and ready to show us where Angsthafn is. He was born there.'

Jurgis looked at Ruth. 'Have you checked him?'

'Of course,' she said. 'He is clean.'

The First Broom gave Villaume a grin. 'Then you're the most welcome face I've seen in this office for a long time. What can you tell us of the place? How will you folks blow it up?'

'We won't blow anything up,' Shaw said quickly, seeing Villaume's face change. 'There are a lot of innocent people involved, and more. We must do it the difficult way. Before I explain, Villaume will show you the place.'

The boy folded his hands in his lap and, sitting up straight, closed his eyes.

'Oh!' Lord Jurgis exclaimed, and then it was silent in the room, while they watched the island grow in their minds.

When he was done, Jurgis swore.

'That's a tough nut,' he said. 'And you want to take that place without a bombardment or anything?'

'Not exactly,' Shaw said. 'I plan to take a small team inside first. We must free those wyrmlings before we attack. They are the key to the whole operation.'

'Why?' Jurgis said.

'For one, because we don't want to face an angry mother wyrm breathing fire at us as we come riding in.'

'Prophecy,' Haai-Bo said firmly. 'Jinn must not have wyrms, or my princess will fail. And Eskandar. Free the brood and the adult one will be grateful. I can talk her into changing sides.'

'That would be helpful,' Shaw said. 'Especially against Nimmendal. I don't see myself attacking a jinni prince with a knife.'

'Tell me about the defenses,' Jurgis said. 'Apart from the big jinni, how many of the beasts are there?'

'With Amir Sostaz dead, there are two others left,' Villaume said. 'Rotokaz is the Supervisor of Cattle, and Jinimir commands the *vatovar*. Of these there are thirty, big and dangerous creatures; warriors all, who devour the bits of cattle the jinn leave for them. They aren't jinn, but creatures like them, and blindly loyal to Great Nimmendal. They command the cannons, with a six of pirates each.'

'How many pirates are there?' Shaw said.

Villaume brought his hands to his chest. 'That depends on the number of ships inside. But never less than a thousand.'

'They are drugged?' Nate said.

'Always,' Villaume said. 'Pirates and vatovar both. Not the cattle though.'

'Why not?' Shaw said.

'Because Great Nimmendal doesn't want them to die from brain rot. He dominates them with his mind alone, like noble Sostaz my master did with me.' Villaume looked at his hands. 'They are in a bad way. Great Nimmendal's domination has broken most minds, and they are as children.'

'A thousand pirates, besides those jinn,' Jurgis said, dismissing the locals for later. 'That's quite a force.'

'We plan to lessen the odds,' Nate said. 'We will let a treasure fleet sail close by and lure those ships out of their snug harbor.'

'Several slow merchant ships and two schooners, laden with gold for Myrlia,' Shaw said. 'That would embolden them to sail.'

'It would,' Villaume said. 'But why would you risk your gold?'

'Ah, there wouldn't really be treasure,' Nate said without even a hint of a smile. 'It would be a ruse. A trap.'

'Mouse trap,' Haai-Bo cackled. 'Sprung by big, fast warrior ships.'

'Oh.' Villaume said. 'I see. And you have those fast vessels?'

'We do,' Shaw said. 'Six of the best.'

'There is one thing you can help us with, Lord Jurgis,' Nate said. 'Spread the word of the treasure fleet.'

'We can do that,' Jurgis said. 'A few whispers, an official drinking too much in some tavern, some mindmages spreading it further; we'll get the story out fast.'

'That would be great,' Shaw said. 'I'll arrange for the treasure fleet. Two schooners and two merchant vessels, sailing from Brisa to Myrlia by way of Yavam Island. I will let you know when they are ready to depart. With a bit of luck, it should tempt all Angsthafn pirates out of hiding.'

She looked at Nate. 'It would be great to be rid of those jinn and their Bokkaners. I'm building a company and I'm darned sick of their beastly tricks!'

CHAPTER 22 — GATHERING

It took a full week for all ships to assemble in Smalkand Bay. *Drakon* and *Marigold* were first; then came *Maiden of Allastar,* the next day followed by *Sashu* and *Glory of Xalt.*

Shaw watched the latter two come in from the beach, with Nate and Captain Wylmer.

'Darn!' Wylmer said. 'What big beast is that?'

'Oh,' Shaw said innocently. 'That's some silly old Qoori frigate we captured.'

'She's the ship that nearly sank Abia's *Drakon*?' Wylmer said.

'If she hadn't had those two magnificent mages on board,' Shaw said. 'But yes, that's her.' She looked at the stout captain. 'Are you interested in commanding her?'

'Of course,' Wylmer said. 'But *Killarn Ranni...*'

'Is a schooner. Any midshipman could command her; we don't need a full-blown captain for that. And if you wonder what Eskandar would say, he'd agree with me. The power is shifting. When we've done away with Angsthafn, we don't need more than one captain at Smalkand. Miya can defend the keep with *Marigold* and one of your juniors in the *Killarn*. We need you at sea, protecting our empire.'

'Our what?' Wylmer said.

Shaw grinned. 'Merchant empire; not the icky political kind. I need big ships. The *Maiden* should go back to trading, and *Drakon* and *Royal Sashu* can't do it alone. Of course we can hire a captain in Seatome, if you don't want the job.'

'Don't be silly; of course I want the job,' Wylmer said. 'But wouldn't Abia...?'

'She won't leave *Drakon*,' Nate said. 'I asked her.'

'In that case, I accept,' Wylmer said. 'Let's go aboard. Who's in command now?'

'She has a handful of Qoori midshipmen,' Shaw said, as she mounted her broom. 'They're quite good but lack experience.'

As they landed in *Xalt*'s small gangway, a young underofficer came hurrying and saluted gravely.

'We arrived, Noble Lady. Welcome. Not speak much, but learn.'

'Good,' Shaw said. 'I am glad. We go to the bridge.' She opened the door to the bridge ladder. 'That guy is the bos'n's mate; one of the seven surviving Qoori leaders.'

On the bridge, they found both midshipmen, with a steersman and a lookout.

'Welcome in Smalkand,' she said. 'Did you have a good voyage?'

Huono saluted. 'Very good, ma'am. Though we request you appoint a captain. Too often we find details escape us; highly embarrassing.'

Shaw nodded. 'I know you are both capable and serious officers,' she said. 'So I thought the matter over and decided to grant your request. Captain Wylmer will take over command of the ship. I suggest he will keep you as first and second officers and see to what training you still need for your certificates. Captain Wylmer, this is Mr. Huono, who was in acting command. The second gentleman is Mr. Tahin.'

Both boys saluted, and Wylmer returned the honor.

'Permission to anchor, Captain?' Huono asked.

'You have the watch, Mr. Huono. Carry on.' Wylmer folded his arms and stepped back into the shadows.

As Huono gave his orders, Shaw winked at the captain. 'We will leave you gentlemen to it.'

The sixth ship, *Wentiibi* arrived near dusk, with the Saeill midshipman Ekiel in command, and Gunno of the *Grimrose* as mate.

'We fulfill our purpose and arrive,' Ekiel said, as Shaw and Nate met them on the beach.

Another kid would've been happy or proud after such a feat of seamanship, but Ekiel sounded as emotionless as before.

At his shoulder, Gunno sighed. 'It was a great journey, and he taught me a lot. If only he could laugh now and then.'

'I'm an officer of the Saeill Invincible Navy,' Ekiel said. 'We are not allowed to laugh. We have our purposes, and each leads to another, for the greater glory of the Saeill.'

'No, no, no,' Haai-Bo cried, dropping down from the sky like a hunting eagle. 'You serve the Lord Bodrus now. He is a jolly god; his divine joy strengthens the soul and the mind. On your knees, young Ekiel. On your knees, for the Sleeping God is here.'

A massive laughter rolled in from the mountains, an all-pervading happiness spread out over the bay and set *Wentiibi*'s crew singing.

'Your purposes are shackles, Ekiel of the Saeill,' a mighty voice said. *'Too heavy weights, carrying you down. By this my word I lift you up. POOF! Your chains are cast off, discarded, gone. You serve ME now, and my command to you is to be happy.'*

A blindingly white light enveloped the boy, and Ekiel cried out.

Then the mighty presence was gone.

'There,' Haai-Bo said. 'Better now?' He chuckled. 'You are honored; it is not easy even for our god to do this while he is asleep.'

Ekiel sat on his knees in the sand, crying his heart out. Shaw dropped next to him and drew her arms around him.

'Crying is good,' she said. 'It brings relief.'

The boy wiped his face on his sleeve. 'My head...' He said in a voice of wonder. 'It's clear. I see no purposes, but... choices. I never had a choice. What do I want? What do *I* want?' He came to his feet. 'I don't know.'

'Don't try to figure it out yet,' Shaw said. 'Let's go inside and meet the others. Take it as it comes.'

'It's a wondrous place, this,' Gunno said. 'Them things in the distance are mountains? They're pretty big, aren't they?' He grinned. 'The world is full of strangeness.'

'It is,' Shaw said. 'Come inside and be comfortable. Almost everybody is here; ships, soldiers, I only need my spies and we're all set.'

They walked into the mess, where Ekiel's unfamiliar blueness caught a lot of attention.

Captain Wylmer stood at the bar with Huono and the other boys from *Xalt*. 'More strange faces,' he said with a broad smile as Shaw pushed the two newcomers forward. 'Welcome!'

'Ekiel is in command of *Wentiibi*,' Shaw said. 'He and the ship are from the Saeill, a country far to the west of Malgarth. They ran into Bokkaners and he is the only survivor of his crew. Gunno here is the skipper of the Tradeport ship *Grimrose*, and acts as Ekiel's first officer for the duration.'

'Good of you,' Wylmer said. 'Come and meet my officers.'

Nate grinned as he steered Shaw away. 'Wylmer is in his element; he was bored to tears here.'

Near midnight, Keena strode in, dressed in a long fur cloak and carrying a sword. 'What's this about burgling Angsthafn?' she demanded as she gripped Shaw's hand.

'Not burgling,' Shaw said. 'We're going to take the place.' She came to her feet. 'Let's go sit somewhere; I'll explain all.'

'Hi, Callogan,' Nate said to the burly mover mage who had followed Keena in. 'You both look true native Peak folks in those smelly pelts.'

'It's cold out there,' he said. 'So we exchanged these at one of the keeps against two copper pans and an ax. I mean, freezing to death is bad for business, so why not?'

'It's fine,' Nate said. 'How is business?'

'People are glad to see us,' Callogan said. 'The gods know where old Sylas gets all those pans, but we're selling stacks of them. Tools, too, and strange enough we're running out of primers fast. I took a stack of children's books, as a hunch, say. People want them, remembering how their grandparents could read, they want to teach themselves and their kids.'

'I'll see who publishes those books,' Shaw said. 'We'll send you a load of them; Eskandar will like that.'

They sat down at a table, and while a serving boy brought cawah, Shaw introduced Villaume. The boy stared fixedly at Keena. 'Mountains,' he said. 'Solitude.'

'Lots of solitude,' Keena said.

'I would like that. Maybe when we're done, I will go with you and learn to live with the silence without masters.'

'We can always use a hand,' Callogan said, mustering the boy.

'We will speak of this again,' Villaume said. 'Now I will show you my home.'

Neither caravaneer said anything while they watched Villaume's image of the pirate base.

When he was done, Keena stretched her legs. 'And you want to capture that? What's our role in it?'

'First, we lure the pirates and most of their force out with our fake treasure fleet,' Shaw said. 'Then the five of us will sneak inside unseen, and free those wyrmlings. Haai-Bo will convince Izo-Ky, that's the big bronze, to join us and she'll hopefully help in the attack.'

'Sneak inside?' Keena looked skeptical. 'How?'

'It depends on Haai-Bo's smooth talking,' Shaw said. 'He'll convince the bronze to let us in. We drop in front of the cage, and you take care of the locks. Then we grab the little ones and warn the fleet. Our broomriders will come, Haai-Bo and the bronze will take care of the inn, while we collect as many of the slaves as we can and take them to safety.'

'That's it?' Keena said. 'That's the whole plan?' She shrugged. 'All right. No details to blow up in our faces; we improvise as we go along.'

'Those slaves, where will they be safe?' Callogan asked.

Villaume focused his eyes on the big mover mage. 'Nowhere,' he said. 'No safe places for cattle. They will flee to their stables and wait.'

CHAPTER 23 — ATTACK

Midshipman Miran turned. 'The treasure fleet is under attack, captain,' he said. 'Ten ships, and some are big 'uns, their communicator reported.'

Abia turned to Shaw. 'This is it. We will close the trap and finish those pirates off.'

A shadowy figure stepped forward, scribbling madly. 'You're going to attack them?' Emmett of the *Gazette* said.

Shaw hadn't seen him before, but she wasn't surprised by his presence. This was a big effort, after all, and his readers surely wanted to know all about it. She looked in the distance, where the volcano lay hidden in the darkness of midnight. 'You'll have to choose, Mister Barlett. Witness the sea battle or the attack on the island.'

'That's no choice,' the young reporter said. 'I'm for the island. The sea battle I can do later, using eyewitness accounts.'

Shaw grinned. 'All right then, Keep your head down, buster. Captain Abbram, we'll go in.' She turned to Nate and the other three. 'Finally.' She brushed Nate's cheek and got out her broom.

'Dear Bodrus, protect us this day, my God,' she thought. *'We're going to battle a bi-ig foe and we don't want to fail you.'*

Villaume sat down in front of her, and she shot up in the air. Higher and higher they rose, and then they set course for the volcano.

'Haai-Bo?'

'Sure,' the wyrmling said. *'Me and young Wiu-To are right ahead of you. I'm trying to locate the bronze... My, she's mad!'*

'What?' Shaw said, and her heart missed a beat.

'Not the spell,' Haai-Bo said quickly. *'Raging mad with despair. I have to be very clear to her.'*

Shaw heard him speak, and she was surprised at the commanding tone he used. The words were incomprehensible, an endless stream both stern and encouraging. Then he broke contact.

'He's a boss,' Villaume said. 'Small, but a boss.'

'Haai-Bo is very highborn,' Shaw said. 'About as high as a male wyrm can be, I think.'

Suddenly a darker shape doomed up. *Haai-Bo, we're there,'* Shaw said, feeling her stomach flip-flop.

'Follow the wall to the left,' Villaume said.

Shaw turned her broom with the side of the volcano barely fifty yards away.

It took another ten minutes before Villaume stirred. 'Careful now.' He whispered, as if afraid the jinn could hear him. There was the cleft in the mountain's side.

'We go in?' she asked.

'Yes,' he said in a voice devoid of emotion.

Shaw entered the cleft, with below her a mass of torches illuminating the hulks with their heavy cannons, and cadaverous monsters even bigger that she'd guessed from the boy's mind.

'Ma'am, she reluctantly gives you fifteen minutes,' Haai-Bo said.

'Faster!' Shaw said and her broom raced across the width of the volcano, over the bay and village. There! The ship, an old trade ship without her masts, with the great bulk of an adult wyrm fidgeting over a large steel cage.

Beside her, Keena dropped without a word and landed in front of the cage door. She was already inspecting the lock when the others joined her. A soft tinkle of her tools told Shaw she'd gone to work.

Then a thin shape stepped from the shadows. 'What are you doing? a high boyish voice said arrogantly.

'We are inspecting the lock,' Villaume said in a subservient voice. 'There is some slight damage; see here.'

'Since when are *you* doing anything important?' the boy sneered. He moved to look closer at the lock, and with one swift blow, Villaume's fist slammed his head hard against the cage. The other boy dropped, and Villaume grabbed him by his tunic and pants, and in one swoop threw him over the railing into the bay. 'Drown, traitor!' he snarled, as the unconscious boy sank from sight.

'Well,' Shaw said. 'That was fast. He wasn't one of the good guys?'

Villaume turned to her, his face impassive again. 'No. The traitor was Amir Rotokaz' boy, who was even crueler than his master. He would have betrayed us in a split second.' He made a brief, chopping motion with his right hand. 'That one was feared by all, and thus unexpecting of violence on himself.'

Overhead, the big dragon rumbled in her throat. 'Darn, those fifteen minutes!' Shaw said.

But Keena hadn't paused in her fiddling, and with a soft click the cage door swung open.

'Quickly,' Villaume said. 'Get those little ones; there will have been an alarm somewhere.'

Shaw plucked a wyrmling from the floor and carried it from the cage. Nate got another one, and Callogan deposited the last two outside. The bronze wyrm crooned, and the biggest of the four wyrmlings lifted its head. It mewled a little, then hopped into the air and flew, to land on its mother's back. The second followed, but the other two didn't manage to get off the ground. They flapped their wings, crying, without success. Nate picked them up and flew to deposit them with their siblings.

'Haai-Bo, ask her to help us. And please tell Captain Abbram to start the assault,' Shaw said. Then they flew up, to hover high over the pirate base.

'We got the ships,' Haai-Bo said. *'At least six captured; the others sunk. Broom boys are under way.'*

'Excellent,' Shaw said. 'As soon as they're here, we must get the slaves to safety.'

It was sooner than she expected when a wave of broomriders came through the cleft in the volcano wall.

'Haai-Bo, ask Izo-Ky to assist,' Shaw said.

The big wyrm jumped in the air and in a few wing beats, she was at the cleft, raining fire down on the vatovar and the pirates lounging at the guns, and they died in their masses.

'A jinni!' Lord Jurgis' voice shouted. 'There's a jinni here!'

Shaw's broom reached the cleft, seeing the wyrm dive, flaming at a blob of lard bigger than any jinn Shaw had seen before. Under her fire he withered, and within seconds, the beast exploded.

'I love that wyrm!' Jurgis cried. 'Gods! What a power.'

'The ca... people,' Villaume said urgently. 'Rotokaz is there, ordering them to die!'

'Back!' Shaw said, her heart in her throat. 'Where is he?'

They found the jinni on the balcony of a wooden building overlooking a corral filled with panicky humans. In his true form he was a buglike creature, with too many limbs and multifaceted eyes, but the same human eyes and mouth in the place where his innards were.

Callogan stood on his broom, his face furious as he pointed at the jinni.

'Wait!' Reporter Emmett steered his broom past the mover mage and a bright light flashed. 'Go ahead,' he yelled to Callogan, his face twisted in a mixture of horror and determination.

Callogan growled. He stretched out a hand and the jinni rose from the roof, squirming and waving his limbs, as the mover mage pulled him higher and higher. Then he sent the jinni crashing down faster than a body should fall. It broke on the bay's surface, and as it sank, a large hole in the water showed where it imploded.

Callogan landed on the roof where the jinni had stood. 'Inside!' he yelled in a mighty voice. 'Get inside!'

A small group of men and women started to run, and in seconds the whole mass poured into the wooden building.

'Darn,' Shaw said. 'What's that Nimmendal guy doing?'

'Hiding, perhaps?' Nate said.

'*Shaw!*' Haai-Bo said sharply. '*Join me at the keep, quick!*'

She stared up and saw him overhead with the bronze wyrm.

'*What's wrong?*' she said, as she steered her broom upward.

'*Nimmendal is on the roof, resurrecting the fallen! Our people will be overwhelmed soon. Izo-Ky will attack, but you must distract him first, to give her time.*'

'*On my way!*' Shaw said, and she raced away, followed by Nate with Villaume.

At the keep she saw the jinni prince for the first time. She had heard the stories of Ozoezd, who Eskandar had killed at Kalbakar; a jinni taller than the warlock tower. This one wasn't much smaller, and the keep seemed barely big enough to hold him. Beside him was a large square shape hidden in blackness.

'Nimmendal!' Shaw cried.

'*Again,*' Haai-Bo said, and Shaw repeated her cry.

'Nimmendal!'

The jinni prince turned as he heard his name echoing through the volcano.

Then he smiled. 'Trade Magnate. Impressive how far you have come. But here it stops. Now you are up against me, and I will win.'

'You're a fool, Nimmendal,' Shaw said. 'You have been a silly idiot from the very beginning. Blundering at WyDir, blundering with Brynnyr Gunny, blundering at Brisa, and now you are blundering here. Darn, overblown puppet; you jinn are stupid beasts!'

The jinni's face had turned a deep red, and he lifted a hand.

'The prophecy will help me this time, you cattle girl!' he yelled. 'Behold the children who will aid my cause. Feeding on their hatred will make me invincible.'

He pointed a fist the size of a dinner table at the blackness, and it dispersed, showing a barred cage full of kids. They were thin, underfed, full of sores, and glaring at the jinni like feral wolves.

'Now you die, child!' Nimmendal said, throwing a wave of incandescence at Shaw.

She dropped just fast enough to feel the heat singing her hair, and then, with a screech that tore the universe, bronze Izo-Ky came down in a near unstoppable mass of muscle and sheer rage. Her claws bit into the jinni's face as she flamed him. Beside her, Wiu-To spat small flames at the jinni's belly face, while two of the little wyrmlings were diving and snapping at the crazy eyes.

'I am undefeatable!' Nimmendal yelled, and it seemed the wyrm fire didn't touch him. 'The prophecy was right! Those cattle calves give me victory!'

'Keena!' Shaw cried. *'I need you!'* She had never before mindcalled anyone but Teodar and Bodrus, and no idea if the other girl heard her. She stared at the kids in the cage, those poor, mistreated kids who were helping their tormentor win with their hate.

Then Keena dropped down beside her. 'My!' she said with a fleeting glance at Nimmendal. 'That's a big 'un, gal.'

Her cool demeanor steadied Shaw. 'Can you get that cage open?' she whispered hoarsely. 'Else we'll lose.'

Keena took a tool from her belt and started on the cage lock. Only then, Nimmendal sensed his danger, for he yelled in anger and reached out a hand to bash Keena. Little Wiu-To dropped from the sky and sent a small mouthful of fire at the hand. The jinni prince screamed a curse and swatted at the wyrmling. But Wiu-To was gone, and the cage lock clicked open.

'Out!' Shaw screamed, her heart pumping like a steam engine. 'Out of that cage! Move! Nate, take those kids into the building. Hurry!'

Nate and Callogan ran forward and herded the kids away.

'Nooo!' Nimmendal yelled as his power weakened, and the bronze wyrm breathed a mighty flame into his face. The jinni's skin and flesh burned away and now only the tinny voice from his belly mouth screamed.

Shaw drew her knives and ran, ducking below the wyrm's claws, she struck twice. Green blood welled up over the horrid face. Then Villaume came, carrying a long spear some soldier must've dropped. His face twisted in terrible anger, he ran the weapon deep into Nimmendal's belly.

The headless body stiffened as its alien brain died and imploded with a sound that shook the very stones.

The wyrm squawked in surprise as her claws held nothing, and Villaume tumbled down in a heap in the powdery dust the jinni prince's downfall had left behind.

CHAPTER 24 — VICTORY

Shaw swallowed a scream as she ran and dropped to her knees beside Villaume. 'Are you all right?'

The boy turned his gray-streaked face toward her, his eyes big and unseeing, and didn't speak.

'Shock,' Nate said. 'Leave him to me; I'll take him to Healer Tymon.' He rose with the boy in his arms. 'Guy must've bird bones; he doesn't weigh much.'

As Nate flew the boy away, Shaw came to her feet and looked up at the wyrm, and the four wyrmlings peering down.

'Thank you,' she gasped, wrestling to steady her breathing. 'Your help made our victory possible, bronze warrior.'

'I... am unused to speech,' the wyrm said. 'Not since Lord Vystyn's days have I spoken aloud. You gave me back my nestlings. You could have demanded my help, by keeping them. Instead, you counted on my honor. Never did any... human... do such, but you. Why?'

'We are of the wyrmcaller's people,' Shaw said. 'We want to help Princess Lothi-Mo and Advisor Haai-Bo restore the wyrms to their proper place in the world.'

'These are things I do not know,' Izo-Ky said, and she sounded perplexed. 'I lack the memories.'

'When we are done here, you must go home with our fleet to Smalkand Bay. It is too far to fly directly, but together with our ships you will have a place to rest when there is need. At Smalkand you will find a Wyrm Ledge and a safe place for your wyrmlings, with many memories.'

'Just so says the noble Haai-Bo,' the bronze said. 'He is wise beyond his years and I trust his word. I will return with your vessels.'

Shaw nodded her thanks and turned around when another voice shouted from the still dark sky over her head.

'There you are!' Lord Jurgis sounded jubilant as he bumped down beside her.

'Well met, bronze wyrm,' he said more quietly. 'You did both humans and your people a great service today.' Then he enveloped Shaw in a small bear's hug. 'We won! It was the weirdest thing; we were fighting those horrible monster warriors and despaired. Every one we killed, rose to attack again, stronger than before. Then all of a sudden the lot of them imploded. The pirates went crazy; crying and fighting us and each other, and the slaves turned into sleepwalkers. All they do is walk around and lament.'

'Nimmendal was resurrecting the fallen,' Shaw said breathlessly. 'Until Izo-Ky and Villaume managed to kill him and shatter his hold over his minions.'

'It was a great fight,' Jurgis said with satisfaction. 'We captured Angsthafn! After all those years we finally captured it. We broke the power of the pirates; the seas are ours again!'

'Now we must get the place back on its feet,' Shaw said. 'We must repair the damage, the locals will need a great deal of care; it will be terribly expensive.'

'Expensive,' Lord Jurgis said. 'But I'm sure you will manage. With your resources...'

'Wouldn't the Weal do it?' she asked innocently.

'Basil is quite content to leave it to you,' Lord Jurgis said. 'The Weal isn't looking for colonies; in fact my brother was just writing the proposal you had discussed for the transfer of Port Naar to your company.'

'Well,' Shaw said. 'If you insist...' She hid a grin. It was all a game; she knew the Weal wouldn't want to pay good gold for a place that was no use to them. But to get Port Naar would be nice. 'We will take charge then,' she said. *'Haai-Bo, would you call the engineer and ask her set up the portal she brought?'*

Villaume came, still looking dazed. 'It's done?' he said. 'The voices died. Now we are all alone. What will happen to us?'

'Alone?' Shaw said. 'Of course not. You are honorable citizens of the Pasandir Peaks, with your own local government and all the good things we can bring you. You will be safe, well-fed and happy.'

'Will we?' he said. 'But our minds aren't used to thinking; our ears have forgotten how to listen and we are drowning in the silence without the jinn.'

'You will soon speak and listen, and we will send help with the silence,' Shaw said. 'Now come; I will first see those kids. Are they your people?'

'No; they are prisoners from captured ships. There are many more of them in the cattle pens,' Villaume said. 'They weren't cattle, and we never knew what their use was.'

Shaw walked into the keep and found herself on the doorstep of a large wooden hall. Doors and much of the furniture were of a size to dwarf even a full-grown Kell; Nimmendal-sized. For a moment she paused. She's been high on fighting spirit, and now she felt empty. Automatically she looked around, but then she remembered Nate was taking Villaume to the healers. She closed her eyes. *Give me strength, lord,* she said. Bodrus didn't answer, but a glow like the coming of spring spread through her body She sighed and walked into the hall.

In the center, the kids from the cage huddled together, their hate drained, and only a few of them looked up as she joined them.

'Hi,' she said. 'I can tell you the jinn and the pirates are all dead.'

Several more looked at her, but no one spoke.

'You are all sailors?' she said.

For a moment they just stared. Then one of them, a hollow-eyed girl with wild, dirty hair, nodded. 'All.'

'There are more of you?'

Again she nodded. 'Many; in the pens.'

'Can you show me?' Shaw said crisply.

The girl came to her feet. 'Yes.'

'Come,' Shaw said, and slowly they walked outside. Here, Shaw got her broom. 'We will fly,' she said. 'Sit down before me.'

The pens were across the bay; an empty expanse of sand and stones, enclosed by a high stockade. At one end stood a large wooden hall, with the balcony where the Rotokaz jinni had stood.

'Inside,' the girl said, her face wet with sweat as if she'd done something strenuous.

Shaw entered the building and stopped in her tracks. 'Oh, gods,' she said. Rows upon rows of rickety wooden bunk beds, each with three or four kids clothed in rags and covered with filth. All had wounds, and open sores; their faces dull with exhaustion and undernourishment. 'Why?'

There was no answer.

'Tymon?' Shaw said urgently, hoping the Smalkand healer would hear her.

'Shaw?'

'You busy?'

'I'm finished with our side. No dead, and most wounded were simple stabs and slashings.'

'I'm at the cattle pens,' Shaw said. *'There are some two hundred kids here, and it's awful. We need a god; no healer can do this alone.'*

'Stay where you are, I'm coming over,' Tymon said calmly.

Shaw had noticed before that their top healer never sounded in a hurry, but that he moved around extremely fast. She barely had time to walk over to the nearest row of crowded bunk beds before he walked in.

Cool and professionally unperturbed, he walked briskly up to her.

'I see what you mean,' he said. 'If we move these people as they are, we lose half of them. Leaving them here is no option either. Are these all?'

Shaw looked at the girl who had brought her here. 'Any more of them?'

Slowly, the girl shook her head. 'Two hundred thirteen,' she said. 'If none died since yesterday's muster.'

Tymon nodded. He walked to the center of the room and held out his arms, hand palms turned outward. He closed his eyes, and Shaw saw his lips move. Around him, a thin white mist gathered, thickening as it spread out across the floor, disregarding the filth. It rose, swirling around the bedposts, covering the prostrate bodies.

The mist avoided her, Shaw saw, and Tymon, but it touched everyone else, until it reached the ceiling. Vague shadows moved around the room, pausing and moving what looked like limbs. It was strange, but not at all creepy, and Shaw watched without fear. Now and then, someone moaned, or coughed rattling, and finally all grew silent. The mist thinned and disappeared.

On the nearest bed, a boy sat up, his eyes large and blinking as he looked around. 'What happened?'

'How do you feel?' Tymon said in his calm physician's voice.

'Trampled by wild buffaloes,' the boy said.

'Elephants,' another guy said. 'Mean, heavy elephants, walking all over me. Oh gods!'

'The elephants are gone,' Tymon said. 'Can you stand?'

The first boy rose, clutching the bedpost as he swayed. 'Force ten,' he said. 'No walking the deck, skipper.'

'Try it,' Tymon said. 'Touch my fingers.' He held out his hands, elbows to his sides.

The first boy frowned and carefully walked to grip the healer's hands like a drunken man.

'Good,' Tymon said. 'You're strong.'

The second boy made a snorting sound. 'I can do that,' he said, and weaved his way to Tymon.

'Very good,' Tymon said. He walked round, asking questions, probing and testing. Finally he walked back to Shaw.

'Not bad at all,' he said. 'Lumentis sent me aid — don't ask me what it was. An army of ghost healers, maybe. It worked; the urgency is gone. All they need is rest, food and fresh air.'

'I can give them that,' Shaw said. 'As soon as our engineer has installed her portal. Let's see what they want.'

She walked to the same spot Tymon had stood. 'Guys,' she said. 'I'm Shaw Harwans; the boss of the Pasandir Trading Co. Rejoice; Angsthafn has fallen. Nimmendal and his cronies are dead, and you are all free.'

'Nimmendal, dead?' someone said. 'Impossible.'

'Not,' the girl who had brought Shaw here said. 'I was there; the wyrm killed him, she did. All fire and claws and he died.'

'So he did,' Shaw said. 'He couldn't withstand a very angry wyrm. Now we have taken over the base. We, that is the PTC's merchant marine and navy.' She grinned. 'A great fight it was, too. Now the PTC will rebuild the island for the local population, like we did at Yavam Island. And you, what do you want? Home? Or a good paying berth?'

'My ship was my home,' a girl said. 'Those beggars killed everyone and stole her. Now where can I go?'

'You're a sailor?'

'Sure,' she said. 'Navigator's mate I was.'

'We need you,' Shaw said. 'I can offer you an acting third mate's ticket, and the schooling to make it stick. Pay according to the official rates, and all the stuff. Think on it.'

She looked at the whole group. 'Guys, you think you can walk to the keep?'

'Try me!' the first boy said. rubbing at a badly healed sore on his arm.

'All right; I'll meet you in the hall,' Shaw said. 'If you have any possessions, don't leave them behind. You'll not be coming back here.'

'Good to see you guys are thinking again,' Tymon said. 'You'll all make it. I'll look in at the locals then.' With a nod and a smile he was off.

Shaw grinned at Villaume as she mounted her broom. 'Tymon is a most powerful healer; he will help your people as he did those kids.'

'There truly was a god?' Villaume said. 'I never heard of a god coming here. Who was he?'

'They couldn't, before; not with the jinn here. This one was Lumentis, God of Knowledge. He is the patron of Vanhaar and most mages follow him. Tymon uses his power for his healing and calls on our own god Bodrus for special cases.'

They touched down at the hall and hurried inside. Nate saw her come in and his eyes lighted up. 'There you are!' he said. 'We just had a miracle. A mist came out of nowhere and touched those kids from the cage. Now look at them!'

Shaw stared at the kids and started to laugh. 'We found a mass of captured guys at the cattle pens, many close to death. Tymon came and called on Lumentis to heal the lot of them. Apparently he did those at the same time.' She walked over. 'Feeling better? The others at the pens are coming here to join you, and then we'll get you away from this place.'

'We got the portal,' Nate said. 'Mage Kier volunteered to man it for the time; he had a replacement in Old Warf, and we need an experienced portal mage here.'

'Excellent,' Shaw said. 'Will you receive those two hundred kids when they come here? I want to hire all who are willing and send home those who won't. Meanwhile I'm going to the ships and see about those prizes. Those kids can man them and sail them home when they've got their strength back.'

'I'll sort them out,' Nate said. 'Groups of ten, and those who want to go home apart from the others.'

Shaw kissed him quickly. 'Thank you. For your patience with bossy me as well.'

He grinned. 'Not bossy, organizing. You're doing great, girl.'

Her step was lighter as she hurried over to Kier. She had been afraid Nate would resent not going with her, but he understood.

'Kier!' she said. 'Am I glad you are here! Can you port me to *Drakon*?'

'Hop in,' he said. 'You're in a heck of a hurry, of course.'

'Ain't I always?' she said, and then she stood in *Drakon*'s portal.

She hurried on deck and looked around. The bogus treasure fleet was under full sail, back to Seatome. There was a cluster of six assorted pirate ships, and around *Drakon* was the rest of their fleet, anchored where they liked.

Aft she found Flag Captain Abia, studying the six pirate ships with her hands to her back.

She smiled when she saw Shaw coming. 'We won,' she said. 'How is it with the base?'

'It's ours,' Shaw said. 'In every way.' Her bad eye was blurry, and she got out her eye patch.

'You've been overdoing it again,' Abia said critically. 'Why don't you go and have a cawah?'

'Later,' Shaw said. The idea was tempting, but she knew she'd never get back up again if she sat down now. She smiled. 'There are some things I must do first. Can you sail those prizes into the base?'

'Sure,' Abia said. 'I'll get on to it directly. What are we going to do with them?'

'We found a mass of captured sailor kids. Healer Tymon got them walking again. I want to sign them on. Those kids can man the prizes and sail them home when they've found their strength back. Tamyas can arrange that; he will know how they feel.'

She found Tamyas on his bridge.

'There you are!' he cried. 'I was about to come and kiss you! What a day! What a glorious day! We wiped them out! We...'

His voice faltered. 'We did get Nimmendal, didn't we?'

'We certainly did,' Shaw said. 'There isn't a pirate or jinni alive around here. Now I have a job for you.'

She told him of the rescued kids, and he stilled.

'Over two hundred?' he whispered. 'So much suffering. They are all like we were, only worse? I must meet them. Put them on board the ships, it will be good for them to be doing familiar things. Amsalon will send food and lemonades from Myrlia, and that will get them back on their feet in a jiffy.' He turned to Wanei, his Qoori first officer. 'Set course for the entrance. And tell Flag we'll be leaving station.'

Wanei passed on the orders to the steersman, and the telegraph jingled. Then *Sashu*'s nose lifted, and she raced away.

The channel into the volcano was full of drifting rubble, broken trees, gun carriages and bodies, but *Sashu* plowed through, and into the round bay.

'Moor in front of the keep,' Shaw said. 'Those kids should be inside, with Nate.'

Without the slightest bump, the ship came alongside the jetty, and sailors sprang ashore to fasten her lines.

Tamyas squared his shoulders inside the long coat with the heavy golden epaulettes he always wore. 'Let's go.' He ran down the ladder and onto the wooden pier.

In the keep hall he stopped and stared around. 'Jinn-sized?'

'This was Nimmendal's home,' Shaw said.

He spat on the ground. 'Burn the stuff,' he growled. Then he saw the mass of kids and hurried over.

'Afternoon,' he said. 'I'm Captain Tamyas, of the PTC ship *Royal Sashu.*'

'I know that coat,' a rake-thin boy said, staring fixedly at Tamyas through the hair that hid half his face. 'That bliddy coat captured me. He wasn't you though. What happened to him?'

Tamyas stroked an epaulet and smiled. 'I'll tell you.' Then he sat down and told them of Allastar Cove, of their raid, and Shaw presenting him with the coat afterward. 'It's a lovely coat,' he said. 'You can see his bloodstains still on the front, where Nate had skewered him. You see, guy, I was a prisoner of those beggars too. Six months rowing that cow *Kokkacir* all over the Emerang Sea until Shaw and her guys came and freed us. They took *Kokkacir* and went on to conquer Yavam Island as well. Most of my guys in *Sashu* were with me on Yavam. We know how it was.'

'He's dead then,' the boy said slowly. 'May I touch his bloodstains?'

'Go right ahead,' Tamyas said.

The boy came forward and caressed the discoloration with his fingers. 'That makes me feel better,' he said.' Thank you, Captain.' Then he went over to Nate. 'May I shake your hand, sir?'

'Sure,' Nate said, and they shook solemnly.

'This is a great day,' the boy said, as he rejoined the others.

'And we'll make it even better,' Tamyas said. 'We captured six of the pirate ships; the rest went to the bottom. Now, seeing how you're all of the sea like me, and I'm a tramp sailor of Port Waid, Ms. Shaw wants you to take over our prizes, put them back into business, and when you're strong enough, sail them to our home port at Smalkand. You'll be paid, fed, clothed and everything. One of our ships will stay here, and escort you. Once in Smalkand, those of you who want to go home, will get some money and free passage. The others can sign on and become sailors of the Peaks.'

'A fair offer,' the girl who had been a navigator's mate said. 'Ms. Shaw promised me a third mate's ticket; I'll take it.'

'The offer stands,' Shaw said. 'You're welcome.'

'Any others who were mates or apprentices?' Tamyas said.

Several hands went up; a master's mate, a bos'n's apprentice, a carpenter's mate, and finally the boy who had touched the coat came and admitted he'd been a Hizmyran midshipman.

Shaw stared at him. 'How do you get here?'

'I was out with the gig, fishing for the captain's dinner.' He clenched his teeth. 'That's not normally a midshipman's duty, but I was under punishment for talking back.'

'Giving a superior lip, you mean?' Tamyas said.

'I did, Captain. I asked my first officer not to call me Bonesy. My name is Bonard, sir, but as I am somewhat thin, I've been called Bonesy quite often. But not by the first lieutenant in front of the whole crew. Still, I should have kept my mouth shut. Anyway, there I was fishing, sitting in an open boat with two sailors for six hours on end and one bottle of water for the three of us. Then the pirate came, bristling with guns. My ship... left, sir.'

'Without you,' Tamyas said, and the anger was clear in his face.

'Yes, Captain,' the boy said. 'The pirate took me, shot the two sailors, and came here. And here I stayed.'

'How long had you been at sea?'

'Six years, sir, of which four as a midshipman.'

'You think you can command a not-too-idiotically-large ship?'

A hint of a smile crossed the boy's lips. 'I think I could sir.'

'I'll let you prove it,' Tamyas said. 'And you will write a report about your being deserted by your superiors. Our Lord Amsalon at Myrlia will pass it on to Crown Prince Meshan, and I'm sure something will be done about it.'

The boy's eyes glinted. 'Thank you, sir,' he said. 'I will, with pleasure.'

Shaw nodded to Tamyas. 'I'll leave you to it, Captain.' She went outside, and nearly bumped into Nate, who came hurrying in again.

'Oops,' he said, embracing her. 'Callogan will be around later; he's cleaning out the debris in the cleft. Fascinating, how he handles those big guns and everything.' He grinned. 'Remember that crystal cutter who skipped it the New Winsproke mine?'

Shaw frowned. 'Yes; number sixteen. What about him?'

'He didn't run. A jinni kidnapped him and he's here, cutting gems that were intended for *Xalt*. We really ruined Nimmendal's plan when we took his ship. He looked well fed, but stiff with stress. So I told him about Wattash and sent him to Alid Jassal with a little note to explain matters. I never saw a guy that relieved.'

Shaw looked thoughtful. 'It stands to reason those beasts had a cutter. Nimmendal wouldn't have his pirates stealing crystals from the Winsproke mine if he hadn't had someone to prepare them. Good, his cutter friends will be glad to have him back.' She clapped her hands together. 'Let's get Villaume and see the locals.'

Moments later, the boy came out. 'I heard my name,' he said simply.

'I was going to call you,' Shaw said. 'Let's see the local people.'

Without a word the boy sat down on her broom, and they crossed the bay to where the locals had been kept.

'At the big hall we are,' Haai-Bo said. *'Healer is getting very tired, but most are people again.'*

Shaw landed and waited for Villaume to get off first. Then she sheathed her broom and took Nate's hand. Together, they went inside the large hall.

The great space was packed, and the stink terrible. Shaw saw Tymon and walked through two rows of people to join him. Hundreds of pairs of eyes followed her, but no one spoke.

Tymon looked up as she came. Tired or not, his face was expressionless as ever. 'There you are. I've done all I could here. They are functioning again, but if you wanted a local government—forget it. First of all those people need lots of rest and plenty of food. But even when they have regained their strength, they won't do more than simple tasks, like tilling the land or hauling goods. They have been under the jinn's dominion too long; it will take another generation before they can start ruling themselves.'

Shaw looked at Villaume. 'I'm sorry, guy.'

The boy nodded. 'I knew it. You couldn't *talk* with them; you see.'

'Everything will be all right,' Shaw said. 'I will ask our Hizmyr director to open a warehouse here, with a manager who can take over the local government. What will you do?'

Villaume looked out over the bay. 'I will go with Keena and Callogan, if they want me. I... I can't stay here.'

'I think they will take you,' Shaw said.

That evening, Shaw and Nate sat in *Drakon*'s messroom, where they had just finished a lavish meal, when Lord Amsalon strode in.

'You did it!' he cried, as he shook their hands. 'You took Angsthafn! The coastal peoples of two seas are rejoicing at your victory. How did you manage to defeat those jinn?'

Shaw caught Nate's glance and sat back, while he told the story.

A serving boy brought cawah, but it didn't break Amsalon's concentration as he listened. When Nate was done, the Hizmyr director sat staring at him and Shaw. 'A heroic victory,' he said. 'And now?'

'I need a manager for Isdor, that's Angsthafn's original name,' Shaw said. 'That's why I asked you to come over.'

Amsalon sipped his cawah. 'I've got two guys,' he said after a pause. 'Twins. I was grooming them for the airship company, but I can find others for that. They're a former guild prince's sons. The one was a minor guildmaster already, his twin a lazy do-nothing — until we found he was a mage. They are nineteen or twenty years old, and together they would be perfect for rebuilding Angst... ah, Isdor.' He hesitated. 'The island is somewhat isolated. Do we have a purpose for that place? Any specialties or whatever?'

'As a naval base it's great.' Shaw said. 'It only lacks a shipyard to be perfect.'

'It's on the Greenwall coast,' Nate said. 'There's a huge river delta right behind it. No one knows it's there, because the jinn kept the whole region well hidden. Some brave explorer could have a crack at opening up the land behind it.'

Shaw sat up. 'I hadn't thought of that! Of course! Isdor as our advance base for the exploration of the Greenwall.' She gripped Nate's hand. 'That's brilliant!'

'I'll ask around,' Amsalon said. He sat back in his chair and watched with fascination how Shaw dipped one cookie after another in a bowl of whipped cream and ate it. 'You really are a most remarkable lady. You build a trade empire like the world never saw before, you defeated the Hizmyran guilds, what none of my countryfolk believed possible, you reorganized young High Queen Agusta's realm, and now you wiped out the pirates who were infesting two oceans. What will you do next?'

'Take a break,' Shaw said. She wiped a dollop of cream from her chin and licked it off her fingers. 'The guys have earned a rest while we wait.'

Amsalon and Nate both stared at her.

'Wait for whom?' Nate said.

'The boss. From now on it's his show. Eskandar will call us for the final battle and we'll go when he does. The prophecy needs us there, with our troops and as many of our kids as we can gather. But the next part is warfare, and that's his beastie.'

Nate nodded. 'Right. I wouldn't mind a break, to be honest. Loaf around, sleep, fish a bit.' He eyed her. 'Together, preferably.'

She patted his hand. 'Together.'

'When that call comes, you can count on me,' Amsalon said. 'You give the word and I'll gather every able-bodied youngster we can muster and join you.'

Shaw grinned. 'I know and I won't forget you, be sure of that.'

'We'll show those man-eating creeps!' Amsalon said. He cocked an eye at her. 'Dear Shaw, Nate; it's none of my business, but that break is a good idea. You two are looking somewhat worn.'

'Like dishrags we are,' Shaw said. 'Old, wrung out dishrags.' Suddenly she knew Nate was right; sleep did sound wonderful. She became aware of the cream-covered biscuit in her hand and her stomach turned with revulsion. 'Enough!' She dropped it on her plate and wiped her hands on her trousers. 'Amsalon, if you want to look the island over, we got a portal in the hall of Nimmendal's keep. Kier from Old Wharf came over as temporary portal mage.'

'I'll go and see him,' Amsalon said.

'Then we're off to bed,' Nate said. He grunted. 'I'm bunking with the crew; Lord Jurgis has my cabin.'

Shaw looked at him. 'Why didn't you tell me? I've got this massive double bed that's far too large for a small girl. There's plenty room for a big hulking boy as well.'

'Who?' Nate said. 'Callogan?'

Shaw gripped his arm. 'Idiot. Good night, Amsalon.'

The Hizmyr director rose and bowed. 'Good night, dear lady; good night, Nate. Have a nice break.'

NOT YET THE END

In **Book #7, Jinnbane,** Eskandar will gather all his forces for the final battle against the lich king and his Jinn minions.

LIST OF NAMES

Abbram, Captain of the PTC Battalion
Abia, Captain of the *Drakon*; sister to Sylas
Agusta, High Queen of Malgarth
Alid Jassal, Director Wattash Mining Comp.
Aliq the Ratboy, mage at the Myrlia warehouse
Amaj Mir, a Kalbakar lordling; Marshall of the Pasandir Army
Amsalon lord Illansor, PTC Director Hizmyr
Ancho-Dar, the Wyrm Queen
Anna, portaller Emporium New Winsproke
Awasuz (D), amir of the Ninth Plane; a jinni lord
Barlett, Emmett, journalist *Weal Gazette*
Barzudan, Duke; a jinni prince at Ozzoon
Basil, Lord Spellstor, Naudin's father
Ber, PTC Lieutenant New Winsproke Defenders
Beth, portaller mage, Smalkand
Bonard, a Hizmyran midshipman
Brigg, a mage school student at Allastar Castle
Brynnyr Gunny, a warlock dowser
Callogan, a mover mage, caravaneer
Cathew, foreman Brisan Building Co
Chagan, Qoori 1Off *Marigold*, Pasandir Navy
Clanger, manager of the New Winsproke shipyard
Clanger, Old Mr. (D) former manager New Winsproke Shipyard
Cornal, Portal mage at Landfalln
Crimmon, mine owner New Winsproke
Darquine of Piright, High Merchant Proprietor of the MCTC
Efena of Rattspir-Volgan, Lady; Lord Rutus' wife
Eghol of Unwaar, ruler, High Singer of Aera
Ekiel, PTC acting captain *Wentiibi*
Elijan, portal hedgemage *Sashu*
Ellogg, PTC broomrider lieutenant New Winsproke Defenders
Enric, portal mage Myrlia
Eskandar, Wyrmcaller of Kalbakar
Ferrazi, Lord; Hizmyran Finance Minister
Gerben of Wrache, Lord Rutus' son
Gorthos, Ducal Commander of troops at Wattash
Gotan, Qoori bos'n's mate *Drakon*
Grim, quartermaster *Sashu*
Gunno, PTC skipper of the *Grimrose*

Haai-Bo, an advisor wyrmling
Hizar, Captain, adjutant of the Hizmyran crown prince
Huono, PTC acting 1Off *Xalt*
Iefan, warehouse manager Wattash
Imooga of the White Shore Clan, Thali engineer, cousin of Ulaataq;
Isambar, PTC captain of *Fayaafa*
Izo-Ky the wyrm of Angsthafn
Jakop, quartermaster *Sashu*
Jathira, Guildlady, a Hizmyran former guild agent
Jem, Princess of Nanstalgarod
Jeppe, a spellscribe mage
Jinnbane, the historic hero who banished the jinn; Skandar Jinnbane
Jonna of Lammark, Agusta's friend
Jurgis of Kell-Spellstor, Lord; First Broom, Kellani's father
Justym of Marroth, mage and former singer; Vystyn's great grandson
Kashim, PTC Lieutenant 5Troop, the babyface
Kavid-Jar, the, Spirit of Mountain; Bodrus' avatar
Keena of the Weevils, mage and caravaneer
Kellani of Kell-Spellstor, 1st broomrider
Kennan, PTC marine captain
Kier, portaller mage, Old Wharf
Lassonder, a noble of Malgarth
Latharom, a mover mage
Leah, mage and warehouse manager Emporium New Winsproke
Leolynn of Kell-Allastar, PTC captain *Maiden of Allastar*
Liom of Morthan, Baron Morthan's son
Lothi-Mo, a royal wyrmling
Lutai, Mrs. (D) former head clerk New Winsproke Shipyard
Lykas, a boy from Ozzoon; ducal envoy
Madogar of Kell-Allastar, PTC 3Mate *Maiden*
Maisy, the various secretaries of the Secretary of the Warlock Tower
Margery, portaller of *Maiden*
Markill, Mage; Renquar general manager
Martha, mage instructor, twin to Tymon
Ma-Ta, a two-fingered red wyrmling
Matijas: PTC 2Mate *Gilded Hind*
Maud of the Kell, Queen, mother of Kellani
Meshan Hathwaari, crown prince of Hizmyr
Miran of New Winsproke, PTC Midshipman *Drakon*
Miyra of Brisa, PTC captain *Marigold*
Morgan, WyDir general manager
Morthan, Baron, leader of the barons faction in Malgarth

Mott, portaller mage, Smalkand
Na'a of the Arrangh, Kell wisewoman, healer of Gathea
Naja, a New Winsproke mine forewoman
Nate, Shaw's partner
Naudin of Maiwar, mindmage
Nimmendal, the Angsthafn pirate boss (jinni prince Hyloman)
Niothe, high priestess of Demetea and chancellor of Ozzoon
Nissha of Kell-Allastar, PTC cadet *Maiden*
Olesha of Port Waid, PTC captain *Gilded Hind*, Tamyas' aunt
Orin, a former guild captive boy
Oskar, PTC Lieutenant, marine battlemage under Kennan
Oychak, Thali engineer at Old Wharf
Ozoezd (D), a jinni prince
Particulus, Magister, mage at the Arcane Emporium
Perre, 2Off *Drakon*, brother to Vence
Phynn, an engineer
Qanan, Lieutenant, Prince of Sashuni, engineer *Sashu*
Rami an Darv. 4Troop, Corporal
Rashaunt XI Hathwaari, King of Hizmyr
Razoon Mir, of Pashwend Keep, one of Aya's scouts
Renquar, supplier of magic paraphernalia
Rhila of Spelley, mage artisan, portaller Port Naar
Ricco, *Drakon*'s purser, a PTC employee
Ruth of Spellstor, Warden of Winsproke, sister to Naudin
Rutus Lord Wrache, chancellor and Court faction leader in Malgarth
Saul of Spellstor, Lord, Warden of Spellstor; Chief Reclaimer
Sem, portal mage *Drakon*
Shar Khali, underminister of Finance
Shar Lowin An-Ushyr, PTC captain *Lion*
Shaw (Ashawta) Harwans, Trade Magnate
Siolde of Seedgraft, Witch, mother of Naudin
Sostaz, Amir (D), an Angsthafn jinni; Villaume's master
Suzie, PTC healer lieutenant of marines
Sylas, Abia's brother, warehouse manager Smalkand
Tamyas, PTC captain *Sashu*
Tazhan, Senior Captain, Hizmyran fleet
Teodar, the Kavid Jar
Tiu-Ti, a wyrmling boy
Tomas, portaller mage.
Tymon, chief healer at Smalkand, twin to Martha
Tyon, Duke of Wattash
Ulaataq of the White Shore Clan, Thali engineer

Ungreff, Baron, a leader of the barons faction, Malgarth
Uthur, the Yavam Island boss
Uyesh, PTC 1Mate *Gilded Hind*
Uzhan, Priest and PTC Lieutenant 3Troop
Varan Lomillor, PTC Director of Malgarth
Vence, 1Off *Drakon*, brother to Perre
Villaume, a boy of Angsthafn
Wador (D), a singer f Unwaar
Wahaz (D), a jinni
Wainschilt, banker at Smalkand
Wallanck of Piright, Overcaptain of the Chorwaynie Archipelago
Wanei Prince of Sashuni, 1Off *Sashu*
Willow, keep boss of Smalkand
Wisp, a young Brisan girl
Wiu-To, a wyrmling boy
Wrachazd, the lich king of Nanstalgarod
Wylmer, Captain Githeon; PTC captain of *Xalt*
Wylmer, Mr., Captain Wylmer's father
Xailin, Qoor 3Off *Drakon*, Imperial Princess of Qoor
Yaboush (D), a hween jinni at Wattash
Yarwan, Commodore; Naudin's father
Yens Rowe-Yens, PTC Lieutenant Seatome Troop
Yerene M'Dannish, of the *Weal Trumpet*, Port Dvarghish
Ylwar An-Ushyr, 1Mate *Lion,* Capt Lowin's brother
Zaotinq, a Qoor warrior with Aya
Zuuni, warehouse manager Myrlia

Aera, Sky Goddess
Amallorad, Father of Gods
Bodrus, the Sleeping God of the Mountains
Chottapan, Sea God
Demetea, Goddess of the Wild Things
Gathea, Nature, the Mother
Gorm & Otha, the Siblings of Battle
Kallianura, Defender of the Home
Lumentis, God of Knowledge
Ratla, Mother of Thieves
Tenaaz, God of Trade
the Thi-a-Yuuk, the Great Grandmother of the Ice
Zenyunthalata, God of the Lands

AZZA, the Universe Maker